About the Author

© Kelly Campbell

BERNARD CORNWELL is the author of the acclaimed *New York Times* bestsellers *Agincourt* and *The Fort*; the bestselling Saxon Tales, which include *The Last Kingdom*, *The Pale Horseman*, *Lords of the North*, *Sword Song*, *The Burning Land*, and, most recently, *Death of Kings*; and the Richard Sharpe novels, among many others. He lives with his wife on Cape Cod.

Stormchild

SHARPE'S COMPANY
Richard Sharpe and the Siege of Badajoz, January to April 1812

SHARPE'S SWORD
Richard Sharpe and the Salamanca Campaign, June and July 1812

SHARPE'S ENEMY
Richard Sharpe and the Defense of Portugal, Christmas 1812

SHARPE'S HONOUR
Richard Sharpe and the Vitoria Campaign, February to June 1813

SHARPE'S REGIMENT
Richard Sharpe and the Invasion of France, June to November 1813

SHARPE'S SIEGE
Richard Sharpe and the Winter Campaign, 1814

SHARPE'S REVENGE
Richard Sharpe and the Peace of 1814

SHARPE'S WATERLOO
Richard Sharpe and the Waterloo Campaign, 15 June to 18 June 1815

SHARPE'S DEVIL
Richard Sharpe and the Emperor, 1820–1821

The Grail Quest Series
THE ARCHER'S TALE
VAGABOND
HERETIC

The Nathaniel Starbuck Chronicles
REBEL
COPPERHEAD
BATTLE FLAG
THE BLOODY GROUND

The Warlord Chronicles
THE WINTER KING
ENEMY OF GOD
EXCALIBUR

The Sailing Thrillers
STORMCHILD
SCOUNDREL
WILDTRACK
CRACKDOWN

Stormchild

A Novel of Suspense

Bernard Cornwell

HARPER

NEW YORK · LONDON · TORONTO · SYDNEY

HARPER

A hardcover edition of this book was published in 1991 by HarperCollins Publishers.

HarperCollins books may be purchased for educational, business, or sales promotional use. For information please write: Special Markets Department, HarperCollins Publishers, 10 East 53rd Street, New York, NY 10022.

FIRST HARPERPAPERBACKS EDITION PUBLISHED 1992.
FIRST HARPERTORCH EDITION PUBLISHED 2005.
FIRST HARPER PAPERBACK PUBLISHED 2011.

Library of Congress Cataloging-in-Publication Data is available upon request.

ISBN 978-0-06-209265-6

11 12 13 14 15   /OV   10 9 8 7 6 5 4 3 2 1

Stormchild is for Art and Maggie Taylor

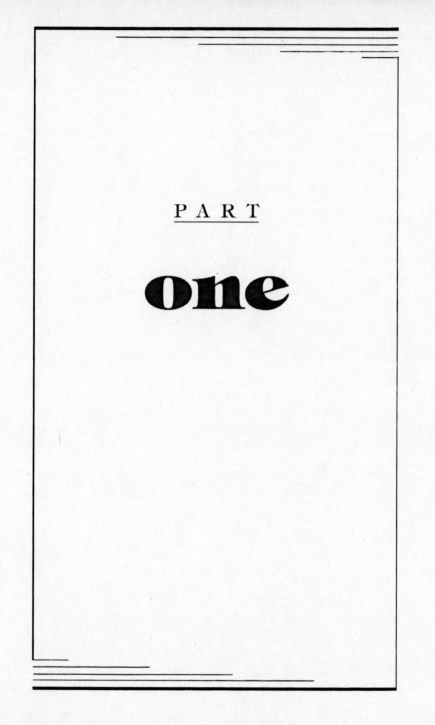

PART

one

The sea was weeping.

It was a gray sea being kicked into life by a sudden wind; a sea being torn into raggedness and flecked white. The fishermen called it a weeping sea, and claimed it presaged disaster.

"It won't last." My wife, Joanna, spoke of the sea's sudden spite.

The two of us were standing on the quay of our boatyard watching the black clouds fly up the English channel. It was the late afternoon of Good Friday, yet the air temperature felt like November and the bitter gray sea looked like January. The deteriorating weather had inevitably brought out the wind-surfers whose bright sails scudded through the gloom and bounced dangerously across the broken waters of the estuary's bar where the high bows of a returning fishing boat battered the sea into wind-slavered ruin. Our own boat, a Contessa 32 called *Slip-Slider*, jerked and pitched and thudded against her fenders on the outer pontoon beneath our quay.

"It can't last," Joanna insisted in her most robust voice as though she could enforce decent Easter weather by sheer willpower.

"It'll get worse before it gets better," I said with idle pessimism.

"So we won't sail tonight," Joanna said more usefully, "but we'll surely get away at dawn tomorrow." We had been planning a night passage to Guernsey, where Joanna's sister lived, and where, after church on Easter morning, my wife's family would sit down to roast lamb and new potatoes. The Easter family reunion had become a tradition, and that year Joanna and I had been looking forward to it with a special relish, for it seemed we had both at last recovered from the tragedies of our son's death and our daughter's disappearance. Time might not have completely healed those twin wounds, but it had layered them over with skins of tough scar tissue, and Joanna and I were aware of ordinary happinesses once again intruding on what had been a long period of mourning and bafflement. Life, in short, was becoming normal, and being normal, it presented its usual crop of problems.

Our biggest immediate problem was a damaged four-and-a-half-ton yawl which had been standing ready to be launched when our crane-driver had rammed it with the jib of his machine. The damage was superficial, merely some mangled guardrails and a nasty gash in the hull's gelcoat, but the yawl's owner, a petulant obstetrician from

Basingstoke, was driving to the yard next lunchtime and expected to find his boat launched, rigged, and ready. Billy, our foreman, had offered to stay and make good the damage, but Billy was already covering for my absence over the Easter weekend and I had been unhappy about adding to his workload.

So the ill wind that had made the sea weep at least blew Billy some good, for I sent him home to his new wife while I towed the big yawl into the shed where wind and rain rattled the corrugated tin roof as I stripped out the damage under the big lamps. I planned the next morning's sail as I worked. If the marine forecast was right and this sudden hard weather abated, we could leave the river at daybreak and endure an hour of foul tide before the ebb swept us past the Anvil and out into mid-channel. We would make Guernsey in time for supper, and the only possible inconvenience in our revised plans was the probability that the visitor's marina in St. Peter's Port would be filled by the time of our arrival and we would have to find a mooring in the outer harbor.

As night fell it seemed improbable that the weather would relent by dawn. The shrieking wind was flaying the river with white foam. The gale was strong enough to persuade some of the Sailing Club members to borrow our launch and tow a gaggle of the club's dinghies off the midstream buoys and into the shelter of our pontoons. Joanna helped them, then spent two hours bringing the boatyard accounts up to date before braving the filthy weather to fetch two bags of cod and chips from the high street. It was while she was gone that Harry Carstairs phoned. "Thank God you're still there," Carstairs greeted me, "I thought you might have gone away for Easter."

Carstairs was a yacht broker who worked out of an air-conditioned office in London's Mayfair. His clients were not the small-boat sailors who were my bread and butter, but rather the hyper-rich who could afford professional skippers at the helm, naked starlets on the foredeck, and stroll-on, stroll-off berths in Monte Carlo. Our yard's normal business was much too paltry for Carstairs's expensive trade, but that year Joanna and I happened to have a great steel-hulled sloop for sale and, though at over a hundred and fifty thousand pounds *Stormchild* was at the very upper range of our stock, she barely scraped in at the slum end of Harry's business. "I've got a likely client who wants to look at the beast tomorrow," he told me in his champagne and caviar accent. "Is that all right with you?"

I hesitated before answering. Of late, as our life returned to normal, Joanna and I had discussed buying *Stormchild* for ourselves. We had dreamed of selling our house, hiring a manager to look after the yard, then sailing away to far white beaches and exotic harbors. *Stormchild* would have been the perfect boat to make those dreams come true, but the trouble was they were only dreams, not plans, and I knew we were not ready to make the change, just as I knew I could not pass up a proper offer for the big steel boat. "*Stormchild*'s still here," I reluctantly told Carstairs, "and the yard's open from eight until six, so help yourself to a viewing. You can get *Stormchild*'s keys from my foreman. His name's Billy and I'll make sure he puts some heat into the boat."

"The customer will be with you at midday"— Harry ignored everything I had said—"and he'll try to knock you down to a hundred and ten, but I told him you wouldn't go a penny below one-thirty."

"Hang on!" I protested angrily. It was not the suggested price that was making me bridle but rather Harry's bland assumption that I would be available to show *Stormchild* to his customer. "I'll be halfway to the Channel Islands by midday tomorrow. Why can't you show the boat yourself?"

"Because I shall be in Majorca, selling a triple-decked whorehouse to a Sheik of Araby," Harry said carelessly. Then, after a deliberately worrying pause, "OK, Tim, if you don't want to sell your sloop, what about that big German yawl at Cobb's Quay? Do you know if she's still available?"

"Sod you," I growled, thus provoking an evil chuckle from Harry, who knew Joanna and I should never have taken *Stormchild* onto our brokerage list. The big yacht was out of our league, but she was an estate sale and the widow was an old friend of the family, and we had been unable to refuse her request that we look after the sale. Out of sentimentality we had even waived our brokerage fee, but not even that concession had shifted the big sloop off our jackstands, and thus, for over a year now, *Stormchild*'s fifty-two-foot hull had taken up precious space in our yard, and she looked like she would be staying for at least another year unless we found a buyer who was immune to Britain's sky-high interest rates. Harry Carstairs knew just how desperately I needed to make room in my cramped yard, which was why he was so blithely confident that I would change my Easter plans. For a few seconds I contemplated letting Billy handle the London lawyer, but I knew my foreman was neither good at nor happy with such negotiations, which meant I would have to stay and deal with the sale myself. "OK, Harry"—I resigned myself to the inevitable—"I'll be here."

"Good man, Tim. The customer's name is John Miller, got it? He's a more than the usually poisonous lawyer but he's rich, of course, which is why I promise I'm not wasting your time."

I put the phone down and ducked into the pouring rain to see if Joanna had returned. The streetlights on the far side of the river shook and danced their reflections in the black water and I thought I saw a moving shadow silhouetted against one of those liquid spears. The movement seemed to be on board *Slip-Slider,* and I assumed Joanna must have taken our supper down into the Contessa's cozy cabin. "Jo!" I shouted toward the shadow.

The yard gate clanged shut behind me. "I'm here." Joanna ran through the pelting rain to the shelter of the yard's office. "Come and eat while it's hot!"

"Just a minute!" I turned on the yard's security lights. Rain sliced past the yellow lamps, but otherwise nothing untoward moved on the wave-rocked pontoons and I guessed the shadow by

Slip-Slider had been my imagination, or perhaps one of the dozen stray cats that had taken up residence in the yard.

"What is it?" Joanna asked me from the office doorway.

"Nothing." I killed the lights, but still gazed toward the rain-hammered river where, at the midstream buoys that the Sailing Club had emptied at dusk, I now thought I could see a big, dark yacht moored, but the smeared afterimage of the bright security lights blurred my sight and made me uncertain whether I was seeing true or just imagining shadows in the darkness.

I went to the office and told Joanna about Harry's prospective customer, and we agreed that the opportunity of selling the big yacht was too good to pass up. The widow of *Stormchild*'s owner was feeling the pinch and, in consequence, we were feeling responsible. That guilt was unreasonable, for the state of the economy was the fault of the bloody politicians, but reasonable or not that guilt meant I would have to sacrifice this weekend's family reunion in an effort to sell the boat. Joanna offered to stay as well, but I knew how eagerly she was looking forward to Easter day, so I encouraged her to sail alone to Guernsey. "Perhaps you can get a flight?" Joanna suggested, though without much optimism for she knew that the chance of finding a spare seat to the Channel Islands on an Easter Saturday flight was remote. "But look on the bright side," Joanna said wickedly, "because now you've got no reason not to hear your brother's Easter sermon."

"Oh, Christ, I hadn't thought of that." My brother David, rural dean in the local diocese and rector of our parish church, frequently complained that while he often patronized my place of work I rarely patronized his. David's muscular Christianity was not entirely to my taste, but, thanks to a London lawyer, it looked as if I would have to grin and bear a dose this Easter.

I left Joanna with the accounts and went back to finish the yawl's repairs. As I ran across the yard I noted that the midstream buoys were empty, which meant that the big yacht I thought I had seen there must have been a figment of my imagination, which made sense for no one in their right mind would have slipped and gone to sea in the teeth of this vicious wind. The weather seemed to be worsening, making a mockery of the marine forecast's promise of a fair morning, but Joanna, more trusting than I, went home at nine o'clock to get a good night's sleep before her early start. When I followed her up the hill three hours later the gale was still blowing the sky ragged, yet, when the alarm woke me before dawn, the wind had indeed veered westerly and lost its spitting venom. "I told you so," Joanna said sleepily. "Did you finish the yawl?"

I nodded. "The bugger'll never know it was hit."

She opened the bedroom window and sniffed the wind. "It's going to be a fast crossing," she said happily. Joanna had grown up in Guernsey where she had learned to sail as naturally as other children learned to ride a bicycle. She relished strong winds and hard seas and, anticipating that this day would bring her a fast wet channel cross-ing, all spray and dash and thumping seas, she was eager to get under way.

I cooked Joanna's breakfast, then drove her down to the river. She was dressed in oilies, while her red-gold hair, beaded by a light shower, sprang in a stiff undisciplined mop from the edges of her yellow woolen watch hat. She suddenly looked so young that, for an instant, her eager face cruelly reminded me of our daughter, Nicole.

"You look miserable," Joanna, catching sight of my expression, called from the cockpit.

I knew better than to mention Nicole, so invented another reason for my apparent misery. "I just wish I was coming with you."

"I wish you were, too," she said in her no-non-sense voice, which acknowledged we could do nothing to change the day's fate, "but you can't. So be nice to the London lawyer instead."

"Of course I'll be nice to him," I said irritably.

"Why 'of course'? You usually growl at cus-tomers you don't like, and I've yet to meet a lawyer you don't treat like something you scrape off a shoe." Joanna laughed, then blew me a kiss. "Perhaps I should stay and make the sale?"

I smiled and shook my head. "I'll be good to the bastard," I promised her, then I released *Slip-Slider*'s bowline and shoved her off the pontoon. "Give me a call when you arrive!"

"I will! And go to David's sermon! And eat properly! Lots of salad and vegetables!" Joanna had released the stern line and put the engine in gear. "Love you!"

"Love you," I called back, and I was struck again by Joanna's sudden resemblance to our daughter, then, after a last blown kiss, she turned to look down river to where the channel waves crashed white on the estuary's bar. I watched her hoist the sails before a gray squall of sudden hard rain hid *Slip-Slider* and made me run for the shelter of my car. I drove to a lorry driver's cafe on the bypass where they made a proper breakfast of blood pudding, eggs, fried bread, bacon, sausage, kidneys, mushrooms, and tomatoes, all mopped up with bread and butter and washed down with tea strong enough to strip paint.

By the time I opened the yard for business the rain had eased and a watery sun was glossing the river where, one by one, the boats hoisted their sails and slapped out toward the boisterous sea. I stripped the tarpaulins from *Stormchild*'s decks and jealously thought how Joanna would be sailing *Slip-Slider* sharp into the wind, slicing the gray seas white, while I swept *Stormchild*'s topsides clean, then put two industrial heaters into her cabins to take the winter's lingering chill out of her hull.

The London lawyer turned up an hour late for his appointment. He was a young man, no more than thirty, yet he had clearly done well for himself for he arrived in a big BMW and, before climbing out, he ostentatiously used the car phone so that we peasants would realize he possessed such a thing. But we were more inclined to notice the girl who accompanied him, for she was a tall, willowy model type who unfolded endless legs from the car. The lawyer finished his telephone call, then

climbed out to greet me. He was wearing a designer oilskin jacket with a zip-in float liner and a
built-in safety harness. "Tim Blackburn?" He held
out his hand.

"I'm Blackburn," I confirmed.

"I'm John Miller. This is Mandy."

Mandy gave me a limp hand to shake. "You're
quite famous, aren't you?" She greeted me.

"Am I?"

"Daddy says you are. He says you won lots of
races. Is that right?"

"A long time ago," I said dismissively. I had
been one of the last Englishmen to win the single-
handed Atlantic race before the French speed-sleds
made the contest a Gallic preserve, then, for a
brief period, I had held the record for sailing non-
stop and single-handed round the world. Those
accomplishments hardly accorded me rock-star
status, but among sailors my name still rang a
faint bell.

"Daddy says it was impressive, anyway," the girl
said with airy politeness, then gazed up at the
deep-keeled *Stormchild* which was cradled by massive metal jackstands. "Golly, isn't it huge!"

"You must stop saying that to me," the lawyer,
who was no more than five foot two inches tall,
guffawed at his own wit, then sternly told me he
had expected to find the boat in the water with
her mast stepped and sails bent on.

"Hardly at this time of year"—I was remembering Joanna's instruction to be nice to this little
man, and thus kept my voice very patient and
calm—"the season's scarcely begun and no one

puts a boat in the water until they need to. Besides," I went on blithely, "I thought you'd appreciate seeing the state of her hull."

"There is that, of course," he said grudgingly, though I doubted he would have noticed if the hull had been a rat-infested maze of rust holes. John Miller clearly did not know boats, and that ignorance made him palpably impatient as I ran down the list of *Stormchild*'s virtues. Those virtues were many; the yacht had been custom built for an experienced and demanding owner who had wanted a boat sturdy enough for the worst seas, yet comfortable enough to live aboard for months at a time. The result was a massive, heavy boat, as safe as any cruising yacht in the world, with a powerful brute of a turbocharged diesel deep in her belly. But *Stormchild* was also a pretty boat, with fine lines, a graceful rig, and decks and coach roofs handsomely planked in the finest teak.

"Which is why," I told the lawyer a little too brusquely, "I'd be grateful if you took off your street shoes before climbing aboard."

Miller scowled at my request, but nevertheless slipped off his expensive brogues. Mandy, who had begun to shiver in the unseasonably cold wind, discarded her stiletto heels before tiptoeing up the wooden boarding stairs and stepping down into *Stormchild*'s cockpit. "She's ever so pretty," Mandy said gallantly. The lawyer ignored her. He was peering at the cockpit instrument display and pretending that he understood what he was seeing.

"You'll take a hundred thousand?" he challenged me suddenly.

"Don't be so bloody silly," I snapped back. My anger was piqued by the knowledge that *Stormchild* was horribly underpriced even at a hundred and fifty thousand pounds, and I felt another twinge of regret that Joanna and I were not ready to buy her.

Miller had bridled at my flash of temper, but controlled his own, perhaps because I was at least fourteen inches taller than him, or perhaps because my fading fame carried with it a reputation for having a difficult temperament. One tabloid newspaper had called me the "Solo Seadog Who Bites," which was unfair, for I simply had the prickly facade that often conceals a chronic shyness, to which I added an honest man's natural dislike of all lawyers, frauds, pimps, politicians, and bureaucrats, and this lawyer, despite his pristine foul-weather gear, was plainly a prick of the first order. "We were thinking of keeping her in the Med"—Miller tapped the compass as though it was a barometer—"I suppose you can deliver her?"

"It might be possible," I said, though my tone implied there could be vast difficulties in such a delivery for, eager as I was to sell *Stormchild,* I was not at all certain that her proper fate was to become a flashy toy to impress Miller's friends and clients. *Stormchild* was a very serious boat, and I loved boats enough not to want this beautifully built craft to degenerate in the hands of a careless owner. "If it's a warm-weather vacation boat that you want," I said as tactfully as I could, "then perhaps you ought to think about a fiberglass hull? They need much less maintenance and they offer better insulation."

"There are plenty of people willing to do maintenance work in the Med," the lawyer said unpleasantly, "and we can always bung some air conditioners into her."

My flash of temper had clearly not discouraged the little runt, so I tried warning him that cooling a boat the size of *Stormchild* would be an expensive business.

"Let me worry about expense," Miller said, then bared his teeth in a grimace that I could, if I chose, translate as a smile. "In my line of work, Blackburn, I occasionally need to impress a client, and you don't do that by being cheap."

"Surely the best way to impress clients is to keep them out of jail?" I suggested.

He gave a scornful bark of laughter. "Good God, man, I'm not a criminal lawyer! Christ, no! I negotiate property deals between the City and Japan. It's quite specialized work, actually." He insinuated, correctly, that I would not understand the specialization. "But the Japanese are pathetically impressed by big white boats"—he glanced at his shivering girlfriend—"and by the girls that go with them."

Mandy giggled while I, suppressing an urge to wring Miller's neck, took him below decks to show off the impressive array of instruments that were mounted above *Stormchild*'s navigation table. Miller dismissed my description of the SatNav, Decca, radar, and weatherfax, saying that his marine surveyor would attend to such details. Miller himself was more interested in the boat's comforts which, though somewhat lacking in gloss, nevertheless met his grudging approval. He especially liked the aft master cabin where, warmed by one of my big industrial heaters, Mandy had stretched her lithe length across the double berth's king-size mattress. "Hello, sailor," she greeted Miller.

"Oh, jolly good." Miller was clearly anticipating the effect that Mandy's lissome beauty would have on his Japanese clients. "Will you take a hundred and ten?" he suddenly demanded of me.

He had obviously smelled that *Stormchild* was a bargain, and I felt a terrible sadness for I knew that, once the boat had been used as the sweetener on a few deals, and once Miller had made his fortune from those deals, she would be left to rot in some stagnant backwater. "Why don't you take a good look at the other cabins," I said with as much patience as I could muster, "then we can negotiate a price in my office. Would you like some coffee waiting for you?"

"Decaffeinated," he ordered imperiously, "with skim milk and an artificial sweetener."

I planned to give him powdered caffeine laced with condensed milk and white sugar. "The coffee will be waiting in the office," I promised, then left them to it.

Billy, who had just finished rigging the repaired four-and-a-half-ton yawl, ambushed me halfway across the yard. His chivalrous concern, like that of every other red-blooded male in the yard, was for the lubricious and goose-pimpled Mandy. "Bloody hell, boss, what does she see in the little fucker?"

"She sees his wallet, Billy."

"Did you see the fucker's oilskin coat?" Billy asked indignantly.

"It can get very rough on the boating pond in Hyde Park," I said reprovingly, then I turned away because a car had just driven past the big sign that read "Absolutely No Unauthorized Vehicles Beyond This Notice," and I was readying myself to shout at the driver, when I realized that the car was my brother's antique Riley.

"They're not racing today, are they?" Billy asked, and my own first thought was that David must have come to the yard to launch his 505 racing dinghy. My reverend elder brother was a lethal competitor and, like others who were addicted to the frail, wet discomfort of fragile racing boats, he pretended to despise the sybaritic conveniences of long-distance sailors like myself. "You mean you have a lavatory on that barge?" he would boom at some hapless victim. "You pee in windless comfort, do you? Next you will inform me that you have a cooking stove on board. You do! Then why not just stay in some luxury hotel, dear boy?"

"You're not taking your eggshell out in this wind, are you?" I greeted David as he opened the Riley's door, then I saw he could not possibly be thinking of taking out the 505, for he was wearing his dog collar and cassock, and even David's mild eccentricities did not extend to sailing in full clerical rig. Instead he was dressed ready for the afternoon's Easter weddings, and I supposed he had come to inveigle me into buying him a pub lunch before he performed his splicing duties. Then the passenger door of the Riley opened and another man climbed out.

It is at that point, just as Brian Callendar climbs out of David's car, that my memory of that Easter weekend becomes like some dark and sinister film that is played over and over in my head. It is a film that I constantly want to change, as if by rewriting its action or dialogue I can miraculously change the film's ending.

Brian Callendar comes toward me. He is an acquaintance rather than a friend, and he is also a detective sergeant in the County Police Force, and there is something about his face, and about David's face behind him, which suggests that the two men have not come to the boatyard for pleasure. The Riley's engine is still running and its front doors have been left open. I remember how the wind was whirling wood-shavings out of the carpenter's shop and across the sloping cobbles of the boatyard's ramp. "Tim?" Callendar said in a very forced voice. I am still smiling, but there is something about the policeman's voice which tells me that I won't be smiling again for a very long time. "Tim?" Callendar says again.

And I want the film to stop. I so badly want the film to stop.

But it won't.

David took my elbow and walked me down to the pontoon where he stood beside me as Callendar told me that a yacht had exploded in mid-channel. Some wreckage had been found, and amongst that wreckage was a yellow horseshoe life buoy with the name *Slip-Slider* painted in black letters.

I stared at the policeman. "No," I said. I was incapable of saying anything else. "No."

"A Dutch cargo ship saw it happen, Mr. Blackburn." Callendar, as befitted a bringer of bad news, had slipped into a stilted formality. "They say it was a bad explosion."

"No." The word was more than a denial, it was a protest. David's hand was still on my elbow. Church bells were clamorous in the town, foretelling the afternoon's weddings.

Callendar paused to light a cigarette. "There are no survivors, Mr. Blackburn," he said at last, "at least none they could find. The Dutch boat has been looking, and the navy sent a helicopter, but all they're finding is wreckage, and not much of that either."

"No." I was staring blindly at the river.

"Who was on board, Mr. Blackburn?"

I turned to look into the policeman's eyes, but I could not speak.

"Was it Joanna?" David sounded uncomfortable, as he always did when raw emotions extruded above the calm surface of life, but he also sounded heartbroken, for he knew exactly who would have been sailing *Slip-Slider*. The question still had to be asked. "Was Joanna aboard?"

I nodded. There was a thickening in my throat. I wanted to turn and walk away as though I could deny this conversation. I looked back to Callendar to see if he was joking. I even half smiled, hoping that the policeman would smile back and it would all turn out to be a bad joke.

"Was anyone else aboard, Mr. Blackburn?"
Callendar asked me instead.

I shook my head. "Just Joanna." I was shaking.
Nothing was real. The world had slipped its gears.
In a second David would laugh and slap my back
and everything would be normal again. Except
David did no such thing, but just looked stricken
and unhappy and embarrassed.

"Oh, Jesus," I said. I had given up smoking fifteen years before, but I took the cigarette from
Callendar's fingers and dragged on it. I supposed
that either the navy or the Dutch boat had called
the Coastguard with *Slip-Slider*'s name, and the
Coastguard would have looked in their card-index
and discovered that I was *Slip-Slider*'s owner. Then
they would have called the police, and Callendar,
being on friendly terms with me, would have vol-
unteered for this horrid duty, but he had first
recruited David to help him. "Oh, Jesus," I said
again, then threw the foul-tasting cigarette into the
river. "When?" I asked. "When did it happen?" Not
that it mattered, but all I had left now were questions which would try to turn tragedy into sense.

"Just after nine o'clock this morning,"
Callender said.

But nothing made sense, Nothing. Except the
slow realization that my Joanna was dead, and I
began to cry.

The film goes scratchy then; scratchy and frag-
mented. I didn't want to watch the film, yet night
after night it would show itself to me until I was

crying again, or drunk, or usually both.

I remember telling the London lawyer and his girl to fuck off. I remember David pouring brandy into me, then taking me to his home where his wife, Betty, began to cry. David had to leave and marry three couples, so Betty and I sat in the cheerless comfort of their childless home while the church bells rang a message of joy into the wind-scoured air. The first reporters sniffed the stench of carrion and phoned the rectory in an effort to discover my whereabouts. Betty denied my presence, but when David came back from his weddings a group of pressmen waylaid him at the rectory gate. He told them to go to hell.

I felt I was already in that fiery pit. David, more comfortable with actions than emotions, tried to find a mechanical reason for Joanna's death. He wondered if there had been a leak of cooking gas on *Slip-Slider*, but I shook my head. "We had a gas alarm installed. Joanna insisted on it."

"Alarms don't always work," David said, as though that would comfort me.

"Does it matter?" I asked. I only wanted to cry. First my son had been killed, then Nicole had disappeared, and now, Joanna. I could not believe she was dead. Somehow, hopelessly, I thought Joanna might still be alive. For the next few days I fiercely tried to imagine that she had been blown clear of the exploding boat and was still swimming in the channel. I knew it was a stupidly impossible scenario, but I convinced myself she would somehow be safe. Even when they found Joanna's remains I tried to convince myself that it was not her.

It was, of course, and when the pathologists were done with what remained of my wife, the undertakers put the scraps in a bag, then into a coffin, and afterward they made up the coffin's weight with sand before David buried her in the cemetery high on the hill where she and I had used to sit and watch the channel. Joanna was buried in the same grave as our son, Dickie, who had also died in an explosion just as a year was blossoming into new life.

A navy boat scooped up what remained of *Slip-Slider,* and the wreckage was brought ashore and examined by forensic scientists, who confirmed what the pathologists had already deduced from their examination of Joanna's remains. My wife had been killed by a bomb.

I remember gaping at Sergeant Brian Callendar when he told me that news, and I again tried to deny the undeniable. "No, no."

"I'm sorry, Tim. It's true."

There was not much physical wreckage for the forensic scientists to analyze; just the life buoy, some shredded cushions from the cockpit, a plastic bucket, the man-overboard buoy, the radar reflector, the dinghy, one oar, the shaft of a boathook, and the wooden jackstaff to which the red ensign, scarred by the bomb blast, was still attached. It was in the shaft of the jackstaff that the scientists discovered a tiny cogwheel which they later identified as coming from a very common brand of alarm clock, and I was able to confirm that to the best of my knowledge there had been no such clock on board *Slip-Slider,* which meant the cheap alarm must have been used to trigger the bomb's detonator.

The police laboratories, despite the paucity of *Slip-Slider*'s remains, were nevertheless able to deduce what kind of explosive had been used, and how it had been detonated. By analyzing where each scrap of wreckage had been stored on board, the forensic men could even tell that the bomb had been planted low down on the port side of the engine block. The blast of the bomb would have driven a gaping hole in *Slip-Slider*'s bilges through which the cold sea must have recoiled in a torrent, but the blast had also erupted razor shards of shattered fiberglass upward and outward to throw whatever and whoever was in the cockpit into the sea. In the same blinding instant the explosion must have filled *Slip-Slider*'s cabins with an intolerable pressure that had blown the decks clean off the hull. The boat would have sunk in seconds, and Joanna, Brian Callendar assured me, would have known nothing.

Callendar had come to the house where he had made me a cup of tea before giving me all the grim details of the forensic findings. "It means they'll bring in the hard men from Scotland Yard"—he paused—"and it means you're going to be run ragged by the press."

The reporters were already besieging me. I protected myself as best I could by taking the phone off the hook and barricading myself in the house where I lived off whiskey, despair, and the sandwiches David brought me. The journalists shouted their questions whenever they saw a shadow at the windows, but I ignored them. I had no answers anyway.

The journalists, just like the police, wanted to know who had planted the bomb. For a time the police suspected me, but when the hard men from London searched the boatyard and the house they found nothing incriminating, and nothing to suggest our marriage had not been happy. The police grilled me about my army experiences, but that was of no help to them either, for my time in the army had been spent almost entirely in David's company playing bone-crunching rugby or going on uselessly strenuous expeditions that had not the slightest military value. David and I had kayaked through the Northwest Passage, dogsledded across Greenland, and climbed allegedly unconquered peaks in the Andes, and all courtesy of the British taxpayer, whose only reward had been press photographs of grinning maniacs with frost-encrusted beards. What I had never done in the army was learn to use explosives.

Nor did I have any motive for destroying *Slip-Slider*. Yet there were other men who might have had a motive to plant a bomb on board the boat; the same men who had constructed the bomb that had killed my son. "But that bomb," Inspector Fletcher said, "was your common or garden Provisional IRA Mark One Milk Churn, remotely detonated by radio and stuffed full of Czechoslovak Semtex. Remind me where it happened?"

"Freeduff." The name still sounded so stupid to me. Freeduff, County Armagh, was the inconspicuous farmlet where Lieutenant Richard Blackburn,

commanding his very first patrol, had been blown
into gobbets of scorched flesh and shattered bones.

"Freeduff," Fletcher said in the voice of a man
recalling old pleasures, "between Crossmaglen and
Cullyhanna. Am I right?"

I gave him a long, meditative look. Inspector
Godfrey Fletcher was the hardest of the hard men
who had been assigned to investigate Joanna's
murder, and he was evidently no ordinary policeman, but an official thug who moved in the
shadowy world of counter-terrorism and political
nastiness. He had the narrow face of a predator
and eyes that were not nearly so friendly as his
manner. The old adage advises that you set a thief
to catch a thief, and on that basis Fletcher was
probably a man well suited to catching murderous
bastards. He was also a man who had clearly
enjoyed his time in Northern Ireland. "What were
you," I asked him after a while, "SAS?"

He pretended not to have heard me, lighting a
cigarette instead. "But the bomb that killed your
wife was not a Mark One Provo Milk Churn, was
it?" His gunfighter eyes stared at me through the
cigarette smoke. "And the Provos never claimed
responsibility for your wife's death, did they?" It
was two weeks after Joanna's funeral and Fletcher
had come to the house to tell me, very grudgingly,
that he no longer suspected me of my wife's murder. But nor, it now seemed, did he think that the
Provisional IRA was responsible.

It had been the press who, in the absence of
any other culprits, began the speculation that the
Provisional IRA had planted the bomb that

destroyed *Slip-Slider*. It was not such a fanciful notion as it might have seemed, for Joanna and I had often loaned the Contessa 32 to British Army crews, who wanted some race experience; *Slip-Slider* had won her class in the last Fastnet Race with a crew of Green Jackets aboard, and some newspapers surmised that the IRA had assumed an army crew would be sailing the Contessa that Easter weekend.

"But this wasn't your average IRA bomb," Fletcher went on. "The Provos are too sophisticated to use mechanical clocks. They like to use silicon-chip timers out of microwaves or VCRs. Using a tick-tock these days is like planting a blackball with a smoking fuse; it's messy and crude."

"Maybe it was a splinter group of the IRA?" I was repeating the press speculation, but without any conviction.

"Then why didn't they claim responsibility? What's the point of slaughtering an innocent woman for the cause of a New Ireland unless you tell the world of your achievement? Because if you don't boast about your murders then the Libyans won't know where to send their money and you've merely wasted a bang, and these days the IRA want bigger bucks for their bangs." Fletcher was standing at the open kitchen door, staring down the long valley toward the restless channel. Joanna had bought the house for that gentle long view toward the sea. Fletcher blew smoke toward the orchard. "No, Mr. Blackburn"—he did not turn round as he spoke—"I don't reckon your wife died for a New Ireland. Your son did, but his death was an explicable act of political terrorism; your wife's death was made to look like an IRA follow-up, but it wasn't. The IRA don't use toytown bombs anymore. So who does? Who are your enemies, Mr. Blackburn?" He turned from the door and stared into my eyes.

"I don't have any enemies," I said.

Fletcher crossed the kitchen in two quick paces and slammed his fist hard on the table. "Who knew about your traditional Easter family reunion?" He waited, but got no answer. "Did someone assume that you'd both be on that boat?" He insisted. "Who tried to kill you and your wife together?" His eyes had the blank cruelty of a hawk's gaze. I still said nothing, and Fletcher despised me for my silence. "Who scoops the pot if you're dead, Mr. Blackburn?" He asked in a scornful voice.

"Don't be so bloody ridiculous," I snapped.

"There must be a fair bit of scratch in your family?" Fletcher's voice was sour as bilge-water. "Your father was a Harley Street surgeon, wasn't he? One of the very best, and one of the most expensive. How much did he leave you and your brother? Half a million each?"

"It's none of your damned business," I snapped.

"Ah, but it is." He leaned forward to breathe cigarette fumes into my face. "Anything's my business, Mr. Blackburn, until I've nailed the fucker who killed your wife. Or was it a bitch who did the killing?"

I said nothing.

Fletcher dropped his half-smoked cigarette into my half-drunk cup of tea. "If you won't help me," he spoke sourly, "then you'll probably cop the next bomb yourself, and frankly, Mr. Blackburn, you'll fucking deserve it unless you tell me where she is."

I looked into his merciless gaze, but said nothing.

"You know it's her, don't you?" Fletcher demanded.

"No," I said. "No!" And once again that simple word became a protest as well as a denial. "No, no, no!"

Fletcher was suggesting that my daughter, Nicole, had murdered her mother. Fletcher was crazy. It was not Nicole. Not my daughter. Not Nicole.

Richard and Nicole were twins. Nicole was always the leader, the braver, the instigator of disobedience and daring, though Richard was never far behind his tomboy sister. At ten years old they had been rescued off the cliffs to the east of the town, though Nicole, who had led her brother on the expedition to find gulls' nests, had defiantly insisted that she and Richard had been entirely safe. At thirteen, in a sudden spring storm, their Heron dinghy had been pulled off the shoals by the town's Lifeboat. The Lifeboat's coxswain, being a good man, had first saved their lives, then given them each a good hiding and said that the next time he would leave them there to drown. Nicole had been furious, not at the coxswain for clapping her ears, but at herself for being trapped on a drying lee shore.

"She's a wild one," the coxswain had told me

the next day, "spat at me like a cat, she did."

Nicole became wild when she was thwarted. She thwarted herself most of all, failing in some ambition she had set for herself. Not that she failed often, for she was a capable and an extraordinarily tough girl. You learn about peoples' characters when you sail with them in small cruising yachts, and I learned a lot about Nicole, even though she prided herself on hiding her feelings. I watched her in gales, in cold, and in fogs, and I never once saw her come near breaking point. The harder a voyage became, the harder Nicole proved. Her brother relied on humor to cushion hardship, but Nicole cultivated a rock-hard endurance. Sometimes that hardness worried Joanna and me, for it spoke of a lack of sympathy in our daughter, yet we also had much to be thankful for. Nicole, like her twin brother, grew into a good-looking adolescent with straight straw-colored hair, sea-blue eyes, and broad shoulders.

The twins had the attractiveness of good health and physical confidence, yet still there was that unsettling streak of ice in Nicole's character. Richard could be immensely giving and understanding, but Nicole was intolerant of any weakness, either in herself or in others. Nicole had to be the best, with one, and only one, exception. Her twin brother Richard, and only Richard, was allowed to be her equal, and even her superior. They were inseparable, the best of friends, and Nicole regarded Dickie's victories as hers, and his defeats as personal slights on her. Once, when Richard was beaten three times in one afternoon's dinghy racing by a newcomer to the town, Nicole was furious. Richard was typically generous in praise of the newcomer, but Nicole regarded his victories as an insult. She swore revenge, but Nicole sailed a Shearwater, a catamaran, while Richard preferred a Fireball, which was a mono-hull. Nicole's Uncle David, who had missed a place on an Olympic team by just one race, and therefore knew a thing or two about dinghy competition, warned Nicole that the newcomer was too good and that her unfamiliarity with the Fireball dinghy would lead to a hiding, but Nicole would have none of it. She practiced for a week and, at week's end, in her brother's boat and with her mother as crew, she routed the newcomer. She won every race and never once, according to Joanna, cracked a smile. "It was war out there," Joanna said. "Terrifying!"

Nicole calmed as she grew older. By her late teens she had learned to put a governor on her temper, and by the time she went to university she could, as her brother lovingly put it, do a passable imitation of a normal human being. Richard had already left home, going, much to my pleasure, into my old regiment. Nicole, who had been suffering from a temporary bout of anti-militarism, had initially disapproved of Richard's career, but the disapproval passed. She herself went to a north-country university where she studied geology. For a time Joanna and I worried that the constraints of scholarship might irritate Nicole into rebellion, but instead she settled down and even displayed an academic aptitude that surprised us both. Not that the old, angry Nicole vanished entirely. She threw herself eagerly into campus politics and succeeded in having herself arrested for throwing eggs at the Prime Minister in a protest against power-station emissions. When I said that it seemed damned silly to be arrested for throwing eggs, I was treated to a half hour's scathing denunciation of my generation, my views, and my carelessness for the planet's future. Yet, despite her passionate intolerance for any views other than her own, Nicole seemed happy and purposeful, and Joanna and I had begun to anticipate the day when we could fulfill our long-held dream of selling the house and buying a boat large enough to live aboard permanently.

Then, in an Irish springtime, when the blossoms exploded white in the deep hedgerows of County Armagh, Richard had died.

And something in Nicole had died with her twin brother.

She abandoned her studies and came home where, like a wild thing, she raged against life's injustices. Joanna and I were advised to give Nicole's grief time to work itself out like some splinter of shrapnel, but instead it seemed to go deeper, and there sour into a grim and hopeless misery. Nicole lost weight, became pale and snappish, and for a time she haunted the local churches, even going so far as to declare an intention of entering a Discalced Carmelite house in Provence. Her Uncle David told her to snap out of it, which she did, but only to hurl herself in entirely the opposite direction. She was arrested for being drunk and disorderly, and three weeks later for possession of marijuana. Joanna and I paid those fines, only to discover that our daughter was pregnant and had no idea who the baby's father was. Nicole herself opted to abort the child, and afterward sank into a sullen, vituperative mood that was worse than her previous extremes of religiosity and carnality.

"It isn't your fault." David tried to reassure Joanna and me, though David, who had no children himself, was hardly an expert on childrearing.

"I could understand," Joanna had said, "if we'd dropped her on her head as a baby, or abused her, or disliked her, but Nickel had a wonderful childhood!" "Nickel" was the family's nickname for Nicole.

"It's just her nature," David had said. "Some people are excessively ambitious and competitive, and Nickel's one of them. It's a Blackburn trait, and you'll just have to endure while she learns to channel it. Right now she's like a motor given too powerful a fuel, but she'll eventually learn to control it, and then you'll be proud of her. Mark my words, Nickel will achieve great things one day!"

Joanna had sighed. "I hope you are right."

Then, that same summer, Nicole met Caspar von Rellsteb. She met him in our boatyard, where he had docked to repair his catamaran's broken forestay. It was a Saturday, and Joanna and I had been trying to hack some order into our tangled garden when, late in the afternoon, Nicole came home and calmly announced that she was leaving

to live with a man called Caspar. "I'm going right
now," she added.

"Now? With Caspar? Caspar who?" an astonished Joanna had asked.

"Just Caspar." Nicole either did not know the
rest of his name or did not want us to know. "He's
an ecologist. He's also a live-aboard like you want
to be," she airily told us, "and he's leaving on this
evening's tide."

"Leaving where?" Joanna asked.

"I don't know. Just leaving." Nicole went into
the house and began singing as she collected her
oilskins and seaboots. For a moment Joanna and I
had just stared at each other, then we had tentatively agreed that our daughter's sudden and
unexpected happiness might prove a blessing, and
that running away with the mysterious seagoing
Caspar had to be better than a life of shoeless des-
iccation in a French nunnery, or of witless drunk-
enness in the town's pubs.

Nicole, her kit bag hastily packed, did not want
us to go to the boatyard to see her off, but she
could hardly stop us, so we drove her to the river
where Caspar's boat proved to be a great brute of a
wooden catamaran called *Erebus*. *Erebus* was a
graceless craft, nearly fifty feet in length, with a
boxy, clumsy appearance that suggested she had
been constructed by an amateur builder who had
compensated for his lack of experience by making
every part of his craft hugely heavy. That precau-
tionary strength must have paid off, for *Erebus* carried the unmistakable marks of long and hard
usage. Her gear was chafed, her hulls were streaked,

and her decks had been blanched by long days of hard tropic sunlight. There was no indication of where the boat had come from, for no hailing port was painted on either of her transoms and her ensign was an anonymous pale green rag that hung listless in the day's sullen heat.

The big catamaran was moored at our visitor's pontoon. Clothes and dishrags were hanging to dry from her guardrails, but there was no other sign of life on board until, quite suddenly, a tribe of very small, very fair-haired and very naked children erupted from the cabin to scream and chase one another across the coach roof and down onto the trampoline netting that formed the catamaran's foredeck. "Are they Caspar's children?" Joanna asked, with what I thought was a remarkable forbearance.

"Yes," Nicole said, as though it was the most normal thing in the world for a girl to wander off and join a ready-made family she had met only two or three hours before.

"So he's married?" I asked.

"Don't be a toad, Daddy." Nicole swung her kit bag onto her shoulder and walked down to the pontoon.

The four naked children on the catamaran's foredeck netting were shrieking with loud excitement, but then a very tall and excruciatingly thin man, who had a pale green scarf knotted around his neck, suddenly appeared in *Erebus*'s cockpit. "Shut up!" He spoke in German, which I had learned years before and still half understood.

The four children were immediately quiet and utterly immobile.

"Oh dear, sweet Lord," Joanna murmured, for the man, apart from the wispy pale green scarf, was bare-assed naked. His skin was tanned the color of old mahogany against which his long white hair and straggly white beard showed bright. He glowered at the cowering children for a few seconds, then turned as he heard Nicole's footsteps on the wooden pontoon. He smiled at her, then held out a hand to assist her on board.

"Time to become the heavy father," I said grimly, then climbed out of the car into the summer afternoon's sunshine. Billy grinned at me from the inner pontoon where he was rerigging a Beneteau, but I did not grin back. Instead I strode down the pontoon, past the fuel pumps, and jumped down into *Erebus*'s cockpit. "Nicole!"

Nicole and the naked man had disappeared into the catamaran's spacious main cabin. I ducked down the companionway into the familiar cruising-yacht reek of unwashed bedding and smelly oilskins. Once in the big saloon my immediate impression was of a tangle of sun-browned skin and greasy hair, then I unraveled the impressions to see that, besides Nicole and the bearded man, there were two other girls in the big cabin. Both girls were about Nicole's age, and both girls were naked. One was completely nude, while the other, a startling redhead, wore nothing but a pale green sarong that was loosely knotted round her waist. That girl seemed to be helping Nicole undress. "What the hell is going on?" I demanded fiercely.

"This is my father," Nicole offered in laconic explanation. The two girls, both as blond as

Nicole, snatched up clothes to cover their naked-
ness, while the man, whom I assumed was the
beguiling Caspar, turned slowly to face me. He
said nothing, but just stared at me with an oddly
quizzical look on his thin face.

"What the hell is going on?" I demanded again.

"Do you want to join us?" the man asked in a
courteous voice.

"Nicole! For God's sake," I said, "come away."

"Daddy! Please go away," Nicole said, as though
I was being tiresome.

"Tim?" That was Joanna, calling me from the
pontoon.

Caspar slowly unfolded himself to stand
upright in the spacious cabin. He found a pair of
faded khaki shorts, which he pulled on, then he
gestured for me to go back to the cockpit. "I would
like to talk with you," he said, and his manner was
so polite that I felt I had no choice but to do as he
requested. "You are unhappy?" he asked when we
were both in the open air. His English was strongly accented with German and held a tone of
pained puzzlement. "You think your daughter is
coming to some harm, yes? I am sorry. It is just
that we are most casual on the boat." He smiled
contentedly, as though inviting me to share pleasure in his explanation.

But I was beyond reason. "You're running a
bloody whorehouse!" I shouted.

Joanna, standing on the pontoon, tried to calm
me down. Caspar offered her the hint of a bow.
"My name is Caspar von Rellsteb"—he introduced
himself—"and I welcome you both on board

Erebus. Your daughter wishes to join our small group, and I am delighted for her and for us." He waved a thin hand about the boat, encompassing the frightened children who huddled together at the catamaran's bows. "We have work to do," he added mysteriously.

"Work?" Joanna asked.

"We do not sail for our recreation," Caspar von Rellsteb said very portentously, "but to measure the damage being done to our planet." His voice was suddenly tougher, and I saw that despite his scrawny build he was no weakling, but had hard muscle under the deeply tanned skin. I guessed he was about my own age, early forties, though it was hard to tell because his long hair, which had gone prematurely white, made him look older, while the lithe movements of his tanned and sinewy body suggested a much younger age.

"Nicole tells us you're an ecologist," Joanna said in her best conversational tone.

"It is a convenient label, yes, though I prefer to think of myself as a surveyor of the planet. My present task is to gauge the extent of pollution and of species-murder. My small boat is ill-equipped to fight such evils, but I monitor them so that the extent of the world's ills will be understood."

"He's not an ecologist," I broke in scornfully, "he's just running a private knocking-shop." I pushed past the tall man and shouted into the cabin's shadows. "Nicole!"

There was no answer. Caspar von Rellsteb half smiled as though Nicole's lack of response was a measure of his victory. "Nicole is an adult, Mr.

Blackburn," he explained to me in a patronizing voice, "and she can choose her own life. You can choose to use violence against me if you wish, but nothing you can do will alter what is ordained." He turned away from me. "Nicole! Do you wish to leave *Erebus* and return to your parents' home?"

There was silence except for the small waves slapping at the twin hulls and the raucous cry of gulls in the warm air.

"Answer me, Nicole!" Caspar von Rellsteb's voice held a sudden heart of steel.

"I want to stay." Nicole's voice was unnaturally timid, as though she feared this skinny man's displeasure, and Joanna and I, hearing such unaccustomed meekness in our daughter's voice, were both astonished.

"Then stay you shall," von Rellsteb said magnanimously, "but first it is only right that you should say farewell to your mother and your father. Come!"

He left us alone with Nicole who was now wearing a shirt and trousers in the pale green that seemed to be the uniform color of the *Erebus* crew, when they wore any clothes at all. "I'm sorry," she said awkwardly, "it's just something I have to do."

"What is?" I demanded too angrily.

"Oh, Daddy." She sighed and looked at her mother, who was making soothing noises and telling Nicole to look after herself.

"You don't know anything about this man!" I attempted one last line of attack.

Nicole shook her head in denial of my anger. "Caspar's a good sailor, and he means to do something about a filthy world, and that's a good thing, isn't it?" Her head went up as she recovered some of her usual defiance. "I want to make a difference. I want to leave the world a better place. Is that so bad?"

Oh God, I thought, but there was no way of dissuading the young when they discovered the world's salvation was in their passionate grasp. "I love you," I said awkwardly, and I tried to give her all the money in my wallet, but Nicole would not take it. Instead she kissed me, kissed her mother, then, cuffing tears from her cheeks, ushered us both ashore.

Joanna and I walked to the car, then drove to the Cross and Anchor from where we could watch the tideway. Joanna nursed a gin and tonic, while I drank beer. After a half hour we saw *Erebus* shove off from the pontoon and motor out into the fairway. All three girls were now on deck, and all were wearing pale green clothes.

"Nicole looks happy," Joanna said wistfully. She had fetched a pair of binoculars from the car and now offered me the glasses. "Don't you think she looks happy? And maybe this is just something she has to work out of her system."

"It's what that superannuated hippie is working into her system that riles me," I said grimly. Then the hippie himself appeared on the catamaran's deck, dressed in his shorts with his white hair tied into a long ponytail. There was something goatlike about him, I thought, and something very disturbing in the girls' matching clothes, which somehow suggested that they had uniformly humbled themselves before von Rellsteb's authority.

"He's a very charismatic man," Joanna said unhappily.

"Balls."

"He defused you." Joanna stroked my hand as the clumsy catamaran motored past us toward the sea. The tide was flooding, which suggested von Rellsteb planned an eastward passage, perhaps back to Germany. I focused the binoculars to see that Nicole, who did indeed look happy, had taken the catamaran's wheel, while Caspar von Rellsteb was winching up the mainsail. The *Erebus*'s sail was banded in broad stripes of white and pale green, the same green as the odd uniform clothes that Nicole and the other girls were wearing.

"She's enlisting in a very good cause, Tim," Joanna said as she watched her daughter sail away.

"She's volunteering for a floating harem," I insisted.

"They're young," Joanna said patiently, "and they're full of idealism and hope. Besides, Nicole's always been an environmentalist, and surely that's better than getting arrested or having abortions?"

"She'll have that goat's baby instead?" I demanded angrily.

"They just want to clean up a polluted world," Joanna said. "What's wrong with that?"

"Nothing," I said. "Except I don't think that bastard's a real environmentalist. He's an opportunist. He knows how desperately the young want a cause, so he attracts them with a load of earnest-sounding claptrap, then turns them into his private harem."

"You don't know that," Joanna said patiently.

"If he's such a wonderful environmentalist," I demanded, "then why are his engines so filthy?" The *Erebus*'s twin exhausts were leaving a dirty cloud of black smoke to drift across the river. "I should have stopped her."

"You couldn't have stopped her," Joanna said, her eyes on the departing catamaran. She paused for a long time, then looked sadly at me. "I've never told you this, Tim, because it's so very unfair and so very stupid, but Nickel blames you for Dickie's death."

"Me?" I stared at Joanna. The accusation was so unexpected and so untrue that, instead of shocking me, it merely surprised me. "She blames me?"

"Because you encouraged Dickie to join the army."

"Oh, Jesus," I swore in exasperation. "Why didn't she talk to me about it?"

"Lord knows. I don't understand the young. I'm sure she knows it isn't really your fault, but—" Joanna, unable to finish the thought, shrugged it away. "She'll be back, Tim."

But I was beyond such hopeful consolations. I was watching my daughter, who blamed me for her brother's death, sail into the unknown. Legally she was a grown woman, able to make her own choices, but she was still our daughter, and now our only child, and I had just lost her to a man I had instinctively hated at first sight. I also knew I had handled my confrontation with Caspar von Rellsteb very badly, but I had not known how else to cope with the man I now thought of as my daughter's abductor.

"Nicole's tough." Joanna tried to find more reassurance as we watched our daughter expertly steer the catamaran through the Bull Sands Channel. "She'll use him and his ideas to get what she wants, and then she'll come home. He's an attractive man, but I doubt he's clever enough to keep her, you mark my words. She'll be home by Christmas."

But Nicole was not home by that Christmas, nor by the next. She did not write to us, nor did she telephone. Our daughter had disappeared, gone we knew not where with a man we could not trace on a boat we could not find. She sailed away and she never came home, though Fletcher, my grimly unpleasant policeman, still insisted that Nicole had come back like a thief in the night to plant a bomb that had killed her mother and had been meant to kill her father, too.

"No." I dismissed Fletcher's allegation scornfully.

Fletcher's knowing smile derided my denial. "Is she still in your will?" he asked. When I did not answer, he assumed correctly that Nicole was. "She gets everything, does she?" he insisted.

"It's none of your business."

"Change your will." Fletcher ignored my anger. "Cut her out. So even if the next bomb does get you, she won't profit from it. We don't want the wicked to flourish, do we, Mr. Blackburn?"

"Don't be so offensive," I snapped at him, but even to myself the retort sounded futile and, for the first time in my life, and despite my fame as a solo sailor, I felt entirely alone.

The public interest in Joanna's murder faded as the months passed and no one was arrested. The newspapers found juicier bones to chew, while the police transferred their efforts to fresher crimes that were more easily solved. Joanna was forgotten.

My life recovered, then limped on. To my astonishment the London attorney, Miller, bought *Stormchild* after all, or rather he and his partners purchased the boat which they announced was to become a "client hospitality facility." The law firm paid a decent price, then offered my yard yet more money to have the boat rigged and launched. Miller demanded that her name be changed from *Stormchild* to *Tort-au-Citron,* which was evidently some kind of legal joke, and though I told him it was bad luck to change a boat's name, he insisted it was not my luck that was at risk but his, and so I had the new name painted on *Stormchild*'s transom. Miller and a group of loud friends came from London to take the newly christened *Tort-au-Citron* on her first voyage. They did not hoist the sails, but merely motored beyond the bar, where they anchored and drank champagne in the summer sunshine before bringing the beautiful boat back to the yard. "Can you keep her until a delivery crew fetches her?" Miller asked me.

"How long?" I asked suspiciously, because I did not want to tie up one of our precious moorings for too many weeks.

"A month at the most. I'm having her delivered to Antibes." He clearly wanted me to know that he did his business in fashionable waters.

I agreed he could keep *Tort-au-Citron* on one of the yard's moorings for a month, but at that month's end no delivery crew had arrived. Then another month passed, and still the abandoned boat swung to her mooring on the changing tides. Autumn winds shivered the river cold, and the first gray frosts of winter etched *Tort-au-Citron*'s rigging white, but still no one fetched her. Her hull became foul with weed and her coach roofs streaked with gull droppings. Telephone calls to Miller's office elicited no instructions, so I sent him a whacking bill for the mooring's rent, but the bill, like the boat itself, was ignored.

Not that I cared very much, for Joanna's death had left me in a state of numbed despair. The house decayed about me, the garden turned rank and wild, and the boatyard only functioned because the staff ignored me and ran it by themselves. I wallowed in self-pity. I had lost a son and a wife, my daughter had disappeared, and I seemed trapped in hopelessness. For weeks I wept in the night, the tears fueled by whiskey. My friends rallied, but it was the friendship of marriage that I missed most; I missed it so much that I often wished I was with Joanna and Richard in their graveyard high above the sea. Christmas was a nightmare, and Joanna's birthday a purgatory. David tried to comfort me, but his efforts did not work; my brother was never a comforting kind of man. To be a comforting man one needs a much greater sensitivity to pain than David either possessed or wanted to possess. "Well at least you might cut your hair," he finally told me, "you look like a damned hippie."

The mention of a damned hippie made me think of Caspar von Rellsteb, then of Nicole, and, for the umpteenth time, I wondered aloud where she was, and how I could send her news of her mother's death. Since the bombing I had renewed my efforts to locate Nicole. I had contacted an old friend who now worked in Army Intelligence, and he had pulled official strings in Germany, but no one there knew of a man named Caspar von Rellsteb, or had heard of a boat called *Erebus*. Nicole had simply vanished. "If she knew her mother was dead," I insisted to David, "she'd come home. I know she would."

David muttered something about letting bygones be bygones. He wanted me to forget Nicole, not because he disliked her, but because he doubted she would ever return home. My brother, with his vigorous view of life, wanted me to dismiss the past and start again, and a year after

Joanna's death he tried to kick-start that new beginning by introducing me to a widow who had moved to our town from Brighton, but I bored the lady by talking of nothing but Joanna and Nicole. I did not want a replacement family; I wanted what was left of my original family.

David finally challenged me over Nicole. "Do you have the slightest evidence that she cares about you? Or wants to have anything to do with you?"

"If she knew her mother was dead," I insisted, "she'd feel differently."

"Dear, sweet God." David sighed. "Has it ever occurred to you, Tim, that Nicole herself might be dead? Perish the thought, but that catamaran she sailed away on doesn't sound like the safest vessel afloat."

"Maybe she is dead," I said listlessly.

"One prays not," David said enthusiastically, "but whatever's happened to Nicole, you simply cannot ruin your life wondering about it. You need a new interest, Tim. You've always liked dogs, haven't you?"

"Dogs?" I gaped at my brother.

"Dogs!" he said again. "I mean I quite understand if Irene wasn't the lady for you"—Irene had been the widow from Brighton—"but Betty's found a charming woman who breeds dogs up on the downs."

"I don't want a dog breeder," I snapped. "I want to find Nicole."

"But I thought you agreed she might be dead?"

"Fuck off," I told my reverend and insensitive brother.

David might have half wanted Nicole to be dead,

yet oddly it was he who found her, or rather who brought me the evidence that Nicole might still be alive. It happened on the Sunday after our brief argument. I was at home, trying to ignore the whiskey bottle as I contemplated opening a can of soup for lunch, when David, still in his cassock, appeared at the back door. "It's me," he said unnecessarily, then dropped the color supplement of one of the Sunday newspapers on the table beside my can of tomato soup. "Mrs. Whittaker gave it to me after Matins"—he explained the newspaper— "because she recognized, well, you can see for yourself. Page forty. Mind if I have a whiskey?"

I did not answer. Instead, with a heart thudding like a diesel engine, I turned to page forty. I knew it was Nicole. David did not need to say anything; there was something in his demeanor that told me my daughter had at long last reappeared.

Nicole was in a photograph that showed a group of environmental activists harassing a French warship on the edge of France's nuclear weapons testing facility in the South Pacific. The picture was part of a long article about the growing militancy of the ecology movement and there, in the very center of the photograph, was Nicole. My heart skipped as I stared at the photograph. Nicole. I wanted to laugh and to cry. The fifteen months of despair and sadness since Joanna's death were suddenly shot through with brilliance, like a spear of lightning slashing through gray clouds. Nicole was alive, and I was not alone. My breath caught in my throat, and my eyes pricked with tears.

The picture, taken in black and white through a

telephoto lens, showed a catamaran that was festooned with banners carrying antinuclear slogans. In the foreground an inflatable boat manned by armed French sailors was motoring toward the catamaran, which was wallowing hove-to in a surging sea. Six young people lined the catamaran's cockpit, all evidently shouting toward the photographer, who had presumably been on board a French warship astern of the inflatable boat. Nicole was one of the six protesters. Her face, distorted by anger, looked lean and tough.

"Oh, God," I said weakly, because seeing my daughter's face after four years seemed something like a resurrection.

"Genesis," David said. He was striding up and down the unwashed kitchen tiles, and was plainly uncomfortable with my emotion.

"Genesis?" I asked him, wondering if I had missed some subtle biblical point.

"Look below the photograph, in the box!" David's tone clearly suggested that he believed this reminder of Nicole's continued existence could do my life no good whatsoever. He drank a slug of my whiskey, lit his pipe, then stared gloomily at the birds in my unkempt orchard.

At the bottom of the page was a box in which the newspaper listed the various militant groups that were using sabotage, which they called "ecotage," to jar the world's governments into paying more attention to the environment. One of those groups was called the Genesis community, presumably, the writer averred, because its members wished to restore the world to its pristine condition. Not much

was known about Genesis except that it was led by a
man called Caspar von Rellsteb, who was one of the
most outspoken supporters of ecotage, and that the
group specialized in seaborne activities. They had
attempted to sabotage the sixty-mile drift nets with
which the Japanese and Taiwanese were obliterating
life in the Pacific Ocean, and were believed to have
attacked two Japanese whaling ships. The group's
activities were confined to the Pacific, where they
had made strong, though futile, efforts to stop
French nuclear testing. "It doesn't say where they're
based!" I protested.

"Obviously in the Pacific," David said.

"Oh, very helpful," I said sarcastically, then
looked again at the photograph as though there
might be some clue in its grainy composition as to
where I might find my daughter. Yet all the picture told me was that Nicole had been alive when
the picture was taken the previous autumn. I recognized the catamaran as the *Erebus* which, nearly
four years before, had taken Nicole out of my life.
I could not see Caspar von Rellsteb in the photograph; if any one of the six protesters seemed to
dominate the scene, it was Nicole herself. The
obsessive look on her face was so familiar to me; a
look of such determination that it veered toward
bitterness. "Buggering up the French bomb, eh?" I
said enthusiastically. "Good for her!"

"If the Frogs want a nuclear bomb," David said
irritably, "then they have to test it somewhere. It's
not doing us any harm, is it?"

"Don't be such a fool," I said. "Good for Nicole!"

David puffed a smoke screen from his pipe. "If

you read the rest of the article," he said in a very guarded voice, "you'll notice that the attacks on the Japanese whaling ships were made with dynamite."

There was a second of silence, then I exploded with indignation at the inference he was making. "Don't be so bloody ridiculous, David!"

"I'm not being ridiculous," he said, "but merely pointing out to you what that damned policeman will undoubtedly notice."

"Fletcher's lost interest," I said. "Besides, if anything, this article proves that Fletcher was wrong! It proves Nicole can't have killed her mother."

"It does?" David asked. "How?"

"She's in the Pacific!" I pointed out. "Even Fletcher will have to admit that it's difficult for someone in the Pacific to plant bombs in England! How's she supposed to have done it? She just popped out one night, sailed halfway round the world, planted a bomb, then sailed back again. Is that it?"

"Of course you're right." David had not intended to trigger my anger, and now mollified it by changing the subject. He picked up the can of soup. "Is this lunch?"

"Yes."

"You'd better come to the rectory instead. Betty's made a loin of pork with applesauce."

"No dog breeders you want me to meet?"

"None at all," he promised.

So I went to Sunday lunch at the rectory, where the three of us discussed the article, examined the photograph, and agreed that Nicole looked wonderfully well. I was feverish with excitement, which worried David and Betty, who both feared that my hopes of a reunion with Nicole might be horribly premature. Yet I could not resist my own pleasure; my daughter was alive and was working to make a better world. Her activities were far away, which suggested she could not have known of her mother's death. "I'm going to find her," I told David. "Find her and tell her."

"It'll be a bit difficult," David warned me. "That article doesn't give you much of a clue where Genesis might be."

But the name was clue enough and, the next morning, still excited, I went to London to find out more.

Matthew Allenby was the secretary, founder, chairperson, inspiration, spokesperson, and dogsbody for one of Britain's largest and most active environmental pressure groups. He was also a remarkably modest and kind man. I did not know him well, but we had sometimes met at conferences where I was a spokesman for the boat trade against the protestors who complained that our marinas polluted coastal waters. Allenby had always treated my arguments fairly, and I liked him for it. Now, though we had not met for at least two years, he greeted me warmly. "I should have written with condolences about your wife," he said ruefully, "and I'm sorry I didn't."

"I couldn't bring myself to read the letters anyway."

He offered me a smile of grateful understanding. "I suppose it must be like that." He poured me coffee, then, after the obligatory small talk, asked me just why I had been so insistent on an immediate meeting.

To answer I pushed the color supplement across his desk. I had ringed Nicole's face with ink. "She's my daughter," I said, "and I want to find her."

"Ah, Genesis!" Matthew Allenby said with immediate recognition. He pronounced the word with a hard "G," and with a note of dismay.

"Genesis?" I was querying the hard "G."

"The German pronunciation," he explained. "I believe the group's leader was born in Germany."

"I've met him."

"Have you now?" Allenby immediately looked interested. "I haven't met von Rellsteb. Not many people have."

I described the circumstances of my encounter with the naked harem on von Rellsteb's catamaran. Allenby seemed amused by my account, and he was a man clearly in need of amusement, for his office was papered with posters that depicted the torn and bloody corpses of seals, dolphins, whales, porpoises, manatees, and sea otters. Other pictures showed poisoned landscapes, fouled rivers, oil-choked beaches, and skies heavy with toxic clouds. It was not a cheerful office, but nor were the evils against which Allenby had devoted his life and which had given him a Sisyphean gravity beyond his years. "What I really want to know," I finished up, "is who Genesis are and where I can find them."

"Genesis"—Allenby still stared at the photograph of Nicole— "is an impassioned community of environmental activists; green militants. They're remarkably secretive and, as a result, somewhat notorious."

"Notorious?" I said with some surprise. "I never heard of them before yesterday!"

Allenby pushed the color supplement back across the desk. "That's because until now the Genesis community has confined its activities to the Pacific, but believe me, within our movement, they are notorious."

"You sound disapproving," I challenged him.

"That's because I do disapprove of them." His disapproval was qualified, perhaps because he did not want to sound too disloyal to a group that espoused his own organization's aims. "Genesis believe that the time for persuasion and negotiation is long past, and that the enemies of the environment understand only one thing: force. It's a view." He shifted uneasily in his chair. "But the trouble with ecotage, Mr. Blackburn, is that it can very easily become eco-terrorism."

"Does Genesis's ecotage involve killing people?" I asked, and hated myself for indulging the suspicion that Nicole had been responsible for her mother's death, but the article's mention of dynamite had sown a tiny seed of doubt that I wanted eradicated.

"No, not that I know of," Allenby said to my relief. "In fact, I think most of their actions have been somewhat clumsy. They've made various attempts to tow paravanes equipped with cutting gear into Japanese drift nets, but I believe they lose their gear more often than they destroy the nets, which is a pity. Do you know about the drift nets?"

"Not much," I admitted, and Allenby described the fifty- and sixty-mile-long monofilament nets with which the Japanese, Taiwanese, and Koreans were destroying sea life in the Pacific.

"Nothing living can escape such a net." Allenby could not disguise his bitterness. "It's the nuclear weapon of the fishing industry, and it leaves behind a dead swath of sea. In the short term, of course, the profits from such a device are phenomenal, but in the long term it will strip the ocean of life. The men who use the nets know that, but they don't care."

"The newspaper says that Genesis used dynamite in some of their attacks?" I said.

"Ah, rumors," he said in a very neutral voice.

"Just rumors?" I probed.

He paused as though weighing the wisdom of retelling mere rumors, then shrugged as though it would do no harm. "Last year two Japanese whaling ships were being scaled in South Korea when bombs destroyed the dock-gate mechanisms. Both ships were effectively sealed inside their dry docks. A dozen green organizations claimed responsibility for the ecotage, but there is substantial evidence which points to Genesis as the responsible group." He frowned thoughtfully. "Of course the Japanese insisted that the whaling ships were being used merely for scientific research, but the Japanese always make that claim. You will detect, Mr. Blackburn, a certain ambivalence in my attitude toward Genesis. On the one hand I believe they do nothing but harm to our movement, alienating the very people whose help we need if we're to achieve our aims, but on the other hand I sometimes find myself applauding the directness of their actions."

I tried to imagine Nicole as a green storm trooper. Could she risk a Korean jail by planting a bomb? And if so, would she risk a British jail for a similar crime? The suspicion that my daughter was a bomb maker, first planted by Fletcher, then nurtured by the newspaper article, would not die in me. "Have you heard of any Genesis activity in the Atlantic?" I asked Allenby, forcing myself to use the German pronunciation with its hard "G."

"None at all, but that doesn't mean they've never operated here. They specialize in hit-and-run tactics and they could, I assume, sail in and out of the Atlantic without any of us being the wiser. You, of all people, must surely appreciate that possibility?"

Crossing the Atlantic, I thought to myself, was a more complicated task than Allenby evidently took it to be. Of course Nicole had not planted the bomb! Of course not! "How do I find Genesis?" I asked Allenby instead of pursuing the possibility of Nicole's guilt.

"I honestly don't know." Matthew Allenby spread long pale hands in a gesture of helplessness. "Part of the group's appeal is their secretiveness. They don't publish an address."

"They must have a base somewhere!"

Again he made the oddly graceful gesture of

helplessness. "For a long time they were based in British Columbia. Von Rellsteb grew up there, of course, so . . ."

"He's Canadian?" I asked with surprise for I had long assumed that von Rellsteb was a German.

"He was born in Germany," Allenby explained, "but he grew up near Vancouver."

"I didn't know," I said, at last understanding why my researches in Germany had turned up nothing.

"But it's no good looking for Genesis in Canada now," Allenby warned me. "They had an encampment on an island off the British Columbian coast, but they left it four or five years ago, and no one seems to know where they went."

My instant guess was that the Genesis community was still in British Columbia, because that coast was a nightmare tangle of islands, straits, and inlets, and if a man wanted somewhere to hide from the world then there were few better places than the waters north of Vancouver.

Allenby was sifting through a heap of business cards he had spilled from a bowl on his desk. "If anyone can help you," he said, "these people can." He offered me a card that bore the name Molly Tetterman and had an address in Kalamazoo, Michigan, USA. Under the name was printed the legend "Chairperson, the Genesis Parents' Support Group." "Mrs. Tetterman's daughter, like yours, joined Genesis and hasn't been seen since," Allenby explained, "and Mrs. Tetterman wrote and asked for my help, but alas, I had no more information to give her than I've been able to give you."

"You've been very helpful," I said politely. I picked up the color supplement which had printed Nicole's photograph and leafed through its pages to find the name of the journalist who had written the article. "Perhaps he can help me?"

"I doubt it." Allenby smiled. "He got most of that information from me anyway."

"Oh." I felt the frustration of a trail gone cold.

"But what I will do," Allenby offered, "is ask around and pass on any information I might discover. I can't really encourage you to be hopeful, but it's odd how things turn up when you least expect them."

"I'd be grateful," I said, but my acknowledgement of his offer was almost as automatic as his making of it, for I could tell from Allenby's tone that he did not truly expect to discover any new information about Genesis. "Perhaps I should talk to this journalist after all." I tapped the article in the magazine. "You never know, he might have found another good source."

"If you talk to the journalist," Allenby said very carefully, "then he'll want to know why you're so interested in Genesis, and even the dullest journalist will eventually connect your inquiry about bombed whaling ships in Korea with an unexplained bomb in the English channel. I'm sure there's no connection," he said gently, "but journalism thrives on such suppositions."

I stared into Allenby's intelligent face and realized how very astute he was, and how very kind too, for he had just saved me from blundering into a heap of unwanted publicity. "There is no connection," I said, loyal to my belief in Nicole's innocence.

"Of course there isn't," Allenby agreed, "but the coincidence is too palpable for any journalist to ignore. So why don't you let me talk to the journalist," he offered, "without mentioning your name, and I'll also talk to some of my Canadian and American colleagues, and if I discover anything, anything at all, then I'll pass it straight on to you. And in the meantime, what you can do, Mr. Blackburn, is to keep on running a nonpolluting boatyard."

I thanked him, and went back to do just that, but despite Allenby's good advice I could not resist trying to discover more about Genesis for myself. I telephoned Fletcher, but he knew nothing of von Rellsteb's organization. "I've heard of a rock group called Genesis, but not a green group," he said sourly, then asked why I was so interested. I revealed that Nicole was a member of Genesis, and I immediately heard a professional interest quicken Fletcher's voice. "You're suggesting that they're connected with your wife's murder?" he asked.

"No, I am not," I said firmly.

"The greens are all so pure, aren't they?" Fletcher had entirely ignored my denial. "But that doesn't mean they're not as bloody minded as anyone else. After all we've got the Animal Liberation Front, who think it's cute to use bombs on humans. I mean I can just about understand the IRA, but blowing up people on behalf of pussycats?" The policeman paused. "Are you going looking for this Genesis mob?"

"There's not much point, is there? I don't know where they live."

"Well, if I hear anything, I'll let you know."

The promise was purely automatic, and I heard nothing more from Fletcher. Even Matthew Allenby could only send me some five-year-old pamphlets written by Caspar von Rellsteb. The pamphlets, printed on recycled paper by an obscure environmental press in California, proved to be savage but imprecise attacks on industry. There was no mention of Genesis, suggesting that the group's name had not been coined when the pamphlets were written, though one of the tracts did outline a communal style of "eco-existence," an "ecommunity," in which children could be raised to think "ecorrectly," and that individual greed would be subsumed by the group's "eco-idealism." The suggestion was nothing more than the old Utopian ideal harnessed to an environmental wagon, and I assumed that the ideas in the pamphlet had become reality in the Genesis community.

The pamphlets provided no clues as to where the Genesis community might have moved when they abandoned their British Columbian encampment. I wrote to Molly Tetterman in Kalamazoo, and in reply received some typewritten and photocopied newsletters from her Genesis Parents' Support Group, but the newsletters added very little to what I already knew. Caspar von Rellsteb had established his Canadian ecommunity on a private island north of the Johnstone Strait, but had since vanished, and the newsletters, far from solving the mystery of the community's present whereabouts, only made it more tantalizing by appealing for anyone with any information to please contact Molly Tetterman in Kalamazoo, Michigan.

"People can't just disappear off the face of the earth!" I complained to David.

"Of course they can. Happens everyday. That's why the Salvation Army has a missing-persons' bureau."

"So what am I supposed to do? Report the Genesis community to the Salvation Army?"

David laughed. "Why not? They're very efficient at finding people."

Instead of the Salvation Army I tried the French navy, politely inquiring whether they had any information about the activists who had harassed their nuclear tests in the Pacific, but their only reply was a formal denial that any such harassment had even occurred. It seemed, as the weeks passed, that von Rellsteb had truly succeeded in vanishing off the face of the polluted earth.

Then Matthew Allenby struck gold.

"Actually I didn't do a thing," he said modestly when he telephoned me with his news. "It was one of our American groups who found him out."

"Where?" I said eagerly.

"Have you ever heard of the Zavatoni Conference?" Allenby asked me.

"No."

"It's a biannual event, a chance for environmentalists and politicians to get together, and it's convening in Key West in two weeks. Most of us would like to hold it somewhere more ecologically significant, but if you don't offer politicians the comforts of a five-star hotel, then they won't turn up for anything. But the point is, Mr. Blackburn, that the organizers sent an invitation to von Rellsteb. . . ."

"They knew where to write to him?" I interrupted angrily, thinking of all my wasted efforts to discover Genesis's whereabouts.

"Of course they didn't," Allenby said soothingly. "Instead they placed advertisements in all the West Coast environmental magazines. But the amazing thing is that he's accepted their offer. He's agreed to give the keynote speech. It's something of a *coup* for the organizers, because most of the ecotage people won't agree to debate with the mainline organizations, and—"

"Where exactly is this conference?" I interrupted Matthew Allenby again.

"I told you, in Key West, Florida." He gave me the name of the hotel.

"So how do I get in?" I asked.

"If you make your own travel and hotel arrangements," Allenby suggested with diffident generosity, "then I'll say you're one of my delegates. But I know that hotel doesn't have any spare rooms, so you're going to have trouble finding a bed."

"I don't give a damn." I could already feel the excitement of the chase. "I'll sleep in the street if I have to!"

"Don't be too eager!" Allenby warned me. "Von Rellsteb might not turn up. In fact, if I had to give odds, I'd say there's less than an even chance that he will actually arrive."

"Those odds are good enough for me!"

"It really is a long shot," Matthew warned me again.

But I reckoned that only by a long shot would I ever find Nicole, and so I bought myself a ticket to Miami. David opined that I was mad, an opinion he hammered at me right until the moment I left England. He drove me to Heathrow in his ancient Riley. "Nicole won't be at Key West! You do realize that, don't you?"

"How do you know?"

"Of course I don't know!" he said. "It is just that like other sensible human beings I predicate my actions, especially the expensive actions, on probabilities rather than on vague hopes that will almost certainly lead to a debilitating disappointment."

"You don't believe in miracles?" I teased him.

"Of course I do," he said stoutly, "but I also believe in the existence of false hopes, disappointment, and wasted efforts."

"All I want to do," I explained very calmly, "is to find Nicole and tell her about her mother's death. Nothing else." That was not entirely true. I also wanted, I needed, Nicole's assurance that she no longer believed I was responsible for her brother's death. That belief of Nicole's might be irrational, but it had snagged in my heart and still hurt. "And to find Nicole," I went on, "I'm willing to waste quite a lot of my own money. Is that so very bad?"

David sniffed rather than answer my question, then, for a few silent miles, he brooded on my obstinancy. "They have pink taxis there, did you know that?" he finally asked as we turned into the airport.

"Pink taxis?"

"In Key West," he said ominously, as though the existence of pink taxis was the final argument that would prevent my leaving. He braked outside the British Airways terminal. "Pink taxis," he said again, even more ominously.

"It sounds like fun," I said, then climbed from the car and went to find my child.

David was right. There were bright pink taxis in Key West.

And I was suddenly glad to be there because it was a preposterous, outrageous, and utterly unnecessary town; a fairy-tale place of Victorian timber houses built on a sun-drenched coral reef at the end of a one-hundred-mile highway that skipped between a chain of palm-clad islands across an impossibly blue sea.

I felt I had been transported out of grayness to a sudden, vivid world that contrasted cruelly with the damp drabness that had been my life since Joanna had died. My hangdog spirits lifted as the pink taxi drove me from Key West's tiny airport into the old town's tangle of narrow streets. I was headed for a private guest house that my travel agent had somehow discovered, which proved to be a pretty house on a tree-shaded street close to the town center. The guest house was owned and run by a man named Charles de Charlus, who, when I arrived, was flat on his back beneath a

jacked-up Austin-Healey 3000. He wriggled backward, stood to greet me, and I saw that he was a
handsome, tall, and deeply tanned man whose
face was smeared with engine oil. "Our visitor
from England, how very nice," de Charlus greeted
me as he wiped his hands on a rag. "You look
exhausted, Mr. Blackburn. Come inside." He ushered me into a hallway lavish with beautiful
Victorian furniture, where he plucked a room key
from the drawer of a bureau. "I'm giving you a
room that overlooks the Jacuzzi in the courtyard.
Do feel free to use it. We have a weight room if
you need some exercise, and an electric beach."
    "An electric beach?"
    "An electric tanning salon. For cloudy days."
    "I doubt I'll have much time for relaxation," I
said, trying not to show the awkwardness that
suddenly flared through me. "I'm here for the
Zavatoni Conference."
    "Oh, you're a green! Well, of course, aren't we
all these days?" Charles led me upstairs and ushered me into a wonderfully comfortable room.
"You'll forgive me if I don't come in and show
you where everything is." In explanation he held
up his hands which were still greasy from his car,
then tossed the room key onto the bed. "Your
bathroom is through the blue door, and the air
conditioner controls are under the window.
Enjoy!" He left me in the cool of the airconditioni-
ing. The curtains were closed, presumably to fend
off the fierce sun, but I pulled them aside to let in
some light and found myself staring down into
the palm-shaded courtyard where the bright blue-

tiled Jacuzzi shimmered and foamed in the heat.
Two men were sprawled in the water. Both were
stark naked. One of them, seeing me, raised a lan-
guid hand in greeting. I let the curtain drop. I could feel myself
blushing. Joanna, I thought, would have been
mightily amused, and I could almost hear her
accusing me of a most ridiculous embarrassment. I
took her framed photograph from my seabag, put
it on the bedside table, and thought how very
much I missed her.

Then I sat on the bed and fished out the visiting card that Matthew Allenby had given me. I
dialed Molly Tetterman's number in Kalamazoo,
Michigan. The phone rang four times, then an
answering machine announced that Molly could
not come to the phone right now so would I
please leave a message. I gave my name and said I
had come to America because Caspar von Rellsteb
was supposed to be giving a speech at the
Zavatoni Conference in Key West, and if the
Genesis Parents' Support Group had any observers
at the conference I'd be very glad to meet them. I
dictated the guest-house telephone number to
Molly Tetterman's answering machine, then, overcome by tiredness, I lay back on the bed's pretty
patchwork quilt and slept.

The next morning, a Monday, was the opening
day of the Zavatoni Conference. I walked to the
conference hotel where I discovered that Matthew
Allenby had left my name with the registration

desk in the entrance foyer. I also found that I was just one of hundreds of other delegates, which surprised me for I had somehow imagined that the event would be a small and rather obscure conference like those I had attended in Britain. The Zavatoni Conference was to be a full-blown celebration of the environment and of the efforts being made to preserve it. The tone was set from the moment I registered and was presented with a badge which read "Hi! I'm Tim! And I Care!" The badge was printed in a livid Day-Glo green. "It's made from recycled plastic," the friendly official reassured me, then directed me to a huge notice board that listed all the day's attractions at the conference.

Most were the predictable fare of such conferences; I could see a film about Greenpeace's work, or attend a lecture on the depredations of the logging industry in Malaysia, or catch a bus that would take delegates to see the endangered Key deer on Big Pine Key. Yet this was also a conference for political action, so there were axes being ground; a Swedish parliamentarian was lecturing on "Environmental Taxes: A Strategy for Fiscal Eco-Enforcement," while the Women Against Meat-Eaters were caucusing with the Coalition for an Alcohol-Free America in the Hemingway Lounge. The European Proletarian Alliance Against Oil Producers was holding a multicultural symposium in the Henry Morgan Suite, where their guest celebrity was a British actress, and I wondered, for the millionth fruitless time, just why the acting profession labored under the misapprehension that trumpery fame gave its members the expertise to tell the rest of us how to conduct our lives.

I decided to give the actress, and all the other meetings, a miss, though I did avail myself of the exhibition in the Versailles Mezzanine where all the environmental groups who were officially represented at the conference displayed their wares. The exhibition ranged from a *tableau vivant* mounted by Mothers Against Nuclear Physics, which showed cosmetically scorched women holding half-melted plastic dolls in rigidly agonized post-disaster poses, to The Land Of Milk And Honey exhibit, which was neatly staffed by well dressed born-again Christian fundamentalists. Matthew Allenby's organization had an intelligently sober exhibit, as did the Sierra Club and a score of other mainline pressure groups, but, despite Caspar von Rellsteb's agreement to address the conference, there was no display illustrating the life and work of the Genesis community.

I went back to the lobby where I was accosted by a woman wearing a clown costume who solicited my signature for a petition demanding an end to offshore oil-drilling throughout the world. Other activists were attempting to ban nuclear power stations, sexism, fur coats, mercury in dental fillings, and pesticides. I signed the petition on fur coats, then spotted Matthew Allenby standing in the open doorway of a crowded room where he was listening to a lecture.

"I feel rather guilty for telling you about this conference," he said. "I rather suspect I've encouraged you to waste a good deal of your money and time. There's absolutely no sign of von Rellsteb, and I'm told it would be very typical of him to agree to attend but then not turn up."

"It won't be your fault if that happens," I said. "Any parent would snatch at the smallest chance of finding his child, wouldn't he?"

"Yes, of course," Matthew agreed, though he still sounded dubious. We had wandered close to the hotel's front door, outside of which a number of demonstrators angrily harangued arriving delegates. The anger was directed at anyone who arrived in a car, and thereby contributed exhaust fumes to global warming. "They're from WASH." Matthew gestured at the angry demonstrators.

"WASH?" I assumed it was a town I had never heard of, or else a contraction of Washington.

"It's an acronym," Matthew explained. "W.A.S.H., or the World Alliance to Save Humanity." He grimaced. "For a time their British branch picketed my office."

"Your office?" I said in astonishment. "What were they accusing you of?"

"They thought my organization should support their call for the abolition of private cars." Matthew sighed. "The green movement is riddled with a holier-than-thou attitude, which means that the extremists are always trying to show how much purer they are than the mainstream groups. It's all rather counterproductive, of course. If we cooperated and agreed on some specific goals then we could make real progress. We could certainly outlaw drift netting in the Pacific. We could probably end the use of CFCs in refrigerators and aerosols, we could seriously reduce carbon monoxide emissions, and we might even save what's left of the rain forests. But what we can't do is ban all cars from the road, and we don't help our cause by saying that we can. Ordinary people don't want to lose their cars, just as they don't want to go cold in winter merely because they're told that oil and coal power stations pollute the air, and nuclear power is unsafe. I know, because I'm an ordinary person and I don't want to stop using a car, and I don't want my children to be cold in winter. The problem with our movement, Mr. Blackburn, is that we're always trying to ban things, but we don't offer alternatives. And I mean genuine alternatives that will heat peoples' homes and apply deodorants to their armpits and propel their automobiles. People will listen to us if we offer them hope, and they'll even pay a few pennies more if they think the extra cost will help the planet, but if we offer them only doom, they'll accept the doom and decide they might as well be comfortable as they endure it. It's the primrose path syndrome; why be uncomfortable if you're going to hell?"

I smiled. "You sound as if you ought to be giving the keynote speech."

"I've been asked to do just that, but only if von Rellsteb doesn't turn up on Wednesday night. Of course my speech won't be as popular, because common sense never is as interesting as fanaticism. If von Rellsteb comes and rants about paying back pollution with violence, then he'll make

every newspaper in the free world, while my real-
ism won't even make two inches in the local
paper."

There was certainly a great deal of press and
television interest in the conference. The numerous reporters were not required to wear the delegates' Day-Glo green name badges, but instead
had official-looking red press tags that, under their
names, announced what newspaper or magazine
they worked for. As Matthew and I stood by the
entrance one such reporter arrived to run the
gauntlet of WASH hatred. She was a pale and flus-
tered-looking girl with something so disorganized
in her looks and so fearful in her expression that I
instinctively felt protective toward her. She was
wearing a long yellow skirt which gave her a fresh,
springlike appearance. She must have arrived by
car or taxi for the WASH demonstrators were giving her a particularly hard time. "You can see,"
Matthew said quietly, "just how easily fanaticism
could spill into terrorism."

"Are you saying WASH are terrorists?"

"No, but they think their cause justifies their
actions, and it won't be long before frustration
with results will demand even more violent
action. No doubt that will be Caspar von Rellsteb's
message on Wednesday night. If he comes."

The frail reporter, her fair hair awry, made it
safely into the hotel where, in her relief, she
spilled a great pile of papers and folders onto the
floor. She looked as if she would burst into tears,
but then a hotel porter hurried to help her pick up
the strewn pile.

"Wednesday night," Matthew repeated to me. "If von Rellsteb is going to come, Mr. Blackburn, you'll see him on Wednesday night. Until then, I suspect, you won't need to bother yourself with these proceedings."

The pale and worried-looking girl, her papers rescued, had disappeared into the crowd, but something about her face stayed in my mind. It was not her beauty that had lodged in my consciousness, for the girl's looks had hardly been striking, but rather it was her vulnerability that made her attractive, or perhaps it was her green-eyed gaze of anxious innocence. I smiled, for that sudden pulse of interest was the first resurgence of something I thought had died with Joanna in the bomb-churned waters of the English channel. Key West, with its vividly improbable happenings, was making me feel alive again, and, Genesis or no Genesis, I was glad to have come.

Next day, trusting Matthew Allenby's intuition that I need not bother with the conference until Wednesday, I explored the pretty tree-shaded streets of Key West, and I thought how much Joanna would have liked the old town. The houses had been built by nineteenth-century shipwrights whose techniques of allowing a ship's timbers to flex with the surge of the sea had enabled the houses to ride out Florida's awesome hurricanes. The facades were intricately carved and shaded by flowering trees. The smell of the sea pervaded every street and courtyard, and the heat was made bearable by the ocean breeze. Charles, my guest-house host, explained Key West's prettiness by saying that for years the old town had been too poor to afford new buildings, and thus had been forced to keep its old ones. Now the beautiful gingerbread houses were reckoned to be American architectural treasures. "Though it took us to realize it," Charles said indignantly.

"Us?"

"You know what the realtors say? Follow the fairies. Because we always find the prettiest, forgotten places, then we fill them with marvelous restaurants and wonderful shops. If you want to increase property values in your hometown, Tim, then invite a gay colony to move in." He saw my fleeting look of alarm, and laughed.

It was Tuesday afternoon and I was sweating with the effort of raising the engine block of Charles's Austin-Healey. Charles had discovered that I had once owned a similar car and knew more than a little about engines, so he had recruited me to help him install a rebuilt clutch. As we worked he drew from me the full story of my journey to Key West—the tale of Joanna and Nicole, and of von Rellsteb's Genesis community. "What will you do if von Rellsteb does show up tomorrow night?" Charles asked me.

"Grab the bastard and ask him to take a message to Nicole." It was not much of a plan, but it was all I could think of.

"Perhaps I'd better come and help you," Charles offered. "I'm good at grabbing men." He flexed his arm muscles and, though I somehow doubted that any physical force would be needed, the thought of Charles's companionship was comforting.

I telephoned the conference organizers the next day, but no one could tell me whether or not von Rellsteb had arrived. If the Genesis leader had come to Florida, he was leaving his appearance until the very last moment. Even when Charles and I drove the repaired Austin Healey to the hotel that evening we still did not know if the guest of honor had actually arrived. Charles was in high spirits, anticipating an adventure, though I suspected the evening promised to bring nothing but disappointment.

Because, as the delegates drifted toward the banqueting hall, von Rellsteb had still not shown up. I found Matthew Allenby frantically polishing his moderate speech in anticipation of having to fill von Rellsteb's shoes. "I'm sorry," he said to me, as though it was his fault that I was to be disappointed.

"It doesn't matter," I reassured him.

"He might yet come," Matthew said, and in that hope Charles and I took our positions at the back of the banqueting hall. We deliberately did not try to find places at the tables, preferring to wait by the room's main doors. If von Rellsteb did come he would enter the room by those doors, and our new plan of attack, enthusiastically proposed by Charles, was that we should grab him as he arrived. I had spent a thoughtful afternoon writing a letter to Nicole; that letter was in my jacket pocket. Charles reasoned that von Rellsteb, ambushed at the door, would agree to take the letter just to be rid of us, but, as the meal went on and there was still no sign of the guest of honor, my letter and Charles's enthusiasm both seemed irrelevant.

The speeches began. The conference chairperson gave a short talk extolling the life of Otto Zavatoni, whose vast brewing fortune, left in trust, made these biannual conferences possible. Then the visiting politicians were introduced and applauded. Most, I noted, came from small European opposition parties and were politicians whose hopes of office had long faded and whose careers therefore could not be hurt by an association with the more extreme green elements. And there was a handful of politicians from the Third World who received the loudest and warmest receptions. The introductions took a long and tedious time and, for want of any better way of entertaining myself, I looked around the huge banqueting hall for the reporter who had been wearing the yellow skirt. I did not see her.

Nor was there any sign of von Rellsteb. Conference officials, still hoping for his arrival, scurried in and out of the banqueting hall. The room was restless. I noted how many reporters were present, clearly drawn by the chance of meeting the mysterious proponent of ecotage. But von Rellsteb still did not show, and, finally, the chairperson stood and bleakly announced that a change of plans was unfortunately dictated by the absence of the guest speaker, but that nevertheless the conference was most fortunate in having the company of Matthew Allenby who had agreed to replace the absent Caspar von Rellsteb. The

applause that greeted the announcement was scattered and unenthusiastic.

Matthew gave his reasonable and sensible
speech. He was a good orator, but, even so, I could
see the more extreme delegates shifting unhappily
as he talked of consensus and education, and of
agreement and cooperation. Many of the delegates
had not come to hear about consensus, but about
confrontation, and five minutes into Matthew's
speech there were the first stirrings of dissent as a
table of Scandinavian activists started to heckle.
Matthew made his voice stronger, temporarily still-
ing his critics. By now it was dark outside, and the
big windows that faced the sea were a black sheen
in which the chandeliers, ablaze with thousands of
light bulbs, reflected brightly. Matthew spoke of
setting attainable goals and of the importance of
not alienating the ordinary man and woman who
wanted to feel they could make a genuine contribution toward repairing the damaged fabric of the
earth. A man who disagreed with the moderation
of Matthew's proposals struck the handle of his
knife against his empty water glass. Someone else
joined the ringing protest, and suddenly the room
was clamorous with dissent. The chairperson called
for order, while a conflicting voice yelled at
Matthew to sit down and be quiet. I was about to
shout my own protest against the protesters, when
suddenly the great room's lights blinked out, the
western sky sheeted a fiery red, and the first guests
screamed with horror.

Genesis had come at last.

$\mathbf{T}$he doors behind Charles and me were kicked violently open. A woman at a nearby table screamed in terror. I turned to see three bearded men silhouetted against the hallway lights that were still shining bright. The three men half stepped over the banqueting hall's threshold. Everything was happening so fast that I was still pushing myself upright from where I had been leaning idly against the wall. Then the three men hurled missiles deep into the darkened room and I twisted awkwardly and frantically aside. I saw smoke trails fluttering behind the objects. Christ! I thought, the bastards are using grenades! and I was instinctively shrinking into a groin-protecting crouch as the first missile cracked apart in a foul-smelling gout of chemical stench. The "grenades" were stink bombs.

"Come on, Tim! Come on!" Charles had recovered more quickly than me, and was already pursuing the fleeing men.

I followed, only to be crushed in the sudden crowd of choking, screaming, and panicked delegates, who fought toward the cleaner air of the hallway. A fire alarm had begun to shrill, its bell filling the hotel's vast spaces with a terrible urgency. The stink bombs were pumping a noxious, gagging smoke that overwhelmed the air conditioner ducts. I heard a crash as a table was overturned. A woman in a sari tripped and fell in front of me. I dragged her upright, shoved her out of my way, then drove my shoulder hard into the press of fleeing people to make a path through them.

"This way, Tim!" Charles was free of the panic and running toward the hotel gardens. The men who had attacked the conference were fleeing through those gardens toward the sea, scattering leaflets in their wake. I could just see the three running figures in the eerie light of the flickering flames that illuminated the hotel grounds.

I tore myself free of the crowd and sprinted after Charles. He had already rammed through a door and jumped off the terrace where the tables were set for breakfast. I leaped after him. Palm trees were burning at the edge of the beach, and I realized it had been their ignition that had sheeted the sky with red flame. The night air stank of burning and of the gasoline I guessed had been used to set the trees alight. The thatched roof of a beach bar had also caught the fire and was furiously spewing sparks into the night wind.

Charles was overtaking the fugitives who ran toward the sea which lay just beyond the burning trees. The three men were wearing green overalls and had ninjalike scarves round their heads, and I realized, with a sudden excitement, that it was the same pale green in which Caspar von Rellsteb had uniformed Nicole when she sailed away on *Erebus*. One of the fugitives, slower than his companions, dodged between the empty lounges beside the hotel's swimming pool, and Charles leaped onto the man's back with a flying tackle that would have made an international rugby player proud. There was a terrible crash as the two men fell into the wooden furniture and I heard the Genesis fugitive cry aloud in pain. "Hold him!" I shouted at Charles in unnecessary encouragement.

The other two men turned back to help their comrade. I reached the pool's apron, ran past Charles and his struggling prisoner, and charged the two men. I shoulder butted the nearest one, who toppled, shouted in fear, then fell backward into the black pool. The second man tried to swerve past me, but I grabbed his arm, turned him, and thumped a fist into his belly. I followed that blow with a wild swing at his face that was cushioned by the man's vast and springy beard into which I tried to hook my fingers, but the man managed to find his balance and tear himself free, leaving a handful of wiry hairs in my right fist. Abandoning his two companions the man sprinted toward the beach.

The man I had pushed into the water was already climbing out of the pool's far side, and I saw that his green overalls were discolored by black streaks which, together with the thick stench that polluted the night air, made me realize that the swimming pool had been deliberately fouled with gallons of black and stinking oil. Behind me Charles suddenly grunted, and I turned to see his captive still desperately struggling. I ran over and thumped a boot into the man's midriff. "Get him into the bushes!" I said.

Conference delegates were flooding into the gardens. I did not want to share my captive with anyone, but instead wanted to force some swift information from the man. Charles dragged the bearded figure into the deep shadows behind the small hut where the hotel's bathing towels were kept. The prisoner made one last frantic effort to twist out of Charles's grip, but only received a smashing punch in the stomach for his pains. He doubled over, but I grabbed his beard and rammed his head back so that his skull thumped painfully against the hut's wall. "Do you want me to give you to the police?" I asked him.

The man said nothing. I could barely see his face, so dark were the shadows, but I could see that our captive was not Caspar von Rellsteb. "Do you speak English?" I asked him.

Still he said nothing. I sensed Charles moving beside me, and the prisoner suddenly gave a small cry of pain. "I speak English," the man said hastily. He had an American accent and breath that smelled rotten.

"Are you from Genesis?" I asked, and, in my excitement, I pronounced it the English way. "Genesis?" I corrected myself.

"Yes!" he said, but with difficulty, for I was holding him by the throat.

"Listen," I said, and slightly released the pressure of my hooked fingers as I spoke. "My name is Tim Blackburn. My daughter is Nicole Blackburn. Do you know Nicole?"

He nodded frantically. I could see the whites of his eyes as he glanced in panic toward the urgent voices of the conference delegates who were milling excitedly by the fouled pool. I could smell the fear in our captive. He had been hurt by Charles and now feared that I was about to add to his pain or, worse, was about to hand him over to a vengeful mob.

"Is Nicole here tonight?" I asked urgently.

He whimpered something that I did not catch.

"Is she?" I insisted.

"No! No!"

"So where is she?" I demanded.

"I don't know!"

"But she's with Genesis?"

"Yes!" he said.

"Where is Genesis!" I hissed at him. "Where's your base?"

He said nothing.

"Answer me!" I said too loudly.

Still the man said nothing, so I rammed a fist into his belly. "Where the fuck is my daughter?" I shouted at him, suddenly not caring if we were overheard. The man stubbornly shook his bearded face. He had evidently decided to act the heroic prisoner; he would give me his name, rank, and number, but he was determined not to reveal where the Genesis community lived. "Where?" I gripped him by the throat and shook him like a dog shakes a rat.

"Hurry!" Charles urged me. Flashlight beams

were raking the nearby bushes, and it could only
be minutes or even seconds before we were seen.
"Hurry!" Charles said again.

"Was von Rellsteb here tonight?" I asked our
prisoner.

"Yes!"

"I want to meet him. Tell him that. Tell him
I've got some important news for Nicole. Ask him
to give her this letter, but tell him I'd like to talk
with him first." I took the letter from my jacket
pocket, then borrowed a pen from Charles and
wrote the guest-house telephone number on the
back of the envelope. Afterward I fumbled about
our captive's overalls until I found a pocket into
which I stuffed the precious letter. "Tell von
Rellsteb to telephone me at the number on that
envelope. Tell him there's no trap. I just want to
meet him. Do you understand?"

The man whimpered his assent. Behind us a
flashlight beam slashed through the bushes, and a
burning frond of palm whipped over our heads.
The hotel's fire alarm was at last silenced, though
somewhere in the night's distance I could hear the
visceral wail of approaching sirens.

"And when you next see Nicole"—I still held
the Genesis man by the throat—"tell her I love
her." The man looked somewhat startled at the
incongruity of those last words, but he managed
to nod his comprehension.

I pushed him away from me. "Go!" I said.

For a split second the man stood astonished, then
he twisted away and ran frantically toward the sea.
He was now a messenger to my daughter, and I

silently urged his escape past the angry conference delegates, who, seeing the fugitive flee from the bushes, shouted the alarm and set off in renewed pursuit.

My messenger almost did not make it to freedom. He ran just inches ahead of his pursuers. I saw him leap off the sea wall, and I thought he must have been overwhelmed by the flood of people who jumped after him, but when Charles and I reached the wall's top we saw that our man was still inches ahead of the hunt. We also saw that there was a large black inflatable boat a few yards offshore with people aboard who were shouting encouragement as our man splashed into the shallows. "Tell Nicole I love her!" I yelled after him, but my voice was drowned by the crackle of flames, the shouts of the crowd, the growl of the inflatable's outboard engine, and the scream of the sirens as Key West's firefighters reached the hotel. The outboard engine roared as the helmsman curved toward the beach, driving the clumsy rubber bow into the surf where the bearded fugitive hurled himself into the face of a breaking wave. "There goes your letter!" Charles said.

The crowd of angry delegates stampeded into the sea after the fugitive. Their feet churned the water white as they charged. The man was swimming now. A woman lunged after him, but fell fractionally short, then hands reached from the inflatable boat, the man was half dragged over the gunwale, and the outboard motor was throttled up so that the lopsided boat thundered away toward the open sea. The man had escaped.

"I think you owe me a drink," Charles said in a

hurt voice. "A big drink. I've ruined a perfectly good pair of pants on your behalf." His white cotton trousers had been ripped, presumably when he had tackled and overpowered our captive.

We left the hotel before anyone could ask us questions and I bought Charles a very stiff scotch in one of the many bars that claimed to have been Ernest Hemingway's spiritual home. I ordered myself an Irish whiskey and, as I drank it, I unfolded and read one of the leaflets that the fleeing Genesis activists had scattered in their wake. The leaflets had been handwritten and copied on an old-fashioned copier that had left smudges of ink on the glossy paper.

"To the Traitors of the Environment," the leaflet endearingly began, "you have Cut and Burned the world's Rain Forests, so we shall Cut and Burn your Fancy Trees. You have Fouled the World's Waterways with Oil, so We shall Take Away your Toy Pool. You have Soured the World's Skies with Noxious Fumes, so We shall Make You Breathe a similar Stench. You Consort with the Enemy, with Politicians, and with their Panders, so how can you Expect a Real Warrior of the World's Ecosystem to Address your Traitorous Conference!" The leaflet went on in a similar vein of capitalized hatred, ending with the boast "We are Genesis. We make Clean by Destroying the Dirt-Makers."

"Very charming," Charles said with fastidious distaste when he had skimmed through the poorly written leaflet. "But why attack fellow environmentalists? Why don't they attack a conference of industrialists?"

"I suppose it's von Rellsteb's way of making a bid for green leadership. He obviously thinks that Greenpeace and all the others are hopelessly respectable, and this is his way of showing it."

"It seems very puerile," Charles said, and so it did. Oil and stink bombs were the weapons of naughty children, not of the eco-warriors the Genesis community aspired to be, yet at least, I consoled myself, they had not used dynamite.

"I'm sorry about your trousers," I said to Charles.

"It was stupid of me to have worn them." Charles looked painfully at the rip in the white cotton.

I could not help grinning at the anguish in his voice. "For a ragged-trousered fairy, Charles," I complimented him, "you're good in a fight."

He looked even more pained. "I'll have you know that Alexander the Great was gay, and who made up the Sacred Band of Thebes? A hundred and fifty fairy couples, that's who, and they were reckoned to be the most lethal regiment that ever marched into battle. And your Lawrence of Arabia knew his way around a Turkish bath well enough, yet he was no slouch in a fight. You should be very glad that we gays are mostly pacifists, or else we'd probably rule the world." He finished his scotch and put the empty glass in front of me. "Perhaps, if you're going to air all your pathetic prejudices about my kind, you should buy me another drink first?"

I spared him my prejudices, but bought him another drink anyway, and wondered if von Rellsteb would call.

*   *   *

No telephone call came on Thursday, and by
that evening I suspected that no call would come.
Why should von Rellsteb contact me? He had gone
to immense trouble to hide himself and his followers from the world, and I could see no reason why
he should risk that concealment by responding to
a plea from the distraught parent of one of his
activists. Besides, the phone number, like the letter, had probably been obliterated by the seawater.

"You tried!" Charles attempted to console me.

"Yes. I tried." And, when no message arrived on
Friday, which was the conference's last day, I realized I had failed. I had lunch with Matthew
Allenby, who ruefully compared the half-inch of
column space that his speech had earned in the
Florida newspapers with the massive coverage that
the Genesis attack had provoked. The local television news had made the Genesis assault their lead
story, reporting that the police and coast guard
had found no sign of the perpetrators. "The publicity is why von Rellsteb does it, of course,"
Matthew Allenby said wistfully.

I thought how Fletcher had talked of terrorists
wanting more bucks for their bangs. "And does
publicity generate cash for Genesis?" I asked.

Matthew frowned. "I don't see how it can. They
publish no address for anyone to send a donation,
yet they must need money. They have to move
around the world, buy their equipment, maintain
their boats, recruit their people. They have to feed
themselves, and the word is that they've got upward

of fifty members. Perhaps they have a secret bene-
factor?" He crumbled a bread roll. "If I was a journalist," he went on slowly, "that's the question I'd
want answered. Where do they get their money?"

I picked listlessly at my salad. Matthew, sensing
my disappointment with the week's events, apologized yet again for tempting me to Key West. "But
maybe he'll still call?"

"Maybe," I agreed, but my flight home left
Miami in less than forty-eight hours, and I knew I
had chased Nicole across an ocean for nothing.

Then, next morning, just when I had finally
abandoned hope, von Rellsteb called.

I had left the guest house to buy some small
presents for David and the boatyard staff. Charles
was out, so one of the kitchen help took the message, which he said was from a man with an unremarkable accent. The message merely said that if I
wanted the meeting I had requested I should wait
at the end of the main dirt road on Sun Kiss Key at
midnight. The caller stressed that I had to be
alone, or else there would be no rendezvous.

I smacked a fist into a palm, showing an excitement that the more cautious Charles did not
share. "You mustn't go on your own!" he insisted,
but I did not reply. I was too excited to care about
caution. "Do you hear me?" Charles asked. "Earth
to Tim! Earth to Tim!"

"Of course I'm going on my own!" I was not
going to risk losing any news of Nicole by disobey-
ing the cryptic orders.

"Suppose it's a trap?" Charles asked.

"Why on earth should it be a trap?" I asked

with stubborn incomprehension.

"Because it's all so secretive," Charles said. "Dirt roads at midnight, no one else to be there. I'd say it was a trap, wouldn't you?"

"Why on earth would they want to trap me?"

"Because we hurt that fellow, that's why, and he probably wants revenge."

"Nonsense!"

"I don't like it, I don't trust it," Charles said unhappily. He had fetched one of the tourist guides from the guest-house reception desk and discovered that Sun Kiss Key was a real-estate name for a proposed housing development on one of the middle keys that lay some twenty miles from Key West. He telephoned a realtor friend and learned that none of the houses had yet been built, and that consequently there was nothing on the island but newly excavated boat canals and a network of unpaved roads. At night it would be deserted. "If I stay a hundred paces behind you," Charles suggested, "then maybe they won't notice?"

"No!" I insisted.

"Then take this." He opened the drawer of a bureau and brought out a holstered revolver. "It's licensed!" he said, as though that made possession of the handgun quite acceptable. I felt the surprise and revulsion that most Europeans feel for handguns, but nevertheless I gingerly reached for the weapon. It was a long-barreled, single-action Ruger, only .22 caliber, but it looked lethal enough. "Have you ever fired a handgun?" Charles asked me.

I nodded, though the last time had been twenty years before in the army, and even then I had only fired six reluctant shots to satisfy an insistent firearms instructor. "I'm sure I won't need this," I said to Charles, though his supposition that von Rellsteb wanted revenge was enough to make me keep the small gun.

"If you don't need it, then just keep it hidden. But if you do need it, then you'll be glad to have it along." Charles took the gun from me and loaded its cylinder with cartridges.

"Why do you keep a gun?" I asked him.

He paused for a second. "Once upon a time," he said, "my car broke down in Texas. I'd decided to drive all the way to San Francisco in an old Packard. It was an antique car, very rare, and someone had told me I could sell it for a lot of money in California, but its back axle broke in Texas. Then two guys stopped in a pick-up. I thought they were going to help me, but . . . " He stopped abruptly, and I wished I had not asked the question, for I saw how the memory pained him, but then he grinned and thrust the revolver toward me. "Fairy firepower, Tim. It shoots slightly up and to the right. And I suppose you'll want to borrow the car as well?"

"Can I?" I asked.

"You may," he said grandly, "indeed you may. But bring it back in one piece. You can be replaced, but Austin-Healeys are rare indeed."

I spent that afternoon writing another letter to Nicole, in case the first was illegible. It was much the same as the first letter. I told my daughter that

I loved her, that I wanted to see her, and that I was lonely for family. I told her I had not killed her brother, and I was sure she knew that, too. It was not a long message, but it still took a long time to write. Then, filled with hope and dread, I waited.

The weather forecast hinted at the possibility of a thunderstorm over the Keys, so I borrowed a black nylon rain slicker from Charles, which I wore over black trousers, black shoes, and a dark blue shirt. "Black suits you," Charles said approvingly.

I growled something ungrateful in reply.

"Don't let a compliment go to your head," he told me, "because your appearance could still take a few basic improvements. A water-based moisturizer for your skin, a decent haircut, and some nice clothes would be a start."

"Shut the hell up," I said, and tucked his holstered gun into my right-hand trouser's pocket. I had Nicole's letter in my shirt pocket, where, if it rained, it would be sheltered by the nylon slicker.

"And for God's sake," Charles went on, "stay under the speed limit on the highway. If the police find you with that gun, we'll both be up to our buns in trouble."

I stayed under the speed limit as I drove up the Overseas Highway which arced on stilts across the channels between the islands. I had left Key West at nine o'clock, wanting to arrive very early at Sun Kiss Key, so that I could scout the rendezvous to smell for even the smallest hint of trouble. Not that I expected trouble, but the strangeness of the occasion and the heaviness of the thundery air gave the whole night an unreal tinge. Ahead of me, like a grim sign of doom, the northern sky was banded by jet black clouds, while overhead the stars pricked bright. There was a half-moon in the east that made the unclouded part of the night's sky lighter than I had anticipated.

I found the dirt road leading off the highway. As I slowed and turned my headlamps flashed across a massive billboard which advertised "Sun Kiss Key, Your Home in the Sun! Waterfront Lots from Just $160,000!" Beyond the billboard the dirt road lay like a white ribbon through the low scrubland. To my left a few pilings had been driven into a cleared patch of land. The pilings were evidently supposed to form the stilts of the development's show house, but work must have come to a standstill, for the pilings were now being used only as supports for a couple of ragged osprey nests. The water in the newly-cut canals was black and still.

I looked in the mirror. No one was following me. Dust from the sport car's tires plumed to drift onto the bushes. I passed another of the canals that was designed to provide boat docks for the planned houses. Behind me the headlight beams blazed and faded along the highway, but no vehicles turned to follow the Austin-Healey onto this lonely and bumpy road.

I came to the end of the track, where I parked the Austin-Healey in a patch of inky shadow.

With the engine switched off the night seemed very silent, then my ears tuned themselves to the noises of a myriad of insects and to the faraway drone of the traffic on the Overseas Highway behind me. I climbed out of the car. The night was warm and still. Far off to my left the sea sucked and splashed at the shallows that edged the keys, while beyond the reefs a motor-cruiser with brightly glowing navigation lights ran fast toward the southwest. To my right, beyond the highway, I could see the lights of the houses on the Atlantic side of the island. The half-moon hung above those houses, while to the north the clouds seemed thicker and blacker. Sheet lightning suddenly paled those dark clouds, hinting at rain over the Everglades. I walked to the water's edge to see that it was a mangrove-edged channel leading to the open sea. Sun Kiss Key was a lonely place for egrets and bonefish, herons and ospreys, but a place doomed to be destroyed by bulldozers and pile drivers, by houses and carports, by power-boats and barbecues.

Waves fretted on the offshore coral. More sheet lightning flickered silent to the north. Someone, I thought, was having a bellyful of bad weather, though the dark clouds did not seem to be spreading any further south. The thought of bad weather gave me a sudden and stunningly realistic image of hard ocean rain falling at sea; an image of clean, fresh water thrashing at a boat's sails and drumming on her coach roof and sluicing down her scuppers, and I wondered just how many months it had been since I had last sailed a boat properly.

It had been too long, I thought, much too long. Apart from the odd delivery job up-channel and shunting boats about the boatyard's pontoons, I had not sailed properly since Joanna's murder. I had not had the energy to provision a boat nor to face the problems of navigation, yet suddenly, in the humid night air of Sun Kiss Key, I missed the ocean. I wanted to feel the chill wind's bite again. I wanted to go far from land into the blank emptiness of the charts where the only guide to life was a belief in God and the high, cold light of His stars. I thought of *Tort-au-Citron, Stormchild* as was, and I resented that she was rotting on a mooring when she and I could have been sailing the long winds of nowhere, and that sudden yearning made me feel that I was at last waking from a nightmare, and I vowed that when I got home I would rig a boat, any boat, and, late though the season was, I would cross the channel and sail round Ushant to where the Biscay rollers would shatter themselves white on my boat's stem.

I smiled at that thought, then looked at my watch. I still had two hours to wait. It had been stupid of me, I thought, to arrive so early, and even more stupid to bring the gun that was a hard lump in my pocket.

"Good evening, Mr. Blackburn."

"Christ!" I jumped like a fearful thing, twisting round to face the sudden voice. I had recognized the voice immediately, for von Rellsteb's German accented English had not changed since my last confrontation with him on the deck of *Erebus*. How the hell had he gotten so close without my hearing him? I could see him now; a dark shape just fifteen yards away. Had he come by boat? Was he alone?

"I'm quite alone." He chuckled as though taking pleasure in anticipating my question. He stepped closer, and I saw by the moonlight that his appearance, like his beguiling voice, had not changed. His face was as narrow and goatlike as I remembered it, and he still had a waist-length ponytail of white hair and a thin straggly beard. He also demonstrated a calm confidence as he reached out to shake my hand. "I rather hoped you would be early," he said. "Midnight seems such a witching hour for a meeting, does it not? But alas, at the time I made the arrangement I did not think I could reach this place any sooner. Luckily things freed up for me. How are you?"

I had warily shaken his hand, but did not respond to his friendly question, preferring to ask one of my own. "Where's Nicole?"

"Ah, she's well! And she's safe!"

"You got my letter for her?"

"It was rather ruined by seawater. The telephone number was written in ballpoint, and decipherable, but the rest? I suspect it was washed away. I am sorry." He shrugged apologetically.

"I have another one for her." I took the letter from my shirt pocket and held it out to von Rellsteb. I was feeling extraordinarily clumsy. Von Rellsteb, not I, had taken charge of this encounter.

Von Rellsteb took the letter and pushed it into a pocket. "You told George that you had important news for Nicole? I assume that news is in the letter?"

"I wanted to tell her that her mother is dead."

"Her mother is . . . " Von Rellsteb began to echo my words, then a look of awful pain shuddered across his face, and I thought of the police suspicion that the Genesis community had planted the bomb that killed Joanna, and I knew that if those suspicions were true, then this man was one of the greatest actors who had ever lived. Von Rellsteb momentarily closed his eyes. "My dear Mr. Blackburn," he said at last, "I am so very sorry. Was it an illness?"

"No." I did not elaborate.

"Poor Nicole!" Von Rellsteb said. "Poor Nicole! And you, too. How very sad. No wonder you are so eager to see her!" He had handled the news of my wife's death with a superb assurance. Most of us, confronted with the mention of death, become tongue-tied and confused, but von Rellsteb's comforting sympathy had been instant and seemingly heartfelt, and I, at last, began to understand how my daughter could have been attracted to this gaunt man. I remembered how Joanna had described him as attractive, and I could begin to see why; his long, thin face had the appeal of sensitivity and intelligence, which made him appear competent to handle the secret hurts of those he met. "You must understand, though," von Rellsteb continued, "that your daughter is frightened."

"Nicole? Frightened?" I asked.

"She thinks you will not forgive her." Von Rellsteb paused to frown in thought. "Sometimes, you know, we do things, and then we find they are gone too far to be retrieved. Do you know what I mean?"

"Not really," I said.

Von Rellsteb gave me a swift, apologetic smile. "I do not always express myself well in English. Nicole is frightened because she did not write or talk to you for so long that each new day makes it harder for her to risk facing the disappointment she knows you must feel."

"But I love her."

"Of course you do." He smiled, complicit with my grief, then stirred the air with his hand as if, frustrated in his efforts to find the right words, he might conjure them from the night's darkness. "I think Nicole knows you love her, but she fears you will be angry because of her absence. She even told me that, perhaps, you had disinherited her!" Von Rellsteb offered a small shrug, as if to share with me the ridiculousness of such a notion, and I did not think to notice that even the mention of disinheritance was an oddity in this admittedly odd rendezvous.

"Disinherit her?" I said instead. "Of course not."

"Not that it matters," von Rellsteb said loftily. "We should be above such mundane matters, yes?"

"And I want to see her!"

"Naturally you do, naturally!" Von Rellsteb said with eager understanding. Behind me the lightning flickered eerily to blanch the rippling water in the mangrove channel. "But it's difficult," von Rellsteb murmured after a pause.

"What is?" I sounded hostile.

"I try to keep the Genesis community separate from the world."

"Why? I thought you wanted to save the world?"

He smiled. "We are not apart from the world, but rather from the people who make the world unclean. The sins of the fathers, Mr. Blackburn, are being visited on their children, so we children must be pure if we are to redeem our fathers' world." His thin, expressive face was suddenly lit by another sheet of lightning which rampaged across the Everglades. "I am expressing myself badly," von Rellsteb went on, "but what I am trying to say, is that we in Genesis have forsaken family, Mr. Blackburn. It is a measure of the seriousness of our purpose."

The pretensions of his words struck me as preposterous. "Seriousness?" I challenged him. "Stink bombs? Oil in a swimming pool?"

He smiled at the accusation. "Of course stink bombs are a joke, but those people at the conference are so, what is the word? Complacent! They talk and talk and talk, and congratulate one another on the purity of their commitment, but while they talk the dolphins are dying and the world's hardwoods are being cut down and oil is being spewed into the seaways. I think it will be the Genesis community, and groups like Genesis, who will cleanse the world, not these fashionable environmentalists with their shrill talk and soft hands. I wanted the journalists at that conference to be aware of the need for extreme measures if the world is to be saved, so I used stink bombs. Would you rather I had used real bombs?"

"Could you have?" I asked him coldly.

"No, Mr. Blackburn, no." His voice was very gentle, as though he dealt with a fractious child.

"Where is Nicole?" I asked him.

"In the Pacific."

"Where, exactly?" I insisted.

Von Rellsteb paused. "I won't tell you." He held up a placatory hand to still my protest, then, as though he needed to move if he was to think and express himself properly, he began pacing up and down the channel's bank. "I have long dreamed of a community that could devote itself to oneness with the earth. A biocentric community, without distractions, living in a silence that might let us hear the echoes of creation and the music of life." He gave me a sudden smile. "You, of all people, know what I mean! You've known the transforming wonder of sitting in a small boat in the center of an ocean in the middle of a night, and suddenly feeling that you steered a vessel among the stars. You could live forever at that moment. There's no history, no anger, no pride, just you and creation and a terrifying, exhilarating mystery. If I am to pierce that mystery, and find its meaning, then I must live in the center of silence. That's what we do." He paused, seeking a further explanation that would satisfy me. "Perhaps we're making the first eco-religion? Perhaps the new millennium will need such a faith? But to forge it, we must live without distraction, and so our first rule, our golden rule, is that we keep ourselves private. That, Mr. Blackburn, is why I will not tell you where we live."

He had almost seduced me with his gently beguiling voice, but some part of me, a robust part of me, would not be sucked into his vision. "You call lacing a swimming pool with oil living in the center of silence?"

"Oh, dear." Von Rellsteb seemed disappointed with me. He was quiet for a few heartbeats, then offered a further explanation. "We don't want to be selfish. We don't want to withdraw totally from the world. Most of the community does stay separate, but a few of us, like myself and Nicole, have to go into the world and deliver shocks to those people who would fill the planet with noise and disgust and dirt and rancor. One day, Mr. Blackburn, the whole world will live in harmony, and the Genesis community both anticipates that era and tries to bring it about. But if I told people where we lived, then I know visitors would come to us, and distract us, and maybe weaken us."

"You don't have much faith in your vision, do you?"

"I have no faith in those who do not share my vision," von Rellsteb said firmly. "And even though I am sure you are not hostile to it, you are still not one of us. Unless you'd like to join us?"

"No!"

He laughed, then stepped back. "I'll give Nicole your letter. I know she'll be pained about her mother."

"I want to see her!"

"Maybe you can." Von Rellsteb stepped back another pace. He was going into the darkness.

"What the hell does that mean?" I demanded.

"If she wants to see you, then you will see her." He stepped further back.

I felt my chances of seeing Nicole slipping away with von Rellsteb's retreat. "Tell her I love her!" I called to him.

"The world is love, Mr. Blackburn." Lightning slashed at the sea, drowning the air with its sudden light, and in its slicing brilliance I caught a frozen glimpse of Caspar von Rellsteb's face, and, in that instant, he seemed to be laughing at me with satanic glee. What earlier had seemed comforting and intelligent now looked evil, but, when my eyes adjusted to the dark again, von Rellsteb had vanished. He had come from the night, and seemed to have dissolved back into it.

"Von Rellsteb!" I shouted.

There was no answer. The sea sucked at the mangrove roots.

"Von Rellsteb!"

But there was only silence and darkness.

I turned away. I felt dizzy, almost drunk, as though I had been mesmerized by von Rellsteb's voice, yet I could not shake the memory of that sudden satanic epiphany. Had he been laughing at me? Had his victory this night consisted of fooling a man whose wife he had killed and whose daughter he had seduced? I stopped and, despite the heat, I was shivering. I also realized that my encounter had yielded me nothing. I had achieved nothing, and I had learned nothing.

Then why, I suddenly wondered, had von Rellsteb agreed to meet me? What had been his purpose this night? To mock me? Then I thought of his denial that he might have used real bombs instead of stink bombs, and remembered the real bombs that had stranded the two Japanese whaling ships in their Korean dry docks. Fear surged inside me. Suppose Nicole was dead? Suppose that von Rellsteb had killed her, and Joanna, and now wanted to kill me? Fletcher had been right when he guessed that my father had left David and me comfortably provided for. We were not flamboyantly wealthy, but nor were we stretched for money, and inheritance has always been a motive for murder. And why else, it suddenly crashed on me, would von Rellsteb have raised the subject of Nicole being disinherited! Sweet God, I thought, that was how von Rellsteb made his money, by making heirs and heiresses of his cowed disciples!

God, he was clever! I remembered the uniform-like clothes Nicole had worn on the day she left with von Rellsteb; clothes which suggested a perverted subservience to von Rellsteb's wishes. Did he have some kind of mesmeric hold over his women? And, once they were under his spell, did he manipulate their lives to enrich his own? Even Matthew had wondered where the Genesis community found its money, and now I knew. I knew.

But I had to carry my knowledge off Sun Kiss Key, and if von Rellsteb wanted me dead so that Nicole would inherit my wealth where better to kill me than on this empty Key in the middle of a thunder-ripped night? Fear swamped me. I ran to the car. I freed the revolver from its holster, slid into the driver's seat, and fumbled for the keys. The engine banged reassuringly into life. I was panting. Sweat was streaming down my face as I let out the clutch and the car lurched forward.

Were they waiting for me? Had they thought to

have a backup party guarding against just such an escape as this? I scrabbled Charles's gun close to me, then shifted into second gear. I had left the headlights switched off. The car bounced sickeningly on the rough track. I shifted again, accelerating hard, spewing a plume of white dust behind me as the bright red car charged toward the highway. Moonlight was bright on the dirt track while lightning blazed to the north.

No one fired at me. No gun muzzle sparked and flamed in the night, yet still the irrational panic made me crouch low behind the leather-covered steering wheel as the little car bucked and banged and howled in the night. I could see the headlights of a great truck hammering down the highway, and I knew I should slow down and let the truck go past, but surely the best position for a Genesis ambush was where the track joined the main road? So I ignored good sense and put my foot down to the floor to try and race the truck.

The truck's noise filled the night. Its chrome trim gleamed in the light of the small orange lamps that the driver had strung across his high cab. This beast of a truck was an eighteen wheeler, one of the behemoth super tankers of the highways, and it was thundering south with a tractor trailer attached and I was about to spin Charles's small car under its juggernaut wheels.

Christ, but it was too late to stop now! I shifted down, making the Austin-Healey's reconditioned engine scream in protest. Then I had the back wheels drifting because the main road was close, very close, and still no one fired at me, but it did not matter, for I was about to die anyway under the hammer blow of a Mack truck's impact. The driver flicked his headlights to full beam as he hit the Klaxons, and the blinding night was suddenly filled with the violence of his giant horns. I kept going, and the truck driver stood on his brakes, so that the Mack's rear end slewed across the road as I accelerated into its path. The Austin-Healey's back wheels screamed and smoked on the blacktop, the steering wheel shuddered as the car's right-hand wheels began to lift, and then the little vehicle skidded toward destruction under the truck's massive tires. The big rig was threatening to jackknife, and its towering chrome radiator grille was filling the noisy night just inches from my rear fender. The Klaxons howled at the moon, tire smoke hazed the bitter air, then the Austin-Healey's starboard wheels hit the road and the small car found its traction, and, suddenly, I was accelerating safely away, while behind me the truck driver went on hammering his horns in angry and impotent protest.

I drove a full mile before putting on my lights and slowing down. Sweat was pouring off me. I felt like a fool. I had not panicked like that in years, not since David had pulled me off a rock face in the Dolomites where I had frozen in absolute terror. That had been over twenty years ago, and then I had at least had real reason for the fear, while tonight the panic had been entirely self-induced. My imagination had worked on my fears, turning von Rellsteb's sinister face into a devilish threat that had never existed. I was still shaking.

I slowed down, worried that the truck driver

might have alerted the police with his CB radio, but no patrol car waited for me as I drove back to the warren of Key West's streets, nor as I at last parked in the small driveway of Charles's guest house. I turned off the engine, then sat in the car for a few seconds, feeling the jackhammer beat of my still frightened heart.

The revolver had fallen off the seat when I skidded onto the highway. I groped on the floor for the weapon then, wearily, I climbed out of the car. The guest house was dark, though I was sure Charles would be waiting up for me, even if only to reassure himself that I had not damaged his beautiful Austin-Healey. I closed the car door.

Then, from the deeply shadowed porch behind me, I heard the scrape of a footstep. I turned in a renewed and terrible panic, realizing that of course they would ambush me here, where else? If I died here it would be written off as just another street crime, and so I ripped the gun from its holster, then half fell against the car as I twisted desperately away from the threat of whoever had been waiting for me in the darkness. I used both hands to raise the Ruger and pointed dead center at the shadow, which now moved toward me from the porch.

"No!" It was a girl, who flinched away from the threat of the gun, and who screamed at me in a panic every bit as frantic as my own. "No! Please! No! No!"

It was the girl from the conference, the girl in the yellow skirt, the girl who had obscurely made me feel glad to be alive. And I had almost shot her.

I hate guns!" The girl was gasping in her panic. "I hate guns!"

"It's all right," I said with an urgency equal to her terror, "it's OK!"

"I hate them!" Her fear seemed out of proportion to its cause. She had twisted away so violently from the sight of the gun that she had dropped her huge, sacklike handbag, which had consequently spilled its contents across the path. "Have you put the gun away?" she asked in a stricken voice. She was still shaking like a sail loosed to a gale.

"It's gone," I said.

She dropped to her knees to retrieve the slew of notebooks, pens, tape cassettes, lipstick, chewing gum, and small change that had cascaded from her enormous bag. "Are you Tim Blackburn?" She turned her anxious face up to me.

"Yes"—I stooped to help her collect her scattered belongings—"and I'm sorry I frightened you."

"You didn't frighten me, the gun frightened me. I've never had a gun pointed at me before. I've been waiting for you."

"Why didn't you ring the doorbell and wait inside?"

"I telephoned," she explained as she grabbed coins out of Charles's flower beds, "and someone said you were out, but would be coming back later, so I came straight round here, but there were no lights on downstairs. I thought everyone must be in bed already and I didn't want to disturb anyone. So I waited."

"A long time?"

She nodded. "Long enough."

"I thought journalists didn't care about waking people up?"

She blinked at me in gratifying astonishment. "How did you know I was a journalist?"

"I noticed you at the conference," I confessed, "and saw you had a press badge."

"Wow!" Her amazement seemed to stem from the fact that anyone might have noticed her. She retrieved a last pencil and straightened up. "My name's Jackie Potten. Actually my name is Jacqueline-Lee Potten, but I don't use the Lee because it was my father's name, and he left my mom when I was kind of little, and Molly Tetterman says she's sorry she wasn't at home when you phoned, but she was away in Maine because her son is in college there and she was visiting him all week, and she only got home today, and I phoned her tonight and she told me about your messages on her answering machine, and she asked me to talk to you, which is why I wanted to see you, and I'm sorry it's so late, but I'm leaving tomorrow . . . "

"Whoa!" I held up my hands to check the impetuous flow, found my key, and opened the guest-house door. "Come and have a drink," I told Jackie. I did not yet know her connection with the Genesis Parents' Support Group or exactly why she wanted to see me, but there was something in her disorganized volubility that I liked. Her presence was also good for me because her vulnerability forced me to control the panic that raced had my own heart and filled me with an inchoate fright.

"I don't drink alcohol or coffee," Jackie informed me in an anxious voice, as though I might be about to force those poisons down her throat.

"Come in anyway," I said.

"Tim!" Charles, hearing his front door open, shouted from the private parlor upstairs. He was waiting up for me, as I had assumed he would, so I gave him the news he really wanted to hear, which was that his precious Austin-Healey was unscratched.

"I didn't expect you back so soon." Charles, who was splendidly dressed in a Chinese silk bathrobe, appeared at the top of the stairs. "What happened?"

"He was early," I said, then placed the gun on the hall table. "I didn't need it, but thank you anyway."

"And who on earth are you?" Charles imperiously demanded of Jackie Potten who, faced with the ethereal creature on the stairway, shrank back into the doorway.

"My name's Potten," she said, "Jackie Potten."

"I assume," Charles said haughtily, "that you

are the person who telephoned earlier. You may
wait for Mr. Blackburn in the guest parlor, and he
will help me make a pot of coffee." Charles walked
slowly downstairs. "Come, Tim."

As soon as we were in the kitchen Charles
dropped his absurdly pretentious manner. "So
what happened? Tell me!"

"Not a lot. He was early, we spoke, he took the
letter, and then vanished. I didn't learn a thing."

"Is that all?" Charles was disappointed.

"That's all." I sat on a stool and shook my head.
"I don't know, Charles. For a time there I actually
liked the bastard, then at the end I thought he was
laughing at me." I had also thought that von
Rellsteb had wanted me dead, so that Nicole could
inherit, but there had been no ambush, so even
that theory was wilting.

"You don't need coffee"—Charles saw the
weariness in my face—"you want something
stronger. Your usual Irish?"

"Please."

Charles pulled open a cupboard and sorted
through the bottles. "What do you know about
that creature?" He waved in the vague direction of
the parlor where Jackie Potten waited.

"She's a journalist," I explained, "and I suspect
she must be interested in the Genesis community
because she said Molly Tetterman told her about
me. You don't mind her being here, do you?"

He offered me a dramatic shudder. "Of course I
mind. She's such a drab little thing."

"Drab?" I sounded offended. "I don't think
she's drab at all."

"You don't? That hair? And that awful blouse? And the skirt? That skirt wasn't tailored, Tim, it was a remnant from a chain-saw massacre! Here!" He tossed me a bottle of Jamesons.

"I think she's rather appealing," I said stubbornly.

Charles raised his eyes to heaven, then poured himself a large vodka. "Would you like to find out what this ravishing creature of your dreams wants to drink?"

"She told me no coffee or alcohol."

"A club soda and ice, then," Charles decided. "I'm certainly not wasting designer water and a twist on such a creature."

I carried the soda water back to the parlor, where Jackie was staring very solemnly at an alabaster reproduction of Michelangelo's David. Charles followed me. "So tell us what happened," he instructed me, as though we had not already spoken in the kitchen.

I told, leaving out only the details of my panicked flight from Sun Kiss Key, lest Charles should think I had been anything less than careful with his precious car. Not that there was much to tell, for my meeting with von Rellsteb had been remarkably unproductive. "I should have come with you," Charles said.

"What good would that have done?" I asked.

"I would have pointed the gun at him, and then told him he had five seconds to tell me where the Genesis community lived. What is it?" This last, rather brusque, question was addressed to Jackie.

"The ice cubes." She gestured at her club soda. "Are they made with tap water?"

"Of course."

She blushed. "Do you mind?" She began fishing out the ice, which she dropped into an ashtray. Charles was amused, but pretended to be exasperated. Jackie Potten, once the offending ice was safely out of her drink, took a tentative sip, then searched through her capacious handbag for a notebook and pencil. "How did von Rellsteb travel tonight?"

"I don't know."

"I mean by boat? Car?"

"I don't know. He sort of appeared, then vanished."

"By broomstick," Charles said happily.

"Gee." Jackie frowned at me. "I mean they had a boat the other night, so I guess they must have come to Florida by sea. I hired a motorboat to look for them, and I searched most places from here to Marathon Key, but I didn't see them."

"What were you looking for?" I asked her. *"Erebus?"*

"Erebus?" She frowned. "Oh, the catamaran! They renamed her *Genesis One.* They've got two other boats we know of, *Genesis Two* and *Genesis Three.*"

"How do you know?"

"Molly asked the State Department, and they gave us copies of complaints that Japanese fishing boats had made. It was nothing to do with the State Department really, because none of the Genesis boats are American, but the Japanese complained to them anyway. And sent some photographs."

"And you looked for one of the boats here?"

She nodded. "But I didn't see any of them. I wondered if von Rellsteb and the others flew here.

Maybe I should try and find their records in the airline computers?"

She seemed to be asking my advice, but I knew nothing of such matters and had nothing useful to say, so I merely shrugged. I wished I could have been more helpful because I was finding her oddly attractive. I did not understand why, she was an unremarkable girl, but I was acutely aware of her presence. I decided her eyes were her best feature. They were large and a curious silvery green, though perhaps that was just the reflection of the sea-green lampshades Charles favored in the guest parlor. Otherwise Jackie's face was very narrow in the chin and broad in the forehead. Her skin was chalky pale and she seemed, under the billowy clothes that had so offended Charles, to be painfully thin. Her fair hair was in disarray despite the pins and clips she had used to tame it. I put her age at mid- to late-twenties, but her innocence made her seem more like a fourteen-year-old waif; the orphan of some heartless storm.

"Would you mind telling me," Charles asked in his silkiest voice, "just who you are, Miss Potten?"

"Oh, gee." She was instantly flustered. "I'm here for the Genesis Parents' Support Group." She paused, as if expecting us to respond, and when neither of us spoke, she added a nervous explanation. "I'm Molly's investigator," she added in further reassurance.

"Investigator?" I sounded incredulous.

"I investigate Genesis," Jackie said defensively.

"So you're not a real journalist?" Charles made the question sound like a sneer.

"Oh, yes! I work for a paper in Kalamazoo"—she paused because Charles had sniggered, but then she decided not to make anything of his scorn— "and the editor isn't really sure that the Genesis community is a proper story for our paper. I mean our only connection with Genesis is through Molly Tetterman, but the editor doesn't like Molly very much. Not because she isn't a good person, because she is, but because she can be very insistent, and she keeps on pestering Norman, he's the editor, about the Genesis Parents' Support Group."

"Jackie," I interrupted her very politely, but I was becoming aware that this orphan of the storm could talk the back legs off a herd of donkeys unless she was checked. "What were you doing at the conference?"

"Oh!" She was momentarily confused, as if trying to remember just what conference I was talking about. "I went there because I hoped to get an interview with Caspar von Rellsteb. Which I didn't, of course." She looked at me rather pathetically. "It's been a wasted trip, really."

"And mine," I said as though it might make her feel better.

"Did you ask von Rellsteb where Genesis lived?" Jackie asked me.

I nodded. "But he wouldn't tell me. He just fed me a whole lot of mystical nonsense about how Genesis needed its privacy."

"I think it's Alaska," Jackie said suddenly.

"Alaska?" I asked.

"The Genesis group has always been based in the Pacific," Jackie explained, "and when they left

British Columbia they probably wanted to stay somewhere on that same coast, and von Rellsteb has always been intrigued by Alaska. No one would know if they were there, because parts of that coast are really inaccessible, so they wouldn't need to bother with green cards or anything like that."

"But why Alaska?" I insisted.

"Because I found the man he shared a prison cell with in Texas, and he said von Rellsteb was always talking about Alaska, and how it was the new frontier and a place where a man could . . . "

"Prison!" I interrupted.

Jackie nodded, but, for once, had nothing more to say.

"Why was he in prison?" I asked.

"It was attempted robbery," Jackie said, "but I only found out about it last month, so I haven't had time to write it up in Molly's newsletter. It all happened ten years ago. He served two years of an eight-year sentence, and when he was released they sent him back to Canada because he should never have been living in Texas anyway. He tried to hold up an armored truck. You know, the kind that collects money from stores and banks? But it all went wrong and he didn't steal a penny in the end. The whole thing was really kind of stupid, except he was carrying a gun, which didn't help his defense in court. His lawyer tried to claim that von Rellsteb was alienated, and that he was only protesting against society."

"Did he fire the gun?" Charles asked.

Jackie shook her head. "The police say it jammed, but for some reason the technical evidence about the gun was inadmissible."

"But if the evidence had been admissible," I said slowly, "von Rellsteb might have been arraigned on a charge of attempted murder?"

Jackie nodded slowly, as though she had not thought of that possibility before. "I guess so, yes."

"Bloody hell," I said.

Charles, plainly bored with the night's lack of interesting news, yawned, and Jackie hurriedly said she had to be leaving. She was driving back north the next day and we agreed that she would give me a lift as far as Miami Airport. The hundred-and-fifty-mile journey would give us each a chance to pick the other's brain for more news of Genesis. "Though of what use such a dull creature can possibly be is beyond me," Charles said grandly after Jackie had left for her motel.

She returned at ten o'clock the next morning in a tiny imported Japanese car that was spattered with bumper stickers; so many stickers that they had spread off the fender onto the fading paint of the trunk. "Vegetarians Do It on a Bed of Lettuce," one sticker proclaimed, while another warned "I Brake for the Physically Challenged," which seemed to imply that the rest of us plowed indiscriminately into wheelchairs with merriment aforethought. "Your car?" I asked Jackie.

"Sure. I worked out that it would be cheaper to drive than fly, so long as I stayed in really economical motels." Jackie explained that her editor in Kalamazoo was not interested in Genesis, so she had attended the conference on her own time and on her own and Molly Tetterman's money.

I put my seabag onto the car's backseat, said farewell to Charles, then climbed into the cramped front passenger seat of Jackie's car, where one dashboard sticker thanked me for not smoking and another enjoined me to buckle up.

We took four wrong turns in our mutual attempts to navigate out of town, but eventually Jackie steered the car safely onto the Overseas Highway where she gingerly accelerated to forty-five miles an hour. "Are you really going to drive all the way to Kalamazoo?" I asked in astonishment.

She evidently thought I was being critical of the car rather than of her nervous driving. "It sort of shakes if you go too fast." She began to describe various other symptoms of the car and, while she spoke, I surreptitiously examined her and wondered just what it was that attracted me to her. She did not, after all, have the impact of beauty, and I did not know her nearly well enough to determine her character, yet still I felt an odd excitement in her company. It was, I finally decided, her very touching look of earnest innocence which made her seem so very fragile and which made me feel so very fatherly toward her. She was, after all, just about young enough to be my daughter.

When she had exhausted the problems of car ownership I asked what had first made her interested in Genesis.

"Berenice," Jackie said, as if that would explain everything, then, realizing that it explained nothing, she rushed into more detail. "She's Molly's eldest daughter, you see, and she went off with von Rellsteb about five years ago, and Molly thinks that Berenice was brainwashed by him, because she's never even written her mother a letter, and they were really close! Berenice was my best friend, I mean, we told each other everything! Everything! Which is why I've been trying to find her. I know she wouldn't just have just cut me dead, I mean, people don't do that, do they?"

"Perhaps she wanted some peace and quiet?" I suggested wickedly.

She looked immediately contrite. "I talk too much," she said miserably. "I know I do. My mother always says I do, and so does Molly, and so did Professor Falk, he was my Ethics of Journalism professor."

"There are ethics in journalism?" I asked.

"Of course there are!" She offered me a reproving look, which, taking her gaze off the highway, made us wander dangerously across the center yellow line.

I leaned over and steered the car back toward safety. "So Berenice just ran away?"

"She went to a school in Virginia, where she met this guy, and in her senior year he took her to British Columbia for spring break, which I thought was kind of weird because she'd always gone to Florida before. That's where she met the Genesis people. They weren't called Genesis then, that came later. They were some kind of weird commune, know what I mean? And they just swallowed Berenice alive! No letters, no calls, nothing!"

"And you've been trying to reach her ever since?"

Jackie nodded. "I even visited British Columbia,

but they threatened to call the police and have me arrested for trespassing! I couldn't believe their nerve!" She frowned. "But at least they didn't point guns at me."

I thought she was reproving me for my behavior of the previous night, and I offered yet another apology.

"I don't mean that," she said hurriedly, "but Genesis is heavily into survivalism. Didn't you know that?"

"I don't even know what survivalism is."

She bit her lower lip as she framed her definition. "It's a kind of apocalyptic horror thing, know what I mean?"

"No."

"Survivalists say that the nuclear holocaust is inevitable, but they're determined to survive it, right? So they live in really remote places, and they have guns, so that if any other survivor tries to take their women or food stocks they can fight them off."

"Charming," I said.

"It's kind of freaky," Jackie agreed, then stopped talking as an eighteen-wheel truck, like the one that had nearly killed me the previous night, overtook us in a thunder of vibration and noise. Jackie was plainly terrified by the truck's looming proximity and I wondered how she was ever going to endure the hundreds of miles between here and Kalamazoo.

"Why did they leave British Columbia?" I asked.

She shook her head. "I don't know. Unless they just wanted to be somewhere more remote? Their

island was pretty terrible, sort of cold-water stand-
pipes and mud everywhere and real primitive, but
a sympathizer let them use it for free, and it had a
sheltered harbor for their boats. I guess boats are
important to von Rellsteb. Do you know anything
about boats?"

"A bit," I said, then changed the subject back.
"Who was the sympathizer who gave them an
island?"

"She's a rich widow who's into New Age. You
know, channellers and crystals and all that really
weird stuff? I think she was charmed by von
Rellsteb. I mean she was really cut up when he just
left her without saying anything. He didn't even
tell her where they were going." Jackie paused. "She
must have given him money, and I guess he was
screwing her." She touchingly glanced at me to
make certain I was not embarrassed by her allegation. "She thought that maybe he'd moved Genesis
to Europe, because they disappeared soon after he
came back from his European trip. But I don't think
she's right. I think they're still in the North Pacific."

"With my daughter," I said grimly, and Jackie
then wanted to know about Nicole, and so I spent a
half hour telling my family's story before we
stopped for lunch at a waterfront cafe where Jackie
ordered a salad of celery, lettuce, and a ghastly concoction called tofu, which she told me was made
from soybeans, but looked to me like the foam
insulation that my boatyard sometimes pumps into
the space between a steel hull and the cabin paneling. "I assume you're a vegetarian?" I asked her.

"I haven't eaten flesh since I was six," she said

enthusiastically. "Mom tried to make me eat chicken or turkey, and some fish as well, because she said I needed the protein to grow properly, but I couldn't bear to think of all the suffering, and even at Thanksgiving I used to make my own fake turkey with vegetables and bread. I used to mix them and . . . "

"Jackie . . . !" I said warningly.

"I know." She was instantly contrite. "I'm talking too much." She suppressed a shudder at the size of the steak on my plate, then reverted to the safer subject of the Genesis community. She told me how difficult it was to get even the smallest scraps of information. "We can't even talk to people who used to belong because, so far as we know, not one member of Genesis has ever left the community since they moved out of British Columbia! Not one. A handful left before that, but none of them know where von Rellsteb might have gone."

It took me a few seconds to understand the implication of Jackie's news. "You think he kills them if they try to escape?"

Jackie was unwilling to endorse the implication of murder, but she thought it more than probable that some members of Genesis were being held against their will. "I never got beyond the pier when I visited British Columbia," she said, "but I got this really bad feeling. I mean like von Rellsteb was into control? Like heavy discipline? I spoke to this professor at Berkeley, and he told me that a lot of Utopian groups finish up by substituting control systems for consensus because their leaders aren't really into agreement and compromise, but have this blueprint which they insist will only work if it's followed exactly, and they somehow manage to impose it on the group, then enforce it with rewards and punishments. Do you know what I mean?"

I was nodding eagerly, because Jackie was reinforcing my own theory that von Rellsteb had some kind of sinister mastery over his followers, and Jackie's revelation offered an explanation of my daughter's silence. Nicole had ignored me because she had no choice. Nicole was not a convert, but a convict, and I told Jackie about the unsettling image of the three girls wearing von Rellsteb's strange green uniform on the day Nicole had sailed away.

"It's not just uniforms," Jackie said. "This guy at Berkeley says these groups make really weird hierarchies for themselves. Some groups degrade into slaves and owners, and in others the underlings have to work their way up the hierarchy by pleasing the guys at the top."

"It makes sense!" I spoke enthusiastically, for how else could my Nicole's vivid spirit have been broken except by some brutal methodology? Nicole, I suddenly knew, was a prisoner, and my suspicion that von Rellsteb used his disciples to make himself wealthy seemed overwhelmingly confirmed by Jackie's description of how Utopian ideals deteriorated into fascist regimes.

Jackie suddenly looked very troubled. "Aren't you going to eat your salad?"

"Of course not. I'm not a rabbit."

"It's good for you." She waited to see if that

encouragement would make me relent, then took the salad for herself when it was obvious I was not going to eat it.

I watched as she picked at the lettuce. "Why doesn't your editor want you to write about Genesis?" I asked her.

"Because he doesn't really believe Genesis is as bad as I say, and the paper can't afford to send me all over the world to find out if I'm right, and I haven't got enough proof or experience to persuade a bigger newspaper to let me do it. If I took the story to a Chicago paper they'd just put one of their own staffers on it, which means I'd be passing up my best chance of a Pulitzer, so I'm chasing the story in my own time. And with Molly's help, of course."

"So you can get a Pulitzer?"

"Sure, why not?" She responded as though that achievement was well within her grasp, and I decided there was more to Ms. Jackie Potten than her unprepossessing exterior promised. "It depends on the story, of course," she explained. "I mean if von Rellsteb really is holding people against their will, then it will be a Pulitzer story, but if he's running just another survivalist commune, then it's page thirty-two beneath the fold."

"It's no story at all," I said, "if you can't find him."

"What I'd like to do is track down where he gets his money. Of course I'd like to find where they're all living, but I guess that would be difficult because the coast of Alaska is really huge! And it's got lots of inlets and islands. They could be anywhere, and maybe they're not even in Alaska!" She sounded rather despairing at the difficulty of the task she had set herself, then she cheered up. "But there might be another way of finding them. The paper trail."

"Paper trail?" I asked in bemusement.

"People can't just disappear," Jackie said with renewed enthusiasm. "There are always records! How does the Genesis community get their money? They must use a bank somewhere, and if they use a bank, then the Internal Revenue Service has to know about them, so maybe I should go that route."

"I know where they get their money," I said with some satisfaction.

"Where?" She was immediately interested.

So I told Jackie about my suspicions that von Rellsteb was raising funds by forcing inheritances onto his cowed followers who, in turn, would pass the money to von Rellsteb. After all, if Joanna and I had both died in the English channel then Nicole would have inherited our expensive house that over-looked the sea, our investments, and our boatyard with its healthy cashflow, and if Nicole was indeed a brainwashed prisoner of the Genesis community, as I now believed her to be, then von Rellsteb would have become the effective owner of that plump lega-cy. And I had no doubt that von Rellsteb was still interested in that legacy. Why else, I asked, would he have raised the matter of Nicole's inheritance?

"He did what?"

I told Jackie about von Rellsteb's odd concern that perhaps Nicole might have been disinherited. "Isn't it obvious why he raised the subject?" I asked her.

"I don't know." Jackie was clearly unconvinced

by my theory. "I haven't heard of any other Genesis parents just disappearing, and why would von Rellsteb go all the way to Europe to find a victim? A lot of his followers come from Canada or the States, so why not pick on them?"

"Because," I suggested, "a murder in Europe is far less likely to be traced back to a commune in Alaska."

Jackie was still unconvinced. "It would be a messy way of making money. Think of all the other family members he'd have to deal with, let alone the lawyers. Mind you"—she was clearly worried that I might be upset by her abrupt dismissal of my theory, so she tried to soften it—"we know so little about what makes von Rellsteb tick. I still haven't discovered why he went to Europe four years ago, and it was clearly important, because it was after that trip that the whole commune disappeared."

Jackie was referring to the journey during which he had met Nicole, and I suggested that perhaps von Rellsteb had been on a recruiting trip.

"Maybe," Jackie said, but without enthusiam.

"Perhaps he was going back to Germany," I said. "He must have relatives there."

Jackie stared at me, then, very slowly, laid down her fork. "I bet that's why he went to Europe!" she said in the tone of voice that betrayed the dawning of an idea.

"Why?"

"Oh, boy! Why didn't I think of that?"

"What?"

"Jeez!" She was mad at herself. "Wow! I've been

dumb! You know that? Really dumb! His father!"

"Father?"

"Only his mother emigrated to Canada. There's no record of a father, but I'll bet that's it!" Then, being Jackie, she told me the story from its very beginning, from the time that Caspar von Rellsteb had been born in Hamburg in the very last months of the Second World War, which, I realized with a pang, made him almost my exact contemporary. Jackie confessed that she had discovered nothing about von Rellsteb's real father, but had instead concentrated her research on his mother who had been a German national called Eva Fellnagel. In 1949 Eva Fellnagel had married a Canadian army sergeant called Skinner, and afterward had gone to live with him in Vancouver. Caspar, Eva's son, had traveled with the couple, and, though the marriage to Sergeant Skinner had not lasted long, it had been sufficient to secure both Eva and her son Canadian citizenship. Jackie said she had always assumed Caspar's aristocratic surname had been an affectation wished on him by his mother. "But perhaps there really was a von Rellsteb!" Jackie said excitedly, "and maybe that's why Caspar went to Europe! To find his real father!"

"And if we could find him, too?" I suggested.

"Sure!" Jackie was excited, certain that by retracing von Rellsteb's European footsteps she could track him all the way down to the present. Then her face fell. "There's just one problem," she said ruefully, "I'd have to go to Germany."

"Which you can't afford to do?" I took a guess at the reason for her dubiety.

"I haven't got any money," she confessed, "and Molly's spent almost all her savings."

"I've got money," I said very simply, because suddenly life had become extremely simple. Nicole was being held prisoner by a man who was trying to forge his own insane Utopia. I would find that man's hiding place and I would free my daughter. It would take money, but I had money, and I would do anything to get my daughter back.

I was going hunting.

"You've done what?" David asked me when I told him the results of my American visit.

"I've hired an investigator."

"Oh, good God! You've hired someone! To do what?"

"To find Nicole, of course."

"Good God!" At first I thought David was upset because of my profligacy, but then I realized he was frightened of my obsession with Nicole, expecting it to end in crippling disappointment. "Tell me, for God's sake!"

I told him about Jackie Potten, and the telling took all the way from Heathrow Airport to the coast where, before taking me home, David stopped for lunch at the Stave and Anchor. We sat at our usual table by the fire, where I took pleasure in a pint of decent-tasting beer and David took an equal pleasure in mocking me. "So! Let us celebrate your achievements, Tim. You have permitted some American girl to fleece you of sixteen hundred pounds. I do applaud you, Tim, I really do."

It was lunchtime, but a depression that had brought a gale of wind and rain up the channel had also fetched a mass of clouds that made the pub windows as dark as evening. The lights were on in the bar where a group of idle fisherman amused themselves by listening to our conversation. I tried to defend myself against David's scorn. "Jackie Potten is a very enterprising reporter," I insisted with as much dignity as my tiredness would allow. "That's what I like about the Americans. They're so full of enthusiasm! They're not like us."

"You mean they don't roam the world giving away their wealth to passing females?" David inquired robustly. "Good God, Tim, the trollop must have thought Christmas had arrived early! She must think you are the greatest fool in Christendom! You never did have any sense of financial responsibility."

"I am merely subsidizing Jackie's investigations," I insisted.

"Oh, dear Lord," my brother said in despair. He scratched a match on the stone of the hearth, then laboriously lit his pipe as he prepared his next broadside. "You remind me of Tuppy Hargreaves. Do you remember Tuppy? He had that very rich parish in Dorset, and a rather grand wife, but he abandoned them both to run away with a girl young enough to be his granddaughter, and in no time at all the poor sod was wearing a wig and gobbling down vitamins and monkey-gland extract. He died of a heart attack in Bognor Regis, as I recall, and the floozie drove off with an Italian hairdresser in Tuppy's Wolseley. I took the cremation service in some ghastly place near Southampton. They only paid me two pounds, I remember. Two measly pounds! No doubt a similar fate awaits you, Tim, with this Jackie creature."

"Don't be ridiculous," I said.

"It is not me being ridiculous," David said very grandly, then gave me a most suspicious glance. "Was this child beautiful? Did she bat false eyelashes at you, is that it?"

"I am merely paying for Jackie to continue her investigation of Genesis."

"Her investigation of gullibility!" David pounced gleefully. "Good God, Tim, how gullible can a grown man be? This Miss Potten presents you with a few tattered assumptions about the Genesis community and you reward her with the balance of monies in your pocket, barely leaving yourself enough to buy a pint of ale! Do you really believe she'll travel to Germany on your behalf?" David, despite his calling, had little faith in humankind. "Not that we can do much about the girl now," he went on, "you're home, the damage is done, so now you can do some proper work."

"What does that mean?" I asked suspiciously.

"It means that your boatyard, now that you've had your fling, could profit from a firm managerial touch." David usually kept an eye on the yard while I was away. "Not that Billy doesn't do his best," he added hastily, "because he does, but he hasn't got the swiftest brain I've ever encountered in a parishioner, and he's a hopeless salesman. And that's what you need, Tim, a salesman! You must sell some of the yard's inventory before you entirely run out of space! You won't believe this, but *Tort-au-Citron* is back on the market. God knows what that lawyer thought he was playing at when he bought her, but you've got her back, and doubtless you'll have to haul her out of the water and let her clutter up the yard again."

"*Stormchild* is for sale again?" I asked in mild astonishment.

"*Stormchild*, yes, or *Tort-au-Citron*," David confirmed. "It seems young Miller rather overplayed his hand in buying the boat, and his partners are now understandably keen to get the brute off their books. I warned them that in today's market it won't sell quickly, but if you can find a buyer, Tim, I think they'll be willing to drop their price pretty savagely. In fact I think they'll take a loss just to put the whole embarrassing exercise behind them."

"Maybe they'll go as low as ninety-five?" I wondered.

"Good Lord, no!" David seemed offended. "You'll have to ask a higher price than that! At least a hundred and ten thousand! Remember, Tim, you're on a broker's percentage, and they're lawyers! In the words of the good Lord himself, screw the wretches till they squeal."

"Ninety-five," I said again, "because I've already got a buyer lined up."

David stared at me with a gratifying amazement. "You do?"

"Yes," I said, "me."

That stopped David cold. He gazed at me for a few seconds over the rim of his glass, took a long swallow of ale, then momentarily closed his eyes.

"I could have sworn you said you intended to purchase *Tort-au-Citron* for yourself. Please inform me that I misheard."

Instead of answering I took our glasses to the bar and had them refilled. When I carried the pints back to the table I confirmed David's worst suspicions. "I've decided to sell the house," I said, "put a sales manager into the yard, and buy *Stormchild*." I was damned if I would go to sea in a boat named after some legal jest. She would have her old name back. "With any luck I'll be away before Christmas. Cheers." I raised my glass to David.

"Go and see Doc Stilgoe and have him prescribe you a nerve tonic," my brother advised.

I smiled. "Truly, David, I've had time to think about my life, and I don't want it to trickle on like it is. Besides, I was never any damned good at running the business; Joanna was always the one who did the books, and I'm a much better sailor than I am a salesman, so I'll buy *Stormchild*, then go looking for Nicole."

"You can't just disappear!" David exploded at me.

"Why ever not? Nicole did."

"She was young! She was a fool! She was irresponsible!"

"And I'm alone," I said, "and what responsibilities do I have?"

"You have responsibilities to Nicole, for a start," David said trenchantly. "If the silly girl ever does decide to come home, then it's going to be mighty difficult for her if home is halfway round the globe and still moving!"

"Nickel's not coming home, David. None of the Genesis community has ever left von Rellsteb, at least not since he went into hiding. Maybe some of his followers have tried to escape, but he's made damn sure that none get away to tell any tales."

"So what the hell are you going to do? Just wander away on a boat and grow a beard?"

"I'm going to find Nicole, of course," I said, then held up a hand to stop David from interrupting me. "I believe she's being held against her will. I can't prove that, of course, unless I find her, so that's what I'll do."

David snorted derision. "You are mad." He was scornful, yet I also heard doubt in my brother's voice, as though he knew I was right and was simply reluctant to admit it.

"No," I said very seriously, "I'm doing what you and I have often dreamed of doing. I'm going on an adventure, an old-fashioned quest across far seas, and, perhaps, at the end of it, I shall find Nicole."

"My dear Tim, what terrible things the Florida sun has done to your sanity," David said, though I heard a distinct tone of jealousy in his voice. David often complained that the world had become dull and offered no chances for adventure.

"Why don't you come with me?" I asked him.

He laughed. "My dear Tim, I'm busy."

"God will give you a sabbatical, won't he?"

"I'm overdue for one," he said wistfully, and I could see he was tempted, but he was also frightened of the temptation. In some ways the relationship between David and myself was like the one that had existed between Nicole and her brother. Nicole, like me, was the daring one, the instigator of mischief, while David, like Dickie, was more cautious. My brother, tough as he was, did not like embarking on uncertain endeavors. That, I often thought, was why he preferred dinghy sailing to deep-water cruising. However fast and exciting a racing dinghy might seem, it is almost always sailed within sight of land, in sheltered waters, and in daylight. Blue-water cruisers, on the other hand, go out into the great waters where tempests, darkness, and dangers wait. "Damn it, Tim, I'd love to come," David now said, "but duty forbids."

Outside the pub the gray wind beat bleak rain across the town's roofs and brought the far sound of the wild seas breaking on the river's bar. To me the noise was music, for it was the sound that would take me back to sea, and to the world's far ends and, if God willed it, back to Nicole.

In a boat called *Stormchild*.

I craned *Tort-au-Citron* out of the water, scrubbed her hull clean of a season's weed and barnacles, then gave her a triple coating of antifouling paint. First, though, I took the ridiculous name off her transom and painted her original name in its place. She was *Stormchild* again, and I was sentimental enough to think that the lovely boat was grateful for the change.

I paid ninety-six thousand for her. She was

worth nearly double that price, but I had persuaded Miller's legal partners that she had deteriorated badly. The lawyers should have insisted on a survey, but they took my word on the boat's condition, confirming David's suspicions that Miller's partners were simply glad to be rid of the yacht. Which suited me, for I now possessed a boat superbly suited to my purpose. *Stormchild* was tough, but she was also fast, safe, and comfortable. My plan was to provision her, then, leaving David to tie up the loose ends of my affairs, I would head south across Biscay. I could expect a lively time of that crossing, for it was already very late in the year, but I would be heading into the regions of perpetual summer, and, when the trade wind belt moved north, I would go west toward America.

"You've heard nothing from that wretched child, I suppose?" David never called Jackie by her name. That was not from unkindness, but rather out of David's fear of the unknown, and I, who knew my brother's foibles only too well, knew I would never shake his preconception that Jackie, being young and foreign, was a threat to me.

"I've heard nothing," I confirmed.

"A fool and his money are easily parted," David said with sanctimonious relish. It was five weeks after my return from Florida and, on a bitterly cold day, he was helping me rig *Stormchild*. We had craned her into the water the day before and now she floated, lone and glorious, at the winter pontoons.

"She might contact me yet," I said defensively, though in truth I had rather abandoned hope of

Jackie Potten. I did not for one moment credit David's belief that she had cheated me, but I did fear that her investigatory skills had not proved equal to discovering why von Rellsteb had made his journey to Europe. I had not heard from Jackie, nor from Nicole. I had harbored a secret hope that the carefully written letter I had given to von Rellsteb on Sun Kiss Key would spur Nicole into a reply, but I had to assume that the letter had never been delivered.

"If that wretched girl doesn't come through with the goods," David said acidly, "then you're sailing into the unknown are you not?"

"Not really. I think Alaska or British Columbia are the places to search." I had bought the Admiralty charts for those far, inhospitable, and secretive coasts, and the more I studied the charts, the more I became convinced that von Rellsteb might indeed have taken refuge in one of the tortuous inlets of the North Pacific. In that expectation I now prepared *Stormchild* for desolate and icy waters. I had put a diesel-powered heater into her saloon and new layers of insulation inside her cold, steel hull. I had built extra water and fuel tanks into her belly and crammed spare parts and tools into every locker. I had treated myself to the best foul-weather gear that money could buy, and I was stocking *Stormchild's* galley with the kind of food that fought off winter's gloom: cartons of thick soups, cans of steak and kidney pies, stewed beef, and plum duff. Thus, day by cold day, my boat settled lower in the water.

Some of the equipment I needed was not avail-

able from my own chandlery, or from any yachts-
man's discount catalog. I had been alarmed by
Jackie Potten's description of the Genesis community as survivalists and impressed by her contention
that Utopian communes often became degraded by
the imposition of a controlling discipline, and I did
not want to face such a belligerent group unarmed,
so I quietly put the word about that I was in the
market for a good rifle. Billy, my foreman, solved
the problem by revealing that his father had hoarded two British Army rifles as souvenirs of his war
service. "Silly old bugger shouldn't have them at
all," Billy said, "not at his age. Bloody things ain't
licensed, and all the old fool will ever do is shoot
hisself in the foot one day. You'd be doing me a
right favor to take them out of the house."

He wanted me to buy both rifles. They were
.303 Lee-Enfields, the No. 4 Mark I version, which
was a robust, bolt-action weapon, tough and for-
giving, with a ten-shot magazine and a maximum
range of twelve hundred yards, though only an
optimist would bother to take aim if the target was
much above three hundred paces. The Lee-Enfield
had once been the standard rifle of the British
forces, and was still used by armies that appreciated the merits of its rugged construction. Both guns
still had their army-issue, brass-tipped, webbing
slings, while their stocks and barrel sleevings had
been lovingly polished with linseed oil.

David helped me hide the two guns deep inside
Stormchild; one we placed in a specially disguised
compartment under the generator in the bow,
while the other we hid behind the timber panel-

ing of the after companionway. "It's sensible to take two," David said with a most unchristian relish, "because if one goes wrong, then you can always shoot von Rellsteb with the second one."

"Don't be daft," I said, "I'm not going to shoot him. I'm only taking the guns as a precaution."

"Don't let him shoot first," David warned me. To my brother *Stormchild*'s voyage had transformed itself from an exercise in futility to an enviable demonstration of moral absolutes that would end with good triumphing over evil. David's initial opposition to my expedition had changed when I told him how idealistic communes like the Genesis community often became fouled by the politics of domination. To David, therefore, Nicole had become a pristine maiden victimized by a Prussian villain, and that dislike intensified when I told David of my conversation with von Rellsteb, and how he had expressed a desire to live at one with the planet. That was just the kind of heretical mysticism that brought out the Christian soldier in my straightforward brother, and so, enthused by righteous indignation, he encouraged me to slay the enemy and release Nicole. But that enemy was well armed, and I was sailing alone, which was one of the reasons I wanted David, who was my closest friend as well as my brother, to accompany me. I made my strongest effort to change his mind on the day when, at long last, we took *Stormchild* for a long shakedown sail off the southern English coast. "Nothing would please me more than to accompany you," David said, "but it's impossible."

"Betty wouldn't mind, would she?"

"She's all for it! She says it would do me good." David was standing at *Stormchild*'s wheel, which, in the manner of many brilliant dinghy helmsmen who find themselves sailing a larger yacht, he twitched far too frequently. We had left the river long before dawn and flown up-channel in the grip of a bitter east wind that had now gentled and backed into an evening whisper. *Stormchild* had taken the day's white-topped waves beautifully, while now, serene and beautiful, she ghosted the evening's flood tide homeward. "She sails very sweetly," David said as he glanced up at her towering, sunset-touched main.

"She does," I agreed, "but I still wouldn't mind a second pair of hands aboard."

"Doubtless, doubtless." David crouched out of the small wind to light his pipe, then chucked the dead match overboard. "Even the bishop said a sabbatical might do me good," he added wistfully.

"Then come!" I said, exasperated by his refusal.

"It would be sheer irresponsibility," he said with a touch of irascibility. "Besides, I'm older than you. I don't think I could cope with the discomforts of long-distance cruising."

"Balls."

He shrugged. "If I could find someone to look after the parishes, I would, maybe." He sounded very uncertain.

"I wish you would come. Think of all the bird life in Alaska!"

"There is that," he said wistfully. David and Betty were both ardent ornithologists, and their house was filled with bird books and pictures.

"So come!" I urged him.

He shook his head. "You've been itching to make a long voyage for years, Tim. It's been too long since you sailed round the world. But I'm not itching for the same thing. I've become a creature of habit. People think I'm a curmudgeonly old clergyman, and that's exactly what I want to be. You go, and I'll stay at home and pray for you. And I'll keep a pastoral eye on the boatyard, too."

"If you change your mind," I said, "you can always fly out and join me."

"That's true, that's true."

Our wake was now just a shimmer of evening light, proof how sea-kindly was *Stormchild*'s sleek hull. We were hurrying home in an autumn dusk, sliding past a dark shore where the first lights hazed the misted hills yellow. There was a chill in the air, a foretaste of winter, an invitation to follow the migrating birds and turn our boat's bows south. In front of us the sea was dark, studded by the winking lights of the buoys, while astern of *Stormchild* the empty sea was touched with the dying sun's gold so that it looked like a shining path which would lead to the earth's farthest ends and to where all our secret hopes and wildest dreams might one day come true.

I had *Stormchild*'s compasses swung professionally, then had a technician give her radar a final service. I had learned that the Alaskan coast was prey to ship-killing fogs, so the radar was more

than a frill, it was a necessity. The aerial was
mounted at the mast's upper spreaders and fed its
signal to two screens; a main one above the navigation station at the foot of the companionway,
and a repeater screen that was mounted in the
yacht's center cockpit.

A new spray hood arrived. It was made from stout
blue canvas with clear plastic windows that would
shelter the forward section of *Stormchild*'s cockpit
against the bitter northern seas and shrieking winds.
Stormchild had a small auxiliary wheel mounted in
that forward section of the cockpit, while the main
wheel was further aft. Astern of the large main
wheel was the teak-planked coach roof over the after
cabin. That cabin was the most comfortable aboard,
but not in a rough sea when the motion amidships
was always easier, so I was using the after cabin as a
storeroom. I planned to live, sleep, navigate, and
cook in the main living quarters amidships. On the
starboard side of those midships quarters was the
navigation station, which was equipped with a generous table, good chart stowage, and plenty of space
for the radios and instrumentation. Aft of the navigation table was a shower and lavatory, while opposite, on the port side of the companionway, was a
large galley. Forward of the galley was the saloon
with its two wide sofas, table, and wall of shelves
that held books and cassette tapes. The diesel-powered heater looked something like a small and complex woodstove, and gave the saloon a decidedly
cozy air, a feeling heightened by the framed pictures
and glass-shaded oil lamps.

Forward of the main cabin were two smaller

sleeping cabins that shared a common bathroom. I had turned one of the cabins into a engineering workroom, while the other was crammed with stores. Last were two chain lockers, a sail locker, and a watertight compartment that held *Stormchild*'s small diesel generator, under which one of the two rifles was hidden.

On deck I had a life raft in a container, a dinghy that was lashed to the after-coach roof, and a stout rack filled with boat hooks, whisker poles, and oars. At the stern, on a short staff, I flew the bomb-scarred red ensign which had flown from *Slip-Slider* and which the navy had rescued from the channel. I would take that ragged flag to my own journey's end as a symbol of Joanna.

Stormchild had been rerigged, repainted, and replenished. The work had taken me eight weeks exactly, and now she was ready. The sale of my house was progressing smoothly, the boatyard had a new manager and all I needed now was the right weather to slip down channel and round Ushant. That weather arrived in early November, and I topped up *Stormchild*'s water and fuel tanks, checked her inventory one more time, then went ashore for my last night in England. I stayed with David and Betty, and used their telephone to make a final effort to reach Jackie Potten. There was no answer from Jackie's telephone, and only the answering machine responded when I called Molly Tetterman's house. So much for the ladies of Kalamazoo, I thought, and put the phone down without leaving any message.

The next morning, in a cold rain and gusting

wind, I carried the last of my luggage down to the boatyard where the heavily laden *Stormchild* waited at the pontoon. Friends had come to bid me farewell and cheered when David's wife, Betty, broke a bottle of champagne on *Stormchild's* stemhead. David said a prayer of blessing over the boat, then we all trooped below to drink more champagne. David and Betty gave me two parting gifts: a book about Alaskan birds and the *Book of Common Prayer*. "Not the modern rubbish," David assured me, "but the 1662 version." It was a beautiful and ancient book with a morocco leather binding and gilt-edged pages.

"Too good for the boat," I protested.

"Nonsense. It isn't for decoration anyway, but for use. Take it."

Billy, on behalf of the boatyard staff, then presented me with a ship's bell that he ceremoniously hung above the main companionway. "It's proper brass, boss," he told me, "so it'll tarnish like buggery, but that'll make you think of us every time you have to clean the sod."

We opened still more champagne, though I, who would be taking *Stormchild* down channel when the tide ebbed, only drank two glasses. It was a sad, bittersweet day; a parting, but also a beginning. I went to find my daughter, but I also went to fulfill a dream that had given such joy to Joanna—the dream of living aboard a cruising boat, of following the warm winds and long waves. I was going away, leaving no address and no promise of a return.

At midday, as the tide became fair, my guests

climbed back onto the pontoon. Friends shouted farewells as the rain slicked *Stormchild*'s teak deck dark. I started the big engine. Billy disconnected the shoreside electricity, then slipped my springs, leaving the big yacht tethered only by her bow and stern lines. David was the last to leave the boat. He gripped my hand. "Good luck," he said, "and God bless."

"Are you sure you won't come?"

"Good luck," he said again, then climbed ashore. I looked ahead, past *Stormchild*'s bows, at the rain-beaten river, down which Joanna had sailed to her death, and from where Nicole had sailed into oblivion. Now it was my turn to leave, and I glanced up at the hill where my wife and son were buried, and I said my own small prayer of farewell.

People were shouting their goodbyes. Most were laughing, and a few were crying. Someone threw a paper streamer. Billy had already let go the bow line and David was standing by the aft. "Ready, Tim?" he shouted.

"Let go!" I called.

"You're free, Tim!" David tossed the bitter end of the aft line onto *Stormchild*'s deck. "Good luck! God bless! Bon voyage!"

I put the engine into gear. Water seethed at *Stormchild*'s stern as she drew heavily and slowly away from her berth. Next stop, the Canaries!

"Goodbye!" a score of voices shouted. "Good luck, Tim!" More paper streamers arced across *Stormchild*'s guardrails and sagged into the widening strip of gray-white water. "Bon voyage!"

I waved, and there were tears in my eyes as the streamers stretched taut, snapped, and fell away. One of the boatyard staff was sounding a raucous farewell on an air-powered foghorn. "Goodbye!" I shouted one last time.

"Mr. Blackburn!" A small and determined voice screamed above the racket, and I glanced back across the strip of propeller-churned water, and there, crammed among my friends and dressed in a baggy sweater and shapeless trousers with her bulging handbag gripped in a thin pale hand, was the lady from Kalamazoo. Jackie Potten had surfaced at last. She had not let me down after all. "Mr. Blackburn!" she shouted again.

I banged *Stormchild's* gearbox into reverse. White water foamed and boiled as the propeller struggled to check the deadweight of over twenty tons of boat and supplies. I slung a line ashore, David and Billy hauled, and ignominiously, just thirty seconds after leaving, I and my boat came home again.

Jackie Potten was panting from the exertion of running through the boatyard carrying a suitcase and her enormous handbag. "A man at the marina office said you were leaving, and I just ran," she explained her breathlessness, "and I can't believe I caught you! Wow! This is some boat! Is it yours?"

"Yes, mine." I ushered Jackie into *Stormchild's* cockpit where I introduced her to David and Betty, who, alone of the rather bemused crowd who had come to bid me farewell, had returned on board the yacht. My brother now behaved with an excruciating gallantry toward her. He invited her down into the saloon, enjoining her to watch the stairs and not to crack her skull on the companionway lintel.

"I tried to telephone you from London Airport"—Jackie talked to me all the way down into the saloon—"but they said your home number was disconnected, and then I telephoned the boatyard and they said you were leaving today, and I would have been here hours ago, but British Rail is some kind of joke. They just pretend to run a railroad. Anyway I caught a bus in the end, which was kind of interesting. Is this some cabin! Are those books for real? You read Yeats?"

"The Yeats belonged to Nicole," I said. I had put a lot of Nicole's books onto the shelves, which were equipped with varnished drop bars to hold their contents against the sea's motion.

"Is this really a stove? That's neat. I didn't know you could heat boats. And a carpet! Wow! This is more comfortable than my apartment!"

David, standing beside me at the chart table, watched Jackie explore the big saloon. "I see I did you an injustice," he said softly.

"Meaning?"

"She's hardly a Salome, is she? Or a Cleopatra. Not at all the sultry Jezebel I had imagined."

"I hired her for her journalistic skills," I said testily, "not for her looks."

"Thank God for that," David said with amusement, and Jackie, in her voluminous and colorless clothes, did look more than ever like some drab, wan, and orphaned child, an impression that was not helped by a brown felt hat of spectacular ugliness.

"Can I use this?" Jackie Potten referred to the saloon table, where she sat and spread some crumpled and dirty papers. "I have to account for your money, see? I guess I really did some pretty dumb things, and I'm not really sure that I separated out all Molly's German expenses from mine . . . "

"You took Mrs. Tetterman to Germany?" I interrupted to ask.

"Sure! But not on your money. Really!" She sounded very anxious.

"Guide's honor?" David, instantly divining the girl's innocence, could not resist teasing her.

"Guide's honor?" Jackie frowned at him. "Oh, you mean like Girl Scouts? Sure, Scout's honor. Except maybe some of the receipts got muddled and that's why I need to run through the paperwork with you, Mr. Blackburn, because you never said that Molly should go, but she kind of insisted and she's really hard to turn down, know what I mean? And she speaks German, too, so it was a real help having her along, but we got those tickets you book thirty days in advance and we traveled midweek, only my ticket cost a lot more because I had to come here as well and Molly didn't. She's flying straight back to Detroit, while I've come to report to you. I don't think we were really extravagant. I mean we stayed at this real fleabag. It was weird. They had a pool, which I thought was kind of neat, but the Germans swim naked! These fat guys, right? Really gross! Molly said it was just natural and healthy, and she went skinny-dipping with them, but I couldn't do it, I really couldn't. And the food was awful—they don't know what vegetarian food is—"

"Quiet!" I sang out.

"I was only trying to tell you . . . " Jackie made another valiant effort to keep going, while David and Betty were trying hard not to laugh aloud.

"Quiet!" I had entirely forgotten this girl's capaci-

ty to talk. I put a finger on my lips to keep her silent
as I walked slowly to the cabin table. Once there I
put my hands on the table's edge and bent toward
Jackie Potten's indignant, pale face. "Did you find
out why Caspar von Rellsteb sailed to Europe four-
and-a-half years ago?" I asked her at last.

"That's exactly what I was about to tell you!"
Jackie said very indignantly. "Yes, I did!"

"Oh, blessed girl," I sat opposite her. "So tell me
now."

"I was already telling you!"

"OK." I held my hands up in mock surrender.
"Please, continue."

"Molly insisted on going to Hamburg, because
that was where von Rellsteb's mother came from.
Molly said two heads were better than one, and it
really was a good idea, because she speaks
German, and she found this lawyer and he was
terrific! He had a cousin who lives in Detroit, and I
guess that helped, because we could tell him all
about Detroit and he was really interested, because
he's never been to the States and he was thinking
of going, in fact, he was thinking he might go this
Christmas, and Molly—"

"Jackie!" I snapped. "I do not care where your
God-damned Hamburg lawyer will spend his
Christmas. I want to know about Caspar von
Rellsteb!"

David was half choking with laughter, while
Betty, who was used to organizing the waifs and
strays of society, looked as though she wanted to
tuck Jackie under her arm and carry her away for a
proper feed. Jackie, astonished at my reproof, gazed

wide-eyed at me for a few seconds, then looked contrite. "I'm sorry," she said, "but the thing is that Friedrich, that's the lawyer I was telling you about, was really terrific and he didn't charge us a penny, and that was what I was trying to explain to you, because you've got to review these accounts"—she pushed the untidy pile of scruffy papers toward me—"to see that we didn't spend your money unwisely, and Friedrich, and this is what I've been trying to tell you all along, only you keep interrupting me, knew all about the von Rellsteb legacy, because it was quite a celebrated case, and he dug all the papers out of the archives and he gave Molly and me copies, and, of course, we paid for the photocopying, you'll see it down there at the bottom of page three, there, see? Twenty-nine marks? And that's cheap for photo-copying, because in America you probably pay ten cents a sheet, in fact, a place near my house charges fifteen cents a sheet! Fifteen! And we paid much less for two copies each of a hundred and ten pages. I've got a proper receipt for the photo-copying as well." She dug through her vast bag. "I know I've got it. I remember putting it aside."

David, hugely amused by Jackie, had gone to the table where he leafed through her carefully handwritten accounts. "What's this?" He demand-ed with mock sternness. "Six marks and thirty-seven pfenning on ice cream?"

"Oh, gee." Jackie blushed with embarrassment. "I told Molly we shouldn't have bought the ice cream, but she said it was all right, because we deserved some reward for all our work, and the food was really terrible. All those sausages, which neither of us would eat, and we'd run out of our own money and we just wanted some ice cream. I'll pay you back, Mr. Blackburn, truly I will."

"You can have the ice cream," I said magnanimously, "if you tell me about Caspar von Rellsteb."

She did, though it took her the best part of a half hour. Betty made us all tea and we sat in the big stateroom, listening to the wind sigh in the rigging and to the rain patter on the coach roof and to the small waves slap on *Stormchild*'s hull, as Jackie Potten slowly unveiled the mystery.

Caspar von Rellsteb's father, Jackie said, was not alive, but had died in the air battles at the very end of the Second World War. Caspar von Rellsteb had discovered his father's identity when he went through his mother's papers after her death, and the same papers suggested that he might have a claim on his dead father's considerable property. He had sailed to Germany to make that claim, taking with him a letter, in which, shortly before his death, *Oberstleutnant* Auguste von Rellsteb had bequeathed his whole estate to Caspar's mother, Fräulein Eva Fellnagel. The letter, written from a Luftwaffe station late in the war, was hardly a legal will, but Auguste von Rellsteb left no other instructions for the disposition of his property before he was killed when his Focke-Wulf 190 was shot down by an American Mustang. The legal status of the letter was challenged by the estate's trustees, but the German judges had dismissed the challenge and upheld the validity of *Oberstleutnant* Auguste von Rellsteb's last wishes. Caspar von Rellsteb had won his case.

"So how much did he inherit?" Betty, quite caught up in Jackie's breathless retelling of the story, asked.

"It's kind of hard to say," Jackie answered, then explained that the legacy went back to the early nineteenth century when a certain Otto von Rellsteb, the youngest son of a landed Junker family from East Prussia, had crossed the Atlantic to the newly independent Republic of Chile. Otto von Rellsteb, like thousands of other hopeful Germans, had gone to buy land at the southern tip of South America, an area so popular with German immigrants that it had been nicknamed the New Bavaria. Otto, unable to afford the richer farmland on the Argentine *pampas,* had purchased a huge spread of cheap coastal land in Chile, where he had established his *finca,* his estate, and where he had raised thousands upon thousands of sheep. He had also discovered an easily quarried deposit of limestone on his *finca* and, thus provided by nature, he had prospered, as had his descendants until his great-great-grandson, Auguste, hating the bleak, wild, stormy coast, and detesting the sound of sheep, and loathing the dumb, insolent faces of his workers, had returned to Europe where, glorying in the Reich, he had joined the *Luftwaffe,* impregnated a whore with his son, then died in a blazing aircraft for his führer.

Jackie Potten carefully unfolded a photocopied map that she pushed across *Stormchild*'s cabin table. "It's there," she said, "all that's left of the von Rellsteb *finca.*"

I did not look at the map. Instead my mind was

reeling with the sudden understanding that the Genesis community was not in Alaska after all, but in Patagonia.

"How big is the estate?" David turned the map toward him. It was not a very helpful map, showing hardly any detail, but instead just some shaded-in islands that rimmed the wild western coast of South America.

"Caspar inherited about twelve thousand acres," Jackie said. "The estate lost a good deal of land when Allende was in power, but Pinochet restored most of it to the German trustees. General Pinochet really liked the Germans, you see, and I guess he was kind of hoping that a German might go back and live at the *finca*. There's evidently a really big farmhouse, and there are still some industrial buildings left at the quarry, because they went on extracting limestone right up until the Second World War."

"The land can't be worth anything," David said dismissively.

"But what a perfect hiding place," I said, and I pulled the photocopied map toward me and saw that Otto von Rellsteb had made his *finca* in the Archipiélago Sangre de Cristo, the Islands of Christ's Blood, in the Magellanic region of Chile, at the very end of the earth, in the last land God made, in the remotest region any man might search for his enemies; in Patagonia.

I knew something about the Patagonian coast, because I had once made plans to take a British army expedition there, but those plans had collapsed when the Ministry of Defense had tediously demanded either scientific or military justification for the jaunt. Perhaps I had been lucky in the Ministry's obduracy, for, though there are one or two wilder places than Patagonia, there is no coast on earth where the sea and wind combine to vent such an implacable and relentless anger. Patagonia has a coast out of a nightmare. It is a seashore from hell.

It is a coastline that is still being formed, a coastline being ripped and burned and forged from the clash of volcano and tectonic plate, and of ocean and glacier. On a chart the coast looks as though it has been fractured into islands so numerous they are uncountable. It is a coast of dizzying cliffs, murderous tidal surges, howling winds, whirlpools, sudden fire, and crushing ice. It is the coast where the massive fetch of the great Pacific rollers ends in numbing violence. From the Gulf of Corcovado to the northern limit of the Land of Fire are five hundred miles of ragged islands about which the wild sea heaps and shatters itself white. There are no roads down that coast. A few wild tracks cross the Andes from the grass plains of the Argentine, but no roads can be built parallel to the tortuous Chilean coast, so the only way to travel is by boat, threading the narrow channels between the inland glaciers and the outer barrier islands. Yet even the innermost channels offer no certain safety to a mariner. A Chilean naval ship, taking food to one of the coast's rare lighthouses, was once trapped in such a channel for forty days as the frenzied Pacific waves pounded the outer rocks and filled the sky with stinging whips of freezing spume. Within the channels, where thick growths of kelp clog propellers and thicker fogs blind helmsmen and lookouts, williwaws or *rafagas*, which are sudden squalls of hurricane-force wind, hurtle down the mountainsides to explode the seemingly sheltered waters into frantic madness. Such winds can destroy a boat in seconds.

The coast, inhospitable though it is, still has its few inhabitants. A handful of ranches cling to the islands and mainland hills; there is one fishing settlement with the unlikely name of Puerto Eden, and one surviving limestone quarry which still extracts stone, but otherwise the long savage coast has been abandoned to the seas and to the winds, to the smoking vents of volcanoes, to the glaciers, and to the earth tremors, which reveal that this is a place where a seam of the planet is still grinding and tearing itself into ruin. The nightmare coast comes to its end in the "Land of Fire," the Tierra del Fuego, at Cape Horn where, before the Panama Canal was dug, the great ships used to die, and where the biggest seas on earth still heap and surge through the narrow and shallow Drake Passage which runs between the Land of Fire and the northernmost tip of Antarctica. It is a horrid coast, a bitter coast, a dangerous and rock-riven coast, where men and boats die easily. It was also a coast which, if I was to find my child and let her loose from a madman's thrall, I would have to search.

"Remember Peter Carter-Pirie?" I asked David.

"I was just thinking of him."

"Carter-Pirie?" Betty asked.

"He was a mad Royal Marine," I explained, "who used to sail a wooden boat to unlikely places. David and I met him in Greenland when we were guinea-pigging survival gear for the army, and he rather excited us at the prospect of sailing the Patagonian coast. He'd been there a couple of times, you see, and I remember he told us quite a bit about it."

"And none of it particularly good," David said grimly.

"He said the bird life was remarkable," I reproved David's pessimism. "Lots of condors, steamer ducks, penguins, that sort of thing. If I remember rightly Carter-Pirie went there to prove that Patagonia was the breeding ground for the greater-crested snipe or something like that."

"There is no greater-crested snipe," said Betty, with the easy authority of an expert, "though there is a Patagonian hummingbird; the green-backed firecrown."

Jackie Potten was staring at the three of us as though we had lost our collective marbles. "Hummingbird?" she said faintly.

"I'd rather like to see that hummingbird," David said wistfully.

"Patagonia can't be a very comfortable place for a hummingbird," I suggested. "I thought they sipped nectar in warm climes?"

"It can't be a very comfortable place for von Rellsteb and his Genesis community either"—David was peering at the map—"if indeed they're there?"

"Where else?" I asked.

"But Patagonia means rather a drastic change in your plans, Tim, does it not?" David inquired.

"Not really." I spoke with an insouciance I did not entirely feel. "It just means that I turn left when I reach the Pacific, instead of turning right."

"You mean . . . " Jackie Potten frowned at me.

I glanced across the table at her. "Oh, I'm sorry, I never told you where I was going, did I? When you arrived I was just leaving to find the Genesis community."

"In this?" She gestured round *Stormchild*'s spacious saloon.

"It's a great deal more suitable than a Ford Escort," I said very seriously.

"You were just leaving?" She ignored my feeble jest. "But you didn't know where to look!"

"I had a mind to try Alaska," I explained, "but I would probably have tried to telephone you as soon as I reached the far side of the Atlantic, and I guess you'd have told me to try Patagonia instead."

"So now you'll just go to Chile?" Jackie seemed astonished that such a decision could be made so lightly. "How do you get there?"

"Sail south till the butter melts, then turn right." David offered the ancient joke.

"I'll sail south to the Canary Islands," I offered more sensibly, "and wait there till the trade winds establish themselves, then I'll run across to the West Indies. After that it'll be a brisk sail to Panama, and I'm guessing now, because I'm not familiar with the waters, but I imagine it will be easier to go west into the Pacific, then dogleg back to South America rather than fight the Humboldt Current all the way down the coast. And with any luck I should be in Chile by March next year, which will be toward the end of their summer and, if there's ever a good time to sail in Patagonian waters, late summer is probably that time."

"Wow!" Jackie Potten said in what I took to be admiration, but then it was her turn to astound me. "Can I come?"

Stormchild sailed on the next tide, just after midnight. She slipped unseen down the river with her navigation lights softly blurred by the light rain. Instead of the champagne parting and the paper streamers there had only been David and Betty calling their farewells from the pontoons, and once their voices had been lost in the night there were only the sounds of the big motor in *Stormchild*'s belly, the splash of the water at her stem, and the hiss of the wet wind. That wind was southerly, but the forecast promised it would back easterly by dawn, and, if the forecast held good, I could not hope for a better departure wind. It was blowing hard, but the big, heavily laden and steel-hulled *Stormchild* needed a good wind to shift her ponderous weight.

I raised sail at the river's mouth, killed the engine, and hardened onto a broad reach. The wake foamed white into the blackness astern as the coastal lights winked and faded in the rain that still pattered on the deck and dripped from the rigging. The green and red lights of the river's buoys vanished astern, and soon the only mark to guide *Stormchild* was the flickering loom of the far Portland light. I had lost count of how many times I had begun voyages in just this manner; slipping on a fast tide down-channel, making my way southerly to avoid the tidal rips that churn off the great headlands of southern England, then letting my boat tear her way westward toward the open Atlantic, yet however many times I had done it there was always the same excitement.

"Gee, but it's cold," Jackie Potten said suddenly.

"If you're going to moan all the way across the Atlantic," I snapped, "then I'll turn round now and drop you off."

There was a stunned silence. I had surprised myself by the anger in my voice, which had clearly made Jackie intensely miserable. I felt sorry that I had snapped at her, but I also felt justified, for I was not at all sure that I wanted her on board *Stormchild,* but the notion of Jackie accompanying me had energized David and Betty with a vast amusement, and they had overriden my objections with their joint enthusiasm. Betty had taken Jackie shopping, returning with a carload of vegetarian supplies and armfuls of expensive foulweather gear that I had been forced to pay for. I had ventured to ask the American girl whether she had any sailing experience at all, only to be told that she and her mother had once spent a week on a Miami-based cruise ship.

"But you can cook, can't you?" David had demanded.

"A bit." Jackie had been confused by the question. "Then you won't be entirely useless." David's characteristic bluntness had left Jackie rather dazed.

Dazed or not, Jackie was now my sole companion on *Stormchild*, which meant I had the inconvenience of sharing a boat with a complete novice. I could not let her take a watch or even helm the ship until I had trained her in basic seamanship, and that training was going to slow me down. Worse, she might prove to be seasick or utterly incompetent. All in all, I was sourly thinking, it had been bloody inconsiderate of David and Betty to have encouraged her to join the ship.

There was also another and murkier reason for my unhappiness. I had felt an inexplicable tug of attraction toward this odd little stray girl, and I did not want that irrational feeling to be nurtured by the forced intimacy of a small boat. I told myself I did not need the complication, and that this girl was too young, too naive, too idealistic, too noisy, and too pathetic. "I thought you had a job to go home to," I said nastily, as though, being reminded of her employment, Jackie might suddenly demand to be put ashore. "Aren't you the *Kalamazoo Gazette*'s star reporter?"

"I was fired," she said miserably.

"What for? Talking too much?" I immediately regretted the jibe, and apologized.

"I do talk too much," she said, "I know I do. But that wasn't why I was fired. I was fired because I insisted on going to Hamburg. I was supposed to be writing some articles on date rape in junior high schools, but I thought the Genesis community was a better story, so I left the paper. And now I've got a chance to sail the Atlantic, so you see I was quite right. Molly says that we should always take our chances in life, or else we'll miss out on everything."

"It's a pity to miss out on roast beef," I said nastily. "What is all that sprouting shit you brought on board?"

"It isn't shit," she said in a hurt voice. "You put seeds in the trays, water them twice a day, and harvest the sprouts. It's a really good, fresh source of protein."

I glanced up at the pale mass of the mainsail. "Did you know that Hitler and Mussolini were both vegetarians? And so was the guy who founded the KGB?"

There was a pause, then Miss Jackie Potten showed me another side of her character. "I know you're captain of this ship," she said, "but I think it's important that we respect each other's beliefs, and that we don't mock each other's private convictions. I kind of think that's really crucial."

I had just been told off by a floozy young enough to be my daughter. I was so mortified that I said nothing, but just clung to the big wheel and glanced down at the binnacle to make certain we were still on a course of 240 degrees.

"Because we all need our private space," Jackie went doggedly on, evidently translating my silence as incomprehension, "and if we don't recognize each other's unique human qualities, Mr. Blackburn, then we won't respect each other, and I really believe that we need to share mutual respect if we're to spend so much time together."

"You're right," I said briskly, "and I'm sorry." I meant the apology, too, though my voice probably sounded too robust to convey the contrition I genuinely felt, but I had been boorish and Jackie had been right to protest. She had also been very brave, but it was evident, from the embarrassed silence that followed, that the display of defiance had exhausted her courage. "Is there anything I can do to help, then?" she finally asked me in a very small and very timid voice.

"You can call me Tim," I said, "and then you can go below and make me a mug of coffee, with caffeine and milk, but no sugar, and you can get me a corned beef sandwich with butter and mustard, but nothing else, and certainly with nothing green in it."

"Right, Tim," she said, and went to do it.

By the time we docked in Las Palmas in the Canary Islands, I had developed a healthy respect for the frail-looking Jackie Potten. Not that she looked so frail anymore, for fifteen hundred sea miles had put some healthy color into her cheeks and bleached her mousy hair into pale gold. After her complaint about feeling cold on our first night out she had uttered not a single grievance. In fact she had proved to possess a patient tenacity that was well suited to sailing and, despite her fondness for a diet that might have starved an anorexic stick-insect, she had a stomach that could take the roughest motion of the waves. In the beginning, as

Stormchild had thrashed into the great gray channel rollers with their hissing and bubbling white tops, Jackie had been nervous, especially when the first sullen dawn showed that we were out of sight of land. That, to me, is always a special moment; when at last you can look around the horizon and see nothing but God's good ocean. For Jackie, when all she saw was the cold crinkling heave of the careless waves, her overwhelming sensation was the terror of insignificance.

The terror did not last. Instead she began to enjoy the challenge, and learned to have confidence in the boat and in her own ability to control *Stormchild*. Within two days she was watch-keeping alone, at first only by daylight, but within a week she was standing the night watches and all traces of her initial nervousness had disappeared. She was a natural sailor, and, as her competence grew, her character hardened out of timidity into confidence. She even talked less, and I realized her previous volubility had been merely a symptom of shyness.

We marked off our private territories within the boat. Jackie had excavated a sleeping space among the heaped stores in the starboard forward cabin where she settled like some small cozy animal. Once in a while I would hear her speaking aloud in that cabin. At first I thought she was just chattering to herself, but later I learned she was dictating into a small tape recorder. She was making a record of the journey, but would not let me listen to the tape. "I'm just making notes," she said disparagingly, "only rough notes."

We raced across Biscay where Jackie, equipped with *Stormchild*'s copy of *The Birds of Britain and Europe* learned to identify the various seabirds that kept us company. There were fulmars on either beam, storm petrels flickering above our wake, and handsome, slim-winged shearwaters effortlessly skimming all about us. As Jackie learned to identify the birds, I taught myself more about *Stormchild*'s character. She was a stubborn boat, good in heavy seas, but sluggish and sullen when, ten days into our voyage, we encountered light winds north and east of Madeira. The winds eventually died to a flat calm and the sails slatted uselessly to the boat's motion on the long swell. I was tempted to turn on the powerful engine, but there was no point in wasting fuel, for nothing would hurry the establishment of the trade winds and I reasoned that we might just as well wait it out at sea than pay daily harbor fees of seventy pesetas per foot of boat length in a Canary Islands port.

After three days the winds came again and *Stormchild* dipped her bows to the long ocean swell. The weather had turned fiercely warm. I changed into shorts, but Jackie had no summer clothes so stayed in her usual baggy attire. I stored our foul-weather gear in a hanging locker and suspected that, storms apart, we would not need the heavy warm clothes again until we had long cleared the Panama Canal, for now we were entering the latitudes of the perpetual lotus-eaters and would stay in these warm latitudes for weeks.

We raised the Canary Islands on a Sunday morning and by mid-afternoon we had cleared the

Spanish immigration procedures in Las Palmas. Jackie was wide-eyed with the realization that it was in this ancient harbor that Columbus himself had waited for the trade winds to take him into the unknown west.

Next day, for lack of space in Las Palmas, we moved to the harbor at Mogan, on the island's south coast. Mogan, like all the other island harbors, was crammed with cruising yachts waiting to make the Atlantic crossing. There had been a time when barely a dozen small yachts a year made this passage, but now the Canary Island ports could scarcely keep up with the demand for berth space. Hundreds of boats would cross with us, making a great flock of sails that would speed across the blue heart of the Atlantic.

"So how long do we wait for the trade winds?" Jackie asked.

"A month? Maybe longer."

We collected our mail from the English pub where David, God bless him, had sent every available chart of the Patagonian coast. He had also sent me the details of the Chilean government's regulations for visiting boats, which were complex, together with his advice to see a Chilean consul somewhere in Central America. "I'm going to talk to Peter Carter-Pirie," he wrote to me, "for his advice on sailing the Patagonian channels. I'll have his words of wisdom waiting for you *Poste Restante* in Antigua, with copies to Panama. Betty and I send best wishes to the lady from Kalamazoo, that is if you're still talking to each other!" I could almost hear David's evil chortling as he wrote that sentence.

I took the charts back to *Stormchild* where I planned to spend the afternoon studying the awful coast where the Genesis community had apparently taken shelter. I had *Stormchild* to myself, for Jackie had taken the boat's folding bicycle to explore the nearby countryside and to look for shops where she could buy galley supplies. I had also instructed her to buy herself some summer clothes, for the weather was stifling and she could not go on wearing her shapeless sweaters and capacious trousers. I spread the Patagonian charts in *Stormchild*'s cockpit, over which I had rigged a white cotton awning, then settled down with a tall jug of Bloody Marys.

I discovered the Archipelago of Christ's Blood to be a tortured group of islands some two hundred miles north of Puerto Natales, which was where the settlements of Tierra del Fuego began. I traced my finger northward from Puerto Natales, across a tangle of islands, fjords, channels, and glaciers, and noted the odd mixture of place names. Some were English, legacies of the great naval explorers of the eighteenth and nineteenth centuries; thus there was an Isla Darwin, a Nelson Straits, an Isla Duque de York, and an Isla Victoria. The majority of the names, naturally enough, were Spanish; some pious, like the Isla Madre de Dios, and some ominous, like the Isla Desolación, but a good number of German names were also salted among the Anglo-Spanish mix; I found a Puerto Weber, the Canal Erhardt, the Isla Stubbenkammer and the Monte Siegfried; just enough Teutonic names to record how many

hopeful people had emigrated from Germany to
Chile's bleak and inhospitable coast.

None of the charts marked von Rellsteb's *finca*,
but of the score of islands which made up the
Archipiélago Sangre de Cristo only one seemed
large enough to sustain a ranch. That island bore
the ominous name of Isla Tormentos, the Isle of
Torments, and I wondered if it had been so named
by shipwrecked sailors who had suffered on its
inhospitable coasts. The long Pacific shore of the
Isle of Torments was shown as a stretch of gigantic
cliffs, pierced by a single fjord that reached so deep
into the island it almost slashed Isla Tormentos in
half. The opposite shore of the island was far more
ragged than the ocean-facing cliffs; the eastern
coast was a cartographer's nightmare, for it looked
as though the island had been raggedly ripped
from the rest of the archipelago to leave a tattered,
scattered, and shattered litter of rocks and islands
and shoals, which, in turn, were all navigational
hazards within the forbiddingly named Estrecho
Desolado, the Desolate Straits. The Patagonian
coast was thickly printed with such depressing
names, but the Archipiélago Sangre de Cristo
seemed to have more than its fair share of forbid-
ding nomenclature, suggesting that sailing its
labyrinthine channels would be hard and dangerous work. I traced the difficult course of the
Desolate Straits to find they were not true straits at
all, but rather a blind sea loch that ran uselessly
into the heartland of the Isle of Torments.

I was distracted from these dispiriting researches by Jackie's noisy return. She came laden with

string bags that were crammed with papayas, avo-
cados, tomatoes, leeks, pineapples, cabbages,
bunches of radishes, and the island's small, good-
tasting potatoes. She was clearly delighted with
the Canary Islands. "I got talking to this Dutch
lady, who's on one of the boats moored by the
wall over there, and she speaks Spanish and she
talked to the lady in the shop, and she told us that
everything in the shop was grown organically.
Everything! Isn't that just great, Tim?"

"It's absolutely astonishingly terrifically wonderful," I said with an utter lack of enthusiasm.
"Did you buy some organic meat for your organic
skipper?"

"Yeah, sure. Of course I did." She produced a
cellophane pack, which held a very scrawny por-
tion of tired-looking chicken, then dived enthusiastically down the main companionway with her
purchases. "Chicken's OK, isn't it? They had rabbits, too, but I really couldn't bring myself to buy
a dead bunny rabbit, Tim. I'm sorry." She shouted
the apology up from the galley where she was evidently storing the food into lockers.

"Did the dead bunnies have their paws on?"

There was a pause, then her small, wedge-shaped
face frowned at me from the foot of the companionway. "I didn't look. Why? Is it important?"

"If the paws are still on the carcass, then it
probably is rabbit," I said, "but if the paws are
missing, then it's a pretty sure bet you're looking
at a dead pussycat."

A heartbeat of silence. Then, "No!"

"Cat doesn't taste bad," I said with feigned

insouciance. "It depends on how well the family fed the pussy, really. The ones fed on that dry cat food taste like shit, but the others are OK."

"Gross me out!" But she laughed, then went back to her chores. She began singing, but her voice faded as she went forward to her own cabin. While we were in port I had taken over the stern cabin to give us both some privacy. At sea I could collapse onto a saloon sofa, but in port it was more difficult to preserve mutual modesty if I was sprawled in the boat's main living space.

Silence settled on the boat, and I guessed Jackie was resting after the excitement of discovering organic stick-insect food in the middle of the Atlantic. I sipped my Bloody Mary and looked back to the charts of the Archipiélago Sangre de Cristo. I assumed that if the von Rellsteb *finca* was indeed on the Isla Tormentos, then it must be built on the tangled eastern coast, facing the Desolate Straits, for in the nineteenth century, when the estate wanted to take its fleeces to market, or to ship its quarried limestone to the world, it would doubtless have used coastal sailing vessels to carry the produce north to Puerto Montt. Such ships could never have found shelter on the ocean-fronting western coast, so I could safely assume that the settlement, if it was on the Isla Tormentos, must stand on the eastern shore, where, if the old charts were accurate, several bays looked promising as possible harbors.

"Tim? What do you think?" Jackie's oddly coy voice startled my somnolent researches. She had appeared on deck, but instead of using the main companionway she had climbed through the forward hatch into the bright sunlight of *Stormchild's* foredeck. I looked up from the Estrecho Desolado to blink at the sudden brilliance of the tropical daylight, in which, to my considerable surprise, a very shy Jackie Potten was standing in a newly bought bikini. "You don't like it," she responded anxiously to my half second of silence.

"I think it's very nice," I said with clumsy inadequacy, and I knew I was not referring to the bikini, which was yellow and more or less like any other bikini I had ever seen, but to Jackie herself, who was unexpectedly revealed as sinuous and shapely, and I had to look quickly down at the charts as though I had noticed nothing out of the ordinary. "I hope you bought some good suntan lotion."

"I did. Yes. Lots." She sounded very chastened, and I guessed she had never worn anything as daring as a bikini before. "The Dutch lady made me buy it," Jackie explained. "She said it was silly to wear too many clothes in the tropics. I've bought some shorts and a skirt as well," she added hurriedly, "because the lady in the shop said that it's kind of respectful to look pretty decent in the town, but that the bikini's OK on the beaches or on board a boat. Is it really OK?" She asked very earnestly.

"Yes," I said very truthfully, "it really is OK." She needed still more reassurance. "It's a very, very nice swimsuit," I said inadequately, "and you look terrific," and the realization that I had spoken the truth was suddenly very embarrassing because Jackie was only a year or so older than my

Nicole, and I also realized that I was blushing, so I looked hurriedly down at my charts and tried to imagine the speed of the winds funneling through the Estrecho Desolado, but somehow I could not concentrate on winds and tides and currents. I looked back to the foredeck, but Jackie was lying down, hidden from me by the thick coils of halyards that hung from the cleats at the base of the mainmast. I sighed and shut my eyes. I told myself that bringing her on this voyage was a mistake, that it had always been a mistake, and that now it suddenly threatened to be an even bigger mistake, because I could feel the temptation to make a damn bloody great fool of myself over some crumpet from Kalamazoo.

So I poured myself a great drink instead.

We waited for the winds to take us away. My birthday came, and Jackie had somehow discovered its date and solemnly presented me with a book of Robert Frost's poetry that she had miraculously discovered in a secondhand bookshop in Las Palmas, and that night she served me a birthday dinner of rabbit stew, the cooking of which was a real triumph of friendship over conviction, and she invited the Dutch woman, who had helped her shop, and whose boat was moored nearby, to join us with her husband. The four of us sat round a dining table under the cockpit's awning, and three of us drank wine until, at last, Jackie decided that she would not die if she tried it too, after which four of us drank wine and told tall stories of far seas and I felt the subtly pleasurable flattery of being mistaken for Jackie's lover.

"I didn't realize," Jackie said after the Dutch couple had left us, "that you were kind of famous."

"It's a very fading fame," I said, "if it ever was really fame at all."

The next day, still waiting for the trade winds, we took a ferry to Lanzarote where we hired a car to explore the famous black island. Jackie wanted to ride one of the camels that carried tourists up the flanks of the volcano, and I, who had taken the uncomfortable trip before, let her go on her own. The camels were rigged with curious wooden seats that accommodated three people abreast, one on each side and one perched high on the beast's hump, and Jackie found herself sitting next to a young Frenchman. He was obviously attracted to her, and I watched the animation with which she responded to his remarks and felt a twinge of the most stupid jealousy, but nevertheless a twinge so strong that I had to turn away to stare across the landscape of black lava.

Joanna. I said my wife's name to myself over and over, as though the repetition would prove a talisman to help me. I was tempted to insist that Jackie fly home, except now I did not want her to go. Things would be better, I told myself, when we could leave, for then we would become absorbed in the routine of sailing a boat. At sea, on a short-handed yacht, a crew sees remarkably little of each other. I would be awake when Jackie slept, and she awake when I slept, and in those few moments

when we might share the deck or a meal together,
we would be far too busy with the minutiae of
navigation and ship-keeping to be worried about
my adolescent fantasies.

More and more boats left. I waited, not because
I wished to draw out these lotus-eating days, but
because the winds about the islands were still
depressingly light, and I did not want to motor
the heavy *Stormchild* all the way south to where
the unvarying trade winds blew across the
Atlantic. I was waiting for a northerly wind to take
me away, and each day I haunted the splendid
Meteorological Office in Mogan to study their syn-
optic charts. "Soon, Tim, soon!" one of the duty
weathermen would greet me each morning.

Jackie translated my irritability as an impatience to leave the Canary Islands. She confessed
to some impatience herself, declaring that she had
developed an unexpected taste for sailing. "I mean
I used to watch the yachts on Lake Michigan,
right? But I never guessed I would ever be on one.
I thought yachts were just for the rich, or at least
for the middle class!"

"Aren't you middle class?" I asked idly.

"Jeez, no! Mom works in a hardware store. My
dad left her when we were real little, and he never
sent us any money, so things have always been
kind of tough." Jackie spoke without any touch of
self-pity. She was sitting in a corner of the cockpit
with her bare, brown knees drawn up to her chin.
It was evening, and behind her the sun was setting
toward the high harbor wall, and its light imbued
her untidy hair with a lambent beauty. She

laughed suddenly. "Mom would be really knocked out to see me now."

"Does that mean she'd be pleased?"

"Don't be stuffy, Tim, of course it means she'd be pleased. Mom always said I should get more fresh air, because I guess I was kind of bookish as a kid. My brother was always out-of-doors, but I was the family's nerd. Mom would be really astonished to see me now." She turned to watch a graceful French sloop that was motoring slowly toward the harbor entrance. A lot of boats liked to leave at nightfall, thinking to use an evening breeze to spur them through the doldrums.

"It's strange," I said, "how we don't really know our children. We think we do, but we don't. I never thought Nicole would do anything stupid. Then, of course, her brother died, and she really went berserk."

"She was fond of her brother?"

I nodded. "They were inseparable." I paused, thinking about Nicole's childhood, raking over the ancient coals of guilt to discover whether I had caused her unhappiness. "The trouble is I was away a lot when they were little. I was sailing round the world, being mildly famous. And Joanna was always busy, so the twins were left alone a lot. But they were happy. They did all the things kids are supposed to do." I poured myself another finger of Irish whiskey. "I was really proud of her. She was a tough kid, but I thought she was levelheaded."

Jackie smiled. "And that's important to you, Tim, isn't it? Being levelheaded."

"Absolutely."

"And you think when Nicole ran off with von Rellsteb she wasn't being levelheaded?"

"Of course she wasn't," I said firmly.

"Maybe she was, Tim." Jackie stirred the ice cubes in her glass, then added a shot of diet cola. One of the advantages of being alongside a pontoon was that we could connect the boat's refrigerator to shoreside electricity and thus satisfy Jackie's insatiable American appetite for ice cubes, though Jackie, with her terror of ingesting anything that might harbor a microbe, insisted on freezing only bottled water, and not the perfectly good stuff that came out of the pontoon hose. The pontoon not only had electricity and water, it even had television cables so that the more lavishly equipped boats could watch "Dallas" in Spanish, French, or English. Jackie, her drink suitably chilled into tastelessness, frowned at me. "Just because we both believe that Caspar von Rellsteb is a weird guy, it doesn't mean that his group hasn't achieved some good things. They're surely right to try and stop drift netting and whaling, aren't they?"

"They are," I agreed, "if that's all they do."

Jackie heard the tension in my voice and stared gravely at me over the rim of her glass. "You've really convinced yourself that von Rellsteb planted the bomb that killed Joanna, haven't you?"

I shrugged. "I can't think who else would have done it." That was not the most convincing proof of von Rellsteb's guilt, but it was the only explanation I could find for Joanna's death, and the explanation convinced me. We knew that von Rellsteb had made himself independent of his Canadian benefactress by means of his father's legacy and it made cruel sense to me that, if von Rellsteb found himself in need of more money, he would seek a further inheritance: mine. I also believed Nicole to be in von Rellsteb's thrall, a victim of his malevolent hierarchy, and that she had consequently been unable to prevent his machinations. "We know von Rellsteb uses criminal violence," I began to justify my suspicions, "and we . . . "

"Once!" Jackie interrupted to reprove me. "We know he committed one crime in Texas, Tim, and that was over ten years ago and no one was hurt." She frowned, thinking. "We're going on a journey of discovery, that's what we're doing. We're going to find out just what von Rellsteb is, because we don't really know anything about him. We don't really know if he keeps people against their will, or if he uses violence. We might even discover that he's running a really legitimate operation, a bit fanatical, maybe, but straight."

"Balls," I said.

Jackie laughed. "You're so full of shit, Tim!"

"Listen." It was my turn to speak earnestly. "I'm not sailing halfway round the damn world with an open mind. I'm sailing because I think von Rellsteb is an eco-terrorist. His aims might be good, but you don't approve of terrorists just because you agree with their political aims. That's the mitigating plea offered by every terrorist in the world! The innocent have to suffer so that Ireland can be united, or the whales saved, or

Israel destroyed, or apartheid dissolved, or whatever else is the cause of the month, and the terrorist claims exemption from civilized restraints
on the grounds that his cause is too noble. In fact
he claims not to be a terrorist at all, but a freedom
fighter! But if you disagree with this freedom
fighter, then he'll murder you or kidnap your wife
or blow up your children." I had spoken with a
more venomous anger than the conversation had
deserved, and in doing so I had said more than I
probably believed, for I did not know whether
von Rellsteb was a terrorist or not. For all I knew
he might be nothing more than a holy fool,
though I suspected he was considerably more
dangerous. At best, I imagined, Caspar von
Rellsteb was a manipulative man who sheltered
his activities behind the virtuous smokescreen of
environmental activism, giving even his survivalist notions a dubious respectability by a green
antinuclear stance, but, as Jackie had maintained,
I had no direct proof that he was a terrorist. I saw
that my anger had disconcerted Jackie and, as the
fury ebbed out of me like a foul tide, I apologized
to her.

Jackie dismissed my apology with a shake of her
head. "You're thinking of your son, right?"

"Of course. And of Joanna."

"Oh God, I'm sorry." She stared across the harbor to where a bright painted fishing boat was
chugging toward the sea. "Is this a crusade for
you, Tim?"

"A crusade?" I asked.

"I mean have you condemned von Rellsteb

already? Is that why you're going to Chile? To punish him?"

It was a shrewd question, and I almost answered it unthinkingly by saying that of course I wanted to shoot the goatlike bastard. I remembered that moment on Sun Kiss Key when I thought he was laughing at me and I wondered, as I often did, whether the reason he had agreed to meet me in Florida was just so he could gloat over the fool he had bereaved and whose daughter he had bedded. Of course I wanted to kill him, but, instead, I just said I was going to Patagonia to find my daughter.

Jackie nodded at that answer, then frowned as she swirled her melting ice around her glass. "What if Nicole doesn't want to leave von Rellsteb?" she asked after a while.

"Then she can stay, of course," I said, "so long as she tells me that herself, and so long as I'm convinced von Rellsteb isn't forcing her to say it, or isn't forcing her to stay in Patagonia against her will."

"And what will you do if you think he is forcing her to do what he wants?"

For an answer, and because I remembered her extravagant reaction to the revolver in Key West, I just dismissed the question with a wave of my hand.

But Jackie would not be so easily fobbed off. "You're not thinking of fighting von Rellsteb, are you?" She waited, but got no answer. "You'd better not, Tim, because I told you he used to be into survivalism, and I'll bet he still is, which means he's bound to have a lot of guns." She shuddered at that thought, then shot me a penetrating look. "You don't have a gun, do you?" Her tone was indignant, as though she had already guessed the true answer.

"No," I said too hurriedly, then, like a fool, compounded the lie. "Of course I don't have a gun. I'm English! We don't carry guns like you mad Yanks!"

"You did in Key West," she accused me.

"That was because of Charles. He just wanted me to take care of his precious car."

"Because I really hate guns." Jackie's suspicions were subsiding. "They're just a stupid statement of intent, right? People claim guns are only for defense, but that's bullshit, I mean, you can defend yourself without using a mechanism designed to kill people. Don't you agree?"

"Sure I agree," I said dismissively, because I did not want to talk about guns. I leaned my head on *Stormchild*'s lower guardrail and stared past the awning's edge at the first bright star that was pricking a hole of light in the softening sky. Then, because the sun had dipped below the harbor wall and because I ran an old-fashioned boat, which meant that our bomb-scarred ensign only flew during the hours of daylight, I stepped past Jackie and took the flag off its staff, then reverently folded the faded and torn cotton.

"Are you OK, Tim?" Jackie must have sensed a sudden saddening in me.

"I'm fine." I told another lie, because I was not fine, but rather I suddenly felt lonely, and I told myself that the attack of self-pity had been triggered by the memories that lurked in the sun-warmed weave of the cotton I held in my hands. "I'm fine," I said again, yet that night, lying sleepless in the stern cabin, I heard a couple making love on the next boat and I felt insanely jealous. I heard a woman's warm soft laughter, unforced and full of pleasure, a sound to aggravate puritans and feminists and loneliness, a sound old as time, comfortable, and full of enjoyment. The gentle laughter died into contentment and I consoled myself with the sour thought that it did not matter for we would all die one day, then I tried to sleep as the water slapped petulantly at *Stormchild*'s hull.

The next morning, unable to bear the idle frustration any longer, I sent a fax to David, telling him our next destination and my estimated arrival date, then I slipped *Stormchild*'s mooring lines. Jackie, knowing that the winds were not yet propitious, was puzzled by our precipitous departure, but her respect for my sailing experience made her accept my muttered explanation that, despite the depressing forecast, I was expecting a northerly blow at any minute. We motored our way offshore and suddenly, five miles from land, and against all the careful predictions of the weathermen, a steady northeaster did indeed begin to blow. I killed the motor, trimmed the sails, and let *Stormchild* run free. The unexpected wind proved to Jackie that I was a genius, while I knew I was merely a fraud. Two days later we found the trade winds and turned our bows west and thus we ran in Columbus's path, bound for the Americas.

We furled the big mainsail, lashed the boom down, then whisker-poled our twin headsails, one to port and the other to starboard. The wind came from dead astern, the twin sails hauled us, the wind vane guided us, the flying fish landed on our deck, and *Stormchild* crossed the Atlantic, rolling like a drunken pig, just as every other boat had run the unvarying trade winds ever since Columbus's *Santa Maria* had first wallowed along these same latitudes under the command of a man who insisted he was sailing to the Orient and who, to his dying day, angrily denied that he had ever discovered the Americas.

Jackie and I sailed through sunlit days and phosphorescent nights. We saw no other boats. Hundreds of craft were out there, strung and scattered across the conveyer belt of the trade wind latitudes, but we sailed in apparent solitude, lost in an immensity of warm sea and endless sky under which we fell once more into our watch-keeping routine. I took the first watch from midnight until four, then Jackie would take the deck until ten in the morning. She then slept until nearly six o'clock in the evening, when she would join me in the cockpit for our main meal of the day. At eight I would go below and try to sleep until midnight, when Jackie would wake me for the first watch with a cup of coffee. I was always on call in case of an emergency, but she never needed to rouse me; she claimed that the hounds of hell could not have woken me, so deeply and well did I sleep at sea. My snores, Jackie claimed, began the moment I went below.

I did sleep well. For the first time since Joanna's death I was sleeping the night through, unharassed by regret. There was only one single morning on that whole voyage of two thousand seven hundred miles that I woke early. On that morning my eyes opened just after eight, a full hour before I usually rolled out of my sleeping bag, and for some reason I could not fall asleep again. It was not the solo sailor's instinct for danger that had woken me, because there was nothing wrong with the boat's motion and there were no odd sounds that betrayed a piece of broken rigging, and I could tell Jackie was safe, because I could hear the shuffle and slap of her bare feet on the foredeck. I wondered if she had gone forward to deal with some small emergency that had woken me, and which, before I was fully conscious, she had brought under control. I could think of no other explanation for being awake.

I yawned, wriggled out from behind the lee cloths which held my sleeping body against the boat's rolling motion, and climbed toward the cockpit. I paused at the midpoint of the companionway and turned to look forward, only to see Jackie doing strenuous aerobic exercises on the sun-drenched foredeck. I froze in sudden and acute embarrassment, because she was doing her bends and stretches in the nude. For a few seconds I stared at her, half in amazement and half in admiration, then, before she became aware of my early appearance, I ducked swiftly back into the galley, where I ostentatiously clattered some pots and pans together.

"You're awake early," she called down a few seconds later.

"Couldn't sleep. What's it like up there?" I shouted the question so she would not think I had already been on deck.

"Same as ever. Sunny, warm, and a force-four wind. I've got six flying fish for your lunch."

"Chuck them back!" There comes a point when the taste of flying fish palls. "Do you want your tea now?" I asked her. Jackie had brought on board an herbal concoction of caffeine-free leaves, which I gallantly brewed for her whenever I took over the watch.

"Please!"

By the time I reached the deck she was in her bikini, looking positively overdressed. "You can turn in early, if you like," I said.

"I'm not tired." She sat cross-legged on the far thwart and I was suddenly assailed by a vivid memory of her lithe, tanned body flexing and arching between the foresails' sheets. I stared upward so that Jackie could not see my blush and, high above *Stormchild*'s swinging masthead, I saw a trans-Atlantic jet scratching its white contrail against the sky. "They say you can navigate by those jets," I said, just to distract myself.

"You can do what?" Jackie had been concentrating on harvesting her sprouts which grew in their plastic trays with an astonishing vigor, and which she ate with an equally astonishing enjoyment.

"I'm told that some people have successfully navigated the Atlantic by following the vapor trails of big jets."

She looked up at the white line scratching itself between the puff-ball clouds. "Figures. Cheaper than buying a sextant."

The next morning six dolphins appeared to escort *Stormchild*. Their arrival gave an ecstatic pleasure to Jackie, and I had not seen such joy in another person since the day I had woken Nicole to the exact same sight twelve years before. Nicole's delighted face had shown an unusual softness, and now, with Jackie's enthusiasm to bring the memory into sharp and sudden focus, it did not seem so odd that Nicole had become the disciple of a man who claimed to be a fanatical environmentalist. "Tim, they're so cute!" Jackie enthused.

"They taste good, too."

"Oh, shut up!" She laughed and hit me. There were times when she seemed impossibly young, and I hated those times. Mostly, to hide my feelings, I treated her with an exaggerated formality, and she seemed to reciprocate the courtesy, but, once in a while, as when she watched the dolphins leaping, her polite mask would slip and I would feel the scar being torn from my soul. I convinced myself that Joanna's death had made me unusually vulnerable to a young woman's charms, and I armored myself against any display of that vulnerability by my painfully correct behavior.

Thus we sailed on. *Stormchild* threw us a few problems, but none that were unusually difficult; a steel cotter pin snapped on the self-steering gear so that the boat suddenly rounded up toward the wind and the sails slatted like demented bat wings. Jackie was on watch, and, by the time I was on deck, she had already recovered the helm and had opened the locker where we kept the spare fastenings. Another day I discovered the bilge was slowly flooding and traced the problem to a pinhole leak in a spare water tank. The odd sail seam opened, but nothing that a few minutes with a needle and sailmaker's pad could not mend.

Day by day the pencil line that represented *Stormchild*'s progress inched its way across our chart. I measured its advance by taking running fixes with the sextant, a process that, at first, Jackie had liked to double-check by turning on the satellite receiver and waiting for the small green numerals to betray the ship's position, but gradually she learned to trust the sun more than the clever box of silicon chips, and soon she wanted to master the sextant herself. I taught her, and it was a good day when I was able to congratulate her for fixing our position within fifty miles. She laughed, rightly pleased with her achievement, then she spread her arms as though to encompass all of *Stormchild* and all of the unending sea and sky. "I could do this forever, Tim."

"You mean sail forever."

"Oh, sure." Her eyes were alight.

"There's nothing to stop you," I said, and felt my heart racing with a ridiculous and futile hope.

"Yeah, there is." She turned away. "Money and a job."

"Sure," I said meaninglessly, and the ship rolled to starboard, back to port, and Jackie's plait swung against her shoulder blades with *Stormchild*'s endless motion. Jackie's hair, which had been mousy and bobbed when I first met her, had grown wildly long and had been bleached into a pale white gold by the salt and sun, so that now it lay in startling contrast against her dark-tanned skin. She looked exotic and fit now, and it was hard to see in this lean, bright-eyed and confident girl the nervous, timid, baggy-trousered waif who had first accosted me in Florida.

We sailed on, mile after rolling mile, in what for me was the most perfect trade-wind crossing of the Atlantic I had ever made. I doubt that a single wave broke high enough on our cutwater to wet *Stormchild*'s deck, and only at the end, as we neared the Caribbean, did two squalls briefly soak our topsides with a sudden and drenching rain. Not long after the squalls, as our deck steamed dry under the tropic sun, we at last saw the airy castles of white cloud rising high above the horizon and I told Jackie that the clouds were forming above land. That afternoon an extravagantly tailed frigate bird swooped close to *Stormchild* and both Jackie and I felt the nervousness that is engendered by an approaching landfall. It is a nervousness that comes from a reluctance to abandon the safe security and comforting routine of a ship for the dangers of a strange harbor and its unpredictable people.

I washed our shore-going clothes by sloshing them around in a plastic garbage bag half filled with seawater and detergent. Later, as the clothes dried in the rigging, we loosed the lashed down boom and hoisted the huge mainsail and let *Stormchild* steady onto a port reach. The rolling stopped immediately and the noises of the ship, which had stayed so constant for four weeks, changed with the new motion. I turned on the VHF radio and heard the intrusive babble of voices.

Two mornings later we were safe in Antigua's English Harbour where, blessedly, there was space at the Dockyard Quay. The Dutch couple, with whom we had dined on my birthday and who had sailed from the Canaries a full month before us, took our mooring lines, and Jackie, to celebrate the completion of her first transatlantic sail, insisted on buying a bottle of cheap champagne that we all four drank at lunchtime. "I didn't think you had any money," I said lightly when the friendly Dutch couple was gone.

"I used my last crumpled dollars," she said, "though I do have some plastic, but I'm afraid to use it because the bills would never reach me, and then the bank will have me crucified." She leaned back on the thwart, under the shade of the cockpit canopy that I had rigged once more. "This is fun, Tim," she said with languorous warmth, then reached and lightly touched my hand. "Thank you for letting me come. God, but this is fun!"

A week later, our ship dressed overall with what flags I could muster and with underwear filling in the gaps, we celebrated Christmas. I gave Jackie a coral necklace, and she gave me a woolen scarf that she had been secretly knitting. "I've nothing else to give you," she apologized, "and you said it will be cold in Patagonia."

"It's wonderful," I said, "thank you."

"It isn't much. I bought the wool in the Canaries. It's real nice wool, isn't it?"

I felt an urge to kiss her, just as a thank you, but I did not have the courage to move, or else I had too much sense to move, and Jackie must have intuited that something was out of joint for she looked at me oddly, then smiled and twisted away up the companionway. "It's weird, isn't it," she said, "to be having a hot-weather Christmas?" I suspected she was covering a moment of mutual embarrassment with a meaningless babble of conversation. "I have an aunt who goes to Florida every winter, and she cooks a turkey and all the trimmings, but she has to turn the air-conditioning way up before she can bear to eat it. Oh, wow, look at that!"

"That" was a majestic French yawl, agleam with bright work and brass, that had shaken out its mainsail ready for sea. I envied the French crew, for I, too, would have liked to have been at sea where, somehow, coexistence with Jackie was easier than in port, but I was waiting for David's promised letter which would enclose the sailing directions for the Chilean coast. I telephoned him on Christmas Day, but got no answer. I decided to wait until New Year's Day, after which, letter or no letter, Jackie and I would sail again.

Jackie telephoned her mother on New Year's Eve, and afterward called Molly Tetterman. "She wanted to come down and join us," Jackie said when she joined me outside the telephone office, "but I couldn't bear it! She never stops talking! Never!" Then she burst into laughter as she remembered how I had used to accuse her of the same sin. "Have I changed, Tim?"

"Yes," I said, "you have." We were walking back toward the dockyard in the hard, bright sunlight.

"Is it a good change?" Jackie asked coyly.

"Yes." I smiled. "I think it probably is."

Suddenly, and with what seemed like an impulsive artlessness, she put her arm through mine. "I was so scared of you at the beginning. I suppose I should never have asked to come with you. It was kind of rude of me, right? But once I was on board you were so awful to me!"

"I was not."

"You were! I just happened to mention that I was a tiny bit cold and you jumped down my throat! I thought you were going to throw me off the boat!"

I laughed. "I don't want you to get off the

boat"—I hesitated, knowing I should not say the next word, but I said it anyway—"ever," and immediately after I had spoken it I felt like such a damn fool that I wanted to take the word back. I felt Jackie stop, then pull her arm out of my elbow. She stared up at me looking shocked, and I knew I was blushing.

"Tim?" Her voice was suddenly very serious.

"Look—" I began to try and explain myself, and Jackie began to say something at the same moment, and then we both stopped to let the other carry on, and I was cursing myself for being such a clumsy and insensitive idiot. Then we were both interrupted by a voice that boomed at us from across the street.

"There you are, Tim! Good man! Well done! Don't move! Splendid! And Miss Potten, too! First class! I was on my way to the harbor, piece of luck finding you here!" It was my brother David, who, lugging two enormous seabags, dodged between the bicycles and bright-painted taxis to join us. "I'm signing on," he said as he dropped the bags on the pavement by my feet.

"You've come to join us?" I asked in horror.

"Indeed I have, dear boy. I decided you were right! I need the change. I need the rest. I need the inspiration, my God, do I need that! I have been granted a sabbatical! Twenty years, Miss Potten, I have labored in the Lord's vineyard, and now I am free to sip the wine for a season of idleness." He beamed his pleasure at me. "Betty sends her love."

"She let you off the leash?"

"She cut the leash! She almost insisted that I

come! So I have left her the keys to the Riley, and I have installed a Low Church curate in my place who will probably destroy my congregation's faith, but I care not!" David turned his happy face to Jackie, who, I thought, did not seem overjoyed at his arrival. "My dear Miss Potten, permit me the liberty of observing that you look positively different!"

Jackie forced a smile. "Hi."

"Hi, indeed." David plucked his seabags from the pavement. "The last time I was here the Admiralty Inn served a halfway decent beer and a damn good meal."

"It still does," I said.

"Then show me to it, dear boy. Show me to it."

We found a table in the pub, but there was an immediate awkwardness between the three of us, to which David, full of news of home, seemed oblivious. The boatyard, he said, was surviving my absence. There had been a fire in a hardware store in the town's high street, but no one had been hurt. The bishop had broken his leg on a dry-ski slope in the local shopping precinct. "It was entirely his own fault," David said with unholy relish, "I see the church has to be relevant to modern life, but that doesn't need to be proved by hurtling down plastic ramps."

"The bishop doesn't mind you taking a sabbatical?" I asked David.

"He's all for it. He thinks I've been working too hard. He also believes that rubbing up against some foreign cultures will broaden my horizons, but I told him that was nonsense, I just wanted to do a bit of bird-watching." David rubbed his hands gleefully. "Just think of it, Tim! The green-backed firecrown hummingbird."

"I thought you were feeling too old to cope with a yacht's discomforts," I said accusingly.

"Old?" David laughed. "I'm only fifty! Just three years older than you, Tim." Jackie glanced at me, then looked away quickly. "So!" David spread his arms to encompass the table. "What do the next three months hold for us?"

"You're here for three months?" I gaped at him. I had somehow thought he might have come for just two weeks.

"That should be long enough to settle von Rellsteb's hash," David said happily, "and still give us time to spot a hummingbird or two. But first we have to beard the monster in his Patagonian lair. How do you plan to do that?"

I unfolded a paper napkin, found a pen, and, still dazed by David's blunt happiness, made a crude sketch of South America. "We sail to Panama as soon as possible," I said, "then make a loop out into the Pacific to avoid the Humboldt Current. I'm afraid there won't be any time to make a visit to Easter Island, or to put in at any of the ports in northern Chile, instead we'll go straight to the southern coast, probably to Puerto Montt." I stabbed my crude map low down on the Chilean coast.

"You seem to be in a devil of a hurry." David lit his pipe.

"From everything I hear it's sensible to make a

landfall in Patagonia before the end of February," I
said, "and between now and then we've got the
best part of five thousand miles to go, so yes, I'm
in a hurry." I paused. "It's going to be a very
uncomfortable voyage, David."

David laughed. "He thinks I've gone soft," he
confided in Jackie, then looked back to me. "I
assure you I'm as fit as you are, Tim."

"Who's keeping an eye on the boatyard while
you're away?" I asked with alarm.

"Your new manager. Very good chap, by the
way. Knows his onions."

"Oh, Christ!" I sighed because my elder brother's arrival threatened to tear my life into shreds.
Just three months ago I had been begging for his
company, but now, isolated in the strange relationship I had with Jackie, I did not want David's
loud intrusion. Except he was here now, and
could not be sent back, which meant that the
small fragile bubble in which Jackie and I had
been so delicately existing was about to be obliterated by the great gales of David's bluff goodwill.

Jackie clearly felt the same sense of violated privacy for she had spoken hardly a word since we
sat down in the pub, but now she leaned toward
me with a frown on her sun-tanned face. "I think
maybe you don't really need me anymore, Tim.
Now that your brother's here."

"Of course I need you!" I said hastily.

"Every ship must have a cook!" David put in his
three cents' worth of appalling insensitivity.

"Shut your bloody trap!" I snapped at him, then
looked back to Jackie. "You can't jump ship now!"

"What I was thinking," she said, and without even acknowledging David's presence at the table, "was that I ought to fly home and make sure everything's OK there. With my mom, you know? And with my apartment. I mean, hell, I just walked away from it! Things may need looking after."

"You're abandoning the Genesis community?" I asked in disbelief.

"No! I just ought to visit home, that's all! And when I'm there I'll try and raise the cash to fly down to Chile and meet you. I mean if we really are going to find the Genesis community then I ought to be prepared for it, and I don't even have a camera with me! What kind of a journalist am I without a camera?"

"I have a camera." David seemed oblivious of the effect his arrival had caused, but he had never been a sensitive man. A good man, but not subtle. He unzipped one of his bags and pulled out a 35mm camera that he put on the table. "It's an efficient camera, but if you find it too complicated, my dear, then we can always buy one of those idiot-proof point-and-shoot jobs, isn't that so, Tim?"

I ignored David, while Jackie, who had gone pale under her tan, just continued talking as though my brother had never spoken. "And maybe if I go home, Tim, I can sell the story to an editor. I know a lot more about Genesis than I did before, and maybe a major newspaper will listen to me now?"

"They'll certainly listen if you tell them that the

famous circumnavigator, Tim Blackburn, is sailing to Chile to shoot a bloody ecologist!" David hooted with laughter at his own wit.

"Shut up." I spoke with hissing menace to my brother, then looked back to Jackie. "Why don't you get the story first, then sell it to a newspaper?"

"I don't know, Tim." Jackie glanced very quickly at David, thus suggesting to me that his bluff arrival was her real reason for not staying. She seemed not to have taken his words about shooting von Rellsteb seriously, which was a relief, but David was never a man to let a sleeping dog lie, and now he pushed his camera across the table toward Jackie.

"Take it, dear girl, with my blessing."

"No, really." Jackie tried to push the camera back.

"Of course you must take it. We are one for all and all for one, are we not?" David offered Jackie his most benevolent smile. "Besides, you look much too frail to use one of the rifles. Not that I think we shall need the guns." David palpably changed mental gears and offered me his most serious expression. "I need to talk with you, Tim, about what we plan to achieve in Patagonia. I really don't think I can involve myself in violence. It just wouldn't look good in the *Church Times!* Of course, if we're attacked, and we do have to defend ourselves, then I assure you I'll be shoulder to shoulder with you." He smiled at Jackie. "And frankly those old Lee-Enfields have the devil of a kick, so I doubt you'd be strong enough to fire one. Not that I think we'll need them, but you never know."

"Shut up," I said plaintively, but much too late.

"Lee-Enfields?" Jackie asked. "What are Lee-Enfields, Tim?"

I did not answer. I had been cornered in a lie and I was desperately thinking how to find an elegant way out, but there was none.

"Are they guns?" Jackie demanded of me.

"There are two rifles on board *Stormchild*," I told her very flatly. "I hid them before I left. It seemed a good idea at the time."

"A damned good idea!" David said with an elephantine lack of tact.

Jackie stared at me very coldly. "Are you planning to fight von Rellsteb, Tim? Is that what you've been planning all along?"

"I'm planning to find my daughter," I said as calmly as I could.

"For which purpose you're carrying guns?" Jackie accused me.

"You're the one who warned Tim that these wretched people are survivalists"—David was trying to retrieve the damage he at last perceived he had caused—"and you can't really expect us to face such maniacs unarmed, can you?"

Jackie ignored him. "I'm going to the Archipiélago Sangre de Cristo to secure a story, Tim, and I thought you were going to help me." She paused in an effort to control the fury that was suffusing her voice, but instead of calming down she seemed to shake with a sudden rage. "But now I find that you lied to me! That you're carrying guns! And that you expect me to help you in your stupid macho crusade!"

There was silence. Some Americans at the next table, embarrassed by the intensity of Jackie's words, raised their voices as if to demonstrate that they were not really eavesdropping, while David, realizing that he had sown the wind that had raised this whirlwind, desperately tried to calm the storm. "Dear girl! Please calm down!"

Jackie still ignored him, fixing me with a fierce look instead. "Did you lie about the guns?"

"Yes," I said wretchedly. "I'm sorry."

"So all this time, when you've been talking about finding your daughter and reasoning with her, you were really planning to use violence?"

"No!" I insisted, though weakly, because I was again lying. I believed von Rellsteb had murdered Joanna, and I knew I would take revenge if it was possible. I could see Jackie did not believe my feeble denial, so I tried another and more plausible justification. "If we're attacked," I said, "then we have to be able to defend ourselves."

"Even the act of carrying a weapon is offensive," Jackie said passionately, "and is liable to encourage violence in others."

"Oh, come!" David said. "Does carrying a fire extinguisher make a man an arsonist?"

Jackie threw down her napkin. "I thought we were going to Chile to find a story! To discover a truth! I can't be a part of some stupid scheme to start a fight!" Her eyes were bright with tears and she shuddered, clearly in the grip of an overpowering emotion. "And I will not involve myself in even the smallest part of your futile and primitive violence!" She glared at David. "Not even as a fucking cook!"

Her piercing voice had now attracted the attention of half the bar. Someone cheered her last words.

"For God's sake, girl!" David tried frantically to calm her, but Jackie would not be calmed. She flung her chair backward and stalked away between the tables. An amused group of Americans offered her loud applause and a berth on their own yacht.

"Oh, good Lord," David groaned, "I'm sorry, Tim."

"Look after the bill," I said to him, then hurried after Jackie, but she had run from the pub to the quay, and, by the time I came out into the harsh sunlight, she was already swinging herself down to *Stormchild*'s deck. "Jackie?" I called as she disappeared down the yacht's companionway.

"God damn it, Tim! Leave me alone!"

By the time I had reached *Stormchild*'s saloon Jackie had already locked herself in her forward cabin. "I don't want you to leave!" I shouted through the door.

"I am not going to be part of a killing expedition! That is not why I came! I want to write a good piece of journalism, and I want to help the parents whose kids have run off with von Rellsteb, but that is all I want to do! I do not want to be a part of your violence, so from now on I'll have to make my own arrangements!" I could hear a half sob in her voice.

"Jackie!" I tried to open the door, but its bolt was too solid to be forced. "I don't want to kill anyone," I said, but it sounded a rather feeble defense, even to me.

"Then throw the guns overboard! You know how I hate guns! Will you throw them overboard?"

"Just come out and talk to me," I said, "please."

"Will you throw the guns away?"

"I might if you come out and talk to me," I said, but my halfhearted concession earned nothing but Jackie's silence, or rather the sounds a girl makes when she stuffs a seabag full of dirty clothes. "Jackie!" I rattled the door again.

"Go away."

"You can't leave," I said, "you haven't got any money."

"I've got plastic!" she shouted at me as though I had insulted her.

"I'm sorry," I said. "I'll make you some tea, then we'll talk about it, OK?" I went back to the galley, leaned my hands on the stove, and sighed. God damn it, I thought, God damn it. Then, taking my time so that Jackie would have a chance to calm down, I made a pot of the herbal tea she liked so much. I let the concoction steep, then poured it into her favorite mug—one that showed two cats with twined lovers' tails and surrounded by little love hearts. I carried the tea to her cabin. "Jackie?"

There was no answer.

I knocked harder. "Jackie?"

The silence was absolute.

"Jackie!"

I ran back through the saloon, up the companionway, and onto *Stormchild*'s deck, where I found the forehatch was open and the bird was flown.

She must have climbed on deck while I was making the tea, tiptoed her way aft, then climbed to the quay and disappeared. I ran through the dockyard, but there was no sign of her. I even caught a cab and raced to the island's small airport, but still I did not find her. My shipmate had vanished; she was gone.

"There's an obvious explanation for the girl's behavior," David said to me a week later. It had been an awkward week. We had spoken about such mundane matters as navigation and watchkeeping, but neither of us had spoken about Jackie's abrupt departure. David, realizing that he had behaved in Antigua with the sensibility of a falling rock, seemed to be ashamed of himself for detonating the emotional outburst, while I was just plain miserable. But now, as *Stormchild* slammed into a vicious steep wave, my brother at last tried to break the silence that was so painfully between us.

"Tell me what is obvious," I, at last, invited him.

"The girl was in love with you."

"Thank you, David," I said with a caustic venom, "and now please shut up."

I had waited three days for Jackie to return to *Stormchild,* but she had not appeared. I couldn't raise any answer from her home telephone number, and, finally, believing that action would be a better diversion than anger, I put back to sea where I had crammed on all sail to drive the big yacht through the Caribbean as though the devil himself was in our wake. It was proving a rough passage for the east winds were driving the Atlantic waters into the shallow basin of the Caribbean and heaping them into steep, short waves. David and I had rigged jacklines down either side of the deck, and I insisted that we wore safety harnesses and lifelines if either of us moved out of the cockpit. We had also erected the new spray hood so that the helmsman could crouch behind its view-perspex screens as the seas shattered white at our stem and splattered down the decks like shrapnel. Now, four nights out of English Harbour, David and I were sharing the sunset watch as he steered *Stormchild* fast toward the Panama Canal. He was also trying to repair the breach that gaped between us. "I think you'll find I'm right," he said mildly, "she showed all the symptoms."

"I thought you were a vicar, not an agony aunt."

He crouched to light his pipe. When, at last, the tobacco was drawing sweetly, he straightened up to steer *Stormchild* into the next steep wave. "A man in my job is constantly being tapped for help by people having emotional crises, so one does learn to recognize the symptoms."

I was tempted to observe that an emotionally troubled parishioner seeking David's help was the equivalent of a seriously ill patient calling for the services of a mortician, but I contented myself with asking him how on earth Jackie's behavior had suggested to him a bad case of love. "I would have thought," I continued sarcastically, "that if the girl was in love with me she'd have stayed on board. She'd hardly have run away from me!"

"Love is very mysterious," David said, as though that explained everything. He was in a confident mood, sure that his diagnosis was unassailable. "As you just observed," he went on, "the girl's reaction to the situation was extraordinary, which would suggest to any reasonably intelligent person that she was seeking a reason, any reason, to escape from what she saw as an intolerable and increasingly irksome dilemma."

"What in hell's name are you going on about?"

"Pour me another Irish whiskey, dear boy, and I shall tell you."

I poured him the whiskey, choosing a moment when *Stormchild* was between white-topped crests. "Here!" I served him the whiskey in one of the plastic-spouted childrens' training cups, which saved us from spilling precious Jamesons across the deck.

"As I told you, the American girl"—even now David found it hard to articulate her name—"is in love with you. I saw it in her face the moment I met you both on Antigua. There is a mooncalf quality about the young when they're in love, and she had it. Doubtless she is searching for an authority figure, which is why she finds older men attractive. I daresay her father died when she was young?"

"He abandoned the family."

"Ah! There you are! You don't have to grow a beard and call yourself Sigmund Freud to pluck

the bones out of that one! She's after a father figure, isn't she? You, of course, being a man of
honor, did not return her schoolgirlish crush,
which frustrated her, and, being an innocent child
and uncertain how to surmount the obstacle of
your indifference, she made the wise decision to
cut her losses and skedaddle. It was clearly too
embarrassing a matter for her to explain calmly, so
instead, and quite sensibly in my view, she seized
upon the first convenient excuse to make her
admittedly embarrassing and hasty exit." My reverend brother smiled very smugly at me. "*Quod
erat demonstrandum,* I believe?"

I stared past the streaming drops on the spray
hood's screen to the ragged turmoil of the sea
beyond. "She wasn't in love with me, David," I
said after a long pause, "I was in love with her."

David smiled as if I had made a fine joke, then
he suddenly realized that I might have spoken the
truth and he looked appalled instead. "Oh, dear,"
was all he could say.

"I'm besotted," I confessed. "I'm the mooncalf,
not her."

David puffed fiercely at his pipe. For a moment I
thought I had silenced him, then he glowered at
me from beneath his impressively bushy eyebrows.
"The girl's young enough to be your daughter!"

"You think I don't know that, for Christ's sake?"
I exploded at him. Jackie was just twenty-six, one
year older than Nicole. Indeed, Jackie had not even
been born when Joanna and I had married.

"I blame myself," David said with a noble air of
abnegation.

"You? Why are you to blame?"

"I encouraged her to accompany you, did I not? But only as someone to spare you the cooking and cleaning chores. Good God, man, I didn't think you'd make a prize fool of yourself!"

"Well I did," I said bitterly.

"Then it's a good thing she's cut her losses and run," David said trenchantly. "You said yourself that this was meant to be an adventure, and certainly not some half-baked romance."

"Can we shut up about it?" I begged him.

"Old enough to be her father!" David, abjuring tact, would now try to jolly me out of misery with mockery. "October falling in love with April! My cradle-snatching brother!"

"Shut up!"

We sailed on in silence as David's pipe smoke whipped back in the wind's path. He looked very self-satisfied and very self-righteous. I probably looked miserable. I could not shift Jackie out of my head, and all I could think about was the desperate hope that she might be waiting for us in Colón Harbor at the Atlantic entrance to the Panama Canal.

We reached Colón two weeks later, dropping our sails as we passed through the breakwater entrance, then motoring through a downpour of rain toward the yacht moorings. Thunder bellowed across the sky, and lightning stabbed viciously above Fort Sherman. As soon as the customs and immigration launch had dealt with us, I insisted on unlashing *Stormchild*'s dinghy, dragging the outboard motor up from its locker in the engine room, then going ashore to the Panama Canal Yacht Club. I told David, with a remarkable lack of conviction, that I wanted to speak with the weather service. He gave me a disbelieving look, but did not try to dissuade me, nor did he suggest that I might use *Stormchild*'s radio-telephone to get a forecast. The thunder echoed back from the hills as the little dinghy buffeted its way through the filthy waters. The yacht club was the rendezvous for small boat crews, but Jackie was not waiting there, and the only mail for *Stormchild* was a good luck message from Betty which contained the reassurance that all was well at the boatyard. At that point I could not have cared if the boatyard staff had gone mad and burned the place to the ground. I cared for nothing but Jackie. I rang her home number and, at last, heard her voice, but only on a newly installed answering machine. "Hi! This is Jackie Potten and I'd really like to talk with you, but I can't take your call right now, so please leave a message after the beep. Oh! And have a nice day!"

"This is Tim," I said, "and I would really like to talk with you. We're going through the Panama Canal tomorrow, then heading south to Puerto Montt. But you can leave a message for me at the Balboa Yacht Club"—I fumbled to find the number of the yacht club, which lay at the canal's Pacific end—"that's 52–2524, and we'll be there tomorrow evening."

"So what is the forecast?" David boomed at me when I returned.

"I couldn't get through to the weather people,"

I lied. "It seems the rain has tied up the phone lines." David made a mocking noise, but was mollified when I presented him with a bottle of brandy I had bought ashore. "It's something," I said, "to celebrate our first trip through the canal."

It was a trip I would normally have enjoyed; an extraordinary passage past basking iguanas and through the massive, water-churning locks, where local line-handlers, especially hired for the transit, skillfully held *Stormchild*'s gunwales off the towering walls. We followed a vast German bulk-carrier through the locks and *Stormchild* bucked in the merchantman's wake as though she was stemming a North Sea storm. David let loose a cheer as we cleared the final lock, then uncorked the brandy.

No message waited at the Balboa Yacht Club, and the only response from Jackie's telephone was the sprightly machine that wished me a nice day, so David and I, in a wet wind and on a gray sea, sailed on.

We sailed into sickening calms and contrary currents against which, day by day and inch by inch, we made our slow way out into the vast and empty Pacific until, a week from Panama, a real wind at last plucked us from our lethargy and bent *Stormchild*'s sails toward the sea. Water hissed at our stem and broke into a creamy wake astern.

The wind carried us into the chill airs brought north by the Humboldt Current. Ten days out of Panama I put away my shorts and took out long trousers, and three days later I dragged my heavy

foul-weather gear out of *Stormchild*'s wet locker
where I also discovered Jackie's oilskins. I pushed
them into a kit bag that I stored under the bunk
she had used, and which was now once again
given over to ship's stores. For days I had been
finding her belongings scattered about the boat.
Her sprouting seeds had gone mad, luxuriating
like a tiny forest in their plastic home until I had
tossed the whole mess overboard. I had discovered
her bikini in a wash bag, and that, like her oilskins, I stored aboard. I found an unused sound
tape for her recorder, a pen, her awful felt hat, and
a pathetic pair of pink socks. "Chuck 'em!" David
robustly encouraged me when he saw me holding
the little socks with the reverence that a Catholic
might yield to a scrap of the true cross.

"They're not mine to chuck."

"You are master under God of this ship, which
gives you inalienable rights under international
law over all persons and objects and smelly socks
found in your domain. Allow me to lighten your
ship, Tim, if you lack the resolve." He plucked the
socks from my hand and hurled them far into the
wind. I saw the flash of bright pink wool floating
briefly amongst a mess of white foam on a wave's
grim face, then the socks were gone forever. The
next morning I hurled the silly mug with the loving cats overboard, though I took a perverse comfort from wearing the scarf Jackie had knitted me.

We thumped on, curving round the bulge of a
continent, then steering *Stormchild* hard to the
south. I saw our first albatross, vast, serene, and
riding the sky like an angel. There were whales in

the gray-green sea and strange stars above us as we left the northern hemisphere behind and slashed on into the southern emptiness. Mile after lonely mile we went, with neither a sail nor a ship in sight, nor even an aircraft above us. This was one of the empty seas, as empty as when Alexander Selkirk, who would be transmuted by genius into Robinson Crusoe, was marooned on an island in the middle of its desolation.

The further south we sailed, the worse the weather became. We seemed to have entered a region of perpetual cloud that shadowed the sea with a sinister, slaty cast. Squalls hissed across that gray, dark sea. The wind flecked the water white and lifted spindrift that permeated every inch of *Stormchild*'s cabins. David and I, when on watch, crouched behind the spray hood and tried not to move our heads too much because the skin of our necks, unused to the confining stiffness of the oil-skin's collars, had been chafed to rawness. My mood, already tormented by Jackie's disappearance, was further soured by the weather. My only escape from doom-laden misery lay in sailing *Stormchild* as efficiently as possible, taking pleasure in a skill well done. I could lose myself behind the wheel, imagining that my endless path through the heave and pattern of great waves could last forever.

There was too much cloud for celestial navigation, and I could not be bothered to use the SatNav, yet I knew we were closing on an unseen coast because of the increasing numbers of molly-mawks, gray gulls, terns, and storm petrels that

came near *Stormchild*. One day, miraculously, the
sun shone, but the weather stayed cold and when
I dipped a thermometer into the sea the temperature measured a mere six degrees centigrade,
which meant we had plunged into the very heart
of the icy Humboldt Current which drags tons of
Antarctic meltwater north into the Pacific. I dug
out the red, white, and blue Chilean courtesy
ensign I had bought in Colón and stored it in a
ready locker of the cockpit.

That night the phosphorescence made a dazzling path behind *Stormchild*'s transom. A school
of Chilean dolphins embroidered that starry wake
by weaving trails of shattered light around it, yet
the beauty of the moment was deceptive for the
weather was becoming ominous and the seas still
heavier. So far, in the nine thousand miles of
Stormchild's voyage, I had escaped all the bad
storms, but that night, almost as though the
Genesis community was aware of our coming and
had summoned the spirits of the deep to stop
Stormchild, a black gale came hurtling out of the
northeast. The barometer plummeted, and the sea,
its current fighting against the wind, became
frighteningly steep and confused. The dolphins
flicked one last dazzling curve in *Stormchild*'s
wake, then left.

David, dragged from his bunk, helped me short-
en sail. We were both swathed in oilskins and sea
boots, and had our lifelines clipped to steel rings
bedded in the cockpit's sole. An hour later we took
in all but the storm trysail and jib, yet still the
wind rose, and by midnight we had reefed down

to just the triple-stitched scrap of storm jib which dragged us scudding through the maelstrom of vicious sea and shrieking wind. *Stormchild* rode the storm beautifully. She thumped up those bastard seas, slashing through their confused summits before plunging down into the dark troughs. At times a cross sea would jar the boat sideways and the cockpit would fill with a seething swirl of freezing water, but always *Stormchild* held firm on course to meet the next wind-haunted crest.

The gale seemed to increase its fury. Once, when a flicker of lightning sliced the sky, I saw that David was praying. A few moments later, when the wind was a deafening and demonic screech, he manfully went below and somehow heated soup which he brought precariously back to the cockpit. Rarely had food tasted better. The boat bucked and shuddered in the worst of the seas, but as dawn approached I sensed that the anger was at last dying from the wind. First light showed us mad waters, blown white by the storm's anger, but already the madness was settling and slowly, as the gray day lightened and the wind became tired, we could at last stow the storm jib, set headsails, and turn our weary boat toward the hidden shore. "If all I hear about Patagonia is right," David remarked ominously, "then that little blow is a mere promise of what is to come."

"Indeed."

"But she's a well-named boat," he said with great satisfaction, and indeed she was, for *Stormchild* had worn the gale's quick savagery with an easy confidence. I knew there was worse to come, much worse, for we were approaching a coast renowned for killing ships, yet our baptism of tempest augured well. "I fear the galley is painted with spilled tomato soup," David confessed, but otherwise there was not a great deal of damage. A seam in the storm jib had begun to tear its lock-stitches apart, some ill-stowed wineglasses had shattered, and an errant wave crashing on our stern had carried away one of the two life buoys, but otherwise *Stormchild* had indeed lived up to the promise of her name.

That evening, as we sipped our whiskey and as *Stormchild* hissed and bubbled her quick wake across the long, exhausted swell of an ocean after storm, the far peaks of Chile showed like jagged clouds above the eastern horizon. We had come to our landfall, to the high snowcapped Andean mountains that lay behind the Patagonian coast. David stared at the mountains through binoculars, then raised his plastic cup in a heartfelt tribute to my navigation. "Well done, my good and excellent little brother, well done."

I said nothing at first. Instead I just stared through red-rimmed eyes at the pink sparks of sun-reflecting snow in that far distance, and I thought with what innocent delight Jackie Potten would have greeted this landfall. "It's a funny old world," I said at last, and raised my beaker in response to my brother's compliment. The sea was darkening into night, mirroring the sky's gloom to leave those high, brilliant, snow-white peaks suspended like shards of rosy light in the dusky air. I watched till the last light drained away and we

could see nothing but the strange southern con-
stellations hanging high between the scudding
clouds.

We hove to, not wanting to make an unfamiliar
coast in the darkness. *Stormchild*, as though impatient with our caution, fretted all night in the
short, steep waves until the creeping dawn silhouetted the far peaks black and foreboding, and, at
last, under the mountains' ominous loom, we
loosened *Stormchild*'s sheets, untied her wheel,
and plunged toward the land.

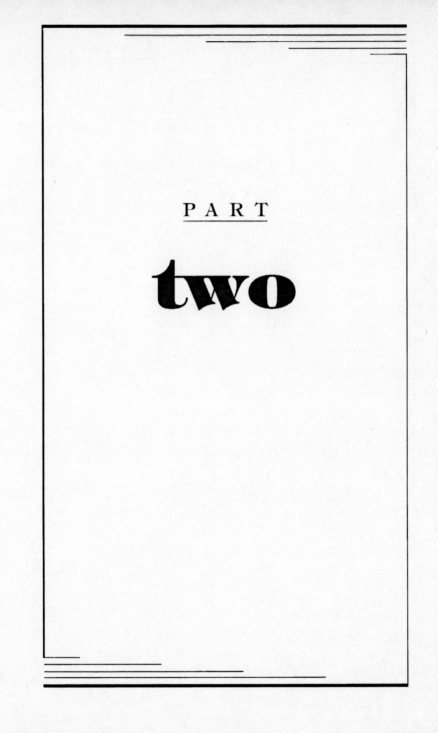

PART

two

Water pounded against *Stormchild's* steel cutwater, then shredded into a thousand ice-cold missiles that rattled down her decks and shattered loud on her spray hood. For hours we had been enduring such hard, cold, frightening, and wearying work. We were fighting against a head wind and a hostile sea, laboring not merely to make progress, but simply to hold our own against the malevolence of an ocean that assaulted us in close-ranked attacking ridges scummed and ribbed with white water. The crests of the ridges were flying maelstroms of wind-whipped spray that mingled with a pelting rain that slashed diagonally out of low, dark clouds. The wave ridges were coming at an angle so that *Stormchild* fought her way up their long, cold slopes, only to corkscrew off their peaks before running fast into their deep gray-green troughs. On the ridge tops the foam was sometimes so

shattered into spray that I could scarcely see
Stormchild's bows. The wind banged and shrieked
and moaned in the rigging, while green water
seethed and broke dirty white in the scuppers and
cockpit drains. This, as Joanna would have
enjoyed telling me, was sailing.

Jackie Potten had not been waiting for me in
Puerto Montt. I had dared to expect her, yet at the
same time had known that I would be disappointed. I telephoned her in Kalamazoo, only to have
her irritating answering machine wish me a good
day. I had also telephoned Molly Tetterman, and
had once again reached nothing more than a tape
recorder.

"You're not pining for the girl, are you?" David
had asked me scornfully.

"That's none of your business."

"Oh, pardon me for living," he said huffily. Our
friendship had been strained, both of us knew it,
and neither of us really knew how to restore it.
David wanted me to forget Jackie, to dismiss her as
though she had never existed, while I was missing
her. I tried to convince myself that my hopes of
any attachment to Jackie had always been as futile
as they were unrealistic, but loneliness nevertheless filled me with a corrosive self-pity. The only
feeling countering that poison was the growing
excitement of sailing ever nearer to Nicole. Each
time I woke for another cold spell of watch duty I
would feel a small frisson of exhilaration at the
realization that every bitter lurch of the hull and
hammering blow of the sea marked a moment
that took me ever closer to my daughter.

Or rather each moment should have been taking me closer, had it not been for this damned head wind and its pounding sea. We were one week and four hundred miles south of Puerto Montt as, with two reefs in the main and the number-two jib winched tight as a board, we were trying to weather Cape Raper. I could see the lowering cape, with its lighthouse, way off on *Stormchild*'s port bow, though our view of the high cliffs was intermittently obscured by the thrashing rain. Once, managing to steady my binoculars on the cliffs, I saw a wave break on the rocks and spume its white water a hundred feet into the air where it was snatched into oblivion by the howling wind.

Cape Raper was the most westerly point of the Chilean mainland and, because it was the one part of that wild coast where there was no inside channel, we were being forced to pass it at sea. Once past the cape we would still have to cross the infamous Golfo de Penas, the Gulf of Sorrows, before we could once again take advantage of the sheltered channels behind the barrier islands, though "sheltered" was hardly the right word because the waterways between and behind the barrier islands were scoured by vicious tides, prey to violent williwaws, and desperately short of good holding for *Stormchild*'s triple anchors. We had already sailed the best part of a hundred miles in such channels, protected from the ocean storms by the wooded Chonos Islands, but now, thanks to Cape Raper, we had to face the great gray open ocean that heaved at us like moving mountain ranges. Seaward of us, and having just as uncomfortable a passage as *Stormchild,* was a big rust-streaked and heavily-laden freighter that must have been carrying limestone north from the Patagonian quarries. Smoke from the freighter's stack streamed ahead in the spray and rain, then I lost sight of her as *Stormchild* plunged off a wave crest to plummet down into a dark trough.

David, sharing the watch with me, gripped a safety bar tight. There was a wariness in his eyes, almost as though, in the great wilderness of wind and water, he was perceiving the wrath of God. We were both dog-tired, both sore, both of us bruised and suffering from the minor injuries of hard sailing: fingers pinched in winches, palms skinned by ropes, and small cuts abraded by salt water. But at least *Stormchild* was taking the seas well; she sailed sweet and true, despite her crew's weariness.

Our last proper rest had been in the fishing town of Puerto Montt, where we had cleared customs and received our ninety-day entrance visas. Then, obedient to Chile's cruising regulations, we had sought a sailing permit from the *Armada,* the Chilean Navy. We had been told to expect a stultifying bureaucracy, but the demise of military government had left the whole process perfunctory. "You're supposed to radio us every day and tell us your position," a black-uniformed *Armada* officer, Captain Hernandez, told us in perfect English, "but I wouldn't bother, because I don't think anyone really cares where you're going. Where are you going, by the way?"

For a heartbeat I had considered lying in case the

Genesis community had contacts within the *Armada*, but Hernandez's friendly manner made the thought instantly ridiculous, so I had told him of our plans to explore the Archipiélago Sangre de Cristo.

"Good God, why?"

"Bird-watching," I lied, for it did not seem entirely sensible to admit that we risked an armed confrontation with a group of survival-minded environmentalists, who, I believed, had murdered my wife and were even now holding my daughter against her will.

"We've come to see the green-backed firecrown hummingbird." David convincingly embellished my lie.

"I'm hardly an expert,"—Hernandez seemed to find nothing particularly strange in the idea of men sailing thousands of miles to spot a bird— "but you might have better luck farther south. Still, I'm sure half the joy of bird-watching lies in the search, yes?"

As Captain Hernandez began to prepare our official papers I wandered to the wall opposite his desk to examine the large scale charts that were pasted together to make a continuous map. I peered very closely at the Archipiélago Sangre de Cristo and particularly at the Isla Tormentos, and saw that someone had inked a small square mark on the shore of the island exactly where I had presumed any settlement might have been built. I tried not to betray any particular interest as I turned towards Hernandez. "Are we likely to find any fishing villages in the islands? I'm thinking of places where we can find provisions?"

Hernandez banged his rubber stamp on our permit, then offered me a dismissive shake of his
head. "There's no fishing village for a hundred
miles, only a community of hippies on
Tormentos. They're an odd lot. They sail off and
make a damn nuisance of themselves to the
Japanese, but they keep well out of our hair. No
bird fouls its own nest, eh?"

"Indeed."

Hernandez had crossed to the wall of charts and
tapped the inked mark, thus confirming my suspicions of where the Genesis community was hiding. "I doubt if the hippies will be of much use to
you if you run short of supplies," he said scathing-
ly. "They seem to live, how do you say—low on
the hog. For all we know they may all be dead by
now. The winters there are hard, very hard. Not
that you need worry. There's plenty of fresh water
in the islands and as many fish as you can catch."
He ceremoniously presented me with *Stormchild's*
sailing permit and wished us both luck.

We went back to *Stormchild* where I copied onto
my own chart the location of the Genesis community's settlement. At last, after all the supposition
and imaginings, we had a destination. I had found
Nicole.

And now, one week later, we were being buffeted by the great seas and drenched by the rain and
whiplashed by the salt spray as we struggled
against a pernicious south wind to round Cape
Raper and gain the Gulf of Sorrows, beyond which
we would discover whether the hippies, low on
their hog, still lived. I was nearing Nicole.

* * *

As we crossed the Gulf of Sorrows the wind and seas became atrocious. We had come to Patagonia in its summer season, but the weather was like a bad northern winter, and our journey had deteriorated into a sodden hell. Squall after squall savaged across the water, the wind rarely dropped below Force Seven and never once veered from due south, and thus it took us three days to claw our way southward across the Gulf. It was three days of hard tacking into a scouring, soaking, dispiriting bitch of a wind, and the misery worsened when I could not find the entrance to the channel that would eventually lead us to the Desolate Straits and to the Isle of Torments. For two whole days we beat up and down that wind-shredded coast till at last a tuna boat radioed us directions.

We escaped the great ocean waves into a network of channels that were bounded by sheer black cliffs, which, during a rare moment when the clouds lifted, I measured with the sextant and found to be over four hundred feet high. The great rock faces cast the narrow seaways into a perpetual gloom through which waterfalls plumed and fell in white smoking streaks. Sometimes it rained so hard that it was difficult to tell where the waterfalls began and the sky ended, and always there was a pervasive mist that permeated *Stormchild*'s cabins so that every surface on the boat became damp and slimy with mold. Even the air seemed sodden.

We motored south in this gloomy, dank world, into which the ocean waves reached to swell and suck green water against the broken black rocks. The tides had a rise and fall as fierce as any in the English channel, yet these tides seemed to follow no set pattern by which we could forecast their surge, for the moon's metronomic tug on the water was confused into craziness by the complexity of the coast's labyrinthine channels. In places, where boulders protruded close beneath the water's surface, the confusion hatched whirlpools and tidal rips that waited in vicious ambush. The whirlpools were glossy, silent, green-black slides inviting a boat to destruction, while the rips looked as though a demented blender was thrashing madly just beneath the waves to explode white spray fifteen or twenty feet into the rain-filled wind. We dared not risk sailing blind into such dangers by traveling at night, so instead we would pick what seemed like a sheltered cove and try to find a lodgement for our heavy anchors which usually just dragged across rock or snagged in the thick floating beds of kelp. One of us would then have to use the dinghy to carry mooring lines ashore, which, because there were rarely shelving beaches, inevitably meant a dangerous scramble across slippery, fissured, weed-slick rocks and an inevitable soaking as a wave surged ice-cold water up the boulders. Whichever of us did that singularly unpleasant mooring duty would then row frantically back to *Stormchild* to be revived in front of the saloon's small diesel heater. "Christ, but I'm too old for this sort of caper," David said one night as he shivered half naked in front of the heater's feeble warmth.

"We used to do it for amusement, remember?"

"We used to do a lot of things for amusement that we can't do now," he said gloomily, then he turned a dinghy-sailor's accusing eye on me. "Isn't yachting supposed to be fun? Isn't that what you cruising sailors always tell me? How you relish the adventures of far waters? I do assure you, Tim, that however wet and cold I make myself in the *Holy Ghost*"—the *Holy Ghost* was David's irreverent name for his beloved racing dinghy—"there is always a welcoming fire and a decent pint of bitter waiting in the Stave and Anchor." He glanced up at the chronometer mounted on the saloon bulkhead and made a swift calculation of what time it would be at home. "I suppose they're just closing up the bar now," he said wistfully, "and John will have a fire going, and a decent fug of pipe smoke, and we're stuck in Patagonia."

Even moored with two lines fore and another two aft, and with our heaviest anchors clutching what grip they could find, we were not at peace. If either of us had miscalculated the length of the mooring lines, and the tide then dropped or rose too fiercely, we would have an unpleasant half hour on deck rerigging the thrumming ropes in the wild, wet darkness. Night winds whistled and howled through the towering gulfs, bringing thick mists or flying clouds that poured sudden downbursts of violent rain on *Stormchild*'s teak deck. Worst of all were the *rafagas*—the sudden gales of deflected wind that, spilling and driving themselves down the sheer cliffs, would strike the water vertically with the speed and force of a hurricane.

Under the impact of the *rafagas* the water would be flattened into a white sheet of shivering foam that was as terrifying to watch as it was to endure. *Stormchild* was hit twice, and both times she was laid right onto her starboard beam as plates and cups spilled in a shattering stream from behind the galley fiddles. David and I, clutching like grim death to whatever handholds we could seize, stared at each other and waited for the inevitable disaster. The first time an awful scraping sound, just audible over the insane shrieking of the wind, betrayed that the big anchors were dragging across rock, but then, slowly, painfully, miraculously, our boat righted herself. In the second knockdown Joanna's portrait, which I had believed to be firmly fixed in its frame, had somehow come loose and its glass had shattered on the saloon floor. I could not work out whether that omen was good or bad. The next morning, when I retrieved the big plough anchor, I discovered its shank had been bent like a hairpin.

In the daylight, when we were under way, the fog would sometimes slam down, or else the rain would be so fierce that we could scarcely see *Stormchild*'s bow pulpit, so we would turn on the radar and try to make sense of the tangle of echoes that confused the screen with its mad green chaos. More often than not the echoes were so jumbled that the set was worse than useless, and while one of us steered, the other would stand in the bows and shout instructions through the wind and fog and rain that formed this Patagonian summer.

Below decks *Stormchild* had become a stinking

pit of wet clothes, mildew, spilled food, damp bedding and diesel fumes. The fumes were my fault. I had been carrying a can of fuel for the saloon's heater when I lost my balance as *Stormchild* lurched, and the diesel oil had soaked into the saloon's carpet. We had tried to air the saloon, but the stench persisted. The Caribbean world of easy cruising and long drinks under *Stormchild*'s cotton awning seemed a million miles away.

Yet the Patagonian waters, though short on the sybaritic comforts of a cruising life, were not without their compensations. On our fourth evening in the channels, when I thought we could not go on fighting the maniacal tides and winds any longer, the weather at last began to relent and the barometer to climb. At dusk the low mist lifted from the settling waters to show us a long view toward a wooded slope a quarter mile away. Then we heard an odd splashing and turned to see a group of sea otters playing in our wake, while at our bows, and fleeing the intrusion of *Stormchild* into their pristine world, a score of steamer ducks paddled wildly at the water with whirling wings. On shore were colonies of rockhopper penguins, while above us thousands of sooty shearwaters flighted to their roosts from the open sea. Just before the darkness was complete we saw two sea lions chasing fish. The sightings proved that we now sailed in one of the world's last great wildernesses, a wilderness in which we saw no other boats and no other signs of human presence. There was a steamer service that ran through the innermost channels to the Tierra del Fuego, but we were well seaward of that boat's route.

The next morning we woke to discover that the weather had indeed relented. Dawn brought sunlight and a delicate, clearing sky. The force of the wind had gentled, and all about us was the sudden sparkle of light on water, a million seabirds, and a scenery so majestic that both David and I felt a catch in our throats. There are few such moments given to us on this earth, moments when we are granted a glimpse of the world as it must have looked at the crowning moment of creation. "'And God saw every thing that he had made,'" David, who, like me, was half bearded now, quoted from Genesis, "'and behold, it was very good.'"

We cast off our moorings, retrieved our anchors from their clinging kelp, and started *Stormchild*'s motor. The sound of the engine seemed an affront to the pure loveliness of the channels. For once we could see clearly and I collapsed the spray hood so that our forward view was unobstructed. The cliffs reared up from the green, shining water and were topped by long wooded slopes. Between the cliffs, where the turmoil of the restless earth had made steep valleys that dropped like chutes toward the tide-hurried water, beech trees grew. In the long, long distance, glimpsed between the scattered islands, the snow-touched peaks showed the spine of a continent. When the channel widened I was able to stop the engine and, for the first time in days, hoist *Stormchild*'s sails so that she glided like some stately pleasure barge across a wide sea-lake that stretched between a group of wooded islands.

The wind was fitful, but the tide was friendly

and pushed us silently along the waterway. We
rounded a corner of glassy water to find another
stretch of wide seaway, along which we ghosted
between small natural meadows, wooded slopes
and sun-touched cliffs. We were like men drunk
on beauty, dazzled by a place as wild, as desolate,
and, for me, as close to God as any place on earth.
Birds of prey with massive ragged wings spiraled
above the scree-edged peaks and beneath the scat-
ter of high white clouds, while black-necked swans
swam from a tree-edged creek to paddle in
Stormchild's placid wake. White mountain streams
cascaded through the trees. It was, so long as the
weather held, Arcadia discovered. The only jarring
note was that one of our two rifles now lay beside
the binnacle, for David, knowing we had entered
the outer islands of the Archipiélago Sangre de
Cristo, had insisted on removing the companionway paneling and retrieving the gun we had hidden there. "Though I doubt very much we shall
need it," David had said as he brought the rifle
topsides.

"You think Genesis will let us come and go in
peace?" I asked.

"I think that naval fellow in Puerto Montt was
right," David said, "and that the Genesis community won't foul their own nest. Why on earth
should they provoke the enmity of the Chilean
authorities by a gratuitous display of violence?"

"So Jackie was right after all?" I asked with as
little malice as possible, "and we don't need
guns?"

"I pray we don't need guns," David said fervently. He was staring forward and, looking at him, I suddenly thought how much this voyage had aged him. There was white in his beard and deep lines about his eyes, so that, for the first time, I saw in my middle-aged brother the signs of old age, and I wondered if I looked the same, and whether Jackie had been offended by my tactless remark on Antigua, and the memory of that remark burned shamefully inside me as I thought what fools old men made of themselves because of young women.

David opened the rifle's butt and took out a pull-through and a bottle of cleaning oil. "I do pray we don't need guns," he repeated, "but that rather depends on how we respond if we meet hostility."

I shrugged as though I did not think it an important question, though increasingly, as the sea miles had slipped beneath *Stormchild*'s keel, that question had dogged me. I had sailed from England with only one clear purpose: to find and rescue Nicole. But as David had just suggested, the completion of that simple purpose depended on what kind of welcome the Genesis community offered *Stormchild*. I suspected that there would be no welcome at all, which was why I was glad David was now cleaning the Lee-Enfield, though whether he would actually fire the gun was plainly another matter. "Are you suggesting I should turn the other cheek?" I asked him.

David tugged a square patch of flannel cleaning cloth through the rifle's barrel. "I think," he said slowly, "that if we are offered violence, then we have to withdraw. We may have to fire in self-defense, but otherwise we must behave with the utmost circumspection." He offered me a wry smile. "I know it's not the most adventurous approach, Tim, but we can't risk causing injury or death."

I knew David was right, but I did not want to admit it. "Back in England," I observed caustically, "you couldn't wait for me to put a bullet between von Rellsteb's eyes. Now suddenly we have to be circumspect?"

"Back in England," he said very simply, "I was wrong."

"You're scared of losing your chance of becoming a bishop, are you?" I accused him nastily. He smarted at that, looking guiltily offended. "Oh, come on, David," I said, "you're a Blackburn! Of course you're ambitious, and murdering environmentalists would really mess up your chances of sitting in the House of Lords and having first pick of the choirboys."

"Don't be ridiculous," he said huffily, "and even if I did want a bishopric, that has nothing to do with the present circumstances."

"Then what does?" I asked him.

He sighed. "The truth, Tim, is that I'm scared of dying. I'm scared of getting into a fight and leaving Betty a widow. I'm not as brave as I was thirty years ago, and I promised Betty I'd do nothing stupid. I intend to keep the promise. I also promised Betty I'd look after you. It's bad enough that we've lost Dickie and Joanna, without losing you."

For a moment I said nothing. It was unlike David to so openly reveal an affection, even toward me, and I was touched. I was also boxed in, for I had not sailed clean across the Atlantic and down to the southern hemisphere just to surrender at the first sign of von Rellsteb's pugnacity. "If I prove that von Rellsteb killed Joanna," I finally told David, "then I'm going to kill him. With or without your help."

"No, you won't," David said very patiently, "because if we discover any wrongdoing, then we will summon the authorities, and if the authorities won't help us, then we will travel to Santiago and enlist the support of the British Embassy. You're famous, and I'm not exactly disreputable, so I assure you the ambassador will listen very closely to us, and if the embassy insists to the Chilean authorities that the Genesis community is sheltering lawbreakers, then it won't take long for the *Armada* to get a patrol boat into these waters."

I shrugged, ceding to his argument. "OK," I said, "no heroics. We go, we reconnoiter, and at the very first sign of hostility, we withdraw." I spoke sourly, but I knew David was right to insist on caution. We were two middle-aged brothers, one of whom wanted to be a bishop, and though an atavistic part of me still wanted to tear the Genesis community apart, common sense suggested we would be hopelessly outgunned and savagely outfought if we took on von Rellsteb's group with our two ancient rifles.

David, seeing my disappointment, smiled. "If we're lucky," he tried to console me, "we'll find

Nicole without any complications."
So, rigged with cautious good sense, we sailed on.

We sailed through the scenery of a suddenly limpid and serene paradise. The wind was dying, and, denied its power, our sails flapped impotently. David went below to make lunch, and, impatient to make progress, I started *Stormchild*'s motor.

By the time we had eaten our meal of pickles, cold salted pork, bread and margarine, the tide had turned against us and *Stormchild* was struggling against a surge of water that poured between two dark headlands which, if my chart was correct, marked our passage into the Desolate Straits.

"Not long now," I said nervously. Our wake was a slash of reflected sunlight against the suddenly dark water.

There was no sign of the Genesis community's presence in these waters; it seemed as though David and I were the first people ever to invade this wilderness. We passed between the twin headlands and the channel widened once more. The water swirled darkly past our hull as kelp geese and black-necked swans paddled desperately away from our intrusion. David, dividing his attention between the birds and the chart, suddenly pointed to a long hilly stretch of land that lay beyond a low rocky promontory and said that, unless he very much missed his guess, those spiky hills were part of the Isla Tormentos.

I stared at the jagged skyline and thought of

Nicole in a burst of sudden, incoherent, and utterly unexpected joy. I was near to rescuing my daughter, and surely all the old love that had been so strong between us would revive when we met, and my heart was so full of love and hope that I dared not express myself for fear of weeping. Nicole, Nicole! I had crossed a world to find her, and now she was so close, and I felt nothing but a welling of love and expectation. David, sensing my feelings, stayed silent.

We turned eastward to cross a wide stretch of open water, then turned southward again into the Desolate Straits proper. In one of the pilot books David had brought from England I had read that the straits took their name from the false hope they offered a mariner. They seemed to promise a sheltered deep-water route clear down to the Land of Fire, while in reality they were merely a long inlet that stretched into the very heart of the Isle of Torments and, once in that stony heart, came to a blind and bitter end. A skipper, thinking to save himself a hard outer passage, but finding, instead, that he had wasted a day's sailing only to reach a dead end, would call these deceptive straits desolate indeed.

Yet here the channel ran straight and inviting. *Stormchild*'s engine purred sweetly, driving her across the now mirror-smooth water, on which our wake fanned in gorgeous silver ripples. To port a black cliff spilled a thin stream of falling white water, while to starboard a slope of sun-drenched trees ended at a beach of white stones. The landscape dwarfed our boat and overwhelmed our senses.

"It'll be nice to see old Nickel again," David awkwardly broke our silence. He had always been fond of Nicole; it had been David, rather than Joanna or myself, who had taught Nicole to sail, and who had first discovered her fierce ambition. David had harnessed that ambition to dinghy racing and often said that, if her brother's death had not skewed her life, Nicole would have achieved what David himself had so narrowly missed: a place on Britain's Olympic sailing team. Nicole, David always maintained, was simply the finest sailor he had ever seen.

"She'll be surprised to see us!" I said. Our conversation was stilted because neither of us could match with words the apprehension we felt for the approaching moment. "Perhaps," I said to cover the clumsiness of our feelings, "we should take in the sails?"

We stowed the canvas. I was becoming increasingly nervous as we came closer to the bay, which had been marked as the site of the Genesis settlement on the charts in Captain Hernandez's office. Fine on *Stormchild*'s starboard bow we could see a rocky headland crowned by a row of wind-splintered pine trees, and, if the Captain's chart was right, the Genesis community lived just beyond that promontory.

David propped the rifle against the folded spray hood, then stooped to light his pipe. "I hope we don't have to use violence," he said nervously, then laughed. "Dear Lord, but I sound just like the American girl, don't I?"

The thought of Jackie gave me a sudden and

astonishing pang, but then even Jackie vanished from my thoughts as *Stormchild* cleared the pine-topped promontory and there, like an evanescent dream given unexpected shape and solidity, was the bay where the first von Rellsteb had made his settlement.

"Oh, God," I murmured, and it was a prayer of thanks as well as a plea for help, for sunlight was dazzling us where it reflected from a windowpane. For suddenly, in one of the last wildernesses of earth, we had found the straight lines of human habitation. There was smoke above a roof. There was a rank smell that was the stench of people.

Stormchild had brought us to Genesis.

I had always imagined the von Rellsteb settlement would be graced by a grand Victorian farmhouse with carved eaves, turrets, and wide verandas. Common sense had told me that no house built to withstand the Patagonian weather could possibly have an exterior as fussily detailed as my imagined Victorian mansion, but nevertheless the fancy had persisted so that when I did at last see the building I felt an immediate disappointment, for it looked like nothing more than a range of overlarge and decaying farm sheds.

The ugly house and its ragged extensions stood in the shelter of a semicircle of low steep hills and above a lawn that sloped down to the bay's shingle beach. The house, which faced eastward toward the water, was made of a limestone so pale that it looked like concrete. It was an immensely

long and disproportionately low house of only
two stories, but with sixteen windows on each of
those two floors. The house might not have
looked as grand as my Victorian fancy had
embroidered it, but the first von Rellsteb had certainly built large. Had he imagined a slew of
grandchildren pounding down his long, echoing
corridors? The building, except for its size, was
otherwise unremarkable, unless one took exception to the bright red corrugated iron roof through
which a dozen stone chimneys protruded. Two of
those chimneys showed wisps of smoke, betraying
humanity's presence.

The house had two single-storied wings, one to
the north and the other to the south. Those two
extensions each added sixty feet to the long facade
of the house before they turned at right angles
toward the protective western hills, presumably
making a huge three-sided yard at the rear of the
house. The two wings were built in the same pale
stone as the house and roofed with the same ugly
sheet metal. The only structure that in any way
matched my original expectations was a cast-iron
gazebo, incongruously like a park bandstand, that
stood in front of the house to offer anyone sitting
in its shelter a long view down the Desolate
Straits. The gazebo was an inappropriate touch,
like a clown's red nose stuck on the waxy face of a
corpse, and its existence added to the sense of
unreality that assailed me as we motored farther
into the bay. All around the settlement were vegetable gardens, which, even in this day's cheerful
sunlight, looked forlorn and unproductive, while

on the steep ridge that lay a half mile behind the buildings was a tall, slender radio mast that was strongly guyed against the island's fierce winds.

"What a godforsaken place," David said in horror. I was thinking of Nicole living in this godforsaken place, and so said nothing. The settlement seemed deserted, the only sign that anyone lived in this awful place was the smoke from the stone chimneys. Nor was there any sign of the catamaran *Erebus*, renamed *Genesis*, though on the southern side of the bay, moored alongside an ancient stone quay, there was an equally ancient looking fishing vessel that was painted a lurid lime-green and had a high bluff bow, a low gunwale amidships, and a stubby wheelhouse astern, from which a tall dark chimney stuck skyward. For an ensign the fishing boat had a pale green scrap of cloth like that I remembered from the day when Nicole had sailed away. The trawler's name, like the renamed *Erebus*, was *Genesis* and had been painted in black untidy letters on her bows. The only other boats I could see were a slew of sea kayaks drawn up on the beach.

I throttled back *Stormchild's* motor as the depth sounder betrayed the bay's steeply shelving bottom.

"We could berth alongside the fishing boat," David suggested.

I shook my head. "I'll anchor and row ashore. You'll stay here?"

"Gladly." David shuddered at the decrepit, uninviting appearance of the settlement. Now that we were closing on the land I could see a row of odd concrete tanks embedded in the sloping lawn in front of the house. David had also noticed the ugly containers and was examining them through his binoculars. "Fish tanks?" he ventured the guess, then gave me the glasses as he went forward to stand beside the main anchor.

I waved to him when the depth sounder showed we were in thirty feet of water. The chain rattled and crashed its way through the fairlead as I killed the engine, then there was a wonderful silence as the chain at last stopped running and as *Stormchild*'s small forward motion dug in the anchor flukes. She tugged once, then gentled as we swung round so that our stern faced the apparently deserted settlement. We were just fifty yards from shore, while the house was another hundred yards beyond the small beach.

"As a garden of earthly delights," David said, "it lacks a certain lighthearted elegance, wouldn't you say?"

"It lacks people, too." I unlashed the dinghy that had been stored on the after coach roof, then splashed the small boat over *Stormchild*'s stern. I did not bother with the dinghy's outboard motor, but instead just lowered myself overboard with a pair of oars and rowlocks. I also took a handheld VHF radio which David would monitor on *Stormchild*'s larger set. He asked if I wanted to take the second rifle with me as well, but I shook my head. "I don't want to antagonize anyone, if anyone's there at all."

"White man come in peace, eh?" David said with a jocularity designed to hide his nervousness, yet there was a hint of truth in his jest, for we both felt like explorers touching a previously unknown shore in an effort to make contact with some elusive and mysterious tribe.

"Wish me luck," I said, then pushed away from *Stormchild*'s side. It was odd to look back at my boat. She had become my carapace, my security, and it was almost unsettling to be rowing away from her sea-battered hull. The woodwork of her cabin roofs looked faded, and her paint was grimed with salt, yet there was still something very lovely about the big yacht as she sat in that unnaturally placid bay with its long view of the Desolate Straits.

A flurry of flightless steamer ducks fled from my dinghy as I neared the shingle beach. My heart was thumping and there was a nervous sourness in my belly. I had thought that my long solo journeys around the world had cured me of helpless fear, yet now I felt a kind of craven panic because I really was rowing into the unknown. I felt a temptation to return to *Stormchild* and let Genesis come to us, but instead I tugged hard on the oars until the dinghy's bows grated at last on the beach. I stepped out and dragged the small boat safely above the tide line. The beach was edged by a seven foot high bluff of stony earth, up which someone had once built a flight of sturdy wooden steps.

I climbed the weathered stairs with a growing sense of unreality. I had sailed ten thousand miles to what? To nothing? To a blast of gunfire? To Nicole? To tears of reconciliation? Or perhaps, if my daughter and I both behaved with true British reticence, to an awkward embrace and an embarrassed conversation.

I reached the top of the wooden steps and started across the springy, short-grassed turf, where I was at once assailed by a stench of manure so overpowering that I almost retched. At first I thought the smell might be coming from the concrete tanks, which I now assumed were sewage settlement chambers, but when I reached the odd tanks I saw that one half were empty while the other half held malodorous and curdled mixtures of oil and water. The smell, distinctly that of sewage, did not emanate from the tanks but from the fields on either side of the house, and I realized that the Genesis community must recycle their own sewage by spreading it as topdressing on the settlement's vegetable plots.

I walked toward the house's central doorway which was framed by a flimsy-looking wickerwork porch, a domestic touch as odd as the strangely festive gazebo. It felt weird to be ashore. The land seemed to be rocking like a boat. I was nervous, yet still no one challenged me, indeed no human sound disturbed the day's peace. A gull screamed, startling me. Then, just as I reached the conclusion that the settlement must be deserted, the double front doors of the house burst open and two bearded men, both wearing identical green garments, emerged into the sunlight.

For a moment we stared at each other. I suddenly felt happy. I was going to see Nicole! And in my happiness I felt an absurd urge to offer the two men a deep bow. "Hello!" I called out instead.

"Go away," one of the two men replied. Both men looked to be in their thirties and had springy, bushy beards. The one who had spoken sported a black beard, while his companion had a brown beard streaked with gray. Neither man appeared to be armed, which was reassuring.

My happiness ebbed as swiftly as it had bubbled up. I started walking toward the two men and an unseen hand immediately slammed the doors of the house shut. I heard bolts slide into place.

"Go away!" The man with the black beard said again.

"Listen," I said in a very friendly tone, "I've just sailed ten thousand miles to see my daughter, and I'm not going away just because you're feeling unsociable. My name's Tim Blackburn. How are you?" I held out my hand. "I'm looking for Nicole Blackburn. Is she here?"

They ignored my outstretched hand. Instead they stood with arms akimbo, daring me to push past them.

"Perhaps you didn't hear me?" I suggested politely. "My name is Tim Blackburn and I've come here to see my daughter Nicole."

"Go away," the man with the black beard said again.

I went to walk round them and the second man raised a hand to push me back.

"Touch me," I told him, "and I'll break your fucking skull."

My sudden hostility made the man skitter out of my path like a frightened rabbit. I walked past him to the odd porch, where I tried to open the front doors that proved to be very firmly bolted. I turned back to the bearded men. "Is Nicole Blackburn here?" Neither man answered, so I peered through the window nearest the door. The glass panes were very grimy, but I could just see into a room that was almost empty except for a bare trestle table on which hurricane lamps stood unlit. The stone window ledge was thick with dead flies. More ominously I noted that the window had stout iron bars set into the stone ledge.

"Tim? This is *Stormchild*, over." The handheld radio suddenly squawked in my oilskin's pocket.

"David? This is Tim, over."

"Tim. I've just seen one green-dressed fellow run to the hills behind the house. He seemed to be carrying a weapon." David's voice sounded ominous, as though the violence he feared had already started. "Do you hear me, over?"

"I hear you," I told him, "and I'll go gently."

"Remember our agreement! We're withdrawing if there's trouble!"

"Perhaps the fellow has just gone duck hunting," I said, then put the radio back in my pocket and smiled at the two bearded men who had edged close to eavesdrop on my conversation. "Where's Nicole?" I asked them.

"Go away!"

Ignoring the monotonous order, I trudged through the muddy soil toward the northern wing of the house. I noticed that all the ground floor windows were protected with the stout iron bars, and the thought occurred to me that this would not be an easy building to break into.

I turned to follow the northern wing where it bent back toward the encircling hills. The single-storied extension was windowless, though here and there, and looking menacingly like loopholes, apertures had been crudely hacked through the limestone blocks. I peered through one such aperture, but could see nothing but darkness inside. My two bearded companions followed a dozen paces behind me, but no longer tried to stop me from exploring the settlement. I walked past rows of carrots, some small bean plants, potatoes, and a wilting patch of red beets. The gardens stretched to the very edge of the escarpment, which formed the near slope of the semicircle of hills toward which David had seen the gunman run.

I walked to the rear of the buildings and saw that the long house and its two wings did indeed form three sides of an open courtyard. I took out the radio and pressed my transmission button. "David? There's a courtyard behind the house. I'm going to have a shufti. I can't see your gunman, so I assume he's holed up on the ridge line. No one will talk to me and the house is locked, so I don't know whether Nicole is here or not. We'll probably lose radio contact when I'm in the courtyard, but if I'm not on the air within fifteen minutes then you'd better break out the guns and all of you should come and look for me. Out." I thought it would do no harm if my unfriendly guardians got the impression that *Stormchild* was crammed with armed men ready to turn their dung-ridden paradise into a killing ground.

I moved into the bare, dank courtyard. Nothing

grew in that depressing space, not even a blade of grass. There was a child's sandpit in one corner, which held some very old and faded plastic toy buckets and spades. Near the damp sandpit were a rusting iron swing, a wooden rocking horse, a doll without its head, and a heap of broken, rusting lobster traps. A cat hissed at me from the roof of one of the two low wings of the house.

From within the yard the two wings of the house looked like rows of stables, each with a Dutch door. In one of the stable compartments were two huge vats and a stench so vile that the homemade manure smelled sweet by comparison. There were bundles of otter pelts hanging on hooks above the vats, and I assumed that this was the settlement's tannery. But a tannery? Why would environmentalists be skinning sea otters?

"You must go away." The man with the black beard was clearly becoming ever more uncomfortable with my brazen snooping.

"Where's Nicole?" I asked him cheerfully and, as before, received no reply. "Is Caspar here?" I asked instead, but with the same result.

I walked to the back door of the house, which, not surprisingly, was locked as firmly as the front entrance. I peered through a barred window to see a kitchen equipped with an ancient wood-fired stove. Bunches of herbs hung from the ceiling beams. I walked on to the next window and saw racks of guns that looked like assault rifles. Some of the spaces in the wooden racks were ominously empty.

I strolled past a vast and disorganized woodpile,

evidence of the community's reliance on timber for their heating and cooking. I heard a child cry inside the house, the first sign that people other than my bearded followers were present at the settlement, but when I shouted a greeting through one of the dusty windows, no one answered.

I explored the southern wing. Hens lived in two of the stablelike rooms, but otherwise I saw nothing alive except the vituperative cat that spat at me from the corrugated, rust-streaked roof. At the corner of the building I stopped to stare at the crest of the escarpment where the radio mast was built, but I could not see the gunman David had spotted, and whom I assumed must now be hidden among the tangle of rocks that crowned the ridge. Just to the north of the radio mast was an earth-faced dam, which suggested a reservoir had been created in a saddle of the escarpment, presumably to control the flow of water from the hills to the settlement's vegetable gardens.

I walked to the building's southern flank and there I stopped in astonishment. A dozen young people were struggling toward the settlement with a big handcart that was stacked high with freshly cut logs. The clumsy cart was being maneuvered along a muddy path by a disconsolate group of women and children who all wore drab and uniformlike gray overalls. The work party was escorted by two bearded men, who, like the two guardians who still dogged my every footstep, wore green trousers and jerkins.

The woodcutting group, who were still a hundred paces from the buildings, saw me and froze.

One of the women gaped in such abject terror that I thought she would faint.

I walked toward them. The man with the black beard tried to call me back, while the small children clung in terror to their mothers' gray trousers. I could not see Nicole among the women, who all looked lank, unhappy, pale, and ill-fed. One of the frightened children began wailing.

"Hello!" I called aloud. "It's all right! I'm a friend!"

"Go away!" One of the green-dressed men seized an ax from the stalled woodcart and started toward me. "Go away!"

I stopped some fifty paces from the big cart. "My name is Tim Blackburn," I shouted, "and I've come here to find my daughter, Nicole. Do any of you know where I can find her?"

None of the group answered. The gray-uniformed women huddled together and seemed to shiver with a collective fear of my appearance. They looked to me like zombies, and I recalled Jackie's assertion how Utopian communities were very often based on one man's idealism, which, to preserve itself, degraded into a fascist system of discipline. These people, the zombies in gray and their bearded guards in green, seemed evidence that von Rellsteb's community was an example of that sad fate. The axman, who had a ginger beard, walked confidently toward me as though he planned to split my skull open. "Is Caspar von Rellsteb here?" I asked him.

"You've got to go." The axman, like the black-bearded man, had an American accent.

"Where's Nicole Blackburn?" I asked him patiently.

"Go away!"

"I'm fed up with all of you," I said dismissively, and tried to walk toward the frightened women. The ginger-bearded man immediately swung his ax at me. His swing was wildly violent and came nowhere close to me. Instead the energy of the blow unbalanced my attacker so that he tottered helplessly backward. I took two quick steps toward him and brought the toe of my right sea boot hard up into his groin.

His breath whooshed out, his eyes opened wide, the ax dropped into the mud, then he followed it with a sudden scream of pure agony. The other bearded men looked as terrified as the women and children.

I picked up the fallen ax. "Where's Nicole!" I demanded of all and any of the green-dressed men.

"Go away." The man with the black beard sounded scared. The man I had kicked was sobbing and whimpering on the ground. David, who could now see me again from *Stormchild*'s cockpit, was insistently demanding to be told what was happening, but the only answer I offered him was a cheerful wave.

Then, because the men were evidently defeated, I tossed the ax into the mud and walked toward the gray-dressed group. "I'm Nicole Blackburn's father," I told them again, and in as comforting a voice as I could manage, but before I could say

another word one of the green-dressed men
ordered them to run.

"Go!" he shouted. "Run! Quick! Go!" He
flapped his hands at them as though he drove a
flock of hens, and the women, with one last look
at me, obeyed. They fled toward the southern
hills, the children clinging to their mothers and
screaming as they ran.

I turned back to the men. "Are you all mad?"

"Go away," one of them said.

"I'll search your house first," I said, and began
walking toward the big sprawl of buildings.

A rifle fired. It was not David on board
Stormchild who had opened fire, but rather the
gunman who was hidden at the crest of the western escarpment. The sound of his gun echoed and
re-echoed around the wide bay, while his bullet
thudded into the ground just five paces in front of
me. At that range it was horribly good shooting
and I hoped it had only been intended as a warning shot, calculated to stop me in my tracks.

If so, it worked. I stopped.

"Tim!" David's voice squawked from the radio.

"Listen." I was not replying to David, but rather
turning to appeal to the bearded men, but my
words were interrupted by a second rifle shot, and
this time the bullet whacked into the damp earth
even closer to me.

"Go," the man with the black beard said.

"Where's my daughter!" I shouted at him, and I
took a threatening pace forward, but immediately
the gunman on the hill fired a third round, and this
bullet hissed menacingly close to my head. I froze.

"For God's sake, what is happening?" David asked plaintively over the radio.

I thumbed the transmit button. "They won't talk, they won't say where Nicole is, and the gunfire is calculated to make me leave."

"I think that might be a very good idea," David said in a dispassionate voice, "because I've spotted another gunman in the house itself. He's on the top floor, left-hand window. I suggest you withdraw, Tim. We've done what we could, now let's do as we agreed."

"Like hell." I was feeling stubborn, stupidly stubborn. I put the radio back into my pocket and looked defiantly at the black-bearded man. "I have sailed ten thousand bloody miles to see my daughter, and I'm not leaving without speaking to her. Where is she?"

The man's only answer was to raise a hand in an evident appeal to the gunman hidden on the escarpment's crest, who now switched his gun to automatic fire and loosed a whole clip of bullets at me. The sound of the shots crackled in the still air as the bullets churned a patch of nearby ground into a morass. The rounds came so close that I instinctively twisted away and half fell.

David, thinking that my fall was evidence that I had been shot, fired back.

The old British army rifle made a much louder report than the gunman's assault rifle, and, long before the echo of his first shot had faded from the bay, David fired again.

The effect was extraordinary. The three men who had been confronting me turned and fled.

Even the man with the ginger beard limped away, still sobbing and gasping. The gunman on the hill began placing single shots very close to me. It was impossible to see where that gunman was hiding because the top of the escarpment was an horrific tangle of rocks and crevices. I decided he was not trying to kill me, but only to drive me away. The Genesis community just wanted to expel me, and, under the encouragement of their marksman's wicked aim, I turned and walked toward the beach. The hidden gunman, seeing my retreat, instantly ceased fire. David, after his first two warning shots, had also ceased fire. I took out the radio as I walked. "It's been a bloody washout," I reported to David.

"Just get back here," he said, and I could hear the nervousness in his voice.

I reached the bluff above the beach. I hesitated there for a few seconds. One part of me, desperate for news of Nicole, wanted to go back and hammer at the door of the house, but when I turned to stare at the ugly building I saw that David was right and that there was indeed a gunman on the upper floor. The man had opened a window and was mutely watching me. The message of his unmoving menace was very clear: that I should go away.

I went away. I climbed down the steps and started hauling the dinghy toward the water and as I did, one of the gunmen opened a furious fire.

David responded.

I stared in horror at *Stormchild*, expecting to see the bullets chewing up her hull and deck, but

Stormchild was untouched, the water around her unscarred by bullets. David, standing in the cockpit, was working the Lee-Enfield's bolt furiously. His shots echoed flat and hard from the far hills.

I left the dinghy and ran halfway up the wooden steps to see what had caused this sudden firefight. Then, crouching so that I was hidden from both Genesis gunmen, I very cautiously peered over the bluff's edge.

A single figure dressed in one of the drab gray boiler suits was running frantically toward the beach. It was a young woman who had run from the woodcutting group and now struggled with extraordinary clumsiness toward the sea. For a second I dared to hope it was Nicole, but then I saw this girl had hair as black as night, while Nicole was fair. The fleeing girl tripped and fell, and I was sure she must have been hit, but then she struggled up again. David kept firing, then the second Genesis gunman, the one in the house, saw the girl and opened fire.

He had seen her too late, and the range was too great. The girl was already close to the concealing bluff. She took one panicked look behind her, then half jumped and half fell over the earthen cliff. For a second I thought she had knocked herself unconscious, but then she struggled up and ran toward me.

I shoved the dinghy into the water. David was now firing at the house and his shots dissuaded the gunman in the upper window. The farther gunman, the one on the high ridge, had also ceased fire, but only, I suspected, because he was reloading. "Anchor!" I yelled at David. "Get the bloody hook up!"

The girl, her eyes huge and terrified, swerved into the shallow waves toward the dinghy. She stumbled and fell full-length into the cold sea. She was gasping as she struggled up and scrambled clumsily over the dinghy's bows. I clambered after her, grabbed the oars, and rowed hard toward *Stormchild*. The girl, sensibly, was curled on the dinghy's floor and hidden from the Genesis gunmen. The one on the ridge had opened fire again, but the range was too great and his bullets went wide. The man in the house could have shredded the dinghy with his fire, and I flinched as I saw his gun's muzzle appear at the windowsill, but then it jerked back as a bullet from David's gun slapped a puff of stone dust and chips from the wall near the window. *Stormchild*'s anchor windlass was thumping away, clattering the pawl-dragged chain over the fairlead. David, who was now standing in *Stormchild*'s bows, fired again at the house. I knew he was not firing to kill, but only to scare, and his tactic seemed to be working.

I rowed to *Stormchild*'s far side. "Over you go!" I told the girl. She obediently tipped herself into *Stormchild*'s scuppers, then slithered into the cockpit. As she wriggled under cover I heard a curious clinking noise and I at last understood why her escape had been so clumsy. She was wearing leg chains.

I followed her on board, tying the dinghy's painter to the nearest stanchion. The girl quivered on the cockpit floor.

"Anchor's clear!" David shouted at me.

He had already started *Stormchild*'s engine, so all I needed to do was ram it into gear. Bullets whiplashed overhead. One clipped the backstay, but did no apparent damage. David fired back. The anchor chain was still clanking aboard, but the anchor was hanging clear of the seabed as *Stormchild* gathered speed. The water at her stern churned white.

"I knew this would end badly," David shouted at me.

"It hasn't ended yet!" I said, then ducked as a stream of bullets whimpered overhead. It was the gunman on the escarpment's crest who was firing, but I suspected we were in much more danger from a group of armed men who were running toward the shabby trawler. Someone must have already been aboard the trawler, because black smoke had started to pour out of its slender funnel.

"They're going to chase us," I warned David.

David stowed the anchor while I pushed *Stormchild* to her top speed. Behind us the decrepit, green-painted trawler clanked away from the quay. David came back to the cockpit and winced as someone on board the ancient fishing vessel fired a clip of bullets toward *Stormchild*'s stern. "Forget the trawler," I told David, "and take our guest below. Use the hacksaw on those chains and give her something to eat."

"Chains!" His eyes widened as he saw the leg irons. "Good Lord above!"

David took the girl into the saloon as a last hopeless clip of bullets from the hills hissed overhead. Then we were hidden from that land-based gunman as *Stormchild* reached the tip of the pine-topped headland where a sudden tidal surge carried her out of danger at the speed of a racing dinghy whipping round a mark. I spun the wheel amidships and, with *Stormchild*'s big turbo-charged engine at full throttle and with her hull borne along by that enormous tide, we traveled quickly away from the trawler. The fishing boat's stack was spewing a filthy plume of greasy smoke, evidence that her old engine was working at maximum effort.

A rifle fired from the trawler and the bullet clanged off *Stormchild*'s transom. A second bullet drove a jagged splinter of teak up from the coaming. That was good marksmanship, too good, and I snatched up David's discarded rifle and fired two quick bullets at our pursuer. The rifle's butt slammed into my shoulder.

"For God's sake! What's happening?" With each rifle shot David could sense potential scandal: a man of God caught fighting a private war in Chile.

"I'm discouraging the ungodly." I fired again.

"How's the girl?"

"She seems to be in shock." David went back below. The gunman on the trawler splashed a clip of bullets into *Stormchild*'s wake.

I fired one more time, then turned back to *Stormchild*'s wheel. The tide swept us on. I was tempted to escape the trawler's laborious pursuit by turning into one of the high-twisting chasms that opened off the wide waterway, but I did not know which of the chasms were dead ends or which held shallows that might ground us, so it seemed wiser to retrace our steps and hope to outrun the trawler in our wake.

"They're calling us on channel sixteen!" David shouted up to me.

"Saying what?"

"That we're kidnapping this girl!"

"Then tell them to fuck off," I told him impatiently.

David doubtless told them to desist from their transmissions, but however politely he phrased his request, its only effect was to provoke another flurry of automatic fire from the trawler. I returned the compliment. The old Lee-Enfield was a wonderfully rugged and reliable weapon, but at that moment I would have given a fair chunk of money to have been equipped with an automatic rifle. Half the trick of winning firefights is to scare the other side with as much noise and mayhem as can be created, and a single-shot, bolt-action rifle was a poor producer of mayhem and noise. But, like David, I had always been a fair shot with a rifle and my slow, deliberate fire unsettled the Genesis gunmen, whose aim was made inaccurate by the labored shuddering of the panting trawler.

"Be careful!" David kept appearing in the companionway to counsel me. "Don't kill anyone!"

In the end it was not my marksmanship that saved us, but rather *Stormchild*. She was by far the faster boat. Our enemies' shots were falling short or going desperately wide, and after a few minutes their firing became sporadic. Their shots echoed forlornly from the cliffs and bluffs that edged the channel. Those shots did no damage, and soon, as *Stormchild* went even farther ahead, they ceased altogether.

Our pursuers still did not abandon their attempts to reach us on the radio. I took out my handheld set and switched it to channel 16 to hear their message. *"Genesis* calling *Stormchild,"* the voice intoned, *"Genesis* calling *Stormchild,* over."* I assumed they had read our boat's name through binoculars.

"Genesis, this is *Stormchild,* over,"* I responded.

"We're requesting that you heave-to." The voice was toneless. "The girl you have on board is a member of our community and needs medical help. Do you understand me, over?"

"Where's Nicole Blackburn?" I asked.

"We're requesting that you heave-to," the voice said again.

"And I'm requesting that you fuck off," I said, "out," and I switched off the little radio. My parting insult produced a last fusillade of rifle fire, but the bullets just plopped exhaustedly in our wake. Five minutes later the trawler's oil-burning engine slowed to a dispirited clank and I saw the craft turn away. We had escaped. It had been a tense few moments, but, as far as I could tell, no one in Genesis had been hurt and we were also safe.

I went down to the saloon to fetch a thermos of coffee and saw that David had cut off the girl's shackles, and that she was now wrapped in one of our blankets and sitting in front of the saloon heater. Her soaking wet gray suit was hanging over the back of the chart table's chair. The girl, who looked to be in her mid-twenties, was glassy-eyed, pale, shivering, and terrified, like a creature dragged back from the grave. "Hello," I said as cheerfully as I could.

She offered me a scared look, but said nothing.

David, his back to the girl, offered me a helpless shrug, as though suggesting that the girl's wits had fled. David was a good pastor, but not a sensitive one. He offered his parishioners a robust certainty of salvation, but left Betty to deal with their emotional crises. David's solution to a broken heart was a good brisk walk followed by a stiff whiskey, which worked with some people, but not with most, and was certainly not going to work with the waiflike creature who now shivered in *Stormchild*'s saloon. "Give her some hot food," I suggested. "I'll come down when I can."

By dusk we were thirty miles north of the Isla Tormentos. Our pursuers had long disappeared, and their final plaintive radio transmissions had subsided into a crackled silence. As the sun shadowed the ravines with a purple haze I nosed *Stormchild* into a narrow passage edged with towering black rocks. We seemed to be at the very bottom of the tide, for thick weeds and bunches of mussels showed high above the waterline at the channel's edges. I crept forward, fearing to hear the scrape of steel on rock as our keel touched bottom, but at last the channel widened into a deep sheltered cove where I was able to rig our mooring lines and drop our anchors. I shut off the engines, and suddenly the world was a place of blessed and wonderful silence. There was not even a wind moaning in the chill, still air. The cliffs soared above us, making an amphitheater of sky in which a thousand thousand seabirds wheeled.

I was tired and cold, but before going below I paddled the dinghy around *Stormchild*'s hull to inspect her for bullet damage. There were some holes in her stern and some long shining scratches on her flanks, but otherwise our escape had been miraculously unscathed. I painted the damage over with white paint, because steel rusts with an appalling swiftness if it is not protected from the salt air, then I went below to find that our guest was now fully dressed in a pair of my trousers and one of David's thick sweaters. She was also weeping hysterically; her thin shoulders heaving and her breath gulping as she huddled on the cabin floor beside the starboard sofa.

"Has she said anything?" I asked.

"Not a word, Tim! Not a whimper!"

David had been unsettled by the girl's tears, so, to relieve him, I gave him the rifle and told him to go topside and keep watch.

"You'll get no sense out of her," he warned me.

"Go," I said, "just go."

He went, and I sat down beside our guest to discover just what she might know about my daughter.

The girl, when I crouched beside her on the diesel-reeking carpet, flinched away as if she thought I was going to hit her. "It's all right," I crooned, "it's all right. I'm not going to hurt you. We're friends, it's all right."

She made a noise halfway between a choke and a sob, but she calmed somewhat as I droned on as softly and reassuringly as I could. She was a dark-eyed, black-haired girl, who, I guessed, had once been pretty, but now that prettiness had soured into a narrow, hurt face with sallow skin against which her sunken eyes were so big and dark they looked like bruises. Her hair hung lank. Her teeth looked caried and in desperate need of cleaning. Her bare ankles, protruding from the legs of my thick flannel trousers, showed horrid patches of open sores where the steel shackles had abraded her skin.

"What's your name?" I asked her.

She opened her mouth, but only succeeded in

making another of the pathetic grizzling sounds.

I raised a hand to stroke her hair, but she immediately flinched away and made another terrified noise. "I'm not going to hit you," I said, "it's all right," and I put my hand very gently on her shoulder and pulled her toward me, and, after a moment's initial resistance, she fell against me and began to sob with huge racking heaves of her thin shoulders. I stroked her long hair, which was sticky with seawater, and kept asking for her name, but she made no response and I began to suspect that she spoke no English, and then, more alarmingly, I feared that she had somehow lost her tongue or vocal chords and could only make the pathetic glottal noises that intermittently punctuated her sobs.

I stroked and soothed her for a full ten minutes before she startled me by suddenly finding her voice. And when she did manage to speak, she did so with an abrupt and astonishing clarity. "Berenice," she said. "My name's Berenice."

"Berenice." I repeated the name, then remembered that Jackie Potten's friend had been called Berenice Tetterman, and I softly pushed the girl away from me so that I could look into her bruised eyes. "You're Berenice Tetterman," I said, "and you come from Kalamazoo in Michigan. I know your friend, Jackie. She's been looking for you. So has your mother."

My words only provoked another flood of tears, but mixed in with the sobs were enough words to confirm that our tattered fugitive was indeed Berenice Tetterman. She told me how guilty she felt about everything, and how she thought her mother might be dead, so I kept repeating that everything was all right now, that she was safe and her mother was alive. Berenice clung with dirty, chipped nails to my sweater, her face buried somewhere in my chest, and slowly, slowly calmed again. She even managed to blurt out a question that seemed immensely important to her. "Are either of you ill?"

"No, of course we're not," I said in the tone one would use to dismiss a child's ridiculous fantasy of gremlins under the bed or ogres in the night garden.

She pulled away to look into my face. "You promise?"

"Cross my heart and hope to die," I said very solemnly, "we're both quite well."

"Because he says that people are dying everywhere. He says the AIDS virus is like the Black Death." Berenice's eyes had widened into terror as she spoke, and then she began to cry once more, but this time without the awful animal intensity that had made her earlier sobbing so distressing. These new tears were ones of exhaustion and sadness, but no longer of despair.

David dropped down the companionway. "All quiet outside," he reported.

"I can't believe they'll find us in this cove," I said, "but I reckon we should keep watch through the night, don't you?"

He nodded. "I'll keep watch until midnight, you until four, then me again?"

"Sure." I was stroking Berenice Tetterman's tangled and salt-ridden hair. "Has she eaten?" I asked David.

"She had some toast and coffee."

"Why don't you make us all some soup?" I suggested.

David switched on the lights in the galley while I went on stroking Berenice's hair, and slowly, so very slowly, drew her story out from the thickets of her terror.

Her first fear had been the risk of catching the awful contagion with which Caspar von Rellsteb had terrified his followers. He had somehow persuaded Berenice and the others in the settlement that the outside world had been so stricken with the AIDS virus that normal life in so-called civilization had become impossible. He had persuaded his disciples that their only safety lay in clinging to his barren island. He had succeeded in using the fear of AIDS as a superbly effective means of control; so effective that, even now, faced with our robust denial of von Rellsteb's terror stories, Berenice half suspected we were deceiving her.

David found a news magazine that had been jammed into a drawer to stop the cutlery rattling. "Look through that," he told her. "I think you'll see the world is still fairly normal."

She leafed through the stained, damp pages, which told of wars and hostages and terrorism, but not of a worldwide plague as awful as those that had decimated medieval Europe. Slowly her look of fear was replaced by one of puzzlement. "We never see magazines or newspapers," she explained, "because Caspar won't let us. He says we mustn't contaminate ourselves with things from outside. We have to stay pure, because we're going to change the world." She was crying very softly again. "Some of us wanted to leave a long time ago, when we first came here, but he wouldn't allow us. One girl tried, and she died, then the AIDS came outside. . . ."

"Who died?" I interrupted her. "What girl died?"

Berenice was puzzled by the swiftness and intensity of my question. "She was called Susan."

"Do you know Nicole Blackburn?" I asked anxiously.

Berenice nodded, but said nothing.

"Was Nicole at the settlement today?" I asked. Berenice shook her head, but again said nothing, and I sensed that the urgency of my questions was somehow frightening her, so I made myself sound calm and reassuring again. "I'm Nicole's father," I explained, "and I've come looking for her. Do you know where she is?"

Berenice seemed scared of answering. "She'd be at the mine, if she was anywhere," she finally said, then launched herself into a long and involved explanation about how she and the others were not really allowed to visit the mine, "although I went there once," she added, "when they wanted us to clean off a boat. It isn't really a mine at all," she explained lamely, "only a limestone quarry with a few shafts, but there are some old buildings there as well."

"And Nicole lives at the mine?" I asked.

"The crews don't really live there"—Berenice frowned as she tried to frame her explanation— "but Nicole does. Most of the crews come to the settlement when they're ashore, but not Nicole.

She stays with the boats, you see, and they shelter at the mine because they had real bad trouble with southerly gales at the settlement. The anchorage at the mine is much safer, and they've got an old slipway there so they can haul the boats out of the water if the weather gets really awful."

David brought us each a mug of oxtail soup and a hunk of hot buttered bread, and I remembered, too late, that both Berenice's mother and erstwhile best friend were vegetarians, which meant this girl could very well be an herbivore as well, but she made no objection to the oxtail; she gulped it down as though she had not eaten in weeks.

Between spoonfuls she told us how strict the division was between the Genesis community's yacht crews and the settlement's workers. The workers, as Jackie Potten had envisaged, were virtual slaves to the privileged crew members. The distinction was even sartorial, for the yacht crews wore the Genesis green, while the workers were given the more utilitarian gray clothes. "He's real strict about that," Berenice said sadly.

She began to tell us about the daily chores of the settlement, but I was not listening. Instead, in a state of half shock, I was assimilating a very unpleasant truth. The same truth had also occurred to David, who now watched me with a troubled expression. We had both traveled to Patagonia in the belief that Nicole was being victimized by von Rellsteb, but from Berenice's description it was clear that our preconceptions had been horribly wrong, and that Nicole, far from being one of von Rellsteb's victims, was one of his privileged crew members. "And Nicole," I finally asked Berenice, "wears green?"

"Of course." Berenice nodded.

Upon which answer hung a slew of other messy deductions, too messy to think about. "And I'll find Nicole at the mine?" I asked grimly.

"Unless she's at sea," Berenice said dubiously, "but we don't really know who's at sea and who isn't most of the time. But Nicole does more sailing than most of the others. She's the skipper of a boat, you see, and they say she's the best sailor of them all, better even than Caspar!"

I smiled, as if acknowledging a compliment to my family, while inside I was trying to come to terms with the destruction of one of my most comforting beliefs. Nicole was not being held prisoner! She was not a victim, but a free agent. She had her own boat. She could come and go where she pleased, and it had never pleased her to find me.

David, realizing how hard it was for me to come to terms with Berenice's news, took over the questioning by asking how many seagoing yachts the Genesis community operated.

"Four," Berenice said. "Two catamarans and two like this one." She waved around Stormchild's cabin. "I saw one of the catamarans a week ago, but I don't know if it's still here." David pressed her for more details of the small fleet's activities, but Berenice knew remarkably little about the movements of the four boats, only that they sailed away to make a better world, and that only those community members who wore green were allowed to crew the yachts.

"How many people are in Genesis?" David asked when it was clear Berenice could tell us nothing more about the four yachts.

"There's thirty-one of us at the settlement, and I suppose there must be at least another thirty in the crews. And there are fourteen children at the settlement." Tears came to Berenice's eyes at the mention of the children.

"Are you a mother?" I guessed at the reason for her tears.

"I had a baby," Berenice said, then her voice choked in a pathetically childlike tone, "but it was stillborn." She began to cry, the tears streaming silently down her cheeks. We waited until she managed to sniff the tears away. "The children have to work," she went on, "mostly they collect seaweed and mussels. And they help with the wood-collecting. We're always cutting wood, and we have to go farther and farther away to find decent trees." She shivered suddenly. "I'm so tired of cutting wood, but Caspar says that since I can't breed children I'm no good for anything except fetching and carrying."

"Dear God," David said in distaste.

"Has Nicole had a baby?" I had to ask.

"I don't think so." She sniffed back her tears and tried to drink more of the soup. "Lisl did."

"Who's Lisl?" I asked.

"She's Caspar's girl," Berenice said, as though it was an important piece of information. "She's German, too. She was the one who made me wear chains." She gestured at the leg irons that David had slung into a corner of the saloon.

"Was that a punishment?" David asked.

"Yes."

"For what?"

"I burned a stew," Berenice said, but in a voice that seemed genuinely penitent for such a grievous offense. She might have fled the Genesis community, but she was still thinking like one of the group, for she hastened to justify her punishment. "Food is very precious, you see, so one of the first rules we learn is never to waste any. It was mutton," she explained, as though that made her offense worse.

"So you cook for the group?" I asked.

"I do everything. I work in the gardens, clean the buildings, collect shellfish, tan the pelts ..."

"Pelts?" David interjected.

"They hunt sea otters," Berenice explained, "and sell the fur in Tierra del Fuego. At first the fur was just for us, because it's so cold, but now they sell it as well."

"Some bloody conservationists," I said angrily, wondering how self-styled ecologists could hunt and kill harmless and playful sea otters.

"He wanted to start a fish farm, but it didn't work, and we used to do experiments"—Berenice paused—"but they failed."

"What experiments?" David asked with a note of dread, expecting, like me, to hear of some awful cruelty imposed on man or beast, but the experiments had merely been efforts to determine a bacteriological method of destroying oil spills at sea. The experiment had been tried in the forlorn concrete tanks in front of the house, but the tests had failed and the experiment had petered messily out. I wondered whether enthusiasm for the experiment, like Genesis's ecological idealism, had been abraded and destroyed by the hardships of surviving the Patagonian winters, but Berenice, despite her desperate eagerness to escape from the settlement, still seemed proud of the community's achievements. The yacht crews, she said, had destroyed drift nets, crippled Japanese whaling ships, and had even made commando-style forays into the Malaysian province of Sabah to spike hardwood trees threatened by the timber industry.

"Spike?" David asked.

"They hammer metal spikes into the trunks of trees marked for felling, and when the chain saw hits the spike it breaks the saw. And they have to stop cutting the tree." Berenice concluded the explanation very lamely.

"What happens," I said laconically, "is that the chain saw rips itself into steel fragments that very often blind the log cutter and are quite likely to kill the poor sod."

"But it stops the forestry!" Berenice said earnestly.

"Oh, whoopee," I said.

"Why did you run away today?" David, who rightly thought my disapproval of Genesis's methodology was a waste of our time, asked Berenice.

The girl tried to frame a sensible answer, but the best she could offer was a jumble of reasons: the horrors of life in the settlement, the eternal cold and damp, how all the luxuries were reserved for the Genesis crews, how tired she was, how she no longer cared whether she lived or died, how she

hated the sight of *cochayuyo* which she said was a
stringy red seaweed that was the settlement's sta-
ple food. She explained how, when she had seen
Stormchild anchored in the bay, she had decided
then and there to run away. "Yours was the first
strange boat I'd ever seen in the bay," she said
with a touching wonder.

"The Chilean Navy never visits?" David asked.

"They did at the beginning," Berenice said, "but I
haven't seen a patrol boat in over two years now."
She hesitated. "There was another boat, I think."
She spoke very nervously, then stopped altogether.

"Go on," I encouraged.

"I didn't see it," she spoke defensively.

"Go on," I said again.

"I only heard Paul talking about it."

"Paul?" I asked.

"He's in one of the crews. He's the nicest of
them." She paused, then evidently decided to
plunge ahead. "Paul said an Australian yacht
arrived at the beginning of the summer, and that
it had three people on board, but they were all carrying AIDS."

"And?" I asked, though I knew the answer
already.

"They took the boat to the mine," Berenice said
in a very soft voice. "That's what I heard, but I
don't know if it's true."

"And the crew was killed?" David asked sternly.

"No!" Berenice looked shocked at the accusation.
"They put the crew into the sick bay, but they died
there." She looked from David's skeptical face to
mine. "They had AIDS!" Again she looked at our

doubting faces. "That's what Paul said, anyway." Her voice tailed away into a silence broken only by the hiss of the cabin heater and the tiny lapping sounds as the small waves rippled down *Stormchild*'s hull.

"What was the name of the Australian boat?" David asked very gently.

"*Naiad*," Berenice said. "It was a catamaran."

My suspicions about the *Naiad*'s fate made me wonder why David and I had not been killed the moment we appeared that morning. Berenice had already told us that Caspar had not been at the settlement when we arrived, and I suspected that, in his absence, no one else had dared initiate the killing. I also suspected that such a decision was reserved to von Rellsteb, for surely, as Captain Hernandez had suggested in Puerto Montt, the Genesis community would need to take great care not to foul their own nests. They could afford to offend many people, but not the country that gave them refuge. But that carefulness would change now, for Berenice was offering us knowledge that von Rellsteb would surely do anything to keep from the ears of the authorities, which meant that if the Genesis community found *Stormchild* all three of us would be dead meat.

"The boat belongs to Nicole now," Berenice said suddenly.

"The boat?" I asked.

"*Naiad*," she said very fearfully. Then, after a long pause. "It's called *Genesis* now, because they all are. Nicole's is *Genesis Four*. Some of us were surprised that she kept that name, because she fell out with Caspar."

"Fell out?" I asked.

"It was after the Australians died." Berenice frowned as she tried to remember the details, then she shrugged helplessly. "That's why Nicole stays at the mine instead of at the settlement. Paul told me that Caspar's frightened of Nicole, but I don't know if that's true." There was another long pause before, in a very timid voice, she asked whether we were going to take her away from the Archipiélago Sangre de Cristo.

"Of course we are," I promised, then, after a pause, I asked where we would find the limestone mine.

She shook her head, but said nothing. David, guessing the purpose of my question, frowned disapproval. He, I was sure, wanted to sail north and fetch help from the authorities, but I still had questions that needed answers.

"Where's the mine, Berenice?" I insisted.

"It's at the very end of the Estrecho Desolada, but you mustn't go there, you mustn't!" The terror that had erupted in her voice was quite genuine. "If you go they'll catch me and they'll punish me. Just take me away, please!" She began to cry again, and out of the sobs came an incoherent wailing that seemed to be about her dead baby, and about her mother, then she began to shake in huge racking sobs, so I laid her down, put her head on a cushion, and draped a blanket over her shivering body. Then, released from the need to soothe and calm her, I stood and stretched my legs and arms to fetch the cramp out of my muscles.

"I think," David spoke softly to me, "that we

now have more than enough evidence of malfeasance to demand action by the Chilean authorities. And we should certainly have this girl's
affidavit delivered to the Australian Embassy in
Santiago.

"Malfeasance?" I mocked David who, as a justice of the peace, liked to use legal terms. "You
think I've just sailed ten thousand fucking miles
to find evidence of malfeasance?"

"Yes!" he said very sharply. "That's what we
agreed, Tim! We agreed to reconnoiter. We have!
We've even succeeded in finding ourselves a first-
rate witness. What more can we possibly hope to
achieve? Our clear duty now is to fetch competent
help."

"What you do is your business," I told him,
"but I'm going on watch." I picked up the rifle
that was propped at the foot of the companionway. "Sleep well," I said.

"We have to alert the authorities," David insisted. "We were lucky today, Tim, because we got
out alive, but we can't rely on our luck holding.
We have to go for help."

"I'll wake you at four." I still would not face his
truth, because I had truths of my own to digest, so
instead I went topside to where a million stars
burned cold above a wilderness, and where, in the
night's sharp darkness, I mourned.

I sat in *Stormchild*'s cockpit with the loaded rifle
across my lap, and I reflected how easily the world
divided itself into the exploiters and the exploited,

and how that crude division was mirrored by the green and gray uniforms of Genesis.

And Nicole, my beloved Nicole, wore green.

Nicole did not have to eat the awful *cochayuyo*, Nicole did not have to work for long, cold, wet hours in the shit-stinking mud of the vegetable gardens, Nicole did not have to wade thigh-deep in ice-cold waters to gather mussels and seaweed, Nicole did not have to cut wood, Nicole did not sleep on an iron-framed cot in a damp dormitory that stank of drying diapers. Instead Nicole wore green and was trusted to sail in far waters. Nicole probably knew of murders. No, worse, and I could not face that last suspicion, but at least I now knew and now accepted that Nicole was not a victim. She was part of the control system. She was an exploiter. I had been wrong about her. I was not sailing to rescue her from von Rellsteb, but from herself.

"High-minded crap," I accused myself aloud when that neat thought occurred to me.

I was sitting dry-eyed and bitter in *Stormchild's* cockpit with my gloved hands resting on the wood and metal of the old rifle. High above me, seen through the wide chimney of the cliffs, a myriad of stars shone bright in the cloudless sky. The moon was hidden by one of the hills, yet it shone a silver light onto the edge of the western cliffs and a little of that light seeped down to shimmer the black water in the narrow entrance channel. Nothing stirred in the night until someone woke below and *Stormchild* moved as the person walked about the saloon. I saw a crack of light show between the companionway washboards, then heard the hiss of the stove. It had to be David who had woken, for I was sure Berenice would not have the courage to light the stove and make herself coffee. I waited, listening to the domestic sounds of spoon and cup and kettle-whistling, then, as the light snapped out, I heard David's footsteps climb the companionway.

"Couldn't sleep," he explained brusquely. "Brought you a coffee." He put the mug beside me, then settled on the opposite thwart. "I'm sorry," he said as curtly as he had explained his presence. He radiated embarrassment.

"Why are you sorry?" I asked him.

"You're wondering about Nicole, aren't you."

He had not, I noticed, described what worried me, but he knew well enough. "She's my daughter, David," I said, "of course I worry about her."

"Then that's why I'm sorry." He was silent for a long time. Water rippled on the hull and the air was cold enough to mist our breath. "I've been thinking, Tim"—David broke the silence—"I guessed you might be too upset to be clear-headed, so I decided to make a few decisions on my own."

"Good. Splendid." I was hardly making it easy for him.

"What we have to do"—he spoke with the forced enthusiasm of a scoutmaster addressing a particularly obdurate troop—"is sail north, get ourselves to Santiago, and enroll some first-class assistance there. Frankly, we've exhausted our options here, and I don't relish our chances of stirring up real action in Puerto Montt, but I've no doubt our embassy in Santiago will listen to us, and I'm sure the Australian government will want to hear the story that girl told us tonight. So, first thing in the morning, I think we should up anchor and sail north. Don't you agree?"

"I never thanked you for making the coffee," I said. "So thank you."

David sighed, but was determined to stay reasonable. "You have something else in mind, Tim?"

"I was just wondering," I said mildly, "what we planned to do about Nicole?"

"She'll have to take her chances with the rest," David said awkwardly.

I turned my head to look at him. "What does that mean?" I asked.

"It means nothing," David said. He, like me, was skirting around the mine field of Nicole's character. "I am sure," David said heavily, "that Nicole has done nothing, and therefore has nothing to fear from the authorities."

"She sails a stolen yacht," I said, "and I'll bet you next Easter's collection that the Australian crew was murdered."

"Oh, come!" David was offended. "We don't know that! And we certainly don't know if Nickel was involved!"

"Indeed we don't," I said, "which is why I want to find her before I condemn her." I paused to stare up at the cold stars. "I don't believe she's a killer," I said at last. "I think von Rellsteb is, but not Nicole. I really can't believe she's a killer. Not my daughter."

"So there can't be any harm in summoning the authorities, can there?" David asked.

"But I want to find out exactly what she is," I went on as though David had not spoken. "I just want to see her before I loose the dogs on her."

"It's not a question of releasing the dogs," David said very awkwardly, then fell into a moody silence. The thin moonlight showed a pale mist seeping off the black water, so that *Stormchild* seemed to float in a silver vapor beneath a canopy of silent starlight. The peace was broken by a bird, roosting somewhere on the cliffs above, making a brief, raucous protest. There was a flap of wings, another indignant squawk, then silence again.

"How's the glass?" I asked suddenly.

David paused, wondering what trick I was playing, then decided to take my question at face value. "It's still rising. I suspect we're in for at least one more day of fine weather."

I rested my head on the safety rail. "If we really intended to run for Santiago, David, we're too late."

"Of course we're not . . ."

"To reach Santiago," I interrupted him icily, "we would have to sail to Valparaíso, which would mean weathering Cape Raper. We have now been holed up in this cove for nine hours, which means that the Genesis boats will already be ahead of us, and they know damn well we need to clear the Cape, so they'll be waiting for us there. I know we can sail far out to sea, and thus try to evade them, but what I'm telling you is that they've already positioned themselves between us and the authorities, and getting past them will be risky."

"We can't be certain of that," he said stiffly.

I turned my head to look at him. "You want to

bet your life on that uncertainty?" There was no
answer. I shrugged. "The settlement will have
radioed the mine, and whatever boats were there
will have left to track us down. They know we
sailed north, so that's the direction they'll pursue,
and they'll know that their catamaran is far faster
than *Stormchild,* so they'll be hoping to overtake
us long before today's dawn. What they don't
know is that we're holed up here, and that consequently they've overshot us."

"Ah!" David suddenly brightened. "You're suggesting we sail south to Puerto Natales instead?
Good idea! There'll be a police post there, I'll be
bound, and we can talk to the embassy by phone.
Not as effective, perhaps, as bashing on the
ambassador's door, but if we make a fuss they're
bound to listen."

"No," I said, "I'm not proposing that we sail to
Puerto Natales, but to the mine."

There was a second's silence before David
exploded in protest. "You're a fool, Tim! We don't
even know if Nicole is there!"

"She probably isn't," I admitted, "but maybe
she is. Berenice saw a catamaran a week ago, and
we know Nicole sails one of their two catamarans.
But even if she isn't there, it's the place where I
can find out about her life. The mine is Nicole's
refuge, her bolthole, and that's where I'll either
discover her, or her belongings."

"And in any case"—David entirely ignored my
explanation—"the mine is at the very end of the
straits and we'll be bottled up there like a mouse
trapped in a Wellington boot! My dear Tim, I

entirely sympathize with your concern, but I must insist that we behave sensibly. We did agree to be prudent, didn't we?"

"The prudent behavior," I said very irritably, "was never to have come here at all, but having come this far I'm not going to go for help to the Chilean authorities. Not before I know what kind of future I'm making for Nicole by bringing in the Chilean police."

David was silent for a long time. His pipe glowed intermittently as he puffed smoke into the rigging, and when he did finally speak his voice had become calm and reflective, as though he knew he could not dissuade me by argument, so would now try a more subtle approach. "Go to bed, Tim. In the morning we'll decide how to escape this trap."

I did not move. "The point is," I said instead, "that I came here to find Nicole, and to talk to her, and it seems very stupid to get this close, then just run away."

"We are not running away," David said very firmly. "We're simply fetching competent assistance. If you discover a wasp's nest in your garden shed you don't go after it with bare hands. Besides, just what chance do you think we have of escaping from the dead end of the Desolate Straits? We'll be trapped there! Come, Tim! Be realistic!"

"I wasn't thinking of using the Desolate Straits," I said very mildly. "I rather thought we might try the Canal Almagro instead."

There were a few seconds of silence as David recalled the chart, then his protest was loud enough to disturb some of the nesting seabirds. "You're crazy!"

"Not if the weather holds," I said gently, "and you said yourself that the glass was rising."

"It's madness, Tim!" David said earnestly. "Madness!"

The Almagro Channel was the deep and winding fjord that pierced the Pacific coast of the Isla Tormentos, and which very nearly cut the island in two. On our best chart the fjord's dead end looked to be only two or three miles from the limestone working, and it would thus carry us very close to the Genesis community's innermost lair, but it was a passage full of danger. The danger was not from the gunmen of Genesis, for they would surely not believe that anyone would be foolish enough to use the fjord, but rather lay in the entrance to the Canal Almagro which was narrow, rockbound, and exposed to the full impact of the massive Pacific rollers. The fjord's entrance would be impassable in rough weather, but there was just a chance that if this fine spell lasted, then the perilous entrance might prove navigable. And it was a chance that seemed worth taking if I was to discover more about my daughter.

"I won't let you do it," David said in his most authoritative manner. "It's far too dangerous. You're not thinking straight—"

"Shut up!" I interrupted him with a savage firmness, "I am master of this vessel. I command here. This is not a democracy. And later today, if the weather holds, Stormchild will sail to the Almagro Channel. If you choose not to stay aboard, then

I'll find a place to put you ashore." I stood. "I'd be grateful if you woke me in two hours time."

"Whatever you say," David said unhappily.

I went to my sleeping bag, but could not sleep. Berenice was sobbing in the cabin that had been Jackie's quarters. David, under the lights of heaven, sat guard in the cockpit. And I lay awake, waiting for dawn and for nightmare.

I took *Stormchild* out of her refuge before first light. There was still scarcely a breath of wind, so we ghosted with an idling engine through a lightening mist that pearled our rigging with silver beads of water. Just as we emerged from the sheltered channel I was alarmed by a heavy splash and I whipped round in fear that our enemies had been waiting in ambush for us, but it was only a sea lion plunging off a rock. The mist became thicker as we nosed into the main channel, which I was forced to navigate by instinct and radar.

David had agreed to accompany me into the Almagro Channel. He came under protest and on the firm understanding that I would turn back at the first sign of real danger. He had also insisted that, when I explored the limestone mine, I would use the utmost circumspection so that our enemies would not suspect our presence on the island. I had solemnly promised that I would indeed be prudent.

Two hours after dawn the mist was gone, shredded by a rising wind that blew us toward the open sea. As we neared the ocean the swells began to make themselves felt in the rockbound waterways. The water surged in great billows between the high walls, gurgling and pouring over black boulders, then sucking and draining as the troughs followed. I hoisted the sails, and, as *Stormchild* emerged into the open sea, the rising wind caught us and carried us fast to where the great waves rose and fell on the rugged cliff faces of the outermost islands. Birds screamed at us. I killed the engine, hardened the sheets, and felt the exultation of a sailor released from rockbound channels into open water.

We sailed five miles offshore, then turned *Stormchild* south. David cooked bacon and eggs, while Berenice, who was now wearing Jackie Potten's oilskins, came to the cockpit and stared in wonder at the open sea and sky. There were no other sails in sight and I suspected that our enemies had gone far to the north, leaving their back door unguarded.

I told Berenice what we planned to do. She looked terrified at the thought of going back to the Isla Tormentos, but I explained that she would not have to go ashore. "I'll walk to the mine," I told her, "and you can stay with David. I'll only be gone a few hours."

"Are you looking for Nicole?" she asked me timidly.

"Yes. Or for news of her."

"She might be there," Berenice said, though without any conviction. Her voice was dull.

I paused to tack ship. For a second the headsails banged like great guns, then *Stormchild* settled on the port tack. A wave shattered on the stem to spray foam down our canted deck. I sheeted in the staysail, then glanced at Berenice. "You don't like Nicole, do you?" I had guessed as much the previous night from the hesitant way in which Berenice had spoken of Nicole.

Berenice seemed taken aback by my challenge, but she did her best to meet it without causing me offense. "She's very fierce," she finally said in a pathetic voice.

"She always was," I said soothingly. "She's very competent and she doesn't have a lot of patience with people who aren't as skilled as she is. I'm not surprised she had a fight with Caspar von Rellsteb." I waited a second, then decided it was worth asking again what the argument had been about. "Was it about the Australian catamaran?" I guessed.

I expected no answer, but to my surprise Berenice was suddenly loquacious. "It wasn't about that," she said, "but because Nicole thinks we ought to be more active. She says it's really counterproductive for all of us to be isolated in South America. She thinks that there ought to be Genesis communities all over the world."

I smiled. "That sounds like Nicole," I said, "ready to organize everyone and take over the world."

"Nicole thinks we aren't achieving enough," Berenice said weakly, then, in a rush of frankness, she admitted that many in the group believed Nicole was right and that von Rellsteb's dream had failed. "It was meant to be different when we moved down here," she said. "We were going to be strengthened by isolation, at least that's what

Caspar said, and we were going to sail out like old-fashioned warriors to put right all the world's wrongs, but it just didn't work." She frowned. "Things are so difficult! Even to organize a meal is hard. And we were supposed to be doing these experiments on degrading oil spills, but they all went wrong, and then he got angry, and somehow nothing works any more. We just survive. Most of us just go from day to day and hope nothing awful happens, but even organizing a meal is hard."

I was appalled at the hopelessness in her voice. "Why the hell didn't you run away sooner? Or protest? Why didn't you rebel!"

"Because if we tried anything like that," Berenice said limply, "we were punished. Not by Nicole," she added for my benefit, "because Nicole's usually at sea. She's by far the most committed of all the crews. I mean if anyone's doing any good, it has to be Nicole."

That, at least, was some good news about my daughter, and it made me dare to hope that, perhaps, I had let my suspicions of Nicole run away with me in the night. Perhaps, in the welter of disappointment and failure that dogged the community, only Nicole was achieving anything worthwhile. Perhaps, I thought, I had no need to explore further, because, if Berenice was right, then Nicole was not tarred with the brush of von Rellsteb's violence.

"Grub up!" David appeared with bacon-and-egg sandwiches, and I made Berenice repeat her description of Nicole's activism. "It doesn't surprise me that she's the most effective," David said proudly, and again I felt the hope that my daughter was struggling to distance herself from von Rellsteb's brutality and failure.

Berenice wanted to know about Jackie. I told her what I could, though had to invent an anodyne answer when Berenice asked why her old friend had abandoned *Stormchild* in Antigua. "I think she just wanted to find a newspaper that would commission a story about Genesis," I lied.

Berenice accepted the answer at its face value, then, after thinking for a few seconds, her face brightened. "Do you think she'll come here to find me? On her own, I mean?"

"Good God, no," David said hurriedly. "She hasn't got the means to come here, has she, Tim?"

"Not unless a newspaper funds her," I said, and bleakly wondered just how the idealistic Jackie would survive in this maelstrom of failure and violence.

By mid morning the wind had freshened into the south and *Stormchild*'s heavy bows were chopping with a perceptible shudder into each new wave. I feared that the rising wind might already have made the fjord's entrance impassable, while David was clearly pessimistic of our chances because the ocean swell was huge and, while such big seas were harmless in the open water, they would be killers where they crashed against the cliffs of the barrier islands to bounce back in complex and tumultuous cross patterns of surge and trough. *Stormchild* would have to be steered through those clashing tons of water and through the cold lash of the wind that would be trying to hurl her against the northern cliffs of the fjord's entrance. The rising wind, reflecting like the water off the cliffs, would be as tricky to negotiate as the sea. I would use the engine to make the passage, but I still faced an immensely difficult piece of seamanship.

Once inside the fjord we would have a fifteen-mile journey to where we could anchor for the night. In the darkness, just before dawn, I planned to go ashore. I hoped to approach the mine in the mists of early morning, make my reconnaissance, then sneak back to the boat unseen and unheard by Genesis. Yet the whole plan, if it could even be distinguished by the word "plan," depended on successfully negotiating the narrow sea gate where the wind and waves waited in awful ambush.

"There," David said somberly in the early afternoon, and he handed me his binoculars and I saw, in the great line of cliffs, a place where the spray was being shattered high into the freshening wind. Beyond that shimmering curtain of broken foam was a dark cleft in the rock. I was looking at the seaward face of Isla Tormentos, and at the desperately narrow crack in its stone coast. I let *Stormchild* fall off the wind, then turned the key to put power into the boat's starter motor. "Go, go!" I murmured encouragement to the big diesel as the starter motor thumped the engine into life.

I suddenly knew this was madness, but I would not turn back. Beyond the shadowed rockbound gut, and beyond the storm of breaking waves, lay Nicole and my confused hopes of her innocence and my equally confused fears for her guilt. And so we plunged toward the rocks.

*   *   *

"God help us!" David, who would have hated me to know he was nervous, could not resist the prayer. I knew he wanted to turn back, but for the moment his pride would not let him make that confession. Instead he just closed his eyes and talked to God.

Berenice, her knuckles blanched white, clung to the safety rail that ran just beneath the collapsed spray hood.

I stood behind the wheel, my legs braced against the boat's savage roll, and tried to make some sense of the titanic battle of ocean waves that barred our passage to the fjord's mouth.

The pattern of that battle began in a simple enough fashion. The great swells, born deep in the Pacific, traveled for thousands of miles to hammer themselves into oblivion against the Patagonian rocks. That oblivion was not instantaneous. When one of the massive waves struck the cliff it dissipated some of its energy as airborne spray, but far more of its energy was bounced outward as a reflected wave that went head-to-head with the next thunderous roller. If the cliffs were irregularly shaped, as these were, then that pattern of wave reflection became tangled and unpredictable. Except I had to predict the pattern, or else *Stormchild* would be tossed aside by one of those waves and splintered into shattered steel against the spray-drenched cliffs.

"Turn back! For God's sake, Tim!" David at last gave way to his fear. "You agreed we wouldn't take any risks! Turn, for the love of Christ, turn!"

"Just pray!" I shouted at him, "pray!" And a second afterward it was too late for anything but prayer for, if we had now turned broadside to the swells, the suction of the waves would have dragged us down into the roots of the cliffs, there to be overwhelmed as thousands of tons of Pacific rollers hammered themselves to death around us.

Where the reflected waves struck the incoming seas there were huge eruptions of foam that were like the explosions of gigantic artillery shells. The noises of the coast were deafening—the hammer blows of water striking rock, the seething clash of seas in turmoil, the racing of our engine, the crack as the wind took our foresail aback, and over it all, like the screams of devils waiting to pluck our souls to hell, the shrieking seabirds who swooped on long, thin wings through the wind-whipped mist of spray and air. The island's cliffs appeared like gigantic ramparts crowned by wheeling seabirds. I whooped defiance, then, more sensibly, looked to make sure that my companions were wearing their lifelines. The boat itself was battened down with every hatch dogged shut and every item on deck double-lashed down, though such precautions were mere cosmetics, for surely nothing on God's earth or in God's sea could save us if I had calculated this approach wrong.

A wave lifted *Stormchild*'s stern and I felt the raw power of a whole wide ocean surge us forward. I raced *Stormchild*'s engine in an attempt to keep her speed high. A mass of water slammed us from the left, breaking white foam as high as the

radar aerial on the mast. The water crashed into
the cockpit and swirled down the scuppers. I
glimpsed the cliff's wet rock face off to port and
instinctively gave the boat some starboard rubber,
but too much, for a reflected wave thumped us on
the port bow and Berenice screamed because it
seemed as if I was now steering the boat straight
for the saw-edged crags on our starboard bow. I
snatched the wheel back, but the helm suddenly
felt loose and soggy, and I knew that the surging
sea was overtaking us and stealing the power from
Stormchild's big steel rudder. Then, just as the great
sea crashed past and just as it seemed that we
must be thrown against the starboard rocks, the
deck seemed to drop away to port like a falling air-
plane, and *Stormchild* slid hard into a trough and
there steadied on her keel. The rudder bit, the
engine raced, and inch by inch we fought our way
into the rock's gut.

Behind us a new sea threw its shadow across
our deck. The wave that had first carried us then
overtaken us broke against the cliffs ahead,
drenching us with water and deafening us with
the sound of its destruction, yet, through the welter of its wind-born foam, I could just see a
smooth, green-hearted black path. The path led to
safety, and I pushed on the wheel's spokes as
though I could personally force *Stormchild* into the
island's calm heart.

The wave that had been thrashing at our stern
now picked us up and threw us forward. The rudder's power vanished again. We had become a
steel missile that was being hurled by a massive

force into a rock cliff. Berenice crouched, David stared wide-eyed, and I felt the wheel quivering in my hands.

For a few seconds we ran in the center of a whirlpool. To starboard a thousand tons of water shattered into flailing scraps. Above us the wet sail flogged. To port a sudden dark hole appeared at the base of a wave to reveal a black, jagged rock thick with seaweed and mussels. I heard Berenice scream in terror, then suddenly there were cliff faces to left and right, a smoothly heaving sea beneath us, and a maelstrom of foam behind us. We had made it.

"Piece of cake," I said, wondering if I would ever manage to uncurl my frozen fingers from the wheel's spokes.

"Nothing to it," David said, but in a voice every bit as shaky as mine. "I'm sorry if I panicked."

"You didn't," I said.

He laughed nervously. "I did, Tim, I did. And I'm already terrified of going back out again."

"That'll be much easier," I said dismissively, which it would, so long as no gale was blowing and so long as we shot the entrance at what passed in these seas for slack water. I throttled back the racing motor. The swells heaved down the channel, while behind us the breaking waves roared and growled and clawed at the fjord's narrow entrance, but we had escaped their fury and were now running into the heart of an island where my daughter and all her secrets lay hidden.

Berenice became demonstrably more nervous as we sailed further up the fjord and closer to the limestone workings. I asked her if anyone from the Genesis community ever visited the fjord, and she shook her head, but then added that such a visit was not implausible. "They've got two cross-country motorbikes," she explained. "the bikes don't always work, and they're usually short of gasoline, but sometimes they ride all over the island."

I still doubted that the Genesis group would think it worth their while to patrol the seaward coast of their island. They had seen us flee northward, and would surely assume we had kept going toward Puerto Montt or Valparaíso. I did my best to reassure Berenice of her safety, but she was almost catatonic with fear as *Stormchild* nosed ever farther into the island's heart.

We used the engine, for, though there was plen-

ty of wind, the fjord's steep sides either cheated us
of the wind's power or else made its direction so
fickle that the sails would have been aback as
often as they might have offered help. The soft
beat of our engine echoed back from massive
black cliffs that were slashed by high white
plumes of narrow waterfalls. Sometimes the fjord
opened unexpectedly into wide lakelike basins
that were dotted with tree-covered islands, and
more than once we had trouble deciding which
waterway from such a lake was the main channel.
The charts were no help. They merely confirmed
that the Canal Almagro existed, but no one, it
seemed, had ever surveyed its tortuous course.
"It's possible," I told David, "that we're the first
boat ever to come here!"

"That's a thought," David said with pleasure. At
my request he had broken out the second rifle
from its hiding place in *Stormchild*'s bows, but
now kept a nervous eye on the depth sounder. He
also noted that the glass was dropping. "It's not
desperately worrying," he said in a voice that
belied his apparent confidence, "but neither is it
entirely reassuring." In any normal circumstance
the fjord, with its bays and anchorages, would
have offered the perfect shelter from a sudden
gale, but any such gale would so heap the seas at
the fjord's narrow entrance that we ran the risk of
marooning *Stormchild* inside. Then, if the Genesis
community did discover our presence, our boat
would be like a rat trapped in a barrel. We could
not risk such a fate so we agreed that, should the
weather threaten to lock *Stormchild* inside the

fjord while I was making my reconnaissance of the
limestone workings, David would take the boat
back to sea and wait for a message from the handheld VHF radio that I would take ashore.

David, even though we had run the major risk
of negotiating the fjord's entrance, was still
opposed to my reconnaissance. "You have no certainty that Nicole will be there," he protested,
"nor that you'll find any news of her!"

"And you've got no certainty to the contrary," I
said. "For God's sake, David, just let me alone for
one day. I promise that if I find nothing, or if
what I find is bad, then I'll sail north with you
and we'll call in the cops."

"But no heroics!" David warned me. "This is
just a reconnaissance, and you are not going to
take any risks, is that a promise?"

"Scout's honor," I said, and gave him the Sea
Scouts salute.

"I know you, Tim!" David said in a slightly
despairing voice. "You're in a stupidly heroic
mood. You think you can swan across the island,
find Nicole, rescue her, then come back here and
open a celebratory bottle of champagne. Well, it
won't work! No battle is won by irresponsibility."

"Of course it isn't," I agreed, but without the
fervor my brother demanded of me.

"Tim! Please!" David said in exasperation. "We
agreed that at the first sign of violence we would
withdraw, and yesterday we were fired on, but did
we withdraw? Did we act upon our agreement? No
we did not. You pulled captain's rank and here we
are taking yet another risk. So I want your promise

that you will try no heroics. No stupidity! I want your promise."

"You have it," I said, and meant it, too.

It was almost dusk as *Stormchild* reached the fjord's blind end where the water widened into a large rippled pool that was surrounded by gently sloping hills. The shingle beaches were edged by belts of woodland, where ferns, moss, and wild fuchsia grew in livid green tangles beneath wind-stunted beech trees. Streams tumbled white and cold from the hills. A kingfisher flashed bright across the gray water as *Stormchild's* anchor rattled down to bite on the bed of a lagoon, where, I guessed, no ship had ever anchored before. The wide lake that terminated the fjord had no name printed on our chart, even the lake was not shown, so I inked in its rough outline and then added a name of my own devising: Lake Joanna.

The evening light was gray and wintry. All day the clouds had been gathering in the west, threatening wind and rain, but suddenly, as *Stormchild* tugged at her bedded anchor flukes, the setting sun emerged from a chasm of smoky vapor to cast a red-gold wash of fierce light across our anchorage. The sunlight made the small mountain streams look like rivulets of molten gold spilling toward a cauldron of liquid silver, above which uncountable seabirds flew on gilded wings toward their nests.

I waited until the glow faded and until the spilling streams of gold had turned back to cold white water again, then I went below. It was my turn to cook, then David would keep watch through the dark hours of the night before, in the first gray light of dawn, I would go to journey's end.

I had been at sea too long. The backs of my legs felt as though they were sinewed with barbed wire, while the breath rasped in my throat and a stitch agonized at my waist. I had plenty of strength in my upper body from wrestling with *Stormchild*'s wheel and hauling on her lines, but my stamina and my leg muscles seemed to have atrophied from the long weeks of being penned up in a small boat.

It was dawn and I was climbing the steep slope above the trees that edged the fjord's beach. I was carrying one of *Stormchild*'s rifles and a bag which held spare ammunition, my rigging knife, a torch, binoculars, the handheld radio, and a few rations. I also had forty feet of half-inch nylon line looped round my upper body, for Berenice had warned that there were places on the island that were inaccessible without a climber's rope.

Behind and beneath me, below the trees and scrub which had soaked me with their dew as I struggled through their entanglement in the night's last darkness, I could just see *Stormchild* in the battleship-gray mist that steamed off Lake Joanna's sheltered surface. It was my first sight of my boat this day, for I had woken and eaten breakfast in the dark, then exchanged my sea boots for an old pair of walking boots, and had put on two sweaters and an old waxed-cotton shooting coat that offered some rudimentary cam-

ouflage, before, still in darkness, David had rowed
me ashore. We had used a lantern to search the
beach till we found a distinctive pale-colored rock
which was the size and shape of a dinner plate,
and we had agreed that, should David be forced to
move *Stormchild* to sea or to a different anchorage,
he would leave me a note hidden under the stone.
Otherwise he expected to see me at dusk. If I came
back after nightfall I was supposed to signal my
whereabouts with the torch. David had stood on
the beach offering me instruction after instruction, all very prudent and laborious, and afterward
he had rather formally shaken my hand and
wished me good luck. "But no heroics, Tim!"

"No heroics," I had agreed.

Now, six hundred feet above *Stormchild* and
beneath a lowering gunmetal sky, I paused to catch
my breath. The ground was uneven, tussocked and
burrowed by nesting birds, while the rifle seemed
to weigh a ton. I glanced up at the sky, wondering
when the rain would come. The wind had suddenly sprung cold and fierce. If I had not known this
to be the southern hemisphere's summer I would
have thought a fall of snow was imminent.

It took me another half hour to reach the crest
of the ridge. Once there I stopped, panting and
sweating, and took out the small handheld radio.
The set was tuned to channel 37, a VHF frequency
that had once been used for contacting marinas
and boatyards in British waters, and which I
doubted anyone other than David would be monitoring. "I'm on your skyline," I told him.

David answered immediately. "Shore party,

shore party, this is *Stormchild, Stormchild*. Took your time strolling up that hill, didn't you? Can you see anything. Over."

"Nothing." Facing me was not, as I had hoped, a long, shallow slope leading down to the mine workings, but rather a wide bleak saddle that looked suspiciously marshy. I took the binoculars from my bag and searched the high plateau, but nothing moved there except the long grasses that rippled under the wind's cold touch. "What's the glass doing?" I asked David.

"Shore party, shore party, this is *Stormchild*. The barometer is still dropping. It is now showing thirty and a half inches. I say again. Three zero point five inches. Over."

"You mean a thousand and thirty-three millibars?" I teased him.

"I mean thirty and one half English inches, and not some ridiculous French standard of measurement." David was incorrigibly old-fashioned in such matters. "Over."

The glass had read 1042 millibars when I woke, which meant that it was dropping more steeply than I had hoped. That drop indicated that a depression threatened us, a threat heralded by the freshness of the wind that I thought was probably stiffening. "If the glass goes on falling at this rate," I advised David, "then you'd better think of making it to sea."

"Shore party, shore party, this is *Stormchild*. I agree. I'll read the glass again in one hour and then decide. May I now suggest you conserve your battery power? Out."

I dutifully switched off the little radio, shoved it deep into my bag, and marched on. From now on I would be out of sight of *Stormchild,* which meant that the VHF radios, which worked only on line of sight, would be blanketed into silence.

The upland saddle proved to be more than just marshland; it was a stretch of ice-cold bog land that sucked at my boots and sapped what little strength I had left. At times, missing my footing on the firmer tussocks, I would plunge up to a thigh in the wet, peaty mess. It had begun to drizzle, but soon that drizzle turned into a chill rain that thickened into a miserable downpour that blotted out the horizon like sea fog. I had not thought to bring one of my old prismatic compasses, but I doubted I would get lost, for if the charts were right then the dead end of the Desolate Straits, where Berenice assured me the limestone workings were built, lay just beyond the saddle's eastern ridge, which, in turn, was no more than a mile away, yet already the marshland had consumed over two hours of painful, wet, slow struggle. I tried to console myself that some people paid small fortunes to be just so discomfited as they stalked deer on the Scottish hills, but the consolation did not help.

At last the going became firmer and the upward slope steeper, evidence that I was reaching the far side of the saddle. Rain was dripping from my hat and my boots squelched with every step. The cold was seeping into my bones, while my heels had been rubbed into painful blisters. Off to my left I could see a rocky peak which looked uncannily like one of the granite tors on Dartmoor, while directly ahead of me the skyline seemed to be crowned with a rampart of ice blocks. It was not until I was within a few paces of the blocks that I saw they were actually pale limestone boulders that were scattered along the ridge line above the quarry and where, winded, sore, and tired, I collapsed onto the wet turf and stared eastward.

Far off, dim through the smearing rain, were the slopes of the Andes, while nearer, though still watered into obscurity, was the labyrinth of islands and twisting channels that made this coast so tangled and broken. It was, despite the rain, a magnificent view, yet beneath me was something that interested me far more—the limestone workings. I had come, at last, to Genesis's inner citadel.

The most obvious, and the ugliest, evidence of the old limestone workings was the quarry itself— a vast open scar that must have been a full half mile across and six hundred feet deep, and which had been ripped out of the hillside to leave a curving artificial cliff that faced toward the headwaters of the Desolate Straits. Trickles of peaty-brown water made miniature falls over the cliff; falls that tumbled hundreds of feet to the quarry floor which was cut into vast terraces so that it looked like an amphitheater for giants, littered with jagged boulders, dotted with pools, and strewn with shale and the detritus of the explosions that had once ripped the limestone out of the hill's belly. Dark holes in the quarry's sides betrayed where mine shafts had been driven horizontally into the mountain. To my left, beyond the big quarry, I could see a second and much smaller quarry, which appeared to face directly onto the straits.

At the seaward side of the larger quarry's floor, where the amphitheater spilled its dark, wet litter of shale toward the sea, was a group of rusting and ugly buildings. The buildings were dwarfed by the quarry's size, yet when I examined them through the binoculars and counted the flights of iron steps that zigzagged up the flank of the largest structure, I realized just how huge the old sheds were. The largest one, a great gaunt structure, seemed big enough to house an airship. The buildings were grouped together, sloping roof touching sloping roof, presumably so that the men who had once lived and worked in this god-awful place would never have needed to expose themselves to Patagonia's merciless weather. I raised the glasses a fraction to see a covered loading ramp sloping down from the large building toward the stone pier that jutted into the Desolate Straits. The profits from limestone must have been huge to have made it worthwhile to bring in all that corrugated iron and timber and machinery.

I could see no one moving around the buildings, or on the hugely stepped floor of the quarry. No boats broke the wind-chopped surface of the straits beyond, though the lip of the quarry hid the closest stretch of water from my high viewpoint. The limestone works seemed deserted; indeed, they looked as though they had been deserted for years, and I felt a twinge of anxiety that Berenice might have invented her story of

Nicole using the mine as her sanctuary.

There was only one way to find the truth, and that was to descend into the quarry. I meant to keep my promise to David, so, before making any move, I used the binoculars to search the lip of the small quarry, then to painstakingly investigate the larger quarry and all its buildings again. I stared hard at every door and window, yet I saw nothing threatening, and the only movement in the quarry was the rippling of the rain-speckled pools under the wind's lash.

Still I waited as the rain pelted onto the empty landscape. I had a flask of cold tea and a great slab of fruitcake that I consumed as a second breakfast while I watched the old workings for any signs of life. I was soaked and chilled to the bone, yet I endured the discomfort for a full hour, seeing neither man nor beast. The only oddity, apart from the fact that the quarry and its buildings existed at all, was a tractor that was parked beside one of the ramshackle sheds, but even with the binoculars it was impossible to tell whether the machine had been abandoned fifty years before or just left there a few hours ago. After a further half hour, during which I became increasingly certain that the limestone works were deserted, I picked up my gun and bag and walked down the right-hand edge of the quarry.

It should have been a moment of heightened apprehension, even drama. For years I had dreamed of finding my daughter, and now, miraculously, half a world away from home, I was carrying a gun into the heart of von Rellsteb's mad empire. Nicole might be just a mile away from me, and, even if she was at sea, I still hoped that I would find some evidence that she was innocent of anything worse than a fanatical desire to cleanse the planet. I tried to buoy up my anticipation, to tell myself that I was on the brink of a dream's fulfillment, but I was too wet and too cold and too aching and too tired to feel the proper apprehension.

So, numbed by cold, I stumbled downhill. I splashed through peaty streams and tripped on thick tussocks of springy grass. My throat was sore and I prayed that it was not the first symptom of a cold. There was still no movement by the huge sheds, which, as I came closer, appeared more and more dilapidated. Whole roof sheets of corrugated iron had been ripped away by the winds to leave rotten holes, in which only the beams were left exposed. Other iron sheets, half loosened by the storms, creaked and flapped in the wind. Rainwater poured off the sloping roofs, cascading through the broken sheets into the shadowed shed interiors. Where there was paint on window frames or doors it was peeling and cracked. The place looked as miserable and deserted as an abandoned whaling station on a remote Antarctic island.

I stopped a quarter mile from the rusted sheds and again examined them through my binoculars, but still I saw nothing to worry me. I gazed for a long, long time, but saw no one move across the sodden quarry floor or past one of the windows. The quarry, and its old works, seemed as empty as the backside of the moon.

I reached the bottom of the hill. Now I was just a hundred yards from the sheds. Still nothing threatened me. If an ambush had been set, then the ambushers were being as silent as the grave, but I felt no instinctive apprehension of danger. I only felt the anticipation of disappointment, for it seemed ridiculous that I might find anything of value in this rusted, derelict place. I looked at my watch and reckoned I had time to search for three or four hours and still be back at the fjord long before dusk, and the thought of returning to *Stormchild* made me long to sit in front of her saloon heater with a hot whiskey-toddy. That tantalizing vision made me wonder whether *Stormchild* would be waiting when I returned. The rain was falling more heavily and the wind blowing more strongly than it had at dawn; the gale David feared might be swirling its way toward the coast and David might already have taken *Stormchild* to safety on the last of the morning's ebb tide. I hoped he would be there nonetheless, for I was soaked through, the rain was leaking down the collar of my coat, and the temptation of *Stormchild*'s spartan comforts was a torment as I paused once more to search the quarry buildings with the binoculars. No one moved there, nothing threatened, and so, throwing caution to the wind, I splashed through puddles made milk-white by limestone dust to push open the nearest door that hung ajar off ancient rusted hinges.

I found myself in an old stable, a reminder that these limestone workings must once have been powered by ponies or mules. No one waited for me. No one shouted a warning. I seemed utterly alone as I walked past the old stalls and under the cacophony of the metal roof being tortured by the rising wind. Water dripped and trickled onto the cobbled floor. Some of the stalls still had their iron feeding baskets, while in a couple there were even frayed head ropes hanging.

Next to the stables, and in equal disrepair, were the bunkrooms where the quarrymen had slept. The windows were broken and the old wooden floor was rotted and covered with bird droppings. A faded calendar was tacked to one wall. I gingerly crossed the room, treading only where nail heads betrayed the existence of joists under the decaying floorboards, and I saw that the yellowing calendar was for the month of *Dezember,* 1931. The script was a big, black, ornate German gothic. There was a photograph, faded almost to invisibility, that showed a tram in front of a big stone building, while two uniformed men, presumably the vehicle's proud crew, stood with chests thrust out by the tram's steps.

I walked through a door on which the faded word *Waschraum* was painted in the same black-letter as the calendar. The washroom consisted of lavatory stalls and two zinc-lined troughs. The lavatories were blackened and broken, while the troughs had collapsed under a welter of old water pipes. The roof of this room was almost entirely missing and the rain poured in to make a huge puddle on the decayed floor. Moss and weeds grew thick in some of the broken lavatories, while the stalls still bore their pre-war graffiti, mute wit-

nesses to the lonely frustrations of breaking limestone from this quarry at the world's bitter end.

I went through another door and edged carefully down a passage from which a number of small
rooms opened to my right. Some of the rooms still
held the rusted metal frames of old cot beds, and I
assumed that the quarry's managers had once
slept here. The windows offered fine views of the
Desolate Straits' blind end where the deceptive
waterway widened into an immense and sheltered
pool and in which a great ship could easily have
turned its full length before docking beside the
quarry's pier. Berenice had told us how Genesis
had begun using this anchorage because it was so
much more sheltered than the bay at the settlement, and I could see the sense of that decision,
for this great sea pool had to be one of the most
secure anchorages I had ever seen. It was also an
empty anchorage, unless I counted a half-sunken
rusted barge that lay at the seaward end of the old
pier. On the southern side of the bay was a stone
quay which was backed by a row of low stone
buildings. Beside the quay was a slipway up which
two steel rails ran, evidence that boats could, as
Berenice had said, be drawn safely out of the water
in this place, but there was no sign of any activity
on the quay or on the slipway. There were no
yachts or dinghies in sight, just the wet wind, the
cold rain, and the empty straits.

The absence of any boats disappointed and
relaxed me. I was disappointed because their
absence surely meant that Nicole was not here,
but it also meant that no one else from Genesis

waited in this dreadful spot, and that, therefore, I
could not possibly be in any danger. I decided my
enemies must have sailed northward, gone to
intercept *Stormchild* off Cape Raper.

I went through another door and stopped in
sheer amazement. I was also overcome with sudden fear because I found myself standing on a
rickety wooden platform high above a machinery
floor. The timbers under my feet creaked ominously, and it seemed as if one more step would
splinter the old wood and tumble me forty feet
down to the floor.

I had entered the largest of all the quarry's buildings, the tall gaunt shed, which I now saw had been
built above and around an excavated pit, and it was
in that huge stone pit, shadowed dark beneath me,
that the quarry's old machinery rusted into powder.

The quarry had been dug to produce limestone.
The great rocks, once they had been exploded and
dragged out of the mountain, had entered the
building to my left and then been processed
through the massive crushers and grinders
beneath me until, turned into rubble and powder,
they had gone spilling down the ramp on my
right and into the holds of ships waiting at the
pier. Then, carried to Europe or to North America
or to Australia, the limestone had been manufac-
tured into cement, lime wash, or fertilizer. There
was still something very impressive about the gargantuan and silent machinery, and its presence in
this lost corner of a vast continent was evidence of
a nineteenth-century determination to conquer
the world and all its resources.

Gingerly, fearfully, I crept down the ramshackle stairs. I became more confident when I saw that the old wooden treads were supported by cast-iron moldings, but it was still with a sense of relief that I reached the machine-hall floor and could walk among the huge, silent engines that were now useless rust. In their day they had been engineering marvels, massively powerful machines that still bore the proud cast-iron plaques that boasted of the towns where they had been forged: Essen, Dortmund, and Bochum. Above the great machines were the giant spindles which had once held the slapping leather belts that had carried power from a bank of huge steam engines built on the pit's lip. Those old steam engines were still there, though they had clearly been the first of the machines to fall silent, their power supplanted by the row of squat diesel generators that looked as if they had come from some First World War battleship. The huge room was like a museum of industrial ingenuity, a great rusting museum. When I kicked a rusting bolt with my right boot the sound echoed forlornly in the huge, dank space.

"How very clever you are to find us, Mr. Blackburn," the voice said when the bolt's last echo died away.

"Oh my God! Jesus Christ!" I blasphemed, twisted down, and huddled into a rust-flaked corner of a machine where I unslung the rifle from my shoulder. My heart was thumping like a runaway jackhammer. I could not see the speaker, and the echoes of the great room made it hard to tell from where he had spoken, but I recognized the voice. It was Caspar von Rellsteb.

"Von Rellsteb!" I shouted.

"Of course! Who else did you expect to find here? Santa Claus, perhaps?" He paused, and, though I looked frantically around, I still could not see him. Von Rellsteb, as if comprehending my panic, laughed. "Or perhaps you expected to find Nicole and the pirated Genesis boats hidden here. Is that what Berenice told you? She has spun that yarn before. Last year she hitched a ride on a visiting Australian yacht and told a wonderful tale of enslavement, and of a worldwide AIDS epidemic, and of pirated boats that we hid at the very end of the Desolate Straits. Such an imagination for a little American girl, eh?" Von Rellsteb laughed again. "Her imagination brought the Chilean police here, and we had two or three weeks of unnecessary trouble before they realized the poor girl was simply unstable. We offered to fly her home to her mother, but, at the last moment, she chose to come back to us. I sometimes regret she made that choice, but we think of all our community's members as family, and, as in every family, love cannot help but take the good with the bad. Isn't that so, Mr. Blackburn?"

I worked a round into the Lee-Enfield's chamber. The rifle's bolt made a very loud noise that echoed menacingly in the tall, dripping, wind-chilled chamber.

I heard von Rellsteb's footsteps grate somewhere close by, but the acoustics of the shed made it almost impossible to detect just where he was. He sighed. "Your caution is misplaced, Mr. Blackburn.

Do come out. I'm entirely alone, and I have no weapons. But I need to apologize to you! My people were stupid to have fired on you when you visited the settlement two days ago. It was purely a reaction of fear and nervousness. Our little community lives a most sheltered life here, and any incursion from the outside world tends to unsettle us."

I slipped off the rifle's safety catch. Was von Rellsteb's voice coming from the right? I peered that way and saw nothing.

"Did you hear me, Mr. Blackburn? I apologize most profoundly, and am only glad that no one got hurt at the settlement. We're re-evaluating our policy on guns, so I hope it will never happen again. Please do come out. Please."

I straightened up, then edged very cautiously round the ponderous rock-crushing machine that had sheltered me. I still could not see von Rellsteb. I thought how furious David would be, for I had done everything I had promised him I would not do, and everything that he had warned me against, which meant that all our careful planning had been shot to hell.

"Good morning!" the voice said behind me, and I whipped the rifle round to see von Rellsteb standing just thirty feet away. He smiled, then spread his empty hands to show that he was indeed unarmed. "Good morning," he said again, and with an intonation that chided me for not responding to his first friendly greeting.

I still did not respond, but just watched him. He was wearing red and black oilskins, sea boots, and a black woolen hat into which he had crammed his long gray hair. He seemed amused by my wary scrutiny. "If I was going to kill you," he said, "I would already have done so. Please put your gun down. I fear that Berenice has filled your head with the most nonsensical fancies. No doubt she told you that Nicole might be found here? Is that right?"

I said nothing. I was again struck by the intelligence in his face, and I had the weirdest and most uncomfortable impression that he was reading my thoughts.

"You've come to see Nicole, of course," he went on as though my silence was an agreeable response to his remarks, "and I know she's delighted that you're here! It was the greatest pity that she wasn't at the settlement when you visited two days ago, but she's waiting there now."

"You lying bastard," I blurted out.

"Oh, Mr. Blackburn." A look of injured sadness crossed von Rellsteb's sensitive face. "What has Berenice told you? That Nicole and I have arguments? That Nicole has taken refuge here, while the rest of us live at the settlement? What nonsense. Nicole very nearly wrote to you after she received the letter you gave me in Florida, but in the end she decided that our policy of separation should be preserved. But when she heard you were here! She was excited, so excited! And she still is! In fact she's waiting at the settlement right now!" Von Rellsteb looked at his wristwatch. "If we hurry we might reach the farm by mid-afternoon, and we can have tea with her. Nicole is very fond of her afternoon tea. It's a rather English trait, and one that the rest of us often tease her about."

I aimed the rifle at his long, thin face. "Say a prayer, you smug bastard."

"Would you rather I brought Nicole here? I will, of course, if you insist." His German-accented voice implied I was being unreasonably difficult, and his self-possession and charm were beginning to make me doubt my own reason. "Fetching Nicole will take time," he went on calmly, as though I was not threatening him with a rifle, "and frankly I can't do it in much under five or six hours." He paused to let me admit the force of his objections, but I said nothing, which prompted von Rellsteb to offer me a disappointed smile. "You're lucky she's here at all," he went on, "because she was planning to spend some days on the lower islands to conduct some seismic studies for the government. That's a great nuisance. When we first came here we were welcomed by the Chilean authorities"—he laughed confidingly, as though he was about to make a private jest that only he and I might understand—"or rather by the old General, *el Presidente*, Pinochet. He liked all things German, you see, so I was definitely flavor of the month." Von Rellsteb enlarged his explanation by clicking his heels together and putting a forefinger like a moustache on his upper lip. He chuckled. "Now we must make ourselves welcome in more useful ways, and the Ministry of the Interior believes there may be silver deposits in the archipelago, and they asked us to make the survey, so, naturally, we're complying. But to be

really honest with you, Mr. Blackburn, I'm not
sure we want to find any mineral deposits, because
exploiting the discoveries is certain to threaten the
ecology of the islands, so I rather think
that Nicole is falsifying the returns!" He chuckled.
"A small deception, but one that is surely justified
by the scenery of these islands. It's magnificent
scenery, isn't it?"

"Does the Chilean government supply you with
the necessary explosives for seismic tests?" I asked.

I had hoped the mention of explosives might
unsettle von Rellsteb, but he seemed entirely
unfazed by my suspicions. "The Ministry of Mines
issues us with the necessary operating permits, of
course, but, in fact, we fetch our dynamite from
commercial suppliers in Valparaíso." He looked at
his watch again. "I'm enjoying talking to you, but
if I'm to fetch Nicole I really should leave."

"Radio the settlement," I said. I was staring at
him through the open ring battle sight of the rifle.

"Alas"—he smiled—"I came here in a sea kayak
and didn't think to bring a radio."

"I've got one," I said.

"Splendid! But I fear it won't transmit from this
rock pit!" Von Rellsteb gestured about the high
walls of the machine hall which would, indeed,
block any transmission. "But if you want to climb
the outside stairs to the roof you can talk to the
settlement. They monitor channel 16. The reception is sometimes a bit erratic, but if you persevere
you should succeed. Please." He took a pace backward and courteously invited me to walk to the
staircase. I did not move. Von Rellsteb smiled and

still held his hand toward the stairs. "Nicole might very well answer herself"—he enticed me—"she often takes a radio watch about this time of day."

I still did not move, nor did I lower the rifle, though in all honesty von Rellsteb had completely unsettled me. He had thrown all my accusations and suspicions out of gear. Had Berenice fed David and me with fantasy? It seemed impossible that von Rellsteb meant me harm, for he was facing me unarmed and he seemed utterly unworried by the threat of my gun. And still he smiled at me, so that I was beginning to feel mesmerized by the piercing blue eyes in his kindly face. Everything he said was so plausible, and I felt my defenses against him weakening.

"Please?" he said again, and gestured to the staircase, then, as though an idea had suddenly struck him, he tapped his hands lightly together. "But this is ridiculous! Your boat must be moored nearby, so why don't you just sail to the settlement! It's ten miles up the straits, that's all. This old mine is such a very uncomfortable place for a family reunion."

"My boat isn't in the straits," I said. My left forearm, bracing the barrel of the Lee-Enfield, was beginning to ache.

Von Rellsteb stared at me with a disbelief that slowly turned into genuine admiration. "Are you moored in the Almagro Channel?" He waited a second, and, when I gave no answer, he shook his head. "No! You can't be! It's never been done!"

I still said nothing. My lips felt dry despite the rain which whirled about the great rusting machines under the broken roof.

Von Rellsteb shook his head in astonishment. "Did you sail up the fjord? Is that what you did? I don't believe it can be done!" He gave me a very suspicious look. "You can't have dared the fjord! I've never risked it, nor has Nicole for that matter, and there isn't much she won't dare in a boat! There can't be more than five feet of water in the entrance to the Almagro Channel!"

"There's over fifty feet!" I said scornfully, and thus I betrayed *Stormchild's* whereabouts to my enemy.

"Thank you, Mr. Blackburn." Von Rellsteb smiled, then abruptly stepped into the shelter of the closest crushing machine as he shouted to his hidden troops. "He's in the Almagro Channel! Johnny? Come with me. Lisl? He's got a rifle, so be careful!" Von Rellsteb was still shouting instructions as he ran away, but he switched into German and it took me a few seconds to make the linguistic transition. I thought he told Lisl to finish me off, then to meet him at the farmhouse.

I had pursued von Rellsteb to the corner of the rock-crushing machine, intending to cut him down, but suddenly the whole high shed echoed with the terrifying sound of automatic gunfire and I saw flecks of brilliant metal appear on the rusting flank of the machine beside my head. It took me a full astonished second to realize that the bright flecks were the strikes of bullets and that the stinging on my cheek was caused by flakes of rusting metal struck off the machine, then I desperately threw myself sideways onto the wet floor, scrabbling in panic for the shelter of the neighboring engine, while all around me the air rang with the ricochet of bullets, the stuttering crash of the gun, and the shout of laughter from the stairway above me. I had a glimpse of a gunman firing at me, the muzzle flames making a pale, bright aureole around the gun's muzzle, then I saw it was not a gunman at all, but a red-haired girl with a long, fierce face. She had to be Lisl, who, I remembered, Berenice had said was Caspar's lover. I tried to bring my rifle to bear on her, but she saw the movement and whipped her fire toward me.

I wriggled desperately into cover. A second gunman opened fire from my right, but his bullets went high and he stopped firing almost immediately. The clangor of the bullets striking the old machinery was much louder than the firing of the guns. I heard people shouting. I thought I identified three voices, one belonged to Lisl, while the other two were mens' voices. Somewhere in the huge machine hall a door slammed hollowly, then I heard the scrape of a huge bolt. From what von Rellsteb had shouted I gathered he must be going to the fjord, where, with one of his gunmen, he would lead the attack on *Stormchild.*

I had to get out, which meant that I had to know where my enemies were so I could get past them. I knew Lisl was above me on the rickety staircase. She had stopped firing, presumably to reload. At least one of the other gunmen was to my right, and the third voice had also seemed to come from that direction. So I should go left toward the landward end of the crushing shed, where the raw limestone had been fed into the huge hoppers. Except my small glimpse of the great machinery room had suggested that the only escape route from the crushing shed was at its eastern end, where the huge ramp angled down toward the sea. So I had to go to my right. I knew I could not stay where I was because my enemies knew where I was hiding, and it could only be moments before they surrounded me.

So run! Yet somehow my tired legs would not move. I was terrified and angry at myself for being gulled by von Rellsteb. The bastard had lied so smoothly, and I had not been able to resist his flattery. Boasting of my achievement I had betrayed *Stormchild*'s whereabouts.

So, to save David, I should run. I knew I had to run. I heard a footfall way off to my right, then, outside the shed, the sudden roar of motorbike engines. I had forgotten about the scrambling bikes, and I cursed myself for thus forgetting because until now I had stood a chance, admittedly very remote, of escaping this place and reaching *Stormchild* before my enemies. But that chance had evaporated with the sound of the bikes as they roared off.

I had to forget *Stormchild* for the moment. My task was to escape this trap, and of all the trap's components I most feared Lisl in her aerie, because to her I was like a mouse under the eye of a hovering falcon. I peered up through a spoke of the nearest machine's huge driving wheel and saw her as a bright-haired shadow in the upper doorway. I raised my rifle, but she saw the movement and opened fire. I flung myself to the left, astonished that there was any strength remaining in my legs, then cannoned off the machine to go in the opposite direction. I ran across the open passage. Lisl was following my abrupt motions with her gun's barrel, hosing bullets across the vast room, but she was too slow and I was safe under cover again.

I crouched, short of breath, terrified, watching the eastern end of the shed where a flood of rainy light showed where the loading ramp spilled its way out of this death trap. Then I saw a man run across that patch of light and I pulled the trigger, much too late, and heard my bullet ricochet off metal to crack against a ceiling girder.

I ran again, and once again Lisl saw me a second too late. Bullets flicked and shrieked and sang and banged through the shed. I sheltered beside a different kind of machine, one that had a crawlspace beneath it. The dank space was no more than a foot high, but it offered me a chance. Lisl would be watching for me in one place, but the crawl space would let me appear in another.

The crawl space was filthy with rust-colored puddles. I hung my bag with its few precious implements about my neck, took a breath, then wriggled my way under the giant machine. The first few feet were easy enough, though I could feel the stinking water soaking through my trousers, but once I was deep under the great mechanism some bolts on its underside snagged on the rope that I still had wrapped about my torso. I dared not use great force to tear myself free, for any noise might betray my predicament.

Instead I slowly edged backward and forward, freeing myself of the obstruction inch by cold inch. I heard voices echoing, the slap of feet again, but my enemies preferred to stalk me rather than rush me, presumably for fear of my rifle. Lisl, worried by my silence or perhaps just trying to flush me out of hiding, fired some shots that rang like bells as they smacked into the iron frame of the machine above me. When she stopped firing I could hear the spent bullets rattle down into the mechanism's rusting bowels.

I paused, watching the passage into which I would emerge. I could see no one there. I twisted my body till it was sideways onto the passage, rolled out, scrambled to my feet, and ran in panicked desperation toward the ramp. It took my enemies a second or two to see me, and another two or three seconds to react. Then Lisl opened fire and her bullets flicked and smacked and whined about me. I knew I did not have time to hurl myself over the ramp's lip, so instead I dived into the shelter of a stone wall that hid me from her deadly perch.

"Where is he?" one of the men demanded.

"Last hopper! This side!" Lisl shouted, then her German-accented voice was abruptly filled with panic. "I said this side! This side!"

Her panic was justified, for the man had mistaken her instructions and now stepped into view just paces from me. He was facing a hopper on the hall's far side and had his back to me, but Lisl's panicked voice whipped him round and his eyes widened with terror as he saw me. He was a broad-shouldered man with a huge and springy beard of tangled brown hair that blossomed wildly across his broad chest. I felt a sudden, wild hope that the bearded man would have the sense to leap back into hiding, thus saving me the need to shoot him, but instead he raised his hands and I saw he was carrying a submachine gun. I was swinging the rifle toward him. I had never shot at anyone in all my life, but he was beginning to flinch as though he feared the noise his own gun would make, and I knew that I had about one second to live if I did not squeeze my trigger first.

So I squeezed my trigger.

He fired, too.

My shot missed. So did his.

The man was screaming as he fired, not because he was hurt, but to disguise his fear. He had fired too soon and his bullets went to my left and kept going away from me as the recoil of the small gun pounded him around. I worked the Lee-Enfield's bolt and heard my ejected cartridge tinkle as it clattered across the stone floor. I raised the rifle, taking better aim then before. The bearded man had managed to control the swing of his gun's shuddering recoil and he was forcing the barrel back toward me. The world was reduced to noise, just noise, a splintering thunder of cartridges and of metal striking stone, and I was probably shouting as loudly as my enemy, then I fired again and the man just leapt backward as though he had been yanked off his feet by a hidden steel cable, and then there was a sudden silence.

Rainwater dripped on the floor. The wind fretted and creaked at a sheet of corrugated iron. The man I had shot took a breath that sounded like the workings of an ancient bellows. I worked the rifle's bolt. I had fired three bullets, or was it four? I knew I should count the magazine down so as not to be trapped without ammunition. I was sure it was three. My breath was coming in panicked gulps. I could see the bearded man's legs protruding from behind a wooden hooper. He was wearing a green jerkin, brown corduroy trousers, and old climbing boots with worn vibram soles. One of his legs was jerking spasmodically. His breathing sounded awful, like bubbles and scraping gravel and unimaginable pain. I thought I was going to be sick. I had a sudden vivid memory of the man's blood pulsing bright in the air as he jerked backward.

"Chris is hit!" Lisl's voice was shocked.

"Where is he?" another voice shouted.

The man called Chris suddenly screamed. It was a terrible scream.

I moved. I ran out from the wall. I turned and looked up. Lisl was leaning over the balustrade. I brought the rifle up and stared at her through the open battle sight. She was turning her gun toward me, then, seeing me and fearing my shot, she leaped backward like a scalded cat.

I turned and ran the few steps to the great ramp that sloped down to the pier and the sea. Wooden steps ran down beside a huge metal-lined chute that had once carried the crushed lime to the waiting ships and now I hurled myself onto its metal lining and slid down as though it was a giant slide in a childrens' playground. Except that this slide was rusted, and bolts snagged me, and I part rolled and part slid and sometimes scrambled my way down to the bottom. I heard something break in the bag of supplies that I still carried about my neck.

The man called Chris still screamed behind me. The sound of his agony faded as I escaped, or almost escaped, for a sudden whine and whipcrack told me that I was being fired at. The sound of the gun echoed down the ramp's tunnel. The bullets missed, then, bruised and bleeding, I spilled over the ramp's end onto the flagstoned surface of the old quay.

I looked up one side of the chute to see another bearded man running down the steps with a gun in his hand. I aimed, fired, and missed. The man suddenly realized how vulnerable he was and turned. I fired again, but the range was long, I was firing uphill into shadows and the man was running fast. I fired a third time, missed yet again and saw the man make an ungainly leap off the stairs and into cover.

I ran down the quay. The rain bounced to make a fine spray on the flagstones. Beneath me, on a small shingle beach where they were concealed from the sea by a ridge of rocks, were four sea kayaks. Two of the slender craft were single-seaters, while the others had two small cockpits apiece. Six paddles lay alongside the kayaks. I jumped down, painfully turning an ankle as I landed. The slender craft were made of fiberglass. I walked past their sharp prows, firing into their bellies. A bullet apiece

was enough to make sure that the kayaks could not
be used in a hurry, but I had to change magazines
to finish the job and the delay betrayed my whereabouts to my enemies. Suddenly their bullets began
whipping at the quay's edge above me, chipping
scraps of stone that dropped around me. I slung the
kayak's six paddles far out into the water, where,
with any luck, they would float away.

Six paddles for six canoeists? If I had understood von Rellsteb's parting instructions, then he
had taken one other person to help capture
Stormchild. Which left four at the mine, one of
whom was screaming with a bullet in his guts.
Was Nicole here? No, I could not believe my
daughter would conspire for my death, though
now, still shivering from the gunfight, I did not
really understand anything except that I had
sailed ten thousand miles to discover nightmare.

Another bullet flicked overhead. I wondered if
one gunman was trying to trap me on the small
beach while the others came down the ramp to
finish me off. I looked to my right and saw that I
could stay in the shelter of the stone quay all the
way to a jumble of dark rocks which lay at the
base of a broken and torn cliff. The rocks extended
far along the shore, and I guessed that once I was
in their cover I would be safe. I limped to their
shelter. It was low tide and the stones were slippery with rain and weed, but I found a deep cleft
that offered me complete protection from any
gunmen in the buildings, and, deep in the cleft's
protective shadow, I paused to catch my breath
and to plan my next move. I was sobbing, not

with pain, but with a kind of self-disgust. Then I forgot my misery for, far above me, and muffled by distance and half drowned by the rush of wind and rain, there was a sudden shot. The screaming of the man called Chris abruptly ended.

"Oh, my God," I murmured in prayer. I had caused a man's death. I had not meant it to be like this. Mingled sweat and rain were running down my face. I refilled the Lee-Enfield's empty magazine. My fingers were cold and clumsy, or perhaps they were shaking because I had killed a man. I was shivering. They would be coming for me. These people were ruthless. Christ! They took no prisoners and left no wounded, not even their own. I knew I must do something. I had to think!

Von Rellsteb had been waiting for me, expecting me. That was the premise from which to start. I had to work out what they wanted, and therefore what they might do, and only then could I decide what I should do, except that whenever I tried to think logically the panic and adrenaline distracted and unnerved me, making me so jumpy that I twisted and almost fired when a kelp goose paddled into view at the seaward end of my hiding place. I tried to relax, but I was shivering uncontrollably.

They had been waiting for me. They knew I would come to the mine and not to the settlement. Why?

They had known I would come to the mine, but they had not foreseen everything. They had expected *Stormchild* to sail up the Desolate Straits, presumably passing the settlement in the darkness, and they had taken care to have their kayaks hidden so that on *Stormchild's* arrival we would have assumed that the limestone workings were abandoned, and once we had gone ashore they would have attacked us because they wanted us silenced, and, doubtless, because they wanted our boat. That was obvious. They wanted *Stormchild.*

They wanted *Stormchild,* yet von Rellsteb's plans to capture her had gone awry when I chose to use the Almagro Channel. But, once my presence in the limestone workings had been detected, von Rellsteb had quickly regrouped his forces and had then dealt brilliantly with me, which meant that by now, unless David had put up a stout fight or had already taken her to sea, *Stormchild* was probably captured, David and Berenice likely dead. But I could not think about those possible disasters, not while a different disaster still threatened to overwhelm me.

I was still not thinking straight. I was shaking and cold and blaming myself. I had been so certain the Genesis boats would sail north to pursue *Stormchild,* but von Rellsteb had known I would come for my daughter. I had done everything he had expected me to do, except for one thing. He had expected me to die, and I was alive.

Now it was time to defy von Rellsteb. It was time, God help me, to fight—for David, for myself, and for Nicole.

It took me about ten minutes to realize that I had trapped myself between a she-devil and a cold, flooding sea. I had thought myself entirely safe in the cleft, which hid me from every landward vantage point, but I had forgotten the tide. The straits, agitated by a strengthening wind, were rising fast, and the icy flooding water would very soon force me out of my hiding place and into the waiting sights of Lisl and her gunmen.

I knew they would be watching for me. They must have realized I was hidden somewhere in the bleak tangle of rocks on the foreshore, and that if I did not break cover soon I would drown or else die of hypothermia in the rising waters. The wind suddenly seemed bitterly cold. It was blowing ever more strongly, gusting close to gale force as it flecked the water behind me white. The deterioration of the weather gave me hope that David

would have decided to take *Stormchild* out through
the fjord's gut into the wide, safe ocean, and
would already be beating his way offshore and
waiting for my radio signal.

The thought of the radio made me remember
how something had broken during my panicked
and bruising descent of the old lime chute. I
opened the bag and fished out the small handheld
radio, which, to my relief, proved to be intact. It
had been the right-hand barrel of my binoculars
that had broken. I shook the scraps of broken lens
and the useless prism out of the barrel and pushed
the now half-useful glasses back into the bag.
Then, in desperate hope, I switched on the radio
and tuned it to channel 37. "*Stormchild, Stormchild!*
This is Tim. Do you read me? Over."

I released the transmitter button and heard
nothing but an empty hiss from the speaker. A
small red light glowed to show me that the radio's
battery was still strong, but rather than waste its
electricity in vain I switched the set off. I was
shadowed by the cliffs and high hills, so only
some freak meteorological condition might have
bounced my signal to wherever *Stormchild* was; if
indeed *Stormchild* still floated, or was in friendly
hands that knew which channel to monitor.

I put the radio in the bag, then ate my last piece
of hoarded fruitcake which I washed down with
the dregs of the cold tea. The incoming tide was
surging up to my feet and I knew I must move
very soon. I peered over the rocks to stare at the
limestone workings. I saw no movement there,
but that did not mean my enemies were not scan-

ning the shrinking shoreline for a sign of me. I ducked down again, slung the bag and rifle on my shoulder, then crawled under the cover of the seaweed-stinking rocks to the base of the cliff.

I had decided that Lisl and her companions would expect me to break cover along the shore, scrambling over the slippery rocks to put more distance between myself and their guns, but I had seen another route out of my predicament, and that route lay directly upward.

In my younger days I had been a halfway decent rock climber. I had never approached the finest standards, but I had been good. When we were schoolboys David and I had often hitchhiked on holiday weekends to the Lake District or Snowdonia and, equipped with a second-hand rope and some scavenged pitons, we would tackle some dangerously severe climbs. I had been the daring one; indeed one word of caution from David had usually been sufficient to send me up some dizzyingly fearful crag while he cringed below. Later, on an army climbing expedition to the Dolomites, I had suffered a crippling bout of vertigo that had persuaded me to abandon rocks in favor of seawater. These days not all the tea in China could have persuaded me onto some of the frightful rock faces I had so blithely climbed as a youth, yet the cliff above the rocky shoreline offered me the only sheltered and unguarded route out of my flooding hideout, so it was time to swallow my fears and start upward.

The cliff, even though it was running with rainwater, was not a difficult climb, but its broken stone made me nervous and my stomach churned sourly as I moved steadily up. It was not the holds that unnerved me—they were firm and wide—but every time I looked down I saw the sea foaming white in the fissures of the rocks, and each such pulsing surge opened the pit in my belly like a greased trapdoor. I forced myself to ignore the seething sea and the clutching wind, and just to keep climbing steadily. I edged northward as I went, going still further from the gunmen, aiming to reach the hill above the quarry. From there I would find a safe place in which to plan my next moves. A good soldier, when in doubt, always goes for the high ground.

But that maxim was also appreciated by my enemies, and they had an easier route than I to that high ground. My first intimation that they were not looking for me from the buildings, but had reached the cliff top before me, was when some stones and turf clattered down the rock face to my left.

I froze. I could hear the voices of a man and a woman above me, and I supposed that Lisl and one of the Genesis gunmen were patroling the cliff's edge in search of me. And, judging by the loudness of the two voices, I had only a few moments before they found me.

To my right I could just see the smaller quarry that I had first glimpsed from the high ridge above the main workings. This smaller excavation was about a hundred feet deep and half as wide across. The smallness of the quarry suggested that it was the place where the first von Rellsteb to colonize this coast had begun his search for limestone, which beginnings he had later abandoned for the more promising deposits to the south. Whatever, the remains of his first diggings provided me with almost perfect cover, and, trying hard not to make any noise, I edged my way toward it. I was aiming for a ledge which ran round the quarry's face like a balcony. The ledge was wide enough to have trapped soil washed from the hill above, and a thick canopy of scrub, stunted beech trees, wild fuchsia, and giant ferns offered me a perfect hiding place. I glanced up, saw nothing of my pursuers, and risked a swift scramble across the soaking rock face.

But the risk proved too great. A shout from above betrayed that I had been seen. I heard Lisl's voice call out in triumph, then a bullet hissed and cracked through the rain not far from my right ear. I swore in panic, then scrambled over the ledge's lip and wriggled deep into the base of the soaking bushes where I burrowed like a desperate animal into the heart of the undergrowth. A nesting bird squawked away in panicked wing beats. I thrust myself into the wet leaves, trying to flatten myself against the cliff face in the hope that I was somehow rendering myself invisible.

I may have been hidden, but my enemies knew they had me trapped. They could shoot me whenever I broke cover. They began firing down at the ledge's thick foliage in an attempt to flush me into the open. I was temporarily safe from their efforts because a slight outcrop of the rock above offered me protection, but that same rock bulge also prevented me from firing back at my enemies.

I shivered. The gunfire snapped angrily, its sound diminished by the rising wind. The bullets flicked the leaves and cracked into stone. Ricochets whined down to the base of the quarry, which, except for a small rain-flecked pool, was as thickly overgrown with scrub as the ledge on which I had trapped myself. I seemed to have a talent for being on low ground with an enemy above me, but I had escaped before, and I would have to escape again. The trick of this escape, I decided, was to persuade Lisl and her companion that they had killed me.

I had been sitting with my knees drawn tight against my body so that no part of me showed under the overhang. I stayed in that cramped position, but slowly, very slowly, and very awkwardly, I unlooped the nylon rope from my torso. Near me was the relatively thick trunk of a stunted beech tree, about which I threaded the forty-foot length of line with a small silent prayer that the beech roots had enough grip in the ledge's damp and friable soil to hold my weight. I then wrapped the two ends of the line round my waist, fastened them in place with bowlines, and concealed the knots beneath my jacket. What I planned depended on my enemies not knowing that I had fashioned this lifesaving tether.

Then, with the knotted rope hidden at my waist, I slithered toward the lip of the small quarry. Once over that lip I would be hidden from the view of anyone at the top of the cliff. The greatest immediate danger was that my enemies would see the movement of the leaves and bushes as I pushed through them, but the wind was heaving the branches and I moved with exquisite care. The rain sheeted down, blinding me and, I hoped, my enemies, too. As I wriggled I shoved the telltale double strand of pale-colored rope under leaves and bushes to further conceal it.

When I reached the lip of the ledge I peered over to discover that the artificially made rock face was an almost sheer drop of forty feet, though I could just see a jagged sloping ledge some eight feet below the lip. That ledge would have to be enough for my survival.

I closed my eyes for a few seconds. I was praying. Unlike my brother I did not often pray, because I believed God's usefulness, like that of any other piece of emergency equipment, decreased according to how often He was used. This moment, poised above the cliff face, was one of those rare occasions when I needed divine aid, so I uttered a fervent prayer that God would hold me in His precious hand for the next few terrifying seconds.

Then slowly, I raised my face until I could see the heads of my enemies. The two of them seemed to be lying full-length at the lip of the cliff to peer down into the quarry. Lisl was recognizable from her bright red hair, while her companion had a shaggy black beard and, tied around his forehead, a bright yellow headband. The two were some sixty feet above me and perhaps fifty feet to my right. I lifted the rifle, then began to stand upright. I was on the very edge of the quarry, its lip and sheer drop just an inch behind my boots. As I stood I twisted my upper body to the right so that I could aim at the black-bearded man. I stood fully upright. The two had still not seen me. The thick, wet ferns reached up to my waist, hiding the twin strands of line that hung beneath my jacket. The two heads were outlined against a dark gray sky, in which the rain slashed silver.

O God of sailormen, I prayed, be with me now, and then I fired. A chunk of rock spat off the cliff's rim just a few inches from the man's unkempt beard. He gasped and jerked back. I worked the bolt, fired again, worked the bolt, and fired a third time. I was no longer aiming, just snapping shots wildly at the place where the two heads had flinched back. Then, blessedly, they both pushed the barrels of their assault rifles over the cliff and, without exposing themselves to take aim, blindly ripped off two full magazines of bullets in my general direction.

God was indeed keeping me safe for the unaimed bullets whipped far above my head.

The crack of the two Genesis rifles was snatched into the wind and rain. I waited till the last ejected cartridge had flickered bright in the day's gloom, then I screamed.

I screamed as though the devil had taken my soul in his bare claws and was tearing it from my guts. I screamed in an awful agony, and, as I made that dreadful shriek into the sky and at the wind, I watched the cliff top and, sure enough, the yellow headband suddenly appeared there, then Lisl's face showed alongside the bearded face, and I had already thrown my arms up in the air, letting the rifle tumble and fall into the void behind me. I followed it, still screaming, and anyone watching me must have thought that I had been hit by a bullet and was now falling backward, spread-eagled, off the rock face and into the deep quarry.

As I fell out of my enemies' sight I scrabbled to get a grip on the doubled rope to soak up some of its impact, and I also twisted around so that my belly and not my spine would take the force of the line's tightening. The rope snaked above me and I had a sudden terror that the line must have come free from the stump. I was certain I must have fallen more than the six feet I had bargained for, but then, abruptly, and with a sickening shock, the rope snapped taut. Being nylon, the doubled line stretched, but still the force was worse than a kick to the belly. I had been screaming as I fell, but the wrench of rope in my belly drove the wind clean out of me so that my tormented dying shriek was abruptly and very convincingly choked off.

In the sudden silence the rifle clattered and banged its way to the bottom of the quarry.

I struck the cliff, swung, hit the rock again, then hung motionless. I dangled like a dead thing hooked in the gut and strung up to be voided of blood. Except I was alive, and I was hurting. I felt as if the rope had ripped my stomach muscles clean out. I wanted to be sick. My vision had sheeted red and I was choking, but I dared not make a sound, or else my enemies would know I was alive and would climb down the cliff to kill me.

So I hung, and I choked back the sobs as I tried

to drag a desperate breath into my aching lungs. I could hear nothing except the thumping of blood in my ears and a small, slight whimpering noise that I suddenly knew was coming from my bile-sour throat, so I clamped my mouth shut.

Then, from above me, the man in the yellow headband whooped in joyous triumph. "Way to go! Did you see that? Oh, shit! That sucker just learned to fly! Fuckin' A!"

The sucker was trying to find a grip on the cliff face. I had levered myself upright by pulling on the taut rope. Then I felt with the tips of my boots until I discovered the small ledge beneath me and, by pushing up with my toes on that ledge, I was able to take some of the weight off the rope that was threatening to cut me in two. I managed to take in a deep and tentative breath. The absence of any sharp pain in my chest persuaded me that at least no ribs were broken, but I still feared I might have torn some muscles. The pain was excruciating, but I had to ignore it because I needed to get down to the floor of the small abandoned quarry before either Lisl or the triumphant man thought to clamber down the upper cliff to search for my corpse.

I found a finger hold for my left hand, then untied one of the bowlines. I was unsupported now and a slip on the wet rock would finish what my enemies thought they had already accomplished. I tried not to think of the void below as, slowly and agonisingly, I lowered myself until I could get a finger hold on the ledge with my right hand. I looked for holds lower down, but the rain and the hurt were blurring my vision and I dared not wait for my sight to clear. Trusting that the holds were there, I pulled the long rope free. It came reluctantly, constantly snagging on some obstruction on the upper ledge, and once it stuck so hard that I thought I might need to use my rigging knife to cut myself free, but I gave the line one last hard, smooth tug and it slithered loose. I dared not pull too hard or fast for fear that the sudden movement in the ledge's foliage would betray my continued existence. Nor did I dare leave the rope in place in case my enemies explored the ledge. I could hear nothing from the cliff top.

The end of the rope at last fell over the rim of the quarry and collapsed on me. I let the rope dangle from my waist as I edged downward with only my toes and fingers touching the wall. The rock wall was sheeted with running water. My fingers were numb. Blood was seeping from a cut on my left hand.

I looked down, blinking my eyes to clear my vision, and I could just see the stock of my fallen rifle showing at the edge of a bush. If it had fallen another four feet to the right it would have plunged into the small pool. The rest of the quarry floor was thickly covered with scrub and my immediate concern was to reach that shelter undiscovered. A stone fell from above, suggesting that one of my enemies was scrambling down the upper and easier cliff face to make certain I was dead. I looked left and saw no quick route down to the quarry floor, then I looked right and saw, just four feet away, a buttress of rock that resembled an oversized and crooked drainpipe clinging to the quarry's face. I made a desperate lunge, risking the emptiness below, and somehow gripped the top of the buttress, then half fell and half shimmied down to the base of the wall. The pain was making me gasp. I knew I was going too fast, and that I risked making a terrible noise as I crashed into the shrubbery on the quarry's floor, but when I tried to slow my descent I only ripped the skin off my right palm. My boots juddered on the rock, then branches whipped at me, and, gasping and whimpering, I rolled off the rock onto a pile of stones that were covered by a thick umbrella of beech scrub. I felt a horribly sharp blow on my left wrist, and heard a distinct snapping noise at the same instant, but I dared not move to investigate the damage.

Instead I lay like a dead man. I was winded and bruised, but I was making neither noise nor movement. I hurt all over; I hurt so much that it was impossible to distinguish any particular pain in my left wrist, and thus tell if it was broken. I kept my eyes tightly closed, as though to open them would reveal unwilling news about my injuries. Rain smashed into the leaves above me, gurgled down stone gullies around me, and hissed on the black pool behind me. Chunks of stone were cascading down the cliff, evidently dislodged by my pursuers as they scrambled down to the ledge. I was sure they would not risk the climb to the quarry floor. They merely wanted some confirmation that I was indeed dead and, even if they could not see me, they would surely assume from the stillness and silence at the bottom of the pit that I had fallen to my death.

I waited. The stones stopped bouncing and falling. At last, faint through the rain, I heard Lisl's voice way above me. "Is that his gun?"

"Yeah."

Silence again.

"Perhaps he fell in the pool?" Lisl again.

"The sucker couldn't fly, and the sucker sure couldn't swim after that fall. In fact, if you think about it, that sucker isn't much fucking good for anything anymore!" The bearded man laughed.

I counted a minute, then another, then a third. I counted to twenty minutes, and still I did not move. Nor did I hear any movement above me, but I had to assume that my enemies might have the patience to outwait me. I counted a further twenty minutes, marking the seconds with a childish chant I had learned as a Sea Scout—one coconut, two coconut, three coconut, and so on up to sixty coconuts, then back to the first coconut again. And I remembered the damp hut where as a boy I had been taught bowlines and sheepshanks and the rudiments of seamanship, and then I started counting off another coconut-marked minute of my life. Surely they had abandoned me for dead by now? Yet still I waited. The rain was remorseless, and I lay under its chill onslaught for a full hour before, bruised and cramped and cold and wet and hurting, I slowly rolled over and stared upward.

The skyline was empty.

I could hear an engine throbbing somewhere in the distance. It was too deep a throb to be one of the motorbikes and too heavy a sound for the tractor I had seen, and I wondered if the Genesis community kept a generator in the old mine buildings.

I stood. It took me a long time, because I ached all over. No one responded to the rustle of leaves and the clatter of stones dislodged by my boots as I struggled upright. It seemed I was alone and, for the moment, at least, safe.

I looked fearfully at my left wrist only to discover that it was my expensive wristwatch that had taken the full force of the blow and had been broken beyond repair. I took it off and tossed it into the black pool.

My stomach was still a belt of agony. The pain lessened if I bent double so, crouching like Quasimodo, I forced my way through the undergrowth to retrieve the rifle. It seemed undamaged, but I dared not fire a shot to test it. At the seaward side of the quarry was a smaller rock face, no more than twenty feet high, that formed the outer wall of the small excavation. It was hard to climb, and even harder because of the pain in my stomach muscles, but I inched my way up and at last I hooked an elbow over the crest and could stare down into the Desolate Straits.

The engine I was hearing belonged to the fishing boat which had vainly pursued *Stormchild* two days before and which now had steamed up the Desolate Straits and was berthed alongside the pier. Black smoke drizzled from her tall chimney.

The sea kayaks that I had holed with bullets were now piled on her deck. Outboard of the trawler was a catamaran, while in the center of the waterway a stained and weathered sloop lay hove-to. I fished out what was left of my binoculars and trained the single lens on the boats. The sloop turned as I watched and, with a burst of troubled water at her stern, began motoring down the straits toward the far settlement.

I panned to the catamaran, daring to hope it was Nicole's boat, but instead I saw that it was the old catamaran in which von Rellsteb had come to my English river so long ago. I recognized neither of the men on board who now cast off from the trawler and, their engines going, turned to follow the sloop.

The trawler alone was left. Lisl was standing on the pier by the fishing boat's gangplank, from where she stared toward the factory ramp down which I had tumbled. It was evident that she was waiting for something or someone. Above her the gulls wheeled and screamed in the rain. The Desolate Straits looked gray, greasy, and cold, while the colors of the far hills, which only two days before had seemed so bright and heavenly, were now dulled by the rain into a dun drab. I shivered.

I assumed that, obedient to von Rellsteb's parting instructions, the Genesis crews were retreating to the settlement. There they could rendezvous and assess what damage, if any, *Stormchild*'s visit had caused them. If von Rellsteb had captured my boat, then that damage would have been minimal, whereas if David was still free and threatening to carry Berenice's testimony to the authorities, von Rellsteb would urgently need to start his pursuit, and I wondered if the departure of the two yachts was the commencement of that urgent pursuit.

It did indeed look as though every Genesis boat and every Genesis crew member was being committed to *Stormchild*'s chase, for, as far as I could tell, they were leaving the mine workings unguarded. That implied there was very little at the workings worth protecting, but it also indicated that Lisl believed me to be dead. That misconception was my one small advantage over Genesis.

I watched Lisl stamp her feet against the cold, then, panning my broken glass right, I saw what it was she waited for. Two men were struggling toward the fishing boat with the body of the gunman I had wounded, and whom, I suspected, the Genesis group had themselves finished off. Now one man held the corpse by the shoulders of its coat while the other grasped the dead man's ankles. The cadaver's bearded head hung backward so that its long hair brushed at the pier's stones and its huge beard jutted pugnaciously toward the rain clouds. Lisl seemed to shudder and back away from the body's passing. The two men very nearly dropped the corpse into the water as they shuffled across the makeshift gangplank, but at last they had the body safe aboard, and Lisl, still keeping her distance from the dead, cast off the trawler's mooring lines. The engine smoke thickened as, with an awful wheezing and clanking, the decrepit vessel steamed away up the wide straits.

When the fishing boat disappeared I rolled over the lip of the quarry.

No one shot at me. It seemed that no one had been left behind to guard the mine against my ghost. I lay panting and pained on the thin turf, then slowly, when my stomach muscles uncramped, I gathered my strength, stood up, and, using the rifle like a crutch, I limped toward the mine buildings, where I still had a daughter to find.

It was in the low stone buildings, which were built into the hillside at the back of the quay, that I found the first signs of Nicole. The buildings were single-storied, and crouched against the spite of the sea wind like a row of Cornish fishermens' cottages. The buildings were locked, but not locked well enough, and inside I discovered crude and uncomfortable living quarters. Some effort had been made to decorate the five bedrooms; one boasted a livid mural showing a humpback whale venting beside an iceberg, while a second was decorated with a painted effigy of an Indian god, its colors bright as the sun, but mostly the rooms were as characterless and cheerless as an army barracks. I wondered which of the beds Nicole used, though the barrenness of the small bedrooms suggested that they were used only when the severity of the weather drove Nicole's crew out of their boat and into the shelter of the cottage's stone walls. There was a small kitchen equipped with a woodstove, a cupboard which held nothing but packets of dehydrated stew, and a battered enamel washing bowl, in which a large evil-looking spider lived. There was also a wooden table, six chairs, and a wall that was covered with peeling paper, or so I thought until I pushed back the kitchen's shutters and saw that the peeling paper was, in fact, rows of curling photographs.

I had found Nicole.

I felt the sudden catch and choke of incipient tears, for there was my daughter's face among the Genesis crews. "Nicole," I whispered her name aloud like an incantation, "Nicole, Nicole." I even reached up a tentative finger and stroked one of the photographs. Suddenly it was all worth it—the voyage, the cold, the pain, and the fear, for here she was, my daughter, and I had found her.

Or rather I had found her face among the photographs, which showed a variety of Genesis activists. In some of the pictures they were attacking fishnets with grapnels and cutting gear, while in another a Genesis group in an inflatable boat was taunting a French naval patrol vessel which had presumably been guarding France's nuclear-testing site in the Pacific. The pictures were amateurish, like fading holiday snapshots, and somehow that suggested that the Genesis eco-terrorists were a group of energetically carefree young people enjoying a most innocent and happy vacation; whenever two people were photographed together they inevitably had their arms about each others' necks, and in almost every snapshot they seemed to be shouting good-natured insults at the camera.

The pictures, I saw, were all of the same crew:

Nicole's. Nicole herself appeared in a dozen of the photographs, and in all but one of those she was either smiling or laughing. One photograph had been taken while she took a bucket shower on her catamaran's foredeck. She had been naked, and had clearly not known that she was being photographed, for the next picture showed her indignant, but good-humored face as she attacked the photographer. In a half dozen of the pictures she was shown with a thin, flaxen-haired boy, who had a blunt face that reminded me uncannily of my dead son. The more I looked, the more the boy in the pictures looked like Dickie. It was unsettling, for there was something about the way in which Nicole and the blond boy had been photographed together that suggested they were lovers.

I tried not to follow those insinuations. Instead I gazed for a long time at those pictures of my daughter, and I wondered just what thoughts and dreams moved her in this new life. None of the happy photographs revealed the answer to that question, but there was a clue in the one unsmiling picture of Nicole. That picture had been taken in an inflatable boat which had been thrashing through a choppy sea beneath a threatening sky. Nicole, sitting in the bows of the rubber boat, had just turned to face the photographer, and the camera had caught her face in a grim and taut expression that put me in mind of Berenice's timid description of my daughter as "fierce." I had a horrible feeling that the grim face was the real face, a face that betrayed no forgiveness nor any love. The picture worried me.

Not two hours before, in the wake of von Rellsteb's ambush, I had been determined to take my revenge, but now I felt an immense hopelessness. Because, at last, I knew just why I had sailed ten thousand miles. The confusions dropped away. I had not come to take revenge for Joanna's death, though revenge would indeed be sweet, nor had I come merely to find Nicole, but rather I had come for love. I had come to see the remorse on my daughter's face. I had come to hear her speak my name. I had come to hear her say that I had not sent her brother to his death. I had come to wipe away her tears. I had brought her my forgiveness, and had never thought she might not want it. I had come to hug and to be hugged, to love and be loved. I had come to fill the void in my life that had been left by a bomb in the English channel. I had come for the worst of all sentimental and self-pitying reasons, but now, staring at my daughter's snarling face, I knew I had wasted my time.

Standing there before the photographs I knew that the very best thing I could do was to creep away. I did not want to know the truth any longer, because the truth would be very hard, and very hurtful. It would be better to remember Nicole as she was in the smiling photographs, to remember her as a cheerful, hard-muscled, and tough activist who sailed the far seas to save dolphins and to raise the world's consciousness by sacrificing her own comforts. That, no doubt, was how she thought of herself, and that was how I should think of her. If I pursued her further, and if

I caught her, then I might discover that she had become someone who believed she knew better than the world, and who was therefore beyond the world's rules and beyond its condemnation. I might find that my daughter had become the tyrant of that one unsmiling photograph. I took that picture down, tore it into scraps, and decided to abandon my hunt. I would leave Nicole to life, as we must all, in the end, leave our children. I smiled at Nicole's happiness in the other photographs, chose two of them as keepsakes, and then I left.

I made a desultory exploration of the remaining buildings, but by now I was merely indulging my curiosity and did not expect to find anything useful, nor did I, though in one room that was stacked with coiled ropes I found an empty cardboard box that was lined with plastic sheeting and which carried the label "Dynamite." The sight of the box encouraged horrible thoughts, so I closed the door of that room and tried to forget what I had seen. In the next room I found a pile of rusted anchor chain, while in a cupboard there was an ancient wooden-handled whaling harpoon with a corroded, but still wicked-looking barbed head. These were the old nineteenth-century storerooms. In the same room as the harpoon was a barrel of nails that had rusted into a solid mass and boxes of Hambro line that fell to pieces the moment it was touched. In yet another room was a cache of empty liquor bottles which had faded labels of long-forgotten brands of whiskey, rum, and aquavit; ancient solaces against the awfulness

of a job at the earth's end. The final rooms, closest
to the old boat lift, were unused and held nothing
but broken barrels, the bones of a rabbit, gull
feathers, and hopelessness.

I left the quay, crossed the twin rails of the boat
lift, and climbed the hill to the mine buildings
where von Rellsteb had ambushed me. The buildings were empty now. I lifted the tarpaulin off the
tractor's engine only to discover that the ancient
cylinder block was a mass of rust. There was nothing more to find, or nothing more that I cared to
find, and so, in the teeth of a rising wind, I left the
mine and, with the rifle slung on my shoulder, I
climbed beside the quarry's northern rim. A small,
black-feathered and bad-tempered bird of prey
screamed at me from a nesting ledge as I began to
slog my way up the sodden hillside.

Once or twice I looked behind me, but the
Desolate Straits stayed empty. The Genesis crews
either were in pursuit of *Stormchild* or were cele-
brating her capture, and I was alone in a wilderness, doomed to a long, cold, soaking walk in the
dying light, and then to a freezing night. I had
stuffed my bag with some packets of the dehydrated stews I had found in Nicole's kitchen, but without a stove the result would be about as appetizing
as pigswill.

I looked behind again and saw that the gray
water of the straits, even though sheltered on all
sides by high hills and wooded bluffs, was being
whipped into whitecaps by the wind, while the
rain, which had now fallen all day, stung my face
with a new and even colder spite. I felt empty and

drained. My quest was over and I was tired and hungry. I had also chosen the wrong route home, for this northern flank of the quarry was much harder going than the southern flank down which I had approached the buildings. The northern slope was striated with rock ledges, broken by small ravines, and made treacherous by slides of scree that forced me to make wide and wearying detours.

Near the top of the slope was the largest and steepest field of scree I had yet encountered, and one which forced me to make a long detour to my right. Ahead of me now was the jumble of rocks that I slowly recognized as the distinctive peak which, only that morning, had so strongly reminded me of Dartmoor's granite tors. I was now so tired that I began to hallucinate that I was back on that Devon moor, and that if I could just keep walking I would soon come to the hiker's inn at Postbridge, where a huge fire would be blazing in the hearth and where I could buy a pint of beer and a deep dish of steak and kidney pie. It was only when I stumbled on a burrow, or when the torn muscles of my belly gave a foul twinge, that the comforting hallucination snapped away and I knew I was alone, wet, and hungry on a Patagonian island.

The torlike stones barred my path westward. I rested for a time at their base, sitting with my back against the rocks and staring at the Desolate Straits, which were now so far beneath me that low clouds, wispy and gray, broke my view of the wind-fretted water.

At last, fighting the temptation to remain in the small shelter of the high rock wall, I tried to go around it, but a steep slope of scree fell away to the north just as it did to the south, so, moving like a somnambulant creature in a nightmare, I clambered slowly up to where the wind and the rain shrieked their cacophony across the tor's summit. The climb was simple, yet as my head poked over the crest the force of the wind almost stole my breath away. I dragged myself over the edge, banging the rifle's butt on the rock as I clumsily moved, and then I went utterly still.

For a second I thought I was dreaming. Then, for another second, I hoped I was dreaming. Then I retched emptily.

A body lay in a cup of the rock.

For a few seconds, for a few whirling seconds of madness, I thought the body was Nicole's, then I saw that this woman had hair as black as the feathers of the bird of prey that had screamed at me on the lower slope.

It was that black hair, which was long and gleaming from the rain, that told me this corpse was that of a woman, because her flesh had been stripped by scavenging birds and animals. The carrion eaters had left some sinews between the yellowing joints, but otherwise she was nothing more than discolored bones in a bleak place. She had been flensed.

I fell to my knees. My sore belly heaved with a last lunge of sour vomit. I wanted to weep, but instead I shuffled forward and made myself examine the skeleton.

There was a ring on one bone finger. I did not touch it. There was also a necklace, which I similarly left alone. The woman's clothes had either been torn by carrion eaters or else had decayed in the weather, for her sweater and jeans were now nothing but faded and threadbare scraps that clung to her yellow bones. The only undecayed object in that high place was a common sack that was still hooked into the bony grip of her dead skeletal hands. One of her leg bones was broken, suggesting she had been unable to reach the shelter of the mine, and instead had died of exposure in this high, bleak place.

I pulled the sack out of her dead grip, making her bones rattle as the frail cloth came free. The first thing I found inside the sack was a blue Australian passport, in which was written the dead woman's name, Maureen Delaney, and her age, twenty-three. The passport photograph showed a round, girlish face that smiled at the world with an astonished happiness.

There was a stub of pencil in the sack, but no sheet of paper or notebook, so I leafed through the passport until I found some faint penciled letters on a blank page that told me how wrong I was. This girl had not died trying to reach the mine, but escaping from it. She had crawled up here, and died, because such a fate was better than staying in the mine. Maureen Delaney had been murdered.

The blank page in the passport was headed *Naiad*, and under that boat's name was a brief and pathetic message. "They killed John and Mark. There were four of them: two Germans, an

American, and an English girl. They let others rape me. And rape me." The words were ill-written and very eloquent, as eloquent as any voice that speaks from the grave. "It is November, " Maureen Delaney's message continued, "they say they'll kill me. The girls won't help me." I turned the passport's stiff page to find some words addressed to her mother.

I closed my eyes as though I could stop the tears.

I tried to persuade myself that there might be another English girl in the Genesis community, or that this Australian girl's dying testimony was mere imagination, but I had deceived myself for long enough, and there could be no more deception. Maureen Delaney's companions had been murdered, and she had been driven to this cold, lonely death, which was as bad as murder, and my daughter had been a participant. For what? For a boat, I assumed, for possession of *Naiad*, because, like all terrorists, my daughter believed that the foulest means were sanctified by the nobility of the cause.

I turned back the passport's pages until Maureen Delaney's smiling, sun-tanned face again stared into mine. She looked, I thought, enthusiastic, like someone who had taken life with both hands as a gift. She must have been an adventurous girl, independent and tough, for she had sailed far seas, keeping the wind's tune and knowing the sea's measure, but then she had been raped and killed. With my daughter's compliance. I imagined the Australian girl begging for help and

Nicole's cold face turning away, and that thought made me want to put the Lee-Enfield's cold muzzle in my mouth and blow my brains out, but instead I put the murdered girl's passport into my pocket. It would have to go to the Australian embassy.

I emptied the last contents of the sack and found the useless remains of a box of matches, and then evidence that Maureen Delaney had planned to take revenge on her tormentors. At the bottom of the sack were six sticks of dynamite, each one wrapped in a sheet of old, pinkish, greasy paper that bore the trademark "Nobel." Maureen Delaney had never found her revenge; instead, after escaping from the buildings by the quay, where, presumably, she had stolen the sticks of explosive, she had fallen and died in this high place.

I said a prayer for her. It was inadequate, but my memorial for Maureen Delaney would be more substantial than prayer, to which end I put the six sticks of dynamite into my bag.

In the cottages, standing in the kitchen where Nicole's photographs decorated the wall, I had persuaded myself that it would be best if I sailed away from the Isle of Torments. I had persuaded myself that I did not need to know what Nicole had become. I had hoped that *Stormchild* would still be free and that I could have sailed away in her and never looked back.

But I could no longer do that. I had found Nicole, and what I had found was evil. David would doubtless say I should give that evidence to the authorities and let the black-uniformed men of the Chilean *Armada* scour out this nest of killers, but one of the killers was my daughter. And a dead Australian girl had given me six sticks of dynamite. So I changed my mind again. I would not, after all, walk away in the solace of ignorance. Instead, as best as I could, I would be a good environmentalist. I would clean up the mess.

I crossed the marshland in the dusk. It still rained, and in places that rain had puddled into the tire tracks left by the two cross-country motorbikes.

I followed the tracks as far as the crest above the fjord. There the thickly ribbed tire marks slewed abruptly northward, almost as though von Rellsteb and his companion had reached this high vantage place and stared down to see that their hunt was over. I, too, gazed down the long, damp slope to see that *Stormchild* was gone. Lake Joanna lay empty, while the land on either bank of the fjord stretched away in broken and deserted folds toward the ocean.

I slid down the hill to the tree line, then charged recklessly through the undergrowth, not caring what noise I made. No one waited in ambush at the hill's foot. I had half expected to find two discarded cross-country motorbikes, but there was only the empty gray-black water that was being stirred into restlessness by the wind and pelting rain.

I looked round the rain-soaked beach until I

found the pale, platelike rock, under which David
had agreed to leave me a message. If *Stormchild*
had been captured then I knew there would be no
such message, and thus I lifted the stone with a
sense of doom which evaporated into instant
relief when I saw the piece of white card that
David had protectively wrapped in a clear plastic
bag. The existence of the message meant that
Stormchild was safe, because David, clearly scared
of the deteriorating weather, had taken her back
to sea.

"08.46 hours." My brother's message was written with ink in block capitals, and began with a
typical punctiliousness. "The glass is still falling
alarmingly, so I propose to take advantage of the
ebbing tide and take *Stormchild* to sea. To save
your radio's batteries I shall listen for your transmissions on the hour, every hour, for precisely
five minutes, on our agreed channel. If I have not
heard from you within seventy two hours, I shall
assume that you have neither read this note, nor
ever will, and I shall go north for help. In the
meantime I have left you a cache of supplies,
which I have concealed in the woodland. You will
find the cache eleven paces due east of this rock.
God bless you, D." The last two sentences had
been written in pencil, just as had the postscript,
which David had evidently scribbled after he had
brought the message ashore. "09.03 hours, Tim! I
have just made my first confirmed sighting of a
green-backed firecrown hummingbird. The bird
had a disappointingly dun plumage, so was probably a female, but it was still a thrill to see! You

might care to look for yourself. Mine was feeding on the wild fuchsias, which are growing among the trees just above your cache."

I saw no hummingbird. I did not even look for a hummingbird. I could not have cared if a whole troupe of hummingbirds had joined wing tips and hummed hallelujahs around my head. I just wanted to find David's cache, which consisted of ten cans of baked beans, ten cans of corned beef, six Kendal Mint bars, a small cooking canteen, a box of Earl Grey teabags, a waterproof container of matches, a can-opener, a groundsheet, and a sleeping bag, all crammed into a rucksack. It was a sensible cache, though I wished he had included one of the cheap, spare quartz watches that I had stored aboard *Stormchild* for the day when all my expensive chronometers gave up their ghosts. David was very sensible in restricting the times when he would keep a radio watch for me, but I no longer had a watch and did not know when the hour was on the hour.

But at least I had food. I opened a can of baked beans and, not bothering to make a fire to heat them, ate them greedily.

Above me a hint of thunder boiled in the low, dark clouds.

With the very last of the day's light I took from my pocket the photographs of Nicole. I stared into her face, trying and failing to understand her. I tried to remember her as a child, but it was as if a veil had drawn itself between those memories and this moment. I did not know my daughter any-more. I did not understand what strange sea change had been wrought in her by her brother's death, nor what she had become in the years since. My daughter was a stranger. I put the photographs away. Night fell in a rage of wind and rain. Lightning flickered briefly to the south.

Except for my brother, my whole family was gone to death or to evil, and I was alone. That knowledge made me feel as though I had passed through a dark gateway into a place where hatred ruled and where any life left to me was bleak and profitless. I crouched in the trees like an animal. I was dirty, soaked, tired, bleeding, and very dangerous.

And I had seventy-two hours, in which to teach the Genesis community that they were not above the law. I had seventy-two hours to destroy them, just as they had destroyed my family. I had been so reluctant to face that truth, but now I would ram it down their throats.

I slept with the Australian girl's legacy of dynamite beside me. I woke long before dawn. I tried to reach *Stormchild* on the radio, but there was no answer, and I dared not drain the battery by leaving the small set switched on in hope of catching any possible transmissions that David might make. Instead I pulled his rucksack onto my back, picked up the rifle, and started walking.

PART

three

It took me most of the daylight hours to cross the Isla Tormentos. I was unsure of my way for I was not returning to the limestone workings, but rather trying to reach the farm settlement. I had no map, no compass, and the sun was hidden all day, so I trudged through the unending rain guided only by guess.

Much of my journey was through marshland for I was using the low ground to avoid the eyes of any Genesis sentinel. I pushed through stands of woodland that were so thick with undergrowth they rivaled a tropical rain forest for impenetrability. I waded rain-swollen, peat-colored streams that were rich with trout, and staggered through deep sloughs under the protests of screaming birds. My blistered feet hurt like hell, so that I hobbled rather than walked. Twice, denied the cover of low ground by rising floodwaters, I was forced up onto the hills, and both times I found the fresh tracks of the cross-country motorbikes, evidence that von Rellsteb and his companion had returned this way, proof, if I needed further proof, that they had failed to capture *Stormchild*.

That failure would be worrying von Rellsteb. He probably believed me to be dead, but that would be no consolation for his fear that *Stormchild* was sailing north to carry Berenice and her damning tales to the Chilean authorities. With my body left to be found, and the Australian girl still missing somewhere on the island, the last thing von Rellsteb needed was any official interest in the Isla Tormentos and he would be doing everything in his power to intercept *Stormchild* in the heavy seas off Cape Raper.

It was that supposition which led me to believe the farm settlement would be largely unguarded. If the community believed I was dead and knew *Stormchild* was at sea, then they would certainly not be guarding their house against an attack from the landward flank. On that assumption I made my plans to make their settlement uninhabitable. Without food and shelter the group would be shattered. I planned to destroy von Rellsteb's legacy. I would murder his dream. I would finish him as he had tried to finish me, and I no longer cared what risks I ran in that destructive revenge because I had nothing left to live for.

I was not entirely bent on suicide. Before attacking, I planned to wait through the rest of David's seventy-two hours, in hope of contacting him on the radio. If I succeeded in reaching *Stormchild* I would persuade David to rescue me when my harrowing of the settlement was finished. I had decid-

ed not to tell my brother what I planned, for fear
that David would summon the authorities before I
succeeded; instead I would merely tell David I was
in safe hiding then arrange a rendezvous with him
somewhere in the Desolate Straits.

But if I could not reach *Stormchild* on the radio,
then damn the consequences.

Because I had nothing left to live for.

I had reached the protective escarpment that
curled about the western flank of the settlement at
nightfall. The last few miles were hard going for I
had entered a nightmarish landscape of rocks,
small gorges, sudden streams and cold black lakes
above which the settlement's crude radio mast
acted as a landmark beckoning me on. I
approached the crest of the escarpment very cautiously, skirting around a wind-fretted reservoir
that was held back by the earthen dam which controlled the water supply. No one challenged my
approach. Once, slipping off a wet rock, my right
foot dislodged a crashing fall of scree, but there
were no guards posted on the high ground to hear
the shattering landslide splash into the lake.

By dusk I had found a hiding place. It was a
deep crevice beneath the rocky peak on which the
radio mast had been built. The crevice was a crack
in the rock eighteen inches high and four feet
deep. Six people could have hidden in its black
shadows and from its eastern lip I could stare
straight down the steep escarpment, across the
vegetable plots, to Genesis community. I made

myself at home in my refuge by spreading out the groundsheet, unrolling the sleeping bag, and stowing my precious food and explosives deep in the dry heart of the rock. I then crept down to the reservoir and had a skimpy wash in its icy water. I had no razor, so my incipient beard, bristly and uncomfortable, had to stay.

Back in my aerie I made a supper of cold baked beans and corned beef as I searched the bay with my half binocular. Neither the catamaran nor the sloop were there, only the decrepit fishing vessel, which suggested the faster yachts had indeed gone north to search for *Stormchild*. They would be having a lively time of it, for the wind was whipping over my rock and shrieking an eldritch sound in the guy ropes of the radio mast, while the landscape beneath me was being beaten by a cold, wind-blasted rain that kept the Genesis community indoors. Just before darkness I saw two of the gray-dressed women hurry with sacks to one of the outhouses, but I saw no one else.

Darkness came and I watched the dim candle lights flicker in the windows of the big house until, one by one, they disappeared and the settlement was swallowed into the wild Patagonian night. After the last light had disappeared I tried to reach *Stormchild* by radio. I counted the seconds, and once every minute for an hour and a quarter I switched on the small set and sent an identifying message, but I heard nothing in reply. It could have been that David and *Stormchild* were too far away, or perhaps the hills of the island were blocking my signal, or maybe the radio was not working. I finally abandoned my efforts and, sheltered from the relentless rain by the tons of rock above me, I tried to sleep, but the best I could manage was a shivering night of intermittent and hallucinatory dozes. I was filled with misery. My feet were in agony, but I dared not take off my boots in case I could not pull them on again over my blistered, bleeding feet.

An hour before dawn I finally abandoned any pretense of sleep and once again tried to radio David, and once again I failed to reach him. I went back to the eastern side of my rock, and, as the gray light seeped into the bowl of the mountains, I watched the settlement stir. A wisp of smoke showed at a chimney. The rain still fell and the wind gusted to make the damp landscape a place of cold misery. I shivered, yet in truth I was so damp and so cold that by now I had almost ceased to notice any further discomfort. During the night my socks had become soaked with blood that now seeped over the edge of my boots.

I contemplated making no hostile move that morning. I needed more rest, and I still had time to reach David. If it was necessary, I planned to spend all day trying to raise him on the radio, but instead, in the morning's early gray light, and just as the first workers went into the fields, everything changed.

For, just after dawn, the most astonishing mournful and trembling sound echoed across the sky like a great shuddering lament. My first prosaic thought was that a lovesick bull sea lion had bellowed his frustration to the new day, but then I realized that this sound was too great for any animal. It was a foghorn.

Minutes later, like the arrival of some phantas-magorical spacecraft from another world, a ship appeared. She was a real, civilized, proper mer-chant ship. I took out my half binocular to see the name *San Rafael* painted on her bows. She looked huge, though in truth she was nothing more than a small coaster, perhaps two hundred feet long and five hundred tons in displacement, but in that bay, where I had thought to see nothing big-ger than *Stormchild,* the *San Rafael* loomed like a Leviathan. She was a smart ship, beautifully paint-ed in a dark blue and gray livery, with the colorful Chilean ensign painted on her funnel. I guessed from the derricks on her foredeck that she was a supply vessel for the oil and gas rigs that edged the Land of Fire, and she looked just the kind of sturdy efficient vessel that such a job would need. She had a high bluff bow, a cargo deck amidships, and a galleried layer of living quarters behind the bridge at her stern. A wisp of steam from her tur-bines drifted across the water as the radar aerial on her short mast whipped busily around. Bilge water spewed from a vent on her starboard side, above which men in blue donkey jackets leaned on her varnished rails to gaze at the isolated settlement.

The arrival of the *San Rafael* had thrown the Genesis community into turmoil. The few gray-dressed women who had already started work in the gardens fled in panic toward the house, while a man in green stared in apparent shock at the cargo boat that now seemed to fill the bay. I shared the man's evident astonishment, for the ship was a stunning reminder that there was a real world somewhere out beyond the tide-scoured channels, a world where people lived by rules and read newspapers and watched television and drove cars and did their shopping. I stared at the wondrous ship, wondering whether I should try to contact her by radio and ask her to pass a message on to *Stormchild*, but even as I was trying to compose a suitable explanation for such an odd request, I saw that the *San Rafael*'s crew was lowering a ship's boat.

I trained my makeshift glass on the coaster. The lens skidded across the group of men at the ship's side, down the flank of the coaster, and at last steadied on the small ship's tender that proved to be a motorized launch about seventeen feet long. The launch's coxswain, a cigarette dangling from his lip, threw off the falls fore and aft, then accelerated the small boat away from the *San Rafael*'s hull toward the beach.

The launch was not bringing supplies to the settlement; she carried neither crates nor fuel drums, but instead she was evidently disembarking two passengers. Those passengers, swathed in yellow rain slickers, huddled nervously together on the boat's central thwart. I could see nothing of the passenger sitting on the port side of the launch, but there was no mistaking the face of the person to starboard, and, upon seeing that face, my heart leapt from its suicidal self-pity into a sudden and very unexpected joy. The face was so very solemn, but it was also so very full of life and enthusiasm and happiness.

Jackie Potten had come to Chile to fetch her Pulitzer.

*   *   *

I switched on my small radio. If I was to talk to the *San Rafael* I would have to call her on channel 16, which was the only frequency I would expect them to monitor, but someone else had already sequestered that channel. I heard a man's voice haranguing the *San Rafael* in quick, agitated Spanish. I could distinguish the ship's name in the man's excited torrent of words, but nothing else, though I hardly needed to know Spanish to understand what was being said; the man was attempting to persuade the *San Rafael* to take the visitors away, but even as his protests became frantic the small launch kept determinedly on toward the beach. As it neared the shore I saw Jackie stand precariously to take a photograph of the settlement.

Two green-dressed men had run to the bluff above the beach and now waved vigorously at the launch in an evident attempt to make it turn round. A third man, this one carrying an automatic rifle, appeared at the back door of the house and began running toward the hills where I lay sheltered, and I realized that the arrival of Jackie and her companion had prompted the same precautions that had attended my own arrival at the settlement. Most of the group stayed protected in the house while a cordon of men tried to make the unwelcome visitors leave. I presumed the gunman on the hill was the precaution of last resort, while the gunman in the house's upper window was posted to dissuade any of the gray-dressed community members from trying to escape.

The green-dressed man began to climb the lower slopes of the hill. I saw that if he kept on his present course he would take up a firing position just twenty or thirty yards away from me. The man wore a yellow headband and had a bushy black beard, and I guessed he was the same man who had tried to kill me from the cliff's top at the limestone working. He was panting as he climbed the steep slope. I had forgotten to switch off my radio, and suddenly the small set squawked and I frantically turned down its volume, but the bearded man, who was probably being deafened by his own hoarse breathing, had not heard the sudden burst of noise. I put my ear close to the speaker to hear a new voice transmitting. I suspected the new speaker was Lisl, for she spoke in German. *"Genesis One, Genesis One,"* she called, "this is the settlement, over."

The catamaran replied after a few seconds. The reception was very faint, indeed almost inaudible, but I was fairly certain that it was von Rellsteb himself who acknowledged the settlement's transmission.

"We have more visitors," Lisl said laconically, and still speaking in German, "two women."

"Then see them off!" I thought I detected a hint of panic or anger in the guttural voice. Von Rellsteb had gone to sea to intercept what he supposed was *Stormchild's* dash for help, but now he was discovering that more unwelcome outsiders had descended on his community.

"The *San Rafael* brought them," Lisl went doggedly on, and my German was not good enough to fully understand all her next words, but I thought she said that the coaster's captain had informed the settlement that the two women had insisted on staying until the ship returned to collect them.

"They mustn't stay!" Von Rellsteb's voice betrayed a terrible anxiety.

"Have you found the English boat?" Lisl asked.

"No."

"Good luck," Lisl said tonelessly. There was no response and, in the silence, I wondered if I should risk talking to the *San Rafael*. I decided against trying, for almost certainly the settlement was monitoring channel 16 and any transmission would betray my presence. So, regretfully, I switched my radio off.

Beneath me the man with the yellow headband had found a firing position on a big, flat-topped boulder close to the concrete dam. He was some twenty yards to my right and well positioned to fire down on any unwelcome visitors.

I looked back to the beach to see that the *San Rafael*'s launch had reached the shingle. Two green-dressed men were trying to push the boat away, but Jackie's companion literally jumped at them, forcing the two men backward. Jackie's companion appeared to be a very heavy woman and a good deal older than Jackie; indeed, I realized with a pang, the larger woman was probably someone of my own age.

Jackie jumped ashore. The launch's coxswain hurled two kitbags onto the shingle, then, with a farewell wave, he reversed his boat off the beach. For a few seconds the bluff hid the confrontation between the visitors and the bearded men from my sight, then the older woman appeared at the top of the wooden stairs that led from the beach. The two men were either trying to drag her back to the sea or, at least, steer her away from the house, but the woman would have none of their interference. She pushed one man aside with a forearm tackle that would not have disgraced a second-row forward playing rugby at Cardiff Arms Park, and shoved the second one back with a thump from her weighted kitbag. Jackie, coming behind, snapped a photograph of the two discomfited men, then ran to catch up with her companion who was now striding purposefully past the gazebo and the concrete tanks toward the front door of the house. I caught a clear glimpse of Jackie's face in my half binocular. Her expression, which blended anxiety and eagerness, was achingly familiar, then she, her companion, and the two men, were all hidden from me by the house itself.

I rested my head on my arms. God damn it! I had thought myself recovered, but one clear glimpse of Jackie's face had sent a shudder of longing through me, and I was suddenly overwhelmed by images from our all too short time together. I remembered her apprehensive excitement as she climbed into the camel's seat on Lanzarote, her shyness when she had shown me her bikini, and her horror on Antigua at the mention of guns. I recalled the guilty glance I had stolen of her as she had exercised naked on *Stormchild*'s foredeck. Oh God damn it, I thought, I was still in love, even though, under the blowtorch of David's scorn, I had tried to forget her.

David. That thought made me switch the radio to channel 37. "This is Tim calling *Stormchild*," I hissed the words scarce above a whisper, "Tim calling *Stormchild*, over." I was watching the man with the yellow headband who was lying behind a makeshift breastwork of loose stones that he had piled as a firing rest on the edge of his flat-topped boulder. The wind must have swallowed my voice, for the man did not look round. "This is Tim calling *Stormchild*." I hissed into the microphone, but there was still no answer. "Come on, you old fart," I said cheerfully, "talk to me!" But insulting the airwaves made no difference, for there was no reply and, alarmingly, the small red battery light had begun to blink, so to conserve what little power was left I switched the set off.

Jackie and her companion, both dressed in their distinctive yellow slickers, now appeared at the corner of the settlement's southern wing. They were clearly behaving as I had behaved when I had first come to the settlement; they had found the front door locked, so now they were working their way round the edges of the buildings. The two men followed forlornly, just as they had followed me.

The older woman marched resolutely across the courtyard toward the back door. I watched through my monocular, expecting to see her try the door and find it locked, but instead, and as much to my surprise as to hers, the back door of the house was suddenly snatched open and an apparent flood of Genesis people ran into view. The red-haired Lisl led their charge.

The Genesis people, who were all wearing

green, spread into a line. The older woman hesitated, while Jackie, a pace or two behind her companion, seemed to have a greater appreciation of
the sudden danger. She twisted round just as the
two men who had followed her from the beach
attempted to snatch her. None of the Genesis people was using a gun, presumably for fear that the
sailors on the *San Rafael* would hear any shots.
The *San Rafael* was still in the bay. She had recovered her launch and the water at her stern had just
begun to foam white as she got under way.

The long low house hid the small drama from
anyone aboard the *San Rafael,* but I could follow
every move. Jackie, trapped by the two men, freed
herself by hurling her heavy kitbag at her closest
attacker. It hit the man in the chest, jarred him
backward, and Jackie began running. Her companion was also trying to run, but the older woman
was so heavy that her flight was more of a lumbering waddle, while Jackie, lithe and fit, easily
dodged her pursuers. After a few sprinted yards
Jackie slowed and turned to shout encouragement
at her companion, but she was too late, for the
older woman had already been swamped by a welter of green-dressed bodies. Jackie hesitated, and I
silently screamed at her to keep on running, then
she must have realized that she could achieve
nothing by continued hesitation, so she turned
and ran like a frightened hare toward the hills.
Three of the men chased after her.

I thought it would prove a desperately close
chase, but Jackie was far fitter and faster than her
pursuers. She twisted among the vegetable patches,

leaped an irrigation ditch, sprinted beside a stand
of pea plants, then was on the lower slopes of the
escarpment and climbing fast. Her three pursuers
had begun their chase just ten paces behind her,
but by the time she reached the slope beneath the
dam they were already thirty yards back and still
losing ground. One of the men stopped altogether
and bent over to catch his breath.

Jackie's companion was being dragged to the
southern wing of the house, evidently to be
locked into one of its stablelike rooms, while Lisl,
whom I supposed von Rellsteb had left in charge
of the settlement, was watching the pursuit of
Jackie. The *San Rafael*, oblivious to the furor its
arrival had initiated, was gaining speed as she
steamed out of the bay.

Jackie glanced behind to see her pursuit was fading, and so slowed down herself. She veered to her
right, jumped the small conduit that spilled from
the dam to carry water to the house, and then
began climbing the steepest part of the escarpment
toward the radio mast. She did not know it, but
she was heading almost directly toward the man in
the yellow headband, who, to prevent her spotting
him, had shrunk back behind his breastwork.

The two men who had kept up the pursuit of
Jackie now stopped. They, like their companion,
were winded, but they also must have realized
that the man in the yellow headband was perfectly situated to ambush the fugitive.

I slid my rifle forward. I was reluctant to fire, for
the shot would betray my presence, but I nevertheless slid the safety catch off and was ready to pull

the trigger if the man aimed his rifle at Jackie. She, thinking herself safe, had reached the crest of the ridge where she turned to look back for some news of her companion, but the older woman had long been thrust inside the stablelike buildings. Jackie, who must have been wondering into just what hell she had precipitated herself, turned away and began walking along the rough, stony track which led beside the reservoir and directly beneath the big, flat rock on which the gunman was perched.

And from where the gunman sprang his ambush.

He did not use his assault rifle. The *San Rafael* had only just disappeared beyond the wooded promontory and any gunshot might still have brought the Chilean vessel back to investigate, so the bearded man abandoned his rifle on the high rock and, instead, leaped down in an attempt to flatten Jackie with his body weight.

She must have sensed something, or else she heard his movement above her, because she broke into a sudden run, leaving the man to sprawl on the path behind her. The man fell heavily, but immediately scrambled to his feet and lunged after her with a demonic burst of energy. Jackie responded by cutting to her right and scrabbling at a steep, stony slope that would surely have defeated her heavier pursuer, except that the man just managed to leap up, catch her right ankle, and pull her back down the slope. I heard her scream as she was dragged down.

"I've got her!" the man shouted triumphantly.

"Bring her down!" One of the two men who

had abandoned the chase, but who were still on the escarpment's face, called back, and, when he heard no reply, he shouted again. "Stephen? Stephen! Are you OK?"

"I'll bring her down in a minute! I've got her! Don't worry!"

The two men waited a few seconds, then, assured that Stephen did have the fugitive in his control, they turned and scrambled back down the escarpment. One of the men raised a thumb toward Lisl, who, understanding the gesture, waved in reply.

Stephen, the man in the yellow headband, had meanwhile forced Jackie to kneel down on the path beside the reservoir. He was standing close in front of her, with his back toward me, and so he saw nothing as I slid from my crevice. I carried the rifle, but very carefully so that its metal bound butt did not clash against the rock. Jackie and her captor were scarcely more than thirty yards from me, but neither of them saw me and neither of them heard me.

Jackie, who was facing me, was too terrified to take notice of anything except her captor, who, with one hand in her hair, seemed to be holding her down on the path. I saw her twist violently to free herself of his grip, but the man cuffed the side of her head with his free hand. He hit her hard and she called out in pain. The man said something, but I could not distinguish his words.

The wind gusted about the rocks, bringing snatches of rain in its cold grip. I slithered down a rock slope, loosening a fall of pebbles with my right foot, but neither the man nor Jackie heard the small avalanche. For a few seconds a dip of land took me out of their sight, and, ignoring the pain in my feet, I ran swiftly across some flat boulders before stopping to peer over a rock barrier to see that Jackie was still kneeling in front of the man who now tentatively took his hand away from her hair. "Stay!" He snapped at her as though she were a dog.

I was now twenty feet away. The man's back was still toward me as I gathered myself to attack.

The man was fidgeting and I thought he must be trying to disentangle a length of rope with which he planned to tie Jackie's hands, but then, because he moved slightly to one side, I saw that he was fumbling to lower his trousers, and I understood why he had wanted Jackie to kneel in front of him.

Jackie understood too, better than me probably, and once again she hurled herself to one side in a frenetic attempt at escape, and this time she very nearly succeeded, except that the bearded man hurled himself full-length after her and managed to wrap his arms round her legs. "Come here, you bitch!" I heard him shout, then he twisted round and his eyes widened in desperate fright.

He had heard my boots as I scrambled over the rock barrier. He turned, and he saw a *revenant* come from the grave. He had seen me fall to my death just the day before, but now, like an apparition ripped from his deepest nightmare, I was reborn. I was charging over the rocks, stumbling on loose stone, but the man did not see my clumsiness, only my face, and he must also have seen my gun and remembered that his own was fifty paces away and lost.

He tried to get up and run, but Jackie tripped him. He scrabbled to free himself of her, half stood, staggered two desperate paces, but then I had pounded past an astonished Jackie and my boot lashed out to catch him in the base of his spine. He yelped in pain and toppled forward. His skull cracked audibly against rock and I saw a spurt of blood splash on stone, but he was still conscious and still ready to fight as he twisted round and balled his fist to lash up at me, but then he froze in terror because the muzzle of a .303 Lee-Enfield No. 4 Mark I rifle was about one half inch from his left eyeball. "Try it, Stephen," I said, "please?"

He gave an infinitesimal shake of his head, but whether to indicate that he was not going to attempt an escape, or whether the response was just pure fear, I could not tell.

"Remember me?" I asked him pleasantly. "I'm the sucker who couldn't fly and couldn't swim either. But I can come back from the dead. And I can kill."

"No," he said, "no. Please!" His fly was undone and showing a length of filthy underpants. I jerked the rifle's muzzle a fraction of an inch and suddenly a stream of yellow piss overflowed from the underpants to soak his trousers. "Oh, Stephen!" I said in offended remonstrance, then I put on the gun's safety catch and reversed it so that I was threatening him with the gun's brass butt instead of its muzzle. "Zip your nasty self up," I said as nicely as I could.

He needed two hands to do up his fly, and,

while he concentrated on the damp zipper, I thumped him over the head with the rifle butt.

I hit him too hard. He saw the blow coming and tried to twist away, which evasion only added desperation to my blow and so the brass cracked on his already bleeding temple with a horrid thud.

He did not immediately flop back unconscious. Instead he groaned and twitched, but I could see the whites of his eyes and knew he would live. More to my purpose I knew he was conveniently out of commission for a few minutes. "Hello, Jackie!" I called over my shoulder.

There was no answer, nor did I dare look round in search of one, for I had to concentrate on Stephen. That was my excuse, though in truth I was almost frightened to look at Jackie for fear of being disappointed, or overwhelmed, or embarrassed. Whatever, I bent over the stricken Stephen whose face had gone horribly white. A fresh trickle of blood, instantly diluted by rain water, spilled from a rapidly swelling bruise on his left temple, and I felt a horrid fear that I might have hit him too hard, and that he was dying after all, but then he gave an awful groan that convinced me he still had a deal of life left in him. I shrugged the nylon rope off my shoulder and swiftly lashed his ankles together, then heaved him onto his belly, dragged his ankles up toward the small of his back, and tied his wrists. He was now trussed as neatly as a dead stag, but I still had to gag him. I tried to rip a length of cloth off his green clothes, but the stitches would not rip and I had left my rigging knife in my hiding place, so I just wrapped the free end of the rope round and round his bearded face, forcing the line between his teeth so that the only sound he could make was a choked gargle. "Fuck you, Stephen," I said cheerfully and patted his head as I stood up. He gargled helplessly, and I decided he was not going to die yet.

"Hello, Jackie," I said again, and this time I did turn round to smile at her. She was still kneeling on the path from where she stared huge-eyed at me. "You'll notice I didn't shoot the scumbag," I said, "but please don't think that's because I've developed moral objections to shooting scumbags, because I haven't, but because the bastards are pretty sure I'm dead and a gunshot would rather give the game away. It might also bring the *San Rafael* back here, and frankly I don't want that. I want to be left alone to make these bastards regret they were ever born. Hello."

She burst into tears. She had no makeup, she was soaking wet, she was crying, and she was spattered with mud, and I thought she was beautiful.

"We can't stand here and chat all day," I went on. "We've got to hide, then fetch Scumbag's gun, and I'm afraid we've got to take Scumbag with us because soon his friends are going to come looking for him and I can't have him telling tales about me. I know you've got the most intense reservations about guns, but would you very kindly carry this one for me? It won't go off." I held the rifle toward her. She hesitated. "Take it!" I snapped, and she guiltily reached out and took it.

"Tim?" she said, as though she did not really believe her eyes.

"It's me," I said, then I bent down and pulled Stephen into a sitting position, before, not without difficulty, hoisting him onto my shoulders. I could have released his ankles and forced him to walk, but I could not afford the time to let him struggle and it was simpler just to carry him. "By the way," I said to Jackie when I had settled Stephen comfortably on my shoulders, "it really is wonderful to see you again."

She immediately started crying again.

It took me ten minutes to get Stephen up to my crevice in the rocks. Once in my deep hiding place I pushed him deep down under the threatening overhang of wet rock. "Shoot the bugger if he gives you any trouble," I told Jackie, then went and retrieved Stephen's assault rifle that turned out to be an American M-16 with two spare magazines. I wriggled back into the crevice where a shivering Jackie had already taken shelter, and where Stephen, still inextricably knotted in my extravagant lengths of nylon rope, lay terrified in the deepest part of the narrow cave. Far beneath us, in the big courtyard of the farm settlement, the worried Genesis people gazed up at the ridge line.

"They probably think Stephen is taking a good long time to rape you," I told Jackie, "but in a few minutes it'll dawn on them that something has gone wrong, and then they'll start looking for him. But I think we'll be safe here as long as we keep our heads down."

"Tim," Jackie said. She was still shedding tears.

"I've been meaning to apologize to you," I said, because I had decided that, on the childish principle of eating the vegetables first, I might as well eat my humble pie quickly. "I should have told you about the guns on *Stormchild*. It was stupid of me. I'm sorry, I really am. I don't blame you for jumping ship, because I really should have been honest with you."

"It wasn't the guns," Jackie said, then, after a sniff, she must have decided that her words had not made much sense. "That wasn't why I ran away," she explained.

"Oh," I said feebly, and I knew I would have to make a much more embarrassing and comprehensive apology, in anticipation of which I felt my face reddening. I was tempted to drop the whole subject, but somehow it seemed important to clear what was left of our relationship, and so I took a deep breath, then launched myself into remorse. "I'm also sorry about what I said to you on Antigua, about wishing you'd stay with me. I never meant to upset you, but sometimes we say things that are stupid, and I'm sorry." The apology sounded lame, but it had been heartfelt and the best I could achieve under these weird circumstances.

Jackie stared at me with her huge and solemn eyes. "I didn't think it was stupid," she said.

"It *was* a stupid thing to say," I insisted, "because all it achieved was to drive you away from me, so it was clearly out of place and I'm really very sorry." My embarrassment had made me turn away from her as I spoke. I was watching Lisl and two men walk toward the escarpment. All three carried rifles. "By the way," I glanced at Jackie, "where the hell did you hide that day on

Antigua? I looked everywhere for you. I even took a taxi to the airport in an attempt to find you."

"I was on that Dutch boat. You remember? The couple we ate dinner with on your birthday?" She sniffed. "I waited with them until you sailed away, then I flew home. I'm sorry, Tim." She sounded close to tears.

"I'm the one who should be sorry," I said very robustly, "because I should never have been so clumsy as to say what I did." I frowned at Stephen who was listening avidly to this exchange of mutual self-blame. His eyes, wide above the loops of gagging rope, seemed to express incredulity for what he heard. "Still"—I went on talking to Jackie—"it really is good to see you again. I missed you."

"I missed you, too," she said.

My heart skipped a beat, but I was determined not to make another fool of myself, so I did not respond to her words, which I was fairly sure were nothing but an expression of politeness. "I'm rather in the habit of missing things at the moment," i told her instead. "David's taken *Stormchild* off to sea, and if I don't get him on the radio soon he's going to sail off and ask for help. He's got your friend with him, Berenice."

"Berenice Tetterman?" Jackie asked in utter astonishment.

"The very same. She ran away. The bastards shot at her, but missed, and we took her on board."

"But that's her mother who was with me!" Jackie paused to take breath. "Molly came because I couldn't persuade any newspaper to send me down here, so Molly sold her car and we used the money to fly to Santiago, and then we had to find our way down here and it was really hard because the car didn't fetch a lot of money, and—"

"Quiet!" I said.

"I'm talking too much," she said in bitter self-reproach.

"No." I pointed down the escarpment to where Lisl and her two companions were climbing toward us. There had been little chance of Jackie's voice carrying that far down the slope, but I wanted Jackie to be aware of the danger. "If we're quiet and still," I said, "they won't find us. Then tonight we'll rescue Molly, if she's still alive."

"Alive?" Jackie said. "You mean . . . " She could not continue.

"I mean they're a murderous bloody bunch, but I don't think they'll kill Molly because they know the *San Rafael* is coming back for you both. But they are killers. I've got proof of it. I also killed one of them. I didn't really, I just shot him and they did the rest, but I suppose it's the same thing." I stopped talking because Jackie was looking so very miserable. "I'm sorry," I said after a while, "but you really don't understand how bad these people are. And Nicole's one of them."

"Nicole?" Jackie stared at me with huge eyes. "You found her?"

I shook my head. "She's at sea." I sounded bleak.

"Maybe she isn't like the others?" Jackie said tentatively.

"She is," I said, "in fact, she may be one of the worst."

"I'm sorry, Tim. God, I'm so sorry." Jackie rested her face on her forearm and I thought she was praying, but then she spoke in a muffled voice. "I'm sorry for everything. I really am."

"Quiet now," I warned her, and I touched Jackie's elbow to reinforce the warning, and she raised her tear-stained face to see that Lisl had climbed onto the dam's embankment not forty yards from our hiding place. "Stephen!" Lisl peered into the rain, seeking her lost gunman. "Stephen!" Lisl shouted again as her two companions joined her on the dam's wall. "Stephen!" They all shouted together.

"Make one little sound, Stephen," I spoke very softly, "and I'll dig your eyes out with a marline-spike."

Stephen, who was staring at us from the cave's recess, made a gurgling sound, which I took to mean his eager agreement to stay silent. "Good boy," I said encouragingly.

Jackie had gone very white. Lisl was close enough for us to hear the click as she cocked her rifle. She raised it in the air and fired off a whole magazine of bullets, then waited for any response from the missing Stephen.

The rain billowed across the reservoir, but no reply came to Lisl's shots. She swore, then scrambled up to the flat-topped rock that Stephen had used as his bastion. She found no sign of him there, nor, from her new vantage point, could she see any evidence of him. "Fuck him," she snapped to her waiting companions, then she jumped down to the path and turned back toward the house. I sympathized with her reluctance to search the torn landscape, for such a search could have taken all day and still have missed hundreds of hiding places such as the one where Jackie and I now sheltered.

"You're just going to abandon him?" One of the men with Lisl called after her.

"For Christ's sake, Paul! He's got a gun! How the hell could anything have happened to him? He'll turn up with the girl in his own time. Now come on."

The three of them scrambled back down the hill and Jackie let out a long, deep sigh of relief.

"I'm afraid they've got an awful lot of guns," I told Jackie, "but you really should understand that I wouldn't be alive today if I hadn't brought a gun myself. I mean I know just how much you disapprove, but the thing is that—"

"Shut up, Tim," Jackie said with a brusque and intense passion.

So I shut up. Jackie added nothing to her bitter command, but instead just stared into the wind and rain.

So, filling her silence, and needing to make my peace with this girl, I tried to explain myself one more time. "I don't like guns any more than you do," I said, "not really, but if some murderous thug is having a go at me I really do—"

"Shut up, Tim, please." Jackie sounded very weary, as though I bored her, and I suddenly realized that I was merely compounding the mistake I had made on Antigua, because my very apologies were a stratagem of love, and, by making the apologies, I was offending her just as I had offended her by the more honest and outright declaration.

So I finally shut up properly and I stared at the house and I thought how lonely life was going to be after all.

"I told you that it wasn't the guns that made me run off," Jackie said suddenly.

"I know that," I said miserably, "it was the other thing," and I felt curdled with shame at the memory, but I made myself define the thing exactly, as though, by eating the last bitter crumbs of the humble pie, I could destroy its memory. "It was my wanting you to stay with me."

"Yes," she said flatly. "That was exactly it."

I stared above the settlement to where the empty waters of the Desolate Straits lay gray and cold. Rain swept in spiteful veils across the distant hills and over the slate-colored tideway. "I'm sorry," I said bleakly. I had already apologized more than enough, but I had not realized till now just how deeply I must have offended Jackie in the crowded Antigua street.

"It frightened me, you see," Jackie said in a voice so soft that I almost did not hear, and when I turned to look at her I saw that she had begun to cry, "because I wanted to say yes."

"You wanted to . . . " I began to echo her words, but she cut me off by shaking her head to indicate that any interruption now might make her lose the thread of her explanation.

"I wanted to say yes"—she went on more strongly—"but it terrified me, Tim. I didn't know if I could make a decision like that so quickly. Do you know what I mean? So I thought, I've got to get away from you to give myself space. At least I thought that once your brother arrived, because he's a bit overpowering. But I couldn't really explain it to you."

I wanted to say something, but could find nothing to say, so kept quiet.

"So I ran away," Jackie went on, "because everything was confusing, especially with your brother there, and I felt in the way, and I thought that if I could just give myself a bit of space I'd find out what I wanted." She stared bright-eyed and serious at me, and I wondered if ever, anywhere on God's earth, a stranger situation had been found for two people to fall in love, and suddenly I began to dare that we were indeed falling in love. Jackie took my silence for an encouragement to speak on. "I mean it's a big decision, isn't it? You wanted me to give up my career, right? And live on a boat? That's kind of a drastic life change! And if I'm going to make that kind of emotional commitment then I want to be sure that I've considered that commitment properly, and you'd want me to do that, too, wouldn't you?"

"Oh, yes, of course," I said, realizing I had forgotten just how much this girl could talk when she was nervous, "or no, perhaps," I went on, and I saw the astonished Stephen was still listening to our every word.

Jackie shook her head in self-recrimination. "I should have explained it all to you on Antigua, but you always seemed so self-sufficient and I thought you'd probably be glad to get rid of me in the end. You see I thought you were just trying to be nice to me, and that you'd change your mind when you really thought about it . . . "

"You thought what?" I asked in astonishment.

"That you didn't mean what you said, and that if you had a few weeks without me you'd think better of it. I mean I couldn't blame you if you did, because—"

"Jackie!" I put a finger on her lips to stop her talking.

She must have thought we were in danger for she stared at me with very wide and very frightened eyes.

I kissed her tears. "I love you," I said, and I think I was close to crying myself.

Only now it was happiness that filled me, and so I kissed her again and I felt relief surging through me as strongly as a flooding spring tide swelling over shoals to render them harmless, and I felt the same relief flood into Jackie as I put my arm about her shoulders and held her close.

Stephen gargled at us. I think he was attempting to be the first to congratulate us on our new found happiness, but I kicked him with my heavy right boot anyway, just to shut him up.

"Oh, Tim." Jackie took a deep breath.

"Does that mean we're sharing a boat now?" I asked her.

"I guess it does." She smiled coyly.

"Whoopee," I said, and just hoped I could get the boat back.

By midday the settlement was sufficiently worried about the missing Stephen to send two men to search the island's interior on the cross-country motorbikes, while another four men, all armed with assault rifles, combed the ravines and rock piles of the high plateau, but no one thought to explore the escarpment's crest immediately above the settlement where the three of us lay concealed. Instead the searchers all went further west, presumably on the assumption that Stephen must have pursued Jackie into the wild landscape that led toward the distant ocean. The search parties had a miserable time of it because the rain was an unending, drumming, thrashing tempest that slashed across the high country and beat the reservoir into frenzy and drowned the vegetable fields at the escarpment's foot.

We kept dry in our crevice, and I told Jackie all I

had learned about the Genesis community from Berenice and from my own exploration of the limestone workings. I told her about the Australian boat, and about the corpse I had found in the high rocks under the cold wind. I showed Jackie the passport, then ungagged Stephen to discover if he knew anything about the Australian girl's death. When Stephen had finished gasping and making a fuss about his strained jaw muscles, I unfolded the blade of my rigging knife and pressed its sharp tip into the soft tissue under his left eyeball. "My father was a surgeon," I told Stephen, "and he taught me that the medical term for what I'm tempted to do is enucleation."

He whimpered, which I decided was a request for further information.

"Enucleation," I told him, "is the operation of removing the eyeball."

He whimpered again, which I translated as an indication that he understood me.

"So unless you want me to begin my new career as an ophthalmic surgeon right here and now, Stephen, talk to me."

What he told us about the Australian boat confirmed Berenice's story. The catamaran *Naiad* had come unexpectedly to the settlement and von Rellsteb, desperate to acquire a fourth yacht, had invited the three Australians to a meal at the mine. Once at the mine the two men had been shot and the girl tossed into a storeroom. "Did you rape her?" I asked Stephen.

He hesitated a split second too long, so I drew blood with the knife's blade. He gave a small scream that was echoed by Jackie. "You bastard," I said to Stephen. "And Nicole? Was she there?"

He nodded.

"Tell me," I said, and I put the point of the stainless steel blade into the newly drawn blood. "Tell me about Nicole," I ordered him.

At the time of *Naiad's* arrival, Stephen said, Nicole had been the navigator for the second Genesis boat, and Stephen had been a member of that same crew, but Nicole, he claimed, had been a difficult shipmate. She was not only a more competent sailor than their skipper, but she was also full of more energy and anger and resolve. Nicole, Stephen said, always wanted to sail the extra mile or take the extra risk. She was desperate to take over command of *Genesis Two,* and the arrival of the big Australian catamaran had seemed a heaven-sent chance for von Rellsteb to prevent a mutiny. Thus the *Naiad* had been pirated and given to Nicole.

"So who killed the Australians?" I asked Stephen.

He stared dumbly at me.

"Who?" I insisted, even though I knew the answer.

"She did," he almost whispered the accusation. "The others hesitated, so she snatched the gun."

"Oh, sweet Jesus," Jackie murmured in a stricken voice.

I stared hatefully at Stephen, wanting to murder him for being the messenger of such news, but then I decided I had better drain the cup to its bitter dregs, so asked him which boat had sailed to Europe two years before.

Again his hesitation was just a fraction too long, indicating not only assent, but guilt.

"*Genesis Two?*" I asked. "Your boat?"

"Yes."

"And Nicole was with you?"

He nodded in terror.

"And you placed a bomb on my boat?"

It would have taken a nerveless creature not to feel terror at the tone of my question, or perhaps it was the cold, sharp steel that pricked at his eye socket that made Stephen shudder and begin to breathe in short, urgent gasps as though he suddenly had to cram a lot of oxygen into what was left of his miserable life. Jackie, fearing what I was about to do, turned away.

"It wasn't me!" Stephen managed to say.

"Was it Nicole?"

"She and her lover." He was gabbling now, eager to prove that he was cooperating with me, eager for my approval, eager to save his sight and his life.

"Her lover?" I remembered the photographs in the radio room at the mine which had showed Nicole with the tall, blond young man who had looked so uncannily like her brother, and I wondered what strange beasts prowled in our lusts when we let them through the gates of inhibition and fed them with our angers. "Is he fair-haired?"

Stephen nodded. "He's called Dominic, and he's her navigator now. They thought that if you died then they would inherit your boatyard and they could start their own group in Europe. Nicole wanted to prove she was better than Caspar, you see, but she needed a base to work from, so she picked your boatyard. Caspar didn't mind, because he always found Nicole difficult, so he said we could take *Genesis Two* to Europe, but only on condition that Nicole called her new group Genesis and acknowledged him as its founder. It almost never happened because we arrived a day late and we thought you'd be gone, and the weather was bad, but Nicole pressed on. She never gave up, never."

I stared into Stephen's terrified face, hating him.

Except it was not this little creep, but Nicole. It had always been Nicole. I had tried to persuade myself that she had been duped by von Rellsteb, while in truth she had been the instigator of all the evil. Why was I so surprised? Fletcher had told me that the vast majority of murders were committed inside the family, and that money and inheritance were motives for murder as old as man, and, from the first moment when I had suspected inheritance as the motive of Joanna's murder, I must have known it was Nicole and no one else. Von Rellsteb could not have profited from my death unless Nicole wished him to. I had tried to convince myself that von Rellsteb had manipulated Nicole, but I should have known better. Nicole had never been manipulated by anybody. It had been Nicole all along; Nicole had killed her own mother and tried to kill me.

"I didn't plant the bomb!" Stephen said in a low, pleading voice.

"Of course not," I said tiredly. It had been Nicole,

probably with her lover, who had stolen up the river in that rain-slatted darkness. It did not matter how, only who, and it could only have been Nicole, for only Nicole would have known that Joanna and I sailed to Guernsey every Easter, and only Nicole would have known just where to find *Slip-Slider,* and only Nicole would have remembered exactly how to get inside the boat to plant the bomb. Had she heard my voice that night? Had she heard her mother and I talking? Had she seen us at that moment when I switched on the yard's floodlamps?

"It wasn't me! It wasn't!" Stephen whimpered.

And, as I thought about Nicole crouching on my boatyard's pontoons, my imagination balked. How could she have done it? Did she think that by saving seals and staunching oil spills and harassing nuclear tests she could atone for murdering her parents? What ungoverned engine of hatred or envy or passion had driven her to such an act? Was it just for money? If Nicole had asked us, we would have helped her, but she had wanted to take all there was and without strings. So she had killed, and if I had not stayed behind to sell *Stormchild* Nicole would be leading her own environmental crusade from my boatyard.

"Tim?" Jackie said very tentatively.

"It wasn't me!" Stephen cried.

"Oh, shut the fuck up," I told him. He had been there. He had been on the boat that had crept up the river to commit murder. This green creep, this self-righteous rapist, had helped sail the boat that took my daughter to kill my wife. "Fuck you," I

said tiredly, then pulled the rigging knife away
and folded its blade. Hurting Stephen would
achieve nothing.

Instead I listened as Jackie questioned him about
Genesis. She had a journalist's curiosity and a
dogged patience, and elicited a sad, but oddly
familiar tale of idealism soured and high hopes
broken. Most of the Genesis activists, like Stephen
himself, had joined von Rellsteb in Canada or on
America's west coast, where, convinced that emotional indignation was a valid replacement for
informed thinking, and fired by the chorus of environmental doom-sayers, they had been attracted to
von Rellsteb's venomous gospel that only by the
most ruthless measures could a polluted world be
restored. For a time, fueled by youthful enthusiasm, von Rellsteb's disciples were convinced their
efforts were making a difference. Every press-cut-
ting that described a drift net sabotaged or a tree
saved encouraged them, yet, as they came to realize they were only doing what a hundred or a
thousand other such groups were doing, von
Rellsteb easily persuaded his followers that their
unique contribution to the environmental crusade
should be a paradigm wilderness community that
would be a forerunner of a new and ecologically
sound world. The Genesis community would show
the way to a better planet. They would live in
peace and organic harmony, hurting not a tree nor
a beast, and loving each other freely.

Patagonia had been the setting for this new
Eden, but, under the environment's hammer
blows of cold, rain, wind, and scarcity, the com-

munity's passionate idealism had first decayed
into petty jealousies and afterward into an author-
itarian hell. Peace was enforced with punishment,
the trees were cut for fuel and beasts killed for fur,
and free love had turned to institutionalized rape,
yet none of the community's leaders, and not
even the majority of its members, would confess
to failure, for to do so would have been to admit
that they were as fallible as other humans. Instead
they had persevered in their losing battle, clawing
small victories from decaying morale. They
harassed the drift netters, and Nicole, Stephen told
us, was even now patrolling the southern seas to
discover which tuna fishermen still killed dolphins. "Nicole will never give up," Stephen added
with a grudging admiration, and he confessed that
he had proved too feeble to join her crew; Nicole
wanted only the hardest and most fanatical people
on her boat. *Genesis Four,* Stephen told us, was
crewed by the community's hard-liners, who,
almost alone now, were still fulfilling some of von
Rellsteb's original aims.

The other members of the community had
given up the fight. Some had weakened and died,
to be buried at the foot of the escarpment, while a
very few had tried to escape, only to discover that
their paradise was too remote and too far from
other human traffic to make such escape possible.

I listened to the hopeless tale and, when Jackie
was finished and Stephen had no more answers to
give, I cut a strip of cloth from his jerkin and
gagged him once again.

Then we lay in silence and stared down at the

world von Rellsteb had made. This was his green
dream. This was the harbinger of the new, pure,
unindustrialized, unpolluted, clean, and lovely
world, where man would live in loving tune with
primal nature. Except nature had other ideas, and
so Jackie and I were staring down at a rain-pound-
ed, shit-stinking failure of flooded vegetable plots
and broken hopes. This, then, was the eco-par-
adise—a place of misery and filth with my daughter at its evil heart. This was Caspar von Rellsteb's
fiefdom, his achievement, and tonight, under the
cloak of darkness, I would destroy it.

The rain smashed down, flooding every hollow
in the uplands and spilling a myriad of rivulets
across the escarpment's edge. This was an earth-
drowning rain, a cataclysm of water, a planet-
drenching misery. We waited as the wan, wet light
faded. Jackie, huddling close beside me for
warmth, told me about her vain attempt to find a
newspaper that would send her south to explore
the Genesis story. Three major papers had been
interested, but each had insisted that a more experienced reporter be assigned to the story. So, she
and Molly Tetterman had decided to go south
themselves. They had flown to Santiago, then,
already worried that their money would run out,
they had bought second-class rail tickets to Puerto
Montt. "The train tickets only cost nine eighty-
five U.S.," Jackie explained, "and the airfare would
have been seventy-two dollars each! So we went
by train, and then we went to the steamship com-

pany and they agreed to bring us here and collect us on their way back from Puerto Natales. They were really great. I thought they were going to charge us a fortune, because the *San Rafael* had to steam miles out of its way to get us here, but they really seemed to want to help us. They're kind of curious about what goes on here."

I asked when the *San Rafael* was arriving to collect them, and Jackie said in ten or eleven days, depending on the weather, and then I thought to ask if, by any chance, she was carrying a watch, and she was, and she was sure it was accurate, and it showed us that the time was just three minutes short of the hour.

I climbed to the very top of the rock where, under the guyed mast and in the wind-whipping lash of the rain, I took out my handheld radio. I knew that the higher I was the more chance David had of hearing me. I switched the radio on and tried to ignore the ominous message of its blinking battery light. I tuned the set to channel 37 then pressed the transmit button. *"Stormchild, Stormchild,"* I said, "this is Tim, this is Tim. Over."

I waited. The red light seemed to be blinking more feebly and I assumed that each wretched blink was draining yet more power from the already weak battery. Rain was seeping inside my collar. "For fuck's sake, David"—I let my tension show—"talk to me!"

A very offended voice suddenly answered. "This is *Stormchild*, this is *Stormchild*. There's no need to use offensive language, Tim. We've been keeping a radio watch for you, but we've had to stand well offshore because of the weather, and there's a bit of westerly in the wind, as you must have noticed, so I didn't dare come too close to the coast." David wittered on, giving me his news, telling me how risky it had been leaving Almagro Channel, and I could not interrupt him, because, so long as he had his transmit button pressed he could not hear my transmissions, so all I could do was wait until he shut up. The small red light on my radio winked tiredly, and still David explained why it had taken him so long to hear my transmissions, but at last he handed the airwave back to me.

"David! I need you at the settlement. David, I say again, I need you at the Genesis settlement. Not at the mine, but at the settlement. Come here now. This radio is on the blink, I can't transmit much longer. Just come here! Do you read me? Over."

All I heard in reply was a hiss and a broken jumble of David's voice, and when the jumble ended I pressed my transmit button. "David! Just come here, just come here, just come here! To the settlement!" The red light was flickering, then disappeared altogether, and, when I released the transmit button, I could hear nothing at all from the set's small speaker. The red light's disappearance showed the radio was dead and I could only pray that with its last weary gasp it had sent the precious message and that David would obey my summons.

I went back to my hiding place where, as the light faded and the rain drummed on, I opened a tin of baked beans for Jackie, a can of corned beef for myself, and nothing at all for Stephen. Our enemies were ever more worried about their missing gunmen and sent two new and bedraggled search parties up into the rocks, but the new searchers still did not look right under their own noses and so discovered nothing. By now, I thought, Lisl would be getting close to panic. *Stormchild* was still on the loose, an unwanted visitor was prowling the island, and she had lost a man and his rifle. I hoped her nerves were shredding.

Before the light faded altogether, and after the last searcher had gone back down the escarpment, I took Jackie to the sheltered lee of the rock, smiled at her, then told her it was time she learned to fire a rifle.

Her eyes widened. "Tim," she began in a very determined voice.

"Shut up," I said in an even more determined voice, then I showed her how to cock the M16, where its safety catch was, and how to fire it in single shots and how to select automatic fire. "I'm surprised they didn't teach you how to do this in Sunday School," I said facetiously. "Doesn't every little American girl learn how to shoot? Now," I went on before she could answer, "the gun isn't loaded, so pick it up and show me how you fire it."

"I couldn't even touch it!" She stared with revulsion at the gun which now lay on the rock between us.

"But you can touch it," I said, "and fire it, and that's exactly what you're going to do tonight."

"No! I can't!" She shuddered. Anyone would have thought I had asked her to eat a steak.

"Listen!" I said, "I need some help tonight. I'm going down to the settlement and I want them to be looking in the wrong direction. In other words, I want you to distract them. So, show me how you select single-shot fire instead of automatic."

"Tim! I can't!"

"For Christ's sake," I said, "I'm not asking you to kill anyone! You don't even have to point the gun at anyone! You just point the damn thing at the stars and shoot the sky! All I want you to do is make a noise with it. Have you got scruples about making a noise?"

She reached out a tentative finger and touched the gun. It did not bite her. "Just make a noise?" she asked.

"Just make a noise," I reassured her.

She actually succeeded in picking the gun up. "You know I won't be able to kill anyone, Tim. I don't mind making a noise with it, but I won't point it at anyone!" She paused, her eyes huge in the damp dusk, and I felt a pang for the passions of youth.

"I told you," I said, "I just want you to make a noise."

"OK," she said bravely.

I gave her a kiss and, once I was sure she understood just how to fire the rifle, I spent the last of the seeping daylight making a weird contraption from parts of the dead radio, from the batteries of the flashlight I still had in my bag, and from five tins of baked beans. Jackie watched me with a puzzled expression. "What is it?" she asked.

"A vegetarian, nonlethal bomb," I told her, then

I pushed the strange contraption into my bag with all but one stick of the Australian girl's dynamite.

The sun sank behind the clouds and slowly, almost imperceptibly, the foul murk of day became the fouler blackness of wet night until, shrouded by the darkness, I wormed my way out of the rock crevice. Jackie gave me a kiss, I promised I would be back within the hour, and then, armed and dangerous, I went to make my mischief.

The first mischief was simply done. I climbed to the rock's peak, where I sawed through the guy wires that held the makeshift aerial upright. I cut two of the twanging wires and the gusting wind did the rest. I heard a splintering torment, then the mast and its aerial crashed down the precipitous slope. For a few seconds the night was filled with the tumble and protest of breaking wood, then there was silence.

"Tim?" Jackie called. "Are you all right?"

"Never better." The aerial's coaxial cable was still trapped on a snag of stone and, just to make sure that the toppled aerial was useless, I slashed the cable through. Now, whatever else might happen in this night's darkness, the settlement could not talk to von Rellsteb. Then, after calling another farewell to Jackie, I clambered from the rocks and slithered down the escarpment's steep face. I carried the Lee-Enfield, some of David's waterproof matches, and one stick of dynamite. I had left Jackie with the rest of the explosives, my vegetarian bomb, the M-16, and stern instructions that, should I not be back within three hours, she was to go north, find another hiding place somewhere on the coast, then use the gun either to signal David as *Stormchild* sailed past or, if *Stormchild* failed to appear, to alert the *San Rafael* when that vessel returned.

I reached the foot of the ridge and began to trudge through the waterlogged vegetable fields. My feet hurt, but I had no choice but to endure the pain. I was also soaked through. The escarpment's steep slope cheated the wind of much of its force, but the rain still fell on these lowlands with the same malevolence with which it crashed among the high rocks. I slipped and fell a dozen times and tried not to remember the feces that were spread on these damp fields. I cursed when I stumbled into a flooding drainage ditch. I shivered, chilled to my bones. The only lights in the wet darkness were the dim, yellow gleam of candles that flickered weakly behind the settlement's barred windows. For the moment I was keeping well clear of the house, preferring to begin my work at the stone wharf where the trawler was berthed.

Astonishingly the fishing boat was unguarded. It seemed that after the mysterious events of the day, the community had retreated into the safe haven of their big house, so, for the moment, I had the night to myself.

I used the heavy rigging knife to slice through all four of the trawler's mooring lines. The last warp parted with a drumming twang to recoil viciously into the darkness where the fishing boat was already drifting away on the strong ebb tide. I could have simply let the tidal current sweep the old boat far away, but I wanted to start a campaign of fear, so I took the tin of waterproof matches from my pocket, and with it the single stick of ancient dynamite with its woven fuse and, praying that the fuse would not burn too swiftly, I knelt down, clumsily struck a match in the teeming rain and, sheltering the fluttering fire under the wing of my coat, I held the dynamite's fuse into the red flame.

For a second the fuse did nothing and the match, assailed by the wind's gusting, almost went out, but then, and with an appalling swiftness, the fuse began to fizz bright sparks. The fuse was only five inches long and it seemed that three of those inches turned to instant ash as soon as the flame took hold, but I steeled myself to keep hold of the pinkish stick as I stood, turned, estimated the distance to the drifting trawler, then threw.

I saw the burning fuse arc through the darkness above the black water, then drop accurately down beyond the trawler's gunwale. I heard the dynamite thump and roll on the wooden deck, then I dropped flat on the quay's wet stones. I covered my head with my arms, closed my eyes tight, and waited.

Nothing happened, and I supposed that the ancient dynamite had been made useless by its exposure to the weather, which was a damned shame for I had predicated much of this night's mayhem on the efficiency of Alfred Nobel's invention and, in my disappointment, and as I tried to work out an alternative course of action, I raised my head to watch the fishing boat's dark shape drift away in the pouring night.

The boat blew up.

Give Nobel a prize, I thought, because the stick of old explosive had worked. Its blast thumped outward with an appalling, breath-stealing force, a force so great that for a few seconds it seemed as though the rain had been blown clean out of the sky, but then the circle of bright explosive light contracted and the hissing rain came back.

The explosion, scything across the trawler's deck, had lifted one of the huge fish-hold hatches and slammed it into the canted windows of the wheelhouse. A bright flame streaked up past the air, up past the boat's derricks, past its aerials, up to where the rain slanted silver and sharp from the low clouds. Another and darker flame was flickering amidst the smoke that was boiling up from the trawler's deck. That smaller flame was dark red, but suddenly it ran and spread to outline the boat's tarred rigging in fire. The sea was illuminated for twenty yards around the burning boat, while, in a much wider circle, scraps of burning debris dropped from the sky.

I slithered away, wriggling far beyond the light of the burning boat before I stood, wiped myself and the gun clean of mud, then began walking back toward the escarpment.

To my right the settlement was in tumult. Lights showed in almost every window. Most of the lights were candles, but there were a few powerful flashlights and two of those stronger lights now bobbed across the front stretch of grass as, too late, the Genesis activists ran around the bay's edge to discover what had happened to their precious boat.

I had thought that the rain might be strong enough to extinguish any fires that the explosion might have started; the very best effect I had dared hope for was that the dynamite might blow in the wheelhouse and shatter the steering lines, but the trawler's old timbers had been so soaked in oil and tar that they were like an incendiary mixture, and now they blazed to dazzle the night. They rippled fire across the bay and flickered a scarlet flame-light against the house front, and across the wet fields, and against the rocks that edged the bay, and up to the low hurrying clouds. The night was suddenly shining, but I was already a shadow in the margins of the lowlands.

I heard them lamenting their loss, but there was nothing they could do. Soon, I thought, their laments would turn to radio appeals for help, but they could not summon their leader, nor could they use their boat to escape. They were trapped, and I had just begun to play.

"How's Stephen?" I asked Jackie, "Giving you grief? You'd like me to kick his head in?"

"He's real quiet." Jackie gazed wide-eyed at the flame-lit scenery. It had taken me the best part of a half hour to climb back up the escarpment, yet still the burning trawler was shuddering the water

with the red reflections of its flames. The boat had
gone aground close to the wooded promontory
where she now slowly burned down to her waterline and from where her death streaked the black
sea with bands of red fire and cast deep shadows
into the settlement's courtyard and into the tumbled rocks by the beach and into the woods above
the burning boat. It was still raining and the
flames gave a dark crimson sheen to the spreading
puddles that made such a misery of the settlement's vegetable gardens.

I now wanted to add to that misery. I had used
one stick of dynamite on the boat, I needed
another later in the night, which left me with four
sticks, which I now made into a single bundle tied
with a strip of green cloth I had cut from
Stephen's trousers. "Getting cold, are you?" I
asked him.

He made an odd guttural noise from inside his
gag. He was shivering. The flames, though burning over half a mile away, were just strong enough
to reflect off his eyeballs. He watched me cut three
of the four fuses off their sticks, then I fashioned
the three into one long fuse which I spliced onto
the fourth. I hoped that I had quadrupled the time
between lighting the fuse and the resultant bang
of the bomb with which I planned to attack the
old earthern dam. I doubted whether the bomb
would be powerful enough to destroy the dam,
but, with luck, it would do enough damage to the
spillway to make the settlement an even more
uncomfortable place to live, and discomfort was
the major weapon I was using to drive von

Rellsteb's followers out to where the world might hold them accountable for their actions.

When the bomb was finished, Jackie and I slithered down from the rocks to the path beside the dam. I left her crouched by a pale boulder, while I walked along the paved pathway which ran across the dam's top.

The dam's purpose was not to conserve water, for water was the one commodity that was never scarce in this land, but rather to save the fields from perpetual flooding by diverting the escarpment's watershed westward instead of eastward. The dam also served as a gigantic header tank for the settlement, for which simple purpose it had no need of complicated sluicegates or turbines. Instead of such refinements I suspected that the dam simply leached its water into pipes buried deeply enough in the earthen wall to make sure that they were never blocked by ice in the wintertime. Some of the pipes would feed the conduits that irrigated the vegetable plots while others went to the house.

To make sure that the reservoir never overflowed to cascade an unwanted rush of water down to the settlement, there was a spillway at the western end of the reservoir which drained the lake's excess water into the island's inner tangle of wetlands. The whole nineteenth-century arrangement was a low-technology water control system of admirable simplicity and efficiency. It was also, I suspected, fairly resistant to sabotage.

That resistance was provided by the dam itself which was a massive wall of earth, doubtless rein-

forced with buried boulders that helped protect
the pipes. I suspected I could not reach those
pipes, so instead I planned to lower the sill of the
dam.

The sill was ten feet wide and had a central
pathway which was paved, but the paving stones
were old, moss-covered, cracked, and uneven, and
it was no trouble to lever one whole slab free.
Then, using my knife, I clawed and scratched and
dug my way down into the dam's sill. I dug like a
dog, desperately scrabbling soil aside as I delved
ever deeper into the cold, damp and hard-packed
mix of shingle and soil. The burning trawler gave
just enough ambient light to let me see what I was
doing.

When I had excavated as far as my arms could
reach, I put the bomb into my newly made burrow, then, taking care to leave the fuse exposed, I
swept loose soil and shingle over the bundled
dynamite. Finally, leaving a space just large
enough for my hand and a match, I pulled the
flagstone back over the half-filled hole.

"Are you ready?" I called to Jackie.

"Go for it!" she shouted back, and I reflected
that for a girl who went loose-kneed at the sight of
a gun she was remarkably sanguine about dynamite.

I glanced toward the settlement. The trawler's
flames were at last losing their battle with the del-
uge of rain and sea, but just enough flickering
light remained to show me the house and its
encircling wings. I could see no flashlights there,
indicating that the Genesis people, knowing their

fishing boat was lost, had withdrawn once more into the protection of the buildings where, doubtless, they were frantically and helplessly trying to reach von Rellsteb on the radio.

So now was the perfect time to feed their panic.

I struck a match in the space I had left under the stone. The flame struggled, then caught, and I touched it to the stub of fuse that suddenly hissed and spat sparks at my knuckles. The fire darted into the loose soil and I hoped to God that there was enough oxygen to keep the fuse burning right down to the old explosives.

I ran. Jackie reached a hand toward me and I threw myself down behind her rock and put an arm about her. "Hold tight," I said in unnecessary warning, then the fire bit into the explosives and the settlement's troubled night became a whole lot worse.

The dying light of the burning trawler was just sufficient to show us what happened. At first I thought the whole energy of the explosive had been wasted into a one-hundred-foot column of flame which belched straight into the sky like an incandescent geyser. Smoke boiled after the spear of flame, then, magically, the smoke seemed to evaporate, leaving nothing except the memory of that startling stab of fire that had pierced the wet sky and momentarily blinded us both.

"Damn," I said softly, thinking that the bomb had failed.

I heard splashes as lumps of soil and scraps of stone pattered down into the reservoir to break the complex geometric design of the radiating rip-

ples that had been generated by the explosive per-
cussion in the dam.

"Damn," I said again, because I had just used
four sticks of dynamite to achieve nothing more
than pretty patterns on a lake.

"No! Listen!" Jackie said excitedly.

I listened and, above the sound of wind and
rain, I heard an odd grinding noise which became
yet louder and louder, and which seemed to come
from the very heart of the mountain beneath us,
and which suddenly turned into a titanic belch
that, in turn, gave birth to an obscenely vast bubble which shattered the black surface of the reservoir hard by the sill itself.

Then, extraordinarily, it seemed as though the
hard-packed soil at the very center of the dam was
being turned into a shivering and gleaming liquid.
Jackie and I, huddled together in the rain,
watched as the apparently solid wall began to
quiver and glisten as the water infiltrated the
bomb-loosened mass of earth. For a second a
smooth, shining, fire-touched lip of water trem-
bled and glittered at the outer edge of the liquefy-
ing dam, then the whole vast agglomeration
collapsed.

The bomb had done better than I had ever
dared anticipate. I had hoped that the explosion
might bite a chunk out of the dam's sill, and that
the consequent erosion of the spilling water
would do the real damage by widening my small
fissure into a gaping breach, but instead the whole
construction now seemed to shatter and collapse
over the escarpment's edge in a single thunderous

avalanche of earth, rocks, and water.

"Bloody hell fire!" I said in delighted awe.

Jackie was gripping my hand with a strength I would not have credited in her.

The water deluged to the bottom of the escarpment, fed now by a veritable Niagara of draining floodwater that slid across the dam's shattered brink. Spray bounced high to meet the rain as what was left of the old earthern dam wall was torn away in chunks the size of houses.

The floodwaters churned across the fields, drowning the vegetables and pouring like a tidal wave toward the house. The released lakewater smashed into the courtyard and flooded into the settlement's lower story as still more water poured in a smooth rush across the rim of the hills. The turbulent flood, touched red and silver by the flames, spread across the plain below, lapped against the big house, and reached with greedy shining streams toward the sea. The flashlights appeared again, but only to bob helplessly above the inundation.

"Aren't you proud of me?" I asked Jackie.

"I'm proud of you," she said, then touched my unshaven cheek with the tips of her fingers. "Be careful, Tim."

"I'll be careful," I promised, for now it was time for me to go down the escarpment again, but this time to visit the flooded settlement itself. Jackie was not coming with me. Instead she would stay safe on the high ground, where, in exactly thirty minutes, she would create a diversion by firing her rifle. She would not fire at the settlement, but into the sky where she could be fairly certain that she would not be shooting any people, bunny rabbits, or roosting sea gulls.

I sent Jackie safe on her nonviolent way, picked up my bag with its baked-bean bomb, shouldered my rifle, and went back down the hill.

I waded through the glutinous slough that I had fashioned from the settlement's vegetable plots. Water still gushed from the destroyed dam, not with the terrible force that had followed the explosion, but still in a strong enough flow to make a curling silver stream that twisted through the mud to make a pool of the courtyard.

I could hear children crying as I neared the house. I could also hear Molly Tetterman hammering on the door of her flooded prison. She was stridently demanding to be released, but I decided she was safer where she was and left her in miserable ignorance while I prowled round to the front of the house.

No one challenged me as I splashed nearer and nearer the pale building. The yellow light of candles and lanterns shivered behind the windows of the upper floor, but the flooded lower story was pitch black. The trawler had at last burned out and the troubled night had slid back into its impenetrable darkness as I took the last remaining stick of dynamite out of my bag. Then I sidled along the front wall of the house and waited.

Children cried above me. I heard a man's angry voice demand that the damned kids be quiet. A woman protested against the man's anger and was immediately hushed, then Lisl's voice, strident and loud, demanded silence. "Listen!" she ordered, and for a second I thought she wanted everyone's attention for some important announcement, but instead she wanted everyone to listen for any more sounds of trouble in the surrounding darkness.

They did not have to wait long.

Jackie fired. She told me later that she had fired the rifle so high into the air that the bullet had probably clipped an angel's wing, but, more to my purpose, the crack of the gun was an unmistakable sound in the wet night and I heard feet stampede across the upper floor to the windows that faced inland. Jackie fired again, and, sure that my enemies had been safely diverted to the back of the house, I struck a match, lit the last fuse, then rolled the dynamite up against the front door before running desperately out onto the soggy lawn to put as much distance as possible between my body and the explosion. I ran twenty paces, then dropped.

"Quiet!" Lisl shouted again, for the brace of rifle shots had prompted a babble of excited voices which, in turn, had started all the infants bawling again. "Look for the muzzle flash!" I heard Lisl shout. I could also hear the fuse of my dynamite spitting angrily, but I saw nothing, for I had my eyes closed and my face pressed hard into the damp ground.

The dynamite blew. I felt the thumping, breath-snatching hot billow of the expanding gasses wash

over me, then my head and shoulders were bom-
barded by scraps of soil. When I raised my head I
saw that the trellised porch had vanished and the
double front doors had been turned into a gaping
and smoking hole. Desperate children were
screaming like tortured banshees in the upstairs
rooms. I worked the Lee-Enfield's bolt, putting a
round into the chamber, then turned the safety
catch off.

"This side!" a voice shouted, and a flashlight
stabbed toward me in the rainy darkness.

I fired. Not at the light itself, but into the window above it. I merely wanted to scare, not to kill.

I heard window glass crash and tinkle as the
light was jerked back inside the room.

I ran toward the house. The door frame was a
smoking mess that led into a hallway inches deep
in floodwater. Light filtered down a stairway to
show me bare walls on which paint of a horrid
institutional green peeled sadly. I pushed into a
room to see the same drab paint. The place
reminded me of the English boarding schools
where David and I had learned the merits of acute
discomfort. I went back into the hall, splashed
past the the splintered front doors that were lying
across the foot of the stairs, and found the
kitchen. Water and mud silted the floor, but the
twin wood-burning furnaces of the long black
range were both alight, making the big room won-
drously warm. I doubted if these twin fires were
ever extinguished for the furnaces probably sup-
plied all the heat and hot water for the entire settlement. I almost burned my hand trying to open

the nearest furnace door, and had to snatch off my woolen hat to use as a hot pad. The heat seared at me from the open door. I found a candle on the table, lit it from the stove's flames, then, my business properly lit, I set about making the room uninhabitable.

I started by hanging my bag, which held my vegetarian bomb, on a beam close to the kitchen door. I carefully arranged the bag's contents, then I extinguished the settlement's fires. I used an old cast-iron skillet to scoop muddy water from the floor and pour it onto the precious flames.

The burning timbers hissed in protest. Water beaded and scurried across the stove's red-hot iron as I went on ladling yet more water into the two furnaces. The kitchen filled with steam and smoke. I had flooded the valley, disabled the radio, now I would deprive them of heat and cooking. Short of burning down the house I could think of few things more calculated to destroy morale in this uncomfortable place.

Once the fires were doused, I used the rifle's butt to sweep plates, bowls, and cups off the dresser. I smashed the crockery into piles of creamy fragments, then yanked down the bunches of herbs that hung from the ceiling beams. I upset huge boxes of stringy red seaweed that, like the herbs, I trampled into the floodwaters. I bashed a metal chimney pipe clean off its stove, then used the rifle's brass-bound butt to hammer through the old lead pipes that brought water to the kitchen. I stove in the windows, then opened a cupboard and spilled more of the settlement's invaluable supplies onto the flooded floor. I tipped over a whole barrel of flour, then hammered at a basket of eggs.

Every few seconds I suspended my activity to listen for the footsteps that would presage a counter-attack by the Genesis people, yet the group was so frightened or else so disorganized that I had virtually finished the wrecking of the kitchen before I at last heard the sound of feet on the stairs. I froze, then heard the scrape of the fallen doors being moved and afterward a cautious splashing in the hallway.

I stepped silently back into a large scullery. A scrap of mirror hung by the door and I saw myself reflected in the tarnished glass, and for a second I did not recognize my unshaven face. It was so smeared with mud that it looked as though I had used a whole tin of army camouflage cream. My bloodshot eyes stared grimly back at me, then I looked away from the glass, raised the rifle, and waited to see who had come to investigate.

Two people stepped through the door. One was a bearded man dressed in faded green, the other, a thin, frightened-looking girl in a baggy gray sweater and lank gray trousers. She hung back behind the man who was carrying a rifle. He stared appalled at the destruction I had caused, while his companion began to whimper. Neither of them saw me in the dark recess of the scullery.

"Drop the gun," I said, "or you're dead."

The bearded man twisted toward me. I fired.

I did not aim to kill. Instead I just filled the room with the noise of the Lee-Enfield, and my bullet buried itself harmlessly in the opposite wall. The girl screamed, I worked the bolt, and the bearded man dropped the rifle into the floodwater as though the gun had suddenly scalded him.

I stepped out of the scullery. "My name is Tim Blackburn"—I held the gun on the man—"and I came here a few days ago seeking news of my daughter, Nicole. No one had the courtesy to give me that news, so I've come back to find it for myself."

The bearded man, his hands in the air, stared at me with a look of pure horror. The girl had cringed back toward the door.

"Lift the flap of the bag above your head," I told the man. "Do it very gently, and don't dislodge the bag, just look under the flap. Quickly now!"

The man very timorously reached up and lifted the canvas flap of my old fishing bag. The room's single candle flickered, but it gave more than enough light to let the man see what lay under the bag's flap, and what he saw terrified him.

He saw my contraption, which consisted of the flashlight's two batteries and one of the printed circuit boards I had taken from the dead handheld radio. I had also ripped out some of the radio's connecting wires and managed to fasten them to the batteries, which, like the circuit board, hung ominously over the lip of the bag. The wires were anchored inside the bag by my unconsumed tins of baked beans. The contraption was entirely useless, yet to the bearded man, who had already witnessed three explosions this night, the device must have looked as devilish as any terrorist's lethal concoction.

"It's going to explode very soon," I told him, "and when it does there'll be nothing left of this house. Do you understand me?"

He made a strangulated noise, then nodded.

"So you're to go upstairs," I told him, "and move everyone out of the house. You're all to go down to the beach and shelter under the bluff, otherwise that bomb will likely kill you. That bag is stuffed with Semtex, and I've equipped it with a trembler switch so that even I can't take it down and defuse it. Do you still understand me?"

He nodded again. If I had told him that the old fishing knapsack was in reality a multiple-targeted independent reentry vehicle equipped with thirty three thermonuclear warheads he would probably have nodded.

"And don't try to radio von Rellsteb for help," I told him, "because I've dismantled your aerial. Now go upstairs and tell Lisl to get everyone out of this house quickly! Go!"

The two of them fled, and I picked the man's discarded M-16 out of the mud. Above my head there were sudden screams, then a stampede of footsteps on the stairs, proof that the threat of the baked bean bomb was working. Somewhere in the darkness, and sounding as if it had been fired from much closer than the escarpment's crest, Jackie's gun suddenly cracked three times and I smiled to think how adventurous she was becoming. The candle on the kitchen table flickered in the draft from the broken windows while upstairs a baby cried. The kids, I thought, were in for a very rough night, but better these few hours of cold misery and hunger than a lifetime of enslavement to von Rellsteb's green tyrrany.

I moved to the kitchen door and saw that a flood of people, gray and ill-dyed green, were scrambling down the stairs, across the broken doors, and out into the rainy darkness. Some carried their children, while others had snatched up blankets. A few green-dressed men carried guns, but they were too intent on escape to use them. Most of the fugitives glanced at me, but they did not speak, they just fled from my threat in the certain knowledge that their house was about to be destroyed, just as their fishing boat and their reservoir had vanished on this night of nightmare.

Lisl was the last to flee. She gave me a cool look, but otherwise offered no defiance. I waited till she was gone and the house was empty, and until the only sounds were those of the rain falling and the wind sighing and of Molly Tetterman demanding her release from her damp prison cell. None of the Genesis people had thought to free Molly Tetterman, but she wasn't in any danger, so I was happy to leave her in her makeshift cell.

So now, other than the imprisoned Molly, I had the house to myself. I had captured von Rellsteb's sanctuary, which, with two guns on my shoulder, I went to explore.

I edged past the shattered and scorched front doors and climbed the stairs. The stairway walls had once been decorated with a dark paper that had since been embellished by the Genesis children with chalk pictures of spouting whales, soaring albatrosses, and waddling penguins. The top of the stairwell had a fine cast-iron balustrade; doubtless one of the many thousands that had been used in the nineteenth century as ballast for empty ships outbound for the southern hemisphere, and which, to this day, so handsomely decorate Australian balconies. The stairs themselves were made of mahogany, a reminder that although the exterior of the house might have been remarkably plain, the first von Rellsteb had clearly spent money on its interior, perhaps so that when he drew his tasseled velvet curtains he could pretend that a wilderness did not press dark against his windowpanes.

The upper landing opened onto a main corridor that stretched dimly on either hand. I walked slowly down the left-hand corridor, pushing open doors to peer into the abandoned rooms. Some of those rooms were still lit by candles and lanterns, and their stark bleakness was another forcible reminder of the boarding-school dormitories of my youth. These bedrooms contained very little beyond cold metal bunks fitted with thin mattresses. Some betrayed a more cheerful touch with homemade rag rugs or curtains fashioned from threadbare bolts of cloth, yet the most comfortable aspect of these sleeping quarters were the ubiquitous otter-fur coverlets on the beds, and I assumed that the sheer misery of the Patagonian cold had driven these self-styled enviromentalists to slaughter. One large room was a nursery and had homemade toys on the floor, bright yellow curtains, and two decrepit sofas, but despite those efforts at domesticity the effect of the living quarters was gruesomely cheerless. I found three bathrooms, all with old-fashioned wooden stands on which chipped enamel bowls rested, big zinc baths hanging from their walls, and tin lavatories that stank because their contents were being saved to fertilize the vegetable fields. The bathrooms, unlike the bedrooms, had no fireplaces, or indeed any other means of being heated. In one bathroom rainwater was dripping to puddle on the ancient cracked linoleum and I shuddered to imagine how in winter these washrooms would be skimmed with ice.

The corridor ended in a window which looked out on the northern hills. I peered into the darkness where Jackie, with an unexpected eagerness, was still banging shots into the night. I half smiled at her enthusiasm, then turned and walked in the opposite direction, past the stairhead and past more spartan rooms. My candle guttered, but its flame cast just enough light to show me that the shorter southern corridor ended, not in a window, but at a handsome mahogany door.

I pushed the door handle down to find it locked.

I took the Lee-Enfield off my shoulder, aimed it at the lock, and fired. In the cinema such a violent act would have sprung the door open with the facility of an exploding bomb, but my shot simply seemed to have jammed the door's mechanism even more firmly. I kicked at the recalcitrant lock with my right heel, but only succeeded in shooting a pang of agony into my already pained foot, then fired a second shot into the tangle of splintered wood and bright bullet-gouged brass. The second bullet, like the first, mangled the mechanism most spectacularly, yet was no more efficient in opening the wretched door than the first shot.

It took me six bullets and a bruised shoulder to finally smash the door open, but, at last, on unoiled hinges, the mahogany swung back and I found myself in the rooms that were evidently reserved for the privileged crew members of Genesis.

It was like passing from a slum to a palace. Whatever lavish comforts and decencies might have mitigated the rigors of this awful place had been put into these rooms. In truth, anywhere other than in

Patagonia, these luxuries would have looked tawdry, but here, on this barren, far island of the world's most bitter shore, the furnishings of these last rooms suggested an air of the most voluptuous carnality, and it was no wonder that the fanatical Nicole had spurned such hedonism to house her crew in the more spartan buildings at the mine.

The floors in von Rellsteb's rooms were covered with a profusion of faded oriental carpets that lent the rooms a feeling of instant opulence. The damp wallpaper was hidden by closely hung paintings and prints, most of which showed romantic German landscapes heavy with gloomy crags, turreted castles, and plunging waterfalls. I suspected that the paintings, like some of the oil lamps that stood on the unwaxed tables, must have been brought to the house by the first von Rellsteb to settle in Patagonia. Between the landscapes hung prints of German cathedrals and etchings of famous Germans; I recognized Blucher, Frederick the Great, Martin Luther, and Goethe, while a plaster bust of Beethoven frowned from the mirror-crowned mantelpiece. Fringed velvet tablecloths were draped over some of the pieces of furniture, while the ancient horse-hair armchairs and sofas were carefully protected by the remnants of lace antimacassars. The furniture had doubtless been intended to convey a sense of Germanic respectability, but now its very incongruity somehow made it seem salacious; a reminder that in frontier territories the first buildings to be lavishly furnished were almost always the brothels. After them came the lawyers' offices, but it was always the whores who had the first carpets.

The two bathrooms that served these privileged rooms were decently equipped with claw-footed tubs and mahogany-seated commodes. The bedrooms were cozy, all with beds so stacked with mattresses that they looked as high as haystacks. One of the smaller rooms was the settlement's radio room; von Rellsteb would never have allowed his farm workers near the transmitters and had taken care to install the equipment behind locked doors. Inside the radio room was a board hung with keys, one of which I supposed would unlock the stable where Molly Tetterman was still imprisoned.

Molly, I decided, would have to wait as I explored these unexpectedly luxurious quarters, of which the final room was by far the most lavish. It was a bedroom with windows facing east toward the sea and south toward the wild moors, and, from the luxury of its furnishings, I guessed that this was where von Rellsteb and Lisl stayed when they were in the settlement. The room was dominated by a vast, carved, wooden bed, on which a grubby white eiderdown floated like a cloud. A cavernous wardrobe stood next to a tile-surrounded fireplace that still held the warm remnants of a log fire. Beside the bed was an antique mahogany dressing table with a huge oval mirror. If it had not been for the rain that dripped from my soaking clothing onto the rugs, and for the two guns on my shoulder I might have thought myself in some Victorian mansion in respectable Frankfurt.

I put my candle into an elegant brass holder on a

bedside table, then paused to listen. Jackie, clearly reveling in her sudden discovery of guns, ripped a whole clip of bullets into the air, but otherwise I heard nothing to alarm me. I knew that some of the Genesis refugees were armed, but I was trusting that they were now so cowed by the night's disasters that they would not dare come back to the house. I also knew their supine inactivity would not last forever, and I therefore could not risk spending too long exploring the house. Yet the temptation to ransack von Rellsteb's own quarters was too great and so I hung the M-16 from my shoulder, tossed the Lee-Enfield onto the bed where it was swallowed in the fluffy billows of the great eiderdown, and then began a feverish search of the big room. I found very little. One drawer of the dressing table had a scrapbook of newspaper cuttings, which told of Genesis's triumphs over their polluting enemies, but the cuttings were few and the victories hardly worth remembering. There were oilskins in the wardrobe and a pile of sweaters in another cupboard, while a small bedside table held a tiny cache of coins and jewels which looked like some tawdry pirate's hoard. It was all so pathetic.

Somewhere in the night a gun fired three deliberate shots. I could not tell whether it was Jackie or one of the Genesis people, so I edged to the eastern window, taking care not to silhouette myself, and stared into the darkness. At first I saw nothing, then, with a horrid shock, I saw a flicker of light out in the bay. My first thought was that the burning trawler had drifted off the rocks, then I realized this new light was too white to be the remnants of any fire.

Then I wondered if *Stormchild* had returned to the
bay and if I was seeing a glimmer of her cabin light,
because the light was certainly made by a ship's
lantern of some kind, but then I forgot the strange
light in the bay because something heavy thumped
on the bedroom's floor behind me.

I turned in panic to see a tin of baked beans
rolling across the carpet toward me.

"Bang," said Caspar von Rellsteb, and laughed.

He leaned in the doorway, dressed in wet oilskins, and with an amused expression on his thin
face. He carried a rifle, as did Lisl, who stood
beside him. She also carried my old fishing knapsack, which she scornfully dropped on the floor so
that another of the baked bean tins rolled pathetically clear. Then, a smile on her face, she turned
her gun's muzzle toward me. "Put the gun down,"
she ordered me, "but do it very slowly!"

I very slowly unslung the M-16 and placed it on
the floor.

"Kick it toward me," von Rellsteb said.

I kicked the assault rifle toward him. It skidded
against a rug, then disappeared under the bed. The
Lee-Enfield, on top of the bed, was concealed by
the folds of the eiderdown, but I was too far from
the bed for the hidden gun to be of any use to me.
I had been trapped by my overconfidence.

Now von Rellsteb had the advantage and I did
not see how he could lose it. "I should have killed
you in Florida," he said in an oddly friendly voice.
"Your daughter was angry that I hadn't. She wants
to inherit your boatyard, you see. She still does, in
fact, though I've told her that you've probably

changed your will by now. Even so, she was right. I should have killed you."

Was he trying to shock me by talking so casually of Nicole's wish to kill me? I refused to rise to his bait, preferring to keep my voice very calm as though we merely talked about the weather. "Was that why you agreed to meet me there? Did you lose your nerve?"

He shook his head. "I met you out of mere curiosity, Mr. Blackburn. You said you had important news, remember, and I wanted to hear it. I was wasting my time, but it was still interesting, and your letter was very pathetic."

"You bastard," I said in impotent anger.

He mocked me with a grimace of feigned sympathy. "I think you have had your revenge here tonight. A pity. It will take us weeks to clear up the mess, but in the meantime we shall feed your body to the hawks."

"It's no good shooting me," I said defiantly, "because the authorities know I'm here."

"Oh, my God! I am so very frightened!" Von Rellsteb laughed. "The authorities! You hear that, Lisl? Perhaps we had better surrender immediately."

"My boat will be in Puerto Natales by now," I plowed on in the face of von Rellsteb's mockery, then tried a little of my own. "You probably thought it was going north?" I smiled, as though I pitied him his misconception.

"Actually," von Rellsteb put a scornful English accent on the word, "I think your boat is on its way here. I suspect it has been hiding offshore for the last two days."

I said nothing. How the hell did he know these things? And once again, just as I had when we confronted each other at the mine, I wondered if this devil was a mind reader.

Von Rellsteb laughed. "Mr. Blackburn, what VHF channel would you monitor if you knew you were dealing with the owner of an English boatyard? Which channel does your daughter prefer when she wants a measure of privacy?" He shook his head as though he was disappointed in my stupidity. "I have been monitoring channel 37 ever since you first arrived in our waters! I thought you might use it to try and reach Nicole, but instead I heard your friend answer your transmission last night. We couldn't hear you, I imagine because you were using a low-power transmitter? Whatever, your friend is now innocently sailing toward us, and I assure you we will prepare a suitable welcome for him; you, I think, will be dead by then. But first, tell me! Are you responsible for the dreadful Mrs. Tetterman being here?"

I tried to look very vague. "Who?"

Von Rellsteb was silent for a second, then shrugged as though he did not really care whether I told the truth or not. "How did you escape at the quarry?"

It was my turn to shrug. "I flew."

Lisl fired a burst of three or four bullets that missed my right shoulder by a whisker. The room was suddenly echoing with noise and stinking with the acrid smell of the gun's propellant. "How did you escape?" she asked harshly.

"When you saw me fall," I confessed, "I had a

rope round my waist. I then climbed to the quarry floor and waited you out."

"Nicole inherited your cunning," von Rellsteb said with a touch of genuine admiration, "and perhaps also your daring. She is very brave. Too brave. I have always thought that one day she will come too close to a Japanese fishing boat and they will ram her. Of all of us, you see, she has caused the most damage to the Japanese nets. There are also times"—he smiled—"when I am tempted to hope that she will come too close to a Japanese fishing boat. She wants to take over from Lisl and me, but luckily for us Nicole does not, how do you say, own the farm? Which is why she went to England. She wanted her own farm." He was watching me very closely. "But you already knew that. How does it feel to have a daughter who wants to kill you? Who killed her own mother? She meant to get you both, of course."

He was trying to rile me, but I said nothing. That was not defiance, but helplessness. My heart was thumping in my chest, my stomach was bitter with defeat, my knees were weak and my mind a blur of hopeless schemes: I could jump to the window, I could leap to the hidden gun on the bed, I could grow wings and fly away. The truth was that I was going to die and von Rellsteb was enjoying the infliction of that truth.

"Why?" I finally managed to find my voice, though it was a very weak and plaintive voice. "Why do you do this? You're supposed to be preserving life, not taking it."

"Now you're being very boring and entirely pre-

dictable," von Rellsteb said. "Do you think that by
enticing me into a sophomoric discussion of my
motives you will gain time? Or perhaps you imagine you can persuade me to let you live? Maybe I
should let you live until Nicole reaches us? She is
coming, you know. I talked to her on the radio
not three hours ago and told her you were here.
Would you like to wait for her?"

"Yes!" I pleaded.

"I think not." Von Rellsteb enjoyed thus contra-
dicting my hopes, "because my people are waiting
outside in the rain, and I would like them to come
inside and get warm, which means I have to kill
you before they return. Most of them are loyal,
but some of them are still naive enough to be
shocked by murder." He aimed the rifle at my face
and I saw Lisl half smile in anticipation of my
death, then Jackie, who must have climbed the
stairs to stand in the doorway that I had blown
open with the Lee-Enfield, ordered von Rellsteb to
put the gun down.

Von Rellsteb stiffened in shock, while an astonished Lisl half turned toward the sudden threat.

"Put the guns down!" Jackie's voice was hysteri-
cal. "I'll shoot!"

Von Rellsteb heard the desperation in that
threat, and he must have realized that Jackie was
almost helpless with nervousness. His eyes flicked
toward me, and I could see what he was thinking,
that he could step out of Jackie's line of sight,
then shoot me, but to do that he would leave Lisl
exposed.

"Shoot him if he moves a finger!" I called to

Jackie, and I wished she would shoot anyway, but I knew she would not. It was a miracle that she had even managed to aim her gun toward von Rellsteb, but she was about as likely to pull her trigger as eat a pork chop. Her sudden appearance had gained me time, but it would be my responsibility to talk Jackie and me out of this unexpected stand-off. "You can't kill me," I said to von Rellsteb, "so you might as well drop your gun. Both of you."

"Why can't we kill you?" Von Rellsteb, despite having Jackie's gun aimed at his back, evidently found my defiance amusing.

"Because the *San Rafael* is coming back here"—I was snatching arguments out of the thinnest air— "and the women who arrived on the *San Rafael* will tell the crew that you murdered me, and that'll be the end of you."

"You are telling me the game is up?" Von Rellsteb mocked me with his use of the stilted cliché.

"Of course the game's up, you fool!" I snapped.

"Not really," von Rellsteb said happily. "I shall radio the *San Rafael* and tell them that their two passengers have decided to join our little band of conservationists, and that therefore they have no need to go so far out of their way. I think they will be grateful to be spared the expense of the fuel, don't you?" He smiled. "I also think, Mr. Blackburn, that if your very nervous rescuer truly planned to kill me, then she would have fired at me already"—he paused to make certain I was directly in his rifle's sights—

"so fare thee well, Mr. Blackburn, fare thee well."
And the gun fired.

Jackie screamed terribly.
Lisl began to turn. I threw myself backward, instinctively falling away from the expected bullets.
Von Rellsteb pitched forward.
Jackie still screamed.
I fell against the wall and bounced back towards Lisl. The sound of gunfire was obscenely loud, echoing off the walls and filling the house. Bullets were chopping across gilt-framed pictures and churning the wall's horsehair plaster into dust and ruin. Picture glass shattered bright, mingling with the blood that was spurting vividly across the room.
It was von Rellsteb's blood, because it had been Jackie who fired.
She had fired her rifle on automatic and, by luck more than judgment, her aim had been perfect. So perfect that her stream of bullets had literally exploded von Rellsteb's chest. She had turned his torso inside out, so that blood and bits of lung tissue and shards of bone and strips of heart were spraying across the carpeted floor.
And Jackie was screaming with horror.
Lisl was falling as she turned. She was smothered in blood, but it was not her blood. She had caught her dying lover's last heartbeat and now she was twisting her rifle toward Jackie whose own gun was now empty. I threw myself forward. My

movements were stiff. My clothes were heavy and waterlogged. My joints ached. I moved like a man underwater.

Lisl saw my movement and began to swing her gun back toward me. I heard Jackie scream again, and Lisl's gun jerked once more toward her. I had sprawled on the bed's thick and fluffy eiderdown that was drenched with von Rellsteb's blood. I scrabbled for the Lee-Enfield. Lisl was ignoring me, aiming at Jackie, and then the heavy rifle was in my hands and I could not remember if the safety catch was on or off, but I didn't have time to find out so I just pointed the barrel and pulled the trigger, and the muzzle was still caught in the eiderdown so that the expanding gasses and the speeding bullet exploded a blizzard of duck feathers, and the bolt would not work because it was also trapped in the thick folds, but I managed to force the bolt to ram another round into the chamber, and I fired again, but Lisl's face had already disappeared in a bright eruption of blood where the first bullet had struck her. The second bullet banged through her gullet, jerking her head forward and back, and then she slumped into a sitting position with her blood pouring thick and shining to make a puddle between her legs.

"Oh, my God!" Jackie was panting. "Oh, my God!"

The room stank of blood and cordite.

Feathers floated in the dusty air. Lisl's red hair had been made a brighter red by her dying blood in which two drifting feathers had stuck to give her an oddly festive look. For a second I thought she was still alive as her hands twitched and I almost fired again until I realized that I was merely watching her fingers contract into the claws of death. They twitched, curled, then she was still.

Jackie was sobbing helplessly.

I disentangled the Lee-Enfield and worked another round into the chamber. There were yet other gunmen at large and I had already foolishly allowed myself to be ambushed once.

Von Rellsteb's dead body voided a long fart.

Lisl's body slumped sideways. The room looked and smelled like a slaughterhouse.

Bile was sour in my throat. I slid off the bed and stood up.

"Oh, my God." Jackie recovered her breath, choked, breathed again, then staggered into the room. "I tried to warn you they were coming"— she was speaking very fast as if she would lose track of her words if she spoke slowly—"because I saw their boat come, so I kept firing the gun. Oh, my God!" She had gasped the words out like a small girl delivering a very important message she did not wholly understand, then she vomited.

The candle guttered. Outside the window a baby was crying. It was still raining.

I stepped over the horror and gathered Jackie in my arms.

And Genesis was almost, but not quite, finished.

By dawn the unhappy Genesis survivors were back in their ruined house. They had no fight left.

As a group they had believed that their aims could best be achieved by violent confrontation, yet, when their methods had been used against them, they had collapsed like a pricked bubble.

Except that Nicole had not collapsed, and, if von Rellsteb had told me the truth, she was even now sailing back for her vengeance. One other Genesis boat had returned in convoy with von Rellsteb and now rode at anchor beside his catamaran in the settlement's bay. That left two Genesis boats still at sea: Nicole's catamaran and the second sloop. I did not fear the sloop's return, for, like the other crews, I suspected their hostility would crumble when they saw the full measure of their community's defeat. But Nicole, everyone assured me, was made of grimmer stuff. Von Rellsteb's radio operator, a glum Californian, confirmed that he had reached Nicole's boat on his single sideband set, but claimed to have forgotten to ask *Genesis Four* for a precise position report. I did not believe him, and, encouraged by the Lee-Enfield's blackened muzzle, he confessed that Nicole's catamaran was hurrying home, but was still some three or four days from making a landfall.

In the wet dawn I disabled the two Genesis yachts by cutting their running rigging and emptying the oil from their engines. I then ran the engines till the pistons seized, hauled in the yachts' anchors, shot the guts out of their radios, then left them to drift until they beached themselves close to the burned-out trawler.

Once the boats were finished I wrapped the

bodies of von Rellsteb and his lover in sailcloth and dragged them through the cloying mud to one of the tanning sheds. I assumed the Chilean authorities would want to see the two corpses. Not that I cared, because I would be long gone.

Jackie, aghast at having killed, went to the sea's edge in the dawn and sat for a long time with her head in her hands. I thought she might have been praying, and perhaps she was, but when her prayers were done, or her thoughts finished, she came and held me very tight. She said nothing and when I tried to speak she just hushed me. She just wanted to be touched.

Molly Tetterman, released from her prison, took it upon herself to organize the dispirited Genesis survivors. Molly could no more resist organizing other people than a bee could desist from making honey, for, while she believed herself to be a nurturing earth mother, she was, in truth, a feminist sergeant-major, who discovered in the sodden wreckage of the settlement a challenge worthy of her talents, and thus she cowed, drilled, and bullied the Genesis survivors into making some small efforts for their own comfort. She rescued food from the ruin I had made of the kitchen and handed out warm clothes from von Rellsteb's wardrobe. She harassed the men into cleaning up the mud-drenched rooms, and used her gentler talents to comfort the scared children. Molly, in brief, was just what a shattered Genesis community needed, and just what I needed, for her bundles of energy freed me from the need to make a similar effort.

Molly looked after the settlement's survivors, while I crippled their boats and wrapped their dead. Then, in mid-morning, I limped through the remains of the vegetable plots toward the escarpment. Stephen, I remembered, was still imprisoned on the ridge.

Jackie caught up with me beside a pond that had been a cabbage patch before I released the reservoir. Where the dam had been there was now nothing but a smooth, high valley that hung above the coastline. A small stream spilt over that lofty rim to glitter in the wan morning light. "What do you think of Molly?" Jackie asked in a tone of voice which implied that she expected to hear my heartfelt expressions of admiration.

"She overwhelms me," I said, "but I'm glad she's here, because she can look after this place till the authorities get here." Once David arrived I proposed to contact the Chilean authorities on *Stormchild*'s radio and tell them about the murder of the Australians, and about the body they would find in the high rocks above the limestone quarry, and about von Rellsteb and Lisl. They would not, however, find me because, as I told Jackie, I intended to take *Stormchild* and intercept Nicole's return.

It took me most of the scramble up the wet escarpment to outline those plans. Once at the top I released the freezing Stephen from the rock cleft. He was pathetically grateful, but less so when I unceremoniously kicked him over the escarpment's brink to tumble him helplessly down the steep slope toward the flooded settlement.

Jackie and I stood together on the rocky summit beside the wreckage of the radio mast. The wind whipped at our coats and drove cold rain toward the empty bay where the burned-out trawler lay like a black scar against the rocks. "Suppose the missing Genesis boats get back here before the authorities arrive?" Jackie asked nervously.

"I'll leave you these two guns. Personally I doubt that you'll need them. I suspect Nicole will follow me, and the other boat will know the game's up. They won't fight you."

It took a tired Jackie a moment before she realized that I planned to sail without her. "You don't want me to come with you?" She asked with a hurt intonation.

"More than anything in the world," I answered truthfully, "but you're not coming."

"Why not?" Her voice was guarded.

"Because Nicole isn't like the rest of Genesis. She's not going to collapse at the first hurdle. She's a fighter, and her boat is crewed by the most fanatical of all von Rellsteb's recruits. I don't think she'll give in without a fight."

"But what does she have to gain by fighting you?" Jackie asked.

"Nothing now," I said, "because it's all over, but she may not see it that way. She's obsessed; she lives in her own world where everyone else is out of step." I paused. "I hope I'm wrong about her, but she could be a very angry and very lethal young woman right now."

"So why are you going to find her?" Jackie asked.

"Because she's my daughter. Because no one else will help her. And because I've come all this way to find her, so it seems stupid not to take the last few steps."

The wind lifted Jackie's fair hair which was still bleached from the sun and salt of our Atlantic crossing. "I think it'll be safe for me to come," she insisted with a gentle defiance. "Nicole must know that the Genesis experiment is finished, and that there's no point in fighting anymore." She looked worriedly up at me. "Besides, you can't sail *Stormchild* on your own, not in these waters."

"Of course I can," I said with a confidence I did not altogether feel, "and David will help me," and even as I added those words, glorious and sudden, and with her great sails white as innocence, *Stormchild* appeared in the Desolate Straits.

David, noticing the empty quay, motored *Stormchild* to the berth vacated by the burnt trawler. He looked exhausted; he was so tired that he could scarce raise the energy to berth the yacht properly. "It's one thing to sail across an ocean," he explained to me, "but trying to stay safe off a lee shore is no joke. I've hardly slept in two nights or days!" He fastened the last fender to protect *Stormchild*'s hull from the stone quay, then stumbled ashore. His eyes were red and his face deeplined.

Berenice Tetterman had already jumped ashore and was running toward her mother, who, in turn, was hurrying toward her daughter. They met, they clasped, they wept, and I felt tears in my own eyes as I realized I would probably never again feel a daughter's clasp. Lucky Molly, I thought, and I tried not be jealous. Mother and daughter hugged each other, both talking at the same time, neither listening, but both happy and both crying.

David, embarrassed as ever by a display of sentiment, turned to stare at the burned-out trawler, the beached yachts, the flooded fields and the gaping hole in the escarpment's ridge where once there had been a dam. "What happened here?" he asked at last.

I described the night's events as we walked toward the house. He grimaced when I told him of Jackie Potten's return, and seemed to flinch when I told him I hoped to marry her. He sighed when I described my bombs, and shuddered when I claimed to have shot both von Rellsteb and Lisl. I took the blame entirely on myself, so that the authorities would not give Jackie a hard time.

David, suddenly alert, smelt something wrong in my story. "They were both armed?"

"Of course. I wouldn't have shot them otherwise."

"They were shooting at you?"

I nodded. "Automatic weapons, too, and all I had was the good old Lee-Enfield."

"So you shot them both from the front?"

It was an odd question, but also a very shrewd one. I hesitated before answering. "No. Well, yes. I shot von Rellsteb in the back, but not the girl."

"So von Rellsteb wasn't shooting at you?"

"What are you?" I asked. "Counsel for the prosecution?"

"The police are going to ask a lot of very awkward questions," David said, "and I just want to make sure you don't tell them lies."

"I won't tell them anything," I said. "I'm sailing away from here and I don't intend to summon any help until I'm well offshore."

David, who had been walking beside me toward the house, suddenly checked. "They're already on their way, Tim. I called them last night."

I stared at him in horror. "You did what?"

"I called the *Armada* last night. Good God, man, what else was I to do? You summoned me here with a radio message that was virtually inaudible! For all I knew, it was a trap! So, of course, I reported the matter to the authorities. The *Armada* should be here later today."

"Oh, God!" I blasphemed.

"Does it matter?" David asked.

"Of course it matters!" I retorted angrily. "Because once the authorities are here they're going to stop everyone leaving. They're going to want statements and fingerprints and God knows what else. We're going to be tied up in Chilean red tape and that means I can't head off Nicole. Not unless I leave now!"

"Where are you going?" David shouted after me. I had begun running back toward the quay.

"I'm going to find Nicole," I turned and explained to him, "because I want to see her alone before she goes to jail. I haven't come this far to run away from her, whatever she might be."

"What do you mean?" David caught up with me.

"I mean," I said, "that Nicole is a killer. She planted the bomb on *Slip-Slider*, David, not von Rellsteb. It was always Nicole."

"Oh, my God." David was stricken. His face went white.

"So I'm going to find her." I turned away.

"No!" David pulled me back, then gestured at the flooded fields and at the the scorched facade of the house. "You've done enough, Tim. There's no need to do more. There's no need to risk more."

I shook my head with exasperation. "You don't understand, David. Nicole is in hell, and only one person can go down and save her now. That's me. I love her, and I can offer her salvation of a kind, but what I can't do is walk away from her."

"You're not God," David said.

"I have to find her," I said, "and touch her before they put her in chains. Is that so bloody bad?"

David held my shoulders with his strong hands. "We agreed," he said urgently, "that if we found evidence of wrongdoing, then we would leave it to the authorities. The Chileans will let you see Nicole. You'll have your chance with her."

I shook myself free. "I make my own chances, David."

"You aren't thinking straight!" He took hold of me again. "You mustn't do this, Tim! No good will come of it! Let the competent authorities deal with it!"

"The competent authorities," I said, "will clap her in jail, and maybe even put her to death. Do they have the death penalty here? I don't know, but whatever happens to her, I first want to go down to her hell, and take her hand, and bring her back to the light. Doesn't your faith approve of that? Or don't you believe in hell anymore?"

"I believe," David said simply, then frowned at me. "You want me to come with you, don't you?"

I ignored his question. "Maybe I'll offer to take her to face British justice," I said, "instead of Chilean."

"And maybe she won't want anything you offer," David said, then he shook his head in a sudden horror. "You mustn't go, Tim! It's too dangerous."

I smiled. "I don't want you to take risks, David. I want you to stay here. I've always thought you should stay here."

Relief showed on his tired face. "Truly?"

"We don't want to risk the bishopric, do we?" I teased him, then turned wearily toward *Stormchild*. "The reason I wanted you to stay here, David," I told him, "is because there's still one other Genesis boat at sea, and just in case it does get here before the authorities, it might be a good idea if you were here to hold the fort. Molly Tetterman seems a very competent lady, but I have a suspicion you'd be a more convincing threat with a gun."

"I think you should stay with me," David said trenchantly.

"I know you do, but I won't." I grinned at him,

then stepped down onto *Stormchild*'s deck. We both went down to the saloon where I helped David collect and pack his belongings. He would deal with the Chilean Navy, then go to Santiago and tell the Australian Embassy about the pirating of the *Naiad*. I gave him Maureen Delaney's passport, then warned him that he would have to field the attentions of some very curious reporters. "If you play it canny," I told him, "you can probably persuade one of the newspapers to pay your fare home in return for some exclusive information."

"Is that how it works?" he asked, though very distractedly. David was not worried about the newspapers, but about me. He thought I was sailing to my death, and he did not know how to stop me.

"Jackie will help you deal with the press," I told him. "This is rather going to be her moment. All those self-important papers who turned her down are now going to be begging for her story."

"Only if they can find me," Jackie said. She had boarded *Stormchild* and now crouched at the head of the companionway. "I'm going with you, Tim."

"No!" I insisted.

Jackie half smiled, then produced one of the guns I had left in the cockpit. It was an M-16 and, with a new-found confidence, she switched it to automatic fire and aimed it at the array of instruments that was mounted above the chart table. One squeeze of the trigger and *Stormchild* would be without radios, log, depth sounder, Satnav, and chronometer. "I'm coming with you, Tim," Jackie said, "or you're not going at all."

"Put the gun down," I said, "please?"

"Well?"

I sighed, then said what I had been wanting to say all day. "Dear Jackie," I said, "please sail with me."

We sailed just after midday, sliding away from the settlement and past the burned-out trawler and out into the swirling eddies of the Desolate Straits. No *Armada* patrol ship had yet arrived. We left David with all our guns except one Lee-Enfield that I stored in a cockpit locker, then, after Molly had embraced Jackie and enjoined me to look after her, we cast off our lines.

We used the big engine, pushing it to the limit in my hurry to escape to the open sea before the *Armada* arrived in the Desolate Straits. By mid-afternoon I had found a narrow channel that, according to the chart, led to the ocean and I plunged into its shadows. I doubted any patrol ship would find us now, and the clouds were too low for any helicopter to be useful. We had escaped unseen, and now hurried between dank, dark cliffs that funneled the gusting wet wind and echoed back the rhythmic pounding of our big engine.

I gave Jackie the helm while I went below and, at last, took off the walking boots and peeled away the blood-encrusted socks. I hobbled into *Stormchild's* tiny head, showered, then used an old cut-throat razor to hack off my stubble. I bandaged my feet, pulled on some reasonably clean and dry clothes, then heated myself a tinned steak and kidney pie and made Jackie a vegetable omelette. I carried the meal to the cockpit where I scoffed down the pie, drank a bottle of beer, stole some of Jackie's omelette, had another beer, made myself two cheese sandwiches because I was still famished, and then, after wolfing down a tin of peaches slathered with evaporated milk, I brewed a pot of tea strong enough to scald the barnacles off a battleship's bum. "Oh, Christ," I said, "but that does feel better."

Jackie went below to wash and change, and I sat alone in *Stormchild*'s cockpit as the engine took us seaward. As we neared the ocean the narrow channel became choppy and, where rocks reared up from the sea bed, the water ran in slick, fast kelds to betray the presence of tidal rips. Jackie joined me on deck where, with our oilskin hoods over our heads, we watched sea otters, kingfishers, fur seals, and geese. "I looked round the galley," Jackie suddenly said in a rather ominous tone.

"So?"

"I couldn't find my sprouting kit."

"Your what?"

"My sprouting kit. You know? The thing that makes fresh sprouts from seeds and beans?"

"It disappeared in a freak wave," I said. "I tried to save it, but alas."

"Tim?" she said sweetly, "you are so full of it, your eyes are brown."

I laughed. I could feel the tremor of the ocean in the way that *Stormchild* was breaking the channel's chop now. We were getting close. Soon, I knew, we would hear the crash of the surf battering against the rocks, and then, under the day's gray shroud of rain and cloud, we would be at sea. At our stern the faded red ensign slapped in the gusting wind. When it was all over, I promised myself, and the last questions had earned their horrid answers, I would let that ensign go into the deep waters and I would buy another flag to mark a new beginning.

In the late afternoon, as the first shearwaters flighted back from the sea to their nests, *Stormchild*'s cutwater thumped into the open water. That first big, cold wave exploded white on *Stormchild*'s bows and ran green down her scuppers. To port and starboard the massive rollers broke ragged on black rocks under a sullen rain as *Stormchild*, like a tiny projectile, arrowed straight from the channel into the vast ocean's wastes. The seas streamed at us in battalion formation, row after row of them, huge and ponderous, each shuddering our boat and making its engine labor, and so, while Jackie took the wheel, I hoisted *Stormchild*'s sails and immediately the yacht stiffened and, when the motor was switched off, settled comfortably into the ocean's own undying rhythm.

By dusk it had stopped raining and the far sun was staining the chasms of a ragged cloud bank with a scarlet touch. The wind was gusting strong and cold from the south, while the endless seas, like restless mountains of liquid slate, heaved *Stormchild* high as they roared blindly beneath her keel. We had left the land far behind, way beyond our sight, as now, alone on a tremendous sea, we reached toward the dying sun to find Nicole.

I had learned the Genesis transmission schedule from von Rellsteb's radio operator, so I knew on what channel and at what times the Genesis Four would listen and so, at nightfall, I went below and turned on Stormchild's big radio. Jackie, at the wheel, peered anxiously down the companionway as I tuned the radio, and, at last pressed the transmitter button. "Stormchild calling Genesis Four. This is Stormchild calling Genesis Four. Over."

Nothing. A great wave rolled past *Stormchild's* flank and I heard the sea scouring down the scuppers. "*Stormchild* calling *Genesis Four*. This is *Stormchild* calling *Genesis Four*. Over."

Still nothing. I sat at the console smelling the pervasive smell of the diesel oil that still reeked in *Stormchild's* saloon carpet. "*Stormchild* calling *Genesis Four*. This is *Stormchild* calling *Genesis Four*. Come in please. Over."

Were the Chileans listening? Was the *Armada* monitoring all the medium and high frequency channels in an effort to find us and intercept us? If they thought I was trying to help my daughter evade their country's justice then the Chilean Navy might very well have a lean, gray patrol vessel somewhere in this wilderness of sea and wind. Yet, I reasoned, the *Armada* would surely talk to me on the radio if they had intercepted this transmission, and so far neither they, nor *Genesis Four,* had replied. Perhaps no one was listening. I pressed the key again. "*Stormchild* calling *Genesis Four.* This is *Stormchild* calling *Genesis Four.* Over."

"We hear you," said the voice from the speaker, and it said nothing more. Just those three words. "We hear you," but it was my daughter's voice, curt and toneless, and I stared at the radio as though it had just transmitted the word of God.

"Nicole?" I transmitted in wonderment. "Nicole?" but there was no reply, and I realized that though my daughter might listen to me, she had nothing to say in return.

So be it. I closed my eyes, pressed the key, and spoke.

I began by saying that I loved her. It sounded stilted, so I said it again, and afterward I told her I knew what she had done, not just to her mother, but to the crew of the *Naiad,* and I said that the evidence of her deeds had been given to her Uncle David, who was making sure it reached the proper authorities. I then explained that the Genesis community had ceased to exist; its leaders were dead, its members were homeless, and its settlement was destroyed. "You can sail back there now and you'll find the Chilean Police and Navy waiting for you, or you can rendezvous with me and we'll either go back together, or sail to the Falklands. I'm not offering you freedom, just a choice between British or Chilean justice. I would also like to meet you and tell you that I still love you, even if I hate what you've done." My words still sounded lame, but the truth so often does limp off the tongue in times of crisis. Just when we most need to speak with the tongues of angels, we stumble with uncertain words.

"I'm sailing southward now," I told Nicole, "and I'll clear the cape in six or seven days. If you meet me, I'll escort you to wherever you want to go and I'll do my best to find you an honest and good lawyer"—I paused—"and I love you, Nicole."

I waited, but there was no reply. "Nicole?" I begged the sky, but still no word came back. I left the radio switched on and its speaker turned full up as I went back to the cockpit, but no voice broke the hissing silence. If Nicole was going to accept my offer, then she was accepting it in silence.

"She said nothing?" Jackie asked.

"Only that she could hear me."

Jackie bit her lip, then gave me a decisive look. "I've been thinking about it, Tim, and I know it's going to be all right. Nicole must know she's got nothing to gain by hurting you? She knows it's over, doesn't she?"

"Yes."

"And she's not a fool, Tim!" Jackie said passionately. "She probably won't even look for us. I mean, the only choice you've offered her is between a British and a Chilean jail, so she's much more likely to sail west, isn't she? To try and lose herself in the Pacific?"

"She might," I admitted, "she very well might," but somehow I did not think that Nicole would resist this final confrontation, and I suddenly wished I had not let Jackie share it with me. I wished I was not driven to the confrontation myself, for, by facing my daughter, I risked my new happiness in exchange for an old relationship that could never be restored.

In the early hours of darkness the wind backed into the east, a sure sign that it would freshen. Jackie and I took in two reefs, and I was glad we did, for within the hour the wind was shrieking in the rigging as we slogged southward on a long port tack. Every slam of the bows reverberated through the steel hull and rattled the crockery in the galley and shivered the floating compass card in the cockpit's binnacle. White spray slashed back to spatter on the spray hood.

I sent Jackie below to rest and noted that, instead of finding a snug refuge in the forward cabin, she took her bag into the aftercabin where my own things were stored. Yet she must have found it hard to sleep, for, shortly after midnight, she came back on deck. The ship was dark as sin for I was sailing without any navigation lights and the stars were cloud-shrouded, so that the only illumination in our whole world was the tiny unobtrusive red glow of the instrument lights.

Jackie groped her way to my side, then snapped her lifeline to the D-ring at the base of the wheel's pedestal. As her night vision came she saw the sliding avalanches of white water that rushed beside our gunwales and the sight made her tremble. "Doesn't it frighten you?" she asked, and I realized that this was her first experience of cold, gale-force sailing.

I smiled in the darkness. "Oh Lord"—I quoted her the fishermens' ancient prayer—"my boat is so small and Thy sea is so big. Protect me."

"That's nice," she said softly.

"Besides"—I gave the wheel a twitch—"you should be cautiously afraid of the sea. A wise old fisherman once said that a man who isn't afraid of the sea will soon be drowned, for he'll go out on a day when he shouldn't sail, but those of us who are afraid of the sea only get drowned every now and again."

She laughed, then was silent for a good long while. Perhaps the mention of drowning had put the thought of Nicole into Jackie's mind, for she suddenly asked just where I thought we would meet Nicole, if we met her at all.

"I know just where she'll met us," I said, because I had thought this whole rendezvous through, and I knew the exact place to which Nicole was even now racing in her fast catamaran. "She'll be waiting at the Horn."

"The Horn!" Jackie echoed the two words, and I heard the wonder in her voice as though she could not truly believe that we were really going to that hell of a seaway where the big ships died

and where the ghosts of sailormen never rested.
We were sailing to Cape Horn.

There are plenty of terrible seas on earth. I
would not lightly sail the Agulhas Current off the
African coast again, for there the sea shudders in a
perpetual rage and its sudden watery chasms can
break the steel spines of the hugest vessels. I
would not willingly sail the North Cape again, for
there the ice storms howl out of a white desert
and the rigging freezes and even boats seem to get
tired of fighting the savagery of that weather. Yet
neither of those places, nor even the storms of the
Tasman or the shallow hell of a North Sea winter
storm can rival the bitter fame of Cape Horn.

Now, racing southward with two reefs tied in
our mainsail, Jackie and I were already in the
cape's feed-chute. Far beyond our eastern horizon
the tip of South America bent ever more sharply
toward the Atlantic, thus forming the northern lip
of a funnel that compressed and savaged the great
Pacific waves that had been fetched across fifteen
thousand miles of roaring ocean, and which were
there forced to squeeze themselves into the shallow gap between Cape Horn and Antarctica. That
gap was the Drake Passage, the coldest, roughest
and most savage waterway on earth. A sober man,
a prudent man, would have taken the Straits of
Magellan, but I would round the Horn, as I had
first rounded it eighteen years before.

Back then, fighting for a record, I had creamed
past the Horn, running west to east, and cutting

the corner close enough to see the flag flying at the small naval post that the Chileans maintained on the Isla de Hornos. My boat had flogged through windlashed spray, plunged through the Horn's steep seas, then disappeared northward toward Plymouth, home and the ephemeral glories of a world record.

Now, with Jackie, I would visit the Cape again, but this time to save a soul. Each cold morning I searched the sea for a sign of a strange sail that waited to intercept us, but all that week, as *Stormchild* neared the Horn, we sailed alone. The wind was cold and unrelenting, the seas gargantuan and dark, and the horizon empty.

Then, at dawn on the seventh day, just as I was beginning to believe that Nicole had spurned my offer of help, I saw, off to our south, a scrap of something pale against the dark water and hideous black clouds. I seized the binoculars and trained them forward, but could make out no details of the far off boat, yet I knew I had seen a sail which waited to meet us at the very place where *Stormchild* must turn eastward to run the treacherous waters of the Drake Passage. I could not be certain yet, but a pursuit that had begun with a photograph in an English Sunday newspaper seemed about to end in the biggest seas God makes.

Jackie, who had the eyesight of a starving hawk, came up from the galley and took the binoculars from me. "It's a catamaran!" she said after a while, then she clung desperately to a stay as a huge sea thundered and foamed under *Stormchild*'s counter.

The seas here were vast, carrying an ocean's pent up violence into battle against two continents.

Genesis Four, if the strange catamaran was indeed *Genesis Four,* sailed northwest to meet us and, a half hour after I had first spotted the strange sail, I could make out the twin hulls flying across the crests of the waves to spew a double cock's comb of high white spray in her wake. The far boat was quick as lightning.

And as mute as the grave. I attempted to talk to the catamaran on the VHF, but there was no reply. I went back topside and tried to calm the idiot excitement that was fusing my emotions. I did not know if I was glad or miserable, only that my daughter was close, and I felt full of love and forgiveness. I wanted to cry, but instead I hunched down from the freezing wind and felt *Stormchild*'s steel hull tremble nervously in the pounding seas.

Those seas were building as they came to their battlefield. The wind was also veering to the west, piling up the seas higher and bringing wicked squalls of black rain which, when they struck, blotted the distant catamaran from our view. The wind, as well as veering, was rising, and the glass was falling, which meant the weather would probably turn even nastier. "Another reef?" Jackie shouted at me.

"I'll drop the main altogether!" I shouted back.

For the last few minutes *Stormchild* had been heeling so far over that her port gunwale had been permanently streaming with green water and her boom, despite being close hauled, had sometimes drawn a gash of white foam in the flanks of leeward waves. I should have reefed a half hour before, but now I would lose the main entirely and depend on our number three jib to pull us through the Drake Passage. Jackie took the wheel while I, wearing twin lifelines, struggled to kill the big mainsail.

And it was a struggle, for we were suddenly in a place of shortening and steepening seas that made *Stormchild*'s motion violently unpredictable. I staggered about the deck to gather in the billowing wet canvas. Spray was being sliced and shredded from the wavetops to mingle with the cold, sleety rain that whipped eastward in the rising wind. I tamed the cold sail, tied it down, then, fearing the rising malevolence of the seas, I bolted the stormplates over the coach roof windows.

"I haven't seen the catamaran for twenty minutes!" Jackie shouted when I returned to the cockpit and the strange boat had vanished somewhere in the welter of spray and rain.

"Go to 150!" I shouted to her. I was turning *Stormchild* back to the southeast, to the course we had been running when the catamaran first saw us. For a second I was tempted to try *Stormchild*'s radar, but I knew the storm-lashed seas would clutter the screen and hide the catamaran among a chaos of confused echoes bounced back from the sharp wavepeaks. Instead I stared south, wondering whether, after all, Nicole and I would now miss each other because of this rising gale that screamed across the sea to make the windward slopes of the waves into maelstroms of foam and broken white water.

Those waves, monstrous after their fifteen-thousand-mile journey, were crashing in from our starboard side to give us a roller coaster ride. When we were on the wave crests it seemed as though we were surrounded by stinging whips of foam that streamed past our bows and smashed home on our starboard flank and filled the sky with white droplets thick as fog. Beneath us the troughs sometimes looked like sudden holes in the ocean with streaked, glossy sides of darkest green, and it seemed inevitable that we would soon topple sideways into one of those great water caverns, and there be buried by a collapsing wave, but *Stormchild* always slid past them to plunge down the next wave's slope. She left a quick white wake that broke into creamy bubbles before it was overwhelmed by the gray spill of broken foam from the wave crests. In the troughs the wind's noise would be noticeably muted, but then we would see the next crinkling, heaving, swelling, and overpowering wave coming to assail our starboard flank, and it seemed impossible that the tons of water would not break to smash down on our mast and sail and deck, but instead we would heave up to the windblown summit from where I would stare anxiously ahead for a glimpse of my daughter's boat.

If indeed it was Nicole we had seen and not some other catamaran thrashing up this lonely coast. After an hour, in which no other sail appeared, I decided that the strange sail had indeed been some other ocean voyager and not Nicole at all.

I took the wheel from Jackie, who, eschewing a
chance to shelter from the wind's cold blast by
going below, stayed with me in the cockpit. I had
collapsed the spray hood to save it from being
destroyed by the wind's fury so that the two of us
stared with salt-stung eyes into the blinding spray
as we searched the mad chaos of wave tops for
another sight of the catamaran.

It seemed to have got much colder, and, despite
the season, freezing rain was now mixing with the
spindrift. I had a towel scarf tight round my neck,
my oilskin hood was raised and its drawstrings
tied, but even so trickles of near freezing water
were finding their way through the defenses to
run chill down my chest. Jackie must have been
similarly afflicted, but she made no complaint;
neither of us spoke, and I think we were both so
frozen and so tired that we were beginning not to
care about the missing boat. I even wondered if
the strange sail had been an hallucination brought
on by the strain of endlessly fighting the cold. My
muscles were cramped and stiff, my thought pro-
cesses glazed, and my corrections to *Stormchild*'s
helm were sluggish and clumsy.

Jackie shouted something. The wind snatched
her words away and it took me an immense effort
of will to turn my head, thus dislodging the temporarily satisfactory arrangement of towel,
sweaters, and oilskins, just to stare blankly at her.

She was gazing forward, her mouth open, her
eyes huge.

I turned to follow her gaze. Then swore.
Because, like a shark slicing in to attack, or like a

weapon aimed at our heart, the strange catamaran was riding up the southern flank of the wave on which *Stormchild* was poised. The catamaran was sailing under a scrap of storm jib and a close-reefed main, but was still traveling at racing speed. She was so close that I could see the pattern of her blue and yellow curtains through her small cabin windows. I could even read the name *Naiad* that had been painted over, but which still showed as ghost lettering under the hull's pale green paint. I gaped at the boat, aware of my racing heart, then suddenly the catamaran turned north to run past our flank, and I saw four figures in her cockpit and I knew that one was my long-lost child.

"Nicole!" I waved like a mad thing. "Nicole!" I shouted, and my voice was lost in the appalling sound of wind and sea and rain and flogging sail-cloth.

"My God!" Jackie screamed, and I suddenly realized that the flogging sound was not sailcloth, but bullets that were smacking across our jib.

I did not move. I was staring at the figure who stood at the catamaran's wheel, and who suddenly pushed back her oilskin's hood to reveal her bright corn-gold hair and blue eyes. "Nicole!" I shouted as the catamaran, its twin wakes spewing quick foam, slashed up the waveslope we had just sailed down. The wheel spun neglected in my hands so that *Stormchild* bridled, jarred sickening-ly, then fell off the wind as the catamaran finally vanished across the crest behind us. My last glimpse was of Nicole's figure, tall and straight, and the name *Genesis Four* painted in crude black letters on the catamaran's starboard transom.

Jackie pummeled my arm. "There were two of them firing at us! Two of them!"

I had not noticed the gunmen, only Nicole. Why shoot at us, I wondered, why? I was their best hope in a world that would hate them. I was their last chance of love, and they wanted to kill me?

"Tim!" Jackie shouted at me, trying to snap me out of my reverie.

"Go below," I told her. "Get on the VHF. Channel 37. Tell her we've come to help her! Tell her I love her!"

I did love her, too, and suddenly my memory registered that Nicole had not just looked at me as her catamaran sliced past *Stormchild,* but that she had smiled at me. "Oh, God." I said the prayer aloud, but could not finish it. I was shaking. I was thinking of Nicole's smile. It had been one of recognition, almost pleasure. Sweet Jesus, but what evil was in us? I had thought to meet her, and to sail with her to where we could talk, but my child had no time for remorse or reunion. She wanted me dead and I did not know why. Was it because I had destroyed Genesis? Or was she so steeped in blood that my death meant nothing more to her? I did not know, I only knew that I was in the worst sea on earth, and pursued by madness.

Stormchild was lying on her side, shaking and pounding in the seas. Her head had fallen off the wind and her one sail was dragging her further round, so I snatched the wheel back and hardened her up into the wind and sea. We were in the foam-ribbed trough of a wave, then, as the hull began to move again, we labored slowly up the next vast slope and I glanced behind just in time to see the vengeful menace of *Genesis Four*'s twin prows, sharp as lances, spear up over the crest behind, then drop to slide down the wave in *Stormchild*'s wake. I heard a popping noise and looked up to see another line of ragged holes rip and tear across *Stormchild*'s jib. Why? I wondered, then I thought to hell with the why, Jackie and I would be dead within minutes if I did not do something. The catamaran was twice as fast as *Stormchild*, and carried twice as many guns. It was no good leaning on sentiment now, I had to fight back, and so I whipped a lashing onto the wheel, slithered across the cockpit, then yanked up the locker lid to find the gun. A bullet clanged off our gunwale and whined up to the clouds. I turned, worked the rifle's bolt, aimed at the catamaran's closest hull, and fired.

Nicole had been overtaking *Stormchild*'s starboard flank. Her boat's superior speed gave her the weather gauge, and she could choose her angle and come as close as she liked, yet suddenly, as I returned the fire and worked the rifle's bolt to fire again, my daughter showed a scrap of good sense and veered her course sharply away from *Stormchild* and my rifle.

"They're not answering the radio!" Jackie shouted, then gave an involuntary scream as a bullet ripped through the coach roof. There were two gunmen in the *Genesis Four*'s cockpit. I recognized one of them as Dominic, Nicole's blond lover, and he seemed to smile as he opened fire again. I heard the sharp crack as his bullets struck our steel hull, then I saw a jagged rent splay open in the metal boom above my head. Another strike of bullets whipped foam from the dark heart of the wave beyond the cockpit. I fired back, but the Lee-Enfield was a slow, clumsy weapon compared with the assault rifles in Nicole's boat.

Stormchild, her wheel lashed now, slashed through the broken crest of another wave. The *Genesis Four* had gone past us and was now racing far ahead of our slower hull. Her two gunmen ceased fire and I knew we would have a few moments peace because Nicole, sailing ahead of us into the shrieking gale, would not dare jibe her boat, but would, instead, have to tack the *Genesis Four* back into our path. I guessed we would not see her for fifteen minutes.

I went below. The cabin was unusually dark because of the stormshields on the windows, and in that unnatural gloom I could see three sparks of daylight where bullets had punched through the hull. I had a sudden terror that Jackie had been hit, and whirled round to see her hunched over the radio consoles. I shouted her name, she did not move, then I saw she was wearing earphones so as to hear better through the gale's turmoil. "They won't answer." She at last saw me and took off the earphones.

"Are you OK?"

She nodded. "I'm OK."

"We won't see them for at least ten minutes," I

promised Jackie, "because even Nicole isn't crazy
enough to jibe a boat in this bitch of a wind." I
took the microphone and pressed its transmission
button. "Nicole! Nicole!"

There was silence, except for the sea's maniacal
fury thundering beyond our steel hull. *Stormchild*
shuddered in a wave, slid through a screaming
horror of foam, then jarred sickeningly into a
trough.

"Nicole!" I called. "Nicole! For God's sake, this
is your father! I'm trying to help you!"

Nothing. Emptiness. Silence. I glanced back up
the companionway, to where the rain slanted
down out of a gray-black sky. At times, as
Stormchild rolled off a wave, I would see a vast cold
sea toppling behind us, and against it the bomb-
riddled ensign would look shatteringly bright.

"Nicole!" I pleaded into the radio, but she was
not listening, or maybe she was listening, but just
refusing to talk to me, and I knew I had just ten
minutes to touch some old nerve of affection in
my daughter, or else she would come back, she
would kill us, and then she would sail away to
take her chances among the far, anonymous
Pacific islands. "Nicole!" I said to her. "I love you,
I love you, I love . . . "

I stopped because a terrible harsh battle percus-
sion was filling *Stormchild* and I twisted, aghast, to
see more holes being punched in the far side of
the saloon and I knew that Nicole had done the
unimaginable; she had jibed her boat in this awful
gale. She was a better sailor than I, and she had a
crack crew, and she had turned her boat in front

of this ship-killing wind, and she had done it to
prove she was a better sailor than I, and that was
why Jackie and I had to die in this awful place.
Suddenly it was all so clear; we had to die so that
my daughter could prove she was a better sailor
than her father.

A bullet ricocheted into the galley. Another
clanged through the stove's stainless-steel chimney. Water pulsed through the bullet holes as
Stormchild dipped to the wind. Jackie screamed.

I ran topside and clipped on my lifeline. I
worked the rifle's bolt, but the Lee-Enfield was
puny against our enemy's automatic fire, and
Stormchild's slow hull was no match for the speed
of my daughter's twin keels, and my seamanship,
God help me, was not a patch on hers. At that
moment, as I watched the slicing hulls come
straight at us, I knew that Nicole was going to kill
us. She would do it to prove she was the better
sailor, and so she was, I thought, as I stared at the
approaching boat that flicked so lightly through
the spume and sea scum. The two gunmen were
using the cabin top as a firing step, the third crew
member was by the sheet winches, while Nicole,
bareheaded and happy, stood tall at the helm
beneath the strange sea-green ensign of Genesis.
Nicole did indeed look happy. She had taken our
measure, and now she would win because she was
more daring than her father.

The *Genesis Four* was sliding toward us down
the face of a wave. *Stormchild* was on the opposing
face. We would meet in the trough. Once again
Nicole held the weather advantage, but this time,

throwing caution to the wind, she would use it to come so close that her gunmen could not possibly miss. They would pour their fire into *Stormchild*'s cockpit, riddling it with ricocheting bullets to overwhelm our cockpit drains with blood. Jackie, terrified of the clangor of bullets down below, had come to crouch beside me. She frowned at my gun, perhaps wondering why I did not fire it, but I knew the rifle would not help me now.

Genesis Four seemed to leap through the water, eager to bring us our death. I laid the gun down in the cockpit and smiled at Jackie. "Hold tight!" I told her, for I had chosen to outdare my daughter.

I stood up straight, not caring about the gunmens' bullets, and I stared at my daughter. If I did not beat her now, then Jackie would die, and I would die, and *Stormchild* would sink to join the legions of Cape Horn's dead.

"Hold on!" I shouted to Jackie, and, with fingers numbed by the cold, I unlashed *Stormchild*'s wheel.

Christ, but the catamaran was close. Jackie held my arm and I could feel her shaking and shivering. And no wonder, for the catamaran was scarcely forty yards away now. Nicole, braced at its wheel, was aiming to slide her starboard hull just inches from our starboard gunwale, and, at that range, despite the jarring of the sea's pounding, Genesis's last gunmen could not miss. Nicole doubtless expected me to turn away and run downwind, and when I did, she would follow. I could see her winch-handler poised to loosen the jib sheets and I knew that the moment I turned to run, the catamaran would pounce on us like a striking snake.

And then we would die, and Nicole would take her chance for freedom in some far, warm sea.

But there was another way.

And I chose it.

I dropped the wheel's lashing, and, when *Genesis Four* was just twenty yards away, I spun the spokes to drive *Stormchild*'s tons of steel straight at the speeding catamaran.

I saw Nicole's eyes widen in alarm. She shouted in anger and snatched at the wheel to turn away, but she was too late. The two gunmen clutched for support at a handrail on the cabin roof and one of their two guns skidded into the scuppers and bounced overboard, then I was shouting at Jackie to hold on for her dear, sweet life.

Someone screamed. I think it was my daughter, because she knew I had beaten her.

Stormchild slammed into the turning catamaran. We smashed her starboard hull, breaking it into splinters of fiberglass. A wire stay whipped skyward. The catamaran's mainsail was suddenly demented, filling a noisy sky with its maniacal thrashing, then, inevitably, the *Genesis Four*'s mast began to topple. I saw Dominic whirl round, face bloody, as the catamaran's severed backstay whipped its frayed metal strands across his eyes. The mast was cracking and falling, and still *Stormchild* was driving into the catamaran's belly like a great killing axe. I heard the tortured screech of steel on steel as our sharp bows slammed into the main beam that spanned the catamaran's twin hulls. I staggered with the impact, while Jackie, her fingers hooked like claws, clung to my arm. *Stormchild*'s forestay snapped, slashing our jib into the ship-killing wind. A sea thundered across our joined decks, sweeping gear off *Genesis Four*'s scuppers and filling *Stormchild*'s cockpit with a crashing, icy whirlpool. Our bows churned sickeningly in the wreckage of the catamaran. I was sobbing for my daughter, for what I had done.

The great sea turned us broadside, thrusting our stern eastward. Our bows were trapped by the catamaran's broken hulls. I threw off *Stormchild*'s jib sheet as the two boats screeched on each other, but our boat was afloat and the *Genesis Four* was breaking apart. Already the catamaran's cockpit was awash and her starboard hull under water. A blue and yellow curtain floated free of the shattered saloon. *Stormchild*'s mast was swaying horribly, but her backstays and shrouds were holding it upright and the damage would have to wait.

"Lifebuoys!" I shouted at Jackie. I could see two yellow-jacketed bodies clinging to the catamaran's wreckage and I could see a third person in the foam-scummed water beyond. I could not see Nicole. The catamaran's mast had collapsed to trail the reefed mainsail and a tangle of lines in the foaming sea.

"Nicole!" I shouted, then hurled a life buoy into the wreckage. I slashed with my knife at the bindings of *Stormchild*'s life raft, and Jackie helped me push the big canister overboard. Another thunderous sea crashed cold across the two boats and when it had passed I saw that the two men who had been clinging to the wreckage were gone. I pulled the life raft's lanyard and watched as the bright orange raft began to inflate.

Another toppling sea hammered like an avalanche at our beam. *Stormchild*'s tortured bows were still buried in the *Genesis Four*, but the lurch and twist of the awful sea loosened and prized us free, then the gale snatched at our jib which still writhed at the end of its halyard, and which now turned us fast downwind. I sliced through the line which tethered the life raft to *Stormchild*, thus leaving the bright orange raft for my daughter. "Engine!" I shouted at Jackie, then I hurled the last buoy overboard and slapped my lifeline onto a jackstay to work my way forward.

Jackie turned on the ignition and, above the throb of our automatic bilge pumps that were dealing with the water let in by the bullet holes, I heard the harsh banging as the starter motor turned over. A wave broke on our counter, swamping the cockpit and crashing white down the companionway. The engine would not start and the wind and sea were carrying us so fast that already the wreck of the *Genesis Four* was hidden by a spume-fretted wave crest.

Jackie advanced the throttle, turned the key again, and this time the motor caught and throbbed. She let in the clutch, then staggered to the wheel to turn *Stormchild* back toward the wreckage, but a great sea, heaped and wind-whipped, slammed us back and almost threw us on our beam ends. Jackie sensibly let the boat run, while I, terrified that our mast would be lost,

sawed with my rigging knife at the jib halyard.
The cut halyard snaked up through the masthead
block to release the jib that sailed away like a
demonically winged monster. The forestay was
streaming ahead of us, carried almost horizontal
by the force of the rising gale, which now leeched
the ocean white and bent *Stormchild*'s tall mast
like a longbow.

I unhanded the mainsail's halyard, took some
bends off the cleat, carried the halyard forward
and shackled it to the foreplate. Then I went back
to the mast and winched the halyard tight so that
I had jury-rigged a new forestay. In harbor that
simple process might have taken three minutes,
but in that insane sea it took closer to half an
hour. Just to shackle the halyard to the foreplate
took immense concentration as the sea tried to
snatch me off the foredeck and over the collision-
bent bars of the pulpit. The wind screamed and
plucked at me, but at last the halyard was secure
and the mast safely stayed and I could crawl back
to the cockpit to discover that the wind and sea
had taken us yet further from the wreckage of
Genesis Four which was now totally lost in the
white hell of sleet and waves behind us. I throttled the engine to full brutal power, and, cursing
the bitch of a sea that fought us, I thrust
Stormchild straight into the throat of Cape Horn's
malevolence.

It took us an hour to find the wreckage of
Genesis Four, and even then we discovered nothing
but scraps: an oar that still had the name *Naiad*
burnt into its blade, a plastic bottle, a sail bag, a

broken pencil. We found *Stormchild*'s life raft, but
there was no one inside. We circled the pathetic
wreckage, enduring the shrieking wind and the
flogging seas and the demonic rain, but though
we found lumps of foam torn from the catamaran's hulls, and though we found our life buoy, we
could not find Nicole. Or any of Nicole's crew. My
daughter was gone. She was drowned. She was
gone to the cleansing sea and it had been I who
had killed her.

And it was I who now wept for her. As a small
child Nicole had been graceful. She had grown
up willful, but Joanna and I had been proud of
her, we had loved her, and we had thought that
our old age would be blessed by her, but then
her brother had been killed by terrorists, and
Nicole, as if to even the score, had become a terrorist herself. Her cause was different from the
cause of those men who had murdered her
brother, but her evil was the same, and now she
was dead.

At last I turned *Stormchild* away from Nicole's
killing place. A new black squall of sleet and rain
clawed across the broken water to overtake and
drive us eastward. I set the storm jib on the staysail halyard, and then we ran the shattering seas
of the Horn in a full gale that blew us through the
night so that it was full darkness when we struck
the first Atlantic waves and turned our scarred and
battered bows north toward the Falklands. Jackie
shared the night watch, huddled beside me in the
cockpit, not talking, but just watching the skirl
and rush of the seething waters.

And in the dawn, as the tired wind calmed, we saw that the sea was weeping.

Much later, months later, when *Stormchild* was tied fore and aft in a warm lagoon, Jackie asked me what we had achieved in that storm off Cape Horn. She asked the question on a night when our mooring lines led to bending palm trees that were silhouetted against the stars of a lambent tropical sky. We were alone and Patagonia seemed a long way off, indeed, so far away that we rarely talked of it, but that night, under the indolent stars, Jackie's thoughts strayed back to Nicole and to Genesis, and, in an idle voice, she asked me just what we had achieved. "We were good environmentalists," I assured her. "We cleaned up some pollution."

For the Genesis community was indeed gone, though it was hardly forgotten, for its misdeeds and its subsequent destruction had made headlines round the world.

Jackie's account of the settlement's harrowing was never published. She had written and rewritten the story, and, in despair of ever capturing the truth, she had torn up version after version until she had finally abandoned her efforts and allowed herself to read the story of the Genesis community in the words of other men and women. Those other journalists had desperately sought Jackie and me, but we had escaped their questions and thus the fate of Nicole and of her crew remained a mystery to the press, though the consensus was that they had simply drowned when *Genesis Four* foundered off the Horn. A few of the more vivid tabloids insisted that Nicole still sailed the murderous seaways, and any mysterious happening anywhere in the oceans renewed the speculation that *Genesis Four* still floated, but the responsible press had long abandoned its search for my daughter. Even the Chilean government, which for a time had made threatening noises about my disappearance, now seemed content to put the whole episode behind them.

Molly Tetterman had taken most of the Genesis community's survivors back to their families in North America, where Molly became something of a celebrity as the battling mother who had rescued her child from the grasp of evil. She wrote to us of her frequent appearances on television talkshows and even said that a network wanted to make a miniseries about her adventures. We wrote back wishing her luck, but heard nothing more of the project.

David wrote to us with news of the boatyard, of the church, and of his hopes that his brief brush with fame might help his chances of a comfortable bishopric. Betty wanted to know when Jackie and I would be married. Soon, I wrote back to them, soon. There seemed to be no hurry. Jackie and I drifted through warm seas, lazy and happy.

Now Jackie leaned against me in *Stormchild*'s cockpit. Beyond our private coral reef the warm waves broke, their sound a quiet murmur of pleasure in the darkness. I sipped whiskey. Jackie had refused a similar nightcap, indeed she had even shaken her head to my offer of wine with the dinner I had cooked at twilight, upon which refusal I had accused her of returning to her teetotaling ways. She denied it, so I had inquired whether this was some new and ghastly self-inflicted dietary prohibition, but she had just smiled tolerantly at my question. Now, in the placid Caribbean night, she reached up to touch my cheek. "Tim?" she asked very solemnly.

"Jackie?" I answered just as solemnly.

"Do you know why I didn't drink today?"

"Because you're an American," I declaimed, "and therefore believe death to be optional. Or else it's because you've just read one of those earnest health articles in a vegetarian magazine, which claims that drinking nine-year-old Cotes du Rhone gives you terminal zits and unsightly hemorrhoids. Or perhaps you're going to become unbelievably boring and tell me that alcohol is a drug and that each of us has a societal responsibility to—"

"Shut up," Jackie said very firmly, "shut up."

I shut up.

She took my hand and kissed it. "You're going to be a father again," she said softly, and I leaned my head on *Stormchild*'s rails and let my tears dissolve the stars.

BOOKS BY BERNARD CORNWELL

THE SAXON TALES

THE LAST KINGDOM

ISBN 978-0-06-088718-6 (trade paperback) • ISBN 978-0-06-112657-4 (abridged CD)
ISBN 978-0-06-075933-9 (large print)

Set during the reign of King Alfred the Great, *The Last Kingdom* depicts a time when law and order were ripped violently apart by a pagan assault on Christian England.

THE PALE HORSEMAN: A Novel

ISBN 978-0-06-114483-7 (trade paperback) • ISBN 978-0-06-078748-6 (abridged CD)

As England is reduced to nothing but a small patch of marshland, a beguiling sorceress and fearful Danish warrior complicate Alfred's desperate plans.

LORDS OF THE NORTH: A Novel

ISBN 978-0-06-114904-7 (trade paperback) • ISBN 978-0-06-115578-9 (abridged CD)
ISBN 978-0-06-088863-3 (large print)

After achieving victory at King Alfred's side, Uhtred of Bebbanburg returns to his home in the North, finally free of his allegiance to the king—or so he believes.

SWORD SONG: The Battle for London

ISBN 978-0-06-088864-0 (hardcover) • ISBN 978-0-06-137094-6 (abridged CD)
ISBN 978-0-06-088866-4 (large print)

Alfred survived the Danish invasions, but fresh Viking ships are arriving to plunder and enslave the Saxons.

THE BURNING LAND: A Novel

ISBN 978-0-06-088876-3 (trade paperback) • ISBN 978-0-06-088875-6 (large print)

The epic story of the birth of England and the legendary king who made it possible.

DEATH OF KINGS: A Novel

ISBN 978-0-06-196965-2 (hardcover) COMING JANUARY 2012!

The sixth volume in the bestselling Saxon Tales series resumes the saga of the birth of a nation.

THE RICHARD SHARPE SERIES

SHARPE'S TIGER
Richard Sharpe and the Siege of Seringapatam, 1799

ISBN 978-0-06-093230-5 (trade paperback) • ISBN 978-0-06-101269-3 (mass market paperback)

The first of Richard Sharpe's India trilogy, in which young Private Sharpe must battle both man and beast behind enemy lines as the British army fights its way through India.

SHARPE'S TRIUMPH
Richard Sharpe and the Battle of Assaye, September 1803

ISBN 978-0-06-095197-9 (trade paperback)

Richard Sharpe must defeat the plans of a British traitor and a native Indian mercenary army in this second volume of the India trilogy.

SHARPE'S FORTRESS
Richard Sharpe and the Siege of Gawilghur, December 1803

ISBN 978-0-06-109863-5 (trade paperback)

In this explosive conclusion to the India trilogy, Sharpe and Sir Arthur Wellesley's army try to conquer an impregnable fort in a battle with stakes both personal and professional.

SHARPE'S TRAFALGAR
Richard Sharpe and the Battle of Trafalgar, October 21, 1805
ISBN 978-0-06-109862-8 (trade paperback)

Having secured a reputation as a fighting soldier in India, Ensign Richard Sharpe returns to England and gets caught up in one of the most spectacular naval battles in history.

SHARPE'S PREY
Richard Sharpe and the Expedition to Denmark, 1807
ISBN 978-0-06-008453-0 (trade paperback)

Sharpe fights once again to keep the treacherous French troops at bay in Denmark.

SHARPE'S HAVOC
Richard Sharpe and the Campaign in Northern Portugal, Spring 1809
ISBN 978-0-06-056670-8 (trade paperback)

Sharpe finds himself in Portugal, fighting the savage armies of Napoleon Bonaparte, as they try to bring the Iberian Peninsula under their control.

SHARPE'S ESCAPE
Richard Sharpe and the Bussaco Campaign, 1810
ISBN 978-0-06-056155-0 (trade paperback)

Sharpe has made enemies among the Portuguese, and when the British army falls back through Coimbra, he and Sergeant Harper are lured into a trap designed to kill them.

SHARPE'S FURY
Richard Sharpe and the Battle of Barrosa, March 1811
ISBN 978-0-06-056156-7 (trade paperback) • ISBN 978-0-06-137416-6 (abridged CD)

Richard Sharpe has been sent by Wellington on a mission to Cadiz, now the capital of Spain, to rescue the British ambassador from a spot of undiplomatic trouble.

SHARPE'S BATTLE
Richard Sharpe and the Battle of Fuentes de Oñoro, May 1811
ISBN 978-0-06-093228-2 (trade paperback)

As Napoleon threatens to crush Britain on the battlefield, Lt. Col. Richard Sharpe leads a ragtag army to exact personal revenge.

SHARPE'S DEVIL
Richard Sharpe and the Emperor, Chile 1820
ISBN 978-0-06-093229-9 (trade paperback)

An honored veteran of the Napoleonic Wars, Lt. Col. Richard Sharpe is drawn into a deadly battle, both on land and on the high seas.

THE NATHANIEL STARBUCK CHRONICLES

REBEL
The Nathaniel Starbuck Chronicles: Book One • Bull Run, 1861
ISBN 978-0-06-093461-3 (trade paperback)

When a Richmond landowner snatches young Nate Starbuck from the grip of a Yankee-hating mob, Nate turns his back forever on his life in Boston to fight against his native North in this powerful and evocative story of the Civil War's first battle and the men who fought it.

COPPERHEAD
The Nathaniel Starbuck Chronicles: Book Two • Ball's Bluff, 1862
ISBN 978-0-06-093462-0 (trade paperback)

Nate Starbuck is accused of being a Yankee spy. In order to prove his innocence and prevent the fall of Richmond, he must test his endurance and seek out the real spy.

BATTLE FLAG
The Nathaniel Starbuck Chronicles: Book Three • Second Manassas, 1862
ISBN 978-0-06-093718-8 (trade paperback)

The acclaimed Civil War series continues as Confederate Captain Nate Starbuck takes part in the war's most extraordinary scenes.

THE BLOODY GROUND
The Nathaniel Starbuck Chronicles: Book Four • The Battle of Antietam, 1862
ISBN 978-0-06-093719-5 (trade paperback)
Nate serves under General Robert E. Lee during the famous battle at Antietam Creek.

THE GRAIL QUEST SERIES
THE ARCHER'S TALE
ISBN 978-0-06-093576-4 (trade paperback)
Determined to avenge his family's honor after a band of raiders brutally pillages his village, Thomas joins the Hundred Years War and embarks on a quest for the Holy Grail.

VAGABOND
ISBN 978-0-06-093578-8 (trade paperback)
Thomas continues his quest as he weaves through the battlefields of the Hundred Years War.

HERETIC
ISBN 978-0-06-074828-9 (trade paperback)
To reclaim what's rightfully his, Thomas finds himself in a murderous race with a black rider.

THE SAILING NOVELS
SCOUNDREL
A Novel of Suspense
ISBN 978-0-06-208238-1 (trade paperback)
A relentlessly suspenseful contemporary thriller set in the lethal world of international terror.

STORMCHILD
A Novel of Suspense
ISBN 978-0-06-209265-6 (trade paperback)
A man must save his daughter from Genesis, a shadowy environmental activist group.

WILDTRACK
A Novel of Suspense
ISBN 978-0-06-146264-1 (trade paperback)
Nick Sandman dreams of sailing away from his troubled life. But to keep afloat, he strikes a devil's bargain with another sailor...

CRACKDOWN
A Novel of Suspense
ISBN 978-0-06-143837-0 (trade paperback)
After accepting a job on a yacht, Nick Breakspear is lured into a web of cocaine, cash, and cold-blooded killings.

STANDALONE NOVELS
THE FORT: A Novel of the Revolutionary War
ISBN 978-0-06-201087-2 (trade paperback)
The story of the Penobscot Expedition, ultimately the largest American naval expedition of the Revolutionary War, has largely been left untold—until now.

AGINCOURT: A Novel
ISBN 978-0-06-157890-8 (trade paperback) • ISBN 978-0-06-078096-8 (unabridged CD)
ISBN 978-0-06-171972-1 (large print)
The inspiring story of that "band of brothers" who survives devastating hunger and disease only to face the horrors of the field of Agincourt.

GALLOWS THIEF: A Novel
ISBN 978-0-06-008274-1 (trade paperback) • ISBN 978-0-06-051628-4 (mass market paperback)
A private investigator in 1820s London explores a murder case that may rescue an innocent man from the gallows.

LISTEN TO
BERNARD CORNWELL

ON AUDIO CD

THE LAST KINGDOM

THE PALE HORSEMAN

LORDS OF THE NORTH

SWORD SONG

SHARPE'S FURY
Richard Sharpe and the Battle of Barrosa, March 1811

AGINCOURT

ON DOWNLOADABLE AUDIO

THE LAST KINGDOM

THE PALE HORSEMAN

LORDS OF THE NORTH

SWORD SONG

SHARPE'S FURY
Richard Sharpe and the Battle of Barrosa, March 1811

SHARPE'S ESCAPE
Richard Sharpe and the Bussaco Campaign, 1810

THE ARCHER'S TALE

VAGABOND

HERETIC

GALLOWS THIEF

AGINCOURT

THE BURNING LAND

THE FORT

Available wherever books are sold, or call 1-800-331-3761 to order.

CPSIA information can be obtained at www.ICGtesting.com
Printed in the USA
LVOW07s1658220716

497319LV00001B/5/P